Praise for *Only Love Can Break Your Heart*

"Set against the backbeat of classic rock hits of the 1970s, Ed Tarkington's pitch-perfect first novel pays tribute to music, love and growing up in small-town America . . . This novel may be a murder mystery wrapped in the cloak of Southern Gothic charm but, at its essence, it's a novel ab̸‾‾‾‾‾‾‾‾‾‾‾‾‾‾‾‾‾‾ informed Tarkington's formativ‾‾ and romantic relationships that ̸

"A clear winner—a taut, engrossing, ‾‾‾‾‾‾ ‾‾‾‾‾‾‾ ‾‾‾‾ ‾‾ ‾‾‾‾ ‾‾‾ abiding love."   —*The Charlotte Observer*

"I've heard it said that all good fiction is about blood, love or money. If that's true, then Ed Tarkington has hit the trifecta with his soulful first novel . . . Plainspoken yet elegant prose, with a heavy dash of good old-fashioned storytelling."
                                          —*Minneapolis Star Tribune*

"A lush mystery-within-a-coming-of-age-tale-within-a-Southern-Gothic . . . Interesting, readable and beautifully written."
                                          —NPR Books

"A coming-of-age story that evolves into a whodunit with tangled roots in three families whose lives collide in 1977 . . . [A] well-plotted, generous inquiry into the intricacies of the human heart."
                                          —*The Atlanta Journal-Constitution*

"Calls to mind a young Pat Conroy . . . Tarkington's fidelity to period and place is matched by his fidelity to human contradictions, to the gray area between heroism and villainy in which most of us reside."   —*Garden & Gun*

"*Only Love Can Break Your Heart* will leave readers stunned, amazed and gasping . . . Highly, highly recommended for all adult book clubs. You won't be able to put it down."   —*El Paso Times*

"This heartbreakingly effective coming-of-age story about the importance of love in one's life is replete with moments of harsh cruelty and tender love . . . Readers will stop and reread paragraphs, not because of confusion but for the pure joy of the language."
—*Library Journal*, starred review

"A rich, moody, moving novel about growing up and growing old before your time. Tarkington's people are rakes, rascals, irascible losers, femmes fatales, rich buffoons, dunderheads, beautiful loons, and one very cool dude, all balanced by the voice of a narrator you come to love as much as he loves his doomed older brother. On top of all that, it's a very fun, deeply satisfying page-turner of a book."
—Brad Watson, author of *The Heaven of Mercury*
and *Aliens in the Prime of Their Lives*

"This addictive tale of abandonment and forgiveness will haunt you long after you've turned the last page."
—Elizabeth Stuckey-French, author of
The Revenge of the Radioactive Lady

"A wonderful, beauty-haunted piece of work. Tarkington's voice in his hard-to-put-down debut novel has a timeless feel to its cadences, the same bittersweet music we hear in the storytelling of the best of our Southern writers who remind us how hard the world can be for dreamers."
—Bob Shacochis, author of *The Woman Who Lost Her Soul*

"From beginning to end, the plotline is intense, never flagging. From the bleeding heart Tarkington stitches on Rocky's sleeve there arises both scandal and rivalry, along with a touch of the paranormal and religious faith." —*Booklist*

"Tarkington's impressive first novel achieves every author's goal: Once you start reading, you can't stop. And as an added bonus for Neil Young fans, Tarkington's riveting tale provides plenty of classic rock riffs, too." —*BookPage*

ONLY LOVE CAN BREAK YOUR HEART

ONLY LOVE CAN BREAK YOUR HEART

a novel

ED TARKINGTON

Algonquin Books of Chapel Hill

2016

Published by
Algonquin Books of Chapel Hill
Post Office Box 2225
Chapel Hill, North Carolina 27515-2225

a division of
Workman Publishing
225 Varick Street
New York, New York 10014

First paperback edition, Algonquin Books of Chapel Hill, November 2016.
Originally published in hardcover by Algonquin Books of Chapel Hill in 2016.
Printed in the United States of America.
Published simultaneously in Canada by Thomas Allen & Son Limited.
Design by April Leidig.

This is a work of fiction. While, as in all fiction, the literary perceptions and insights are based on experience, all names, characters, places, and incidents either are products of the author's imagination or are used fictitiously.

Library of Congress Cataloging-in-Publication Data
Tarkington, Ed, [date]
Only love can break your heart : a novel / by Ed Tarkington.—First edition.
pages cm
ISBN 978-1-61620-382-5 (HC)
1. Teenage boys—Fiction. 2. Stepbrothers—Fiction.
3. Small cities—Fiction. 4. Domestic fiction. I. Title.
PS3620.A735O55 2016
813'.6—dc23   2015017464

ISBN 978-1-61620-526-3 (PB)

10 9 8 7 6 5 4 3 2 1
First Paperback Edition

For Elizabeth-Lee

———

and in memory of my father,
Edward H. Tarkington Sr.

How accidentally a fate is made . . . or how accidental it all may seem when it is inescapable.

— PHILIP ROTH

ONLY LOVE CAN BREAK YOUR HEART

PART ONE

Don't Tell a Soul

1

PAUL WAS MY HALF BROTHER. But I never called him that. This was partially out of loyalty—for I remained devoted to him, despite everything—but mostly because it didn't seem quite enough, having only half of one brother. So I never thought of him that way.

We lived just inside the city limits of Spencerville, on Old Boone's Ferry Road, a long, tree-shrouded drive through the wide, grassy fields and the horse farms on the gentle slope leading out to the Blue Ridge Mountains. The Old Man's house was a two-story brick Georgian set up on a rise at the end of a long gravel driveway. No Colonial manse, mind you—more like the impression of one in the mind of a poor man made good.

There were four bedrooms on the upstairs floor of our house. My room was across the hall from Paul's, facing the side yard. Before I came along, it was used by the Old Man and Paul's mother, and, later, by the Old Man alone in the years between one wife and the next. Whether he ever had any other women up there in his bed I do not know, but I'm highly doubtful. Around the turn of the 1970s, in Spencerville, sleeping over could still do damage to reputations. Even the free and consenting adults of our town were made to feel that it was somehow more unseemly to enjoy each other in the comfort of their own homes than to be caught in the backseats of cars parked at the end of a deserted cul-de-sac, or for said cars to be seen parked outside the Marquis de Lafayette Motel across the river in Munro.

If the Old Man's car was ever among those spotted in one of those areas designated for clandestine carnal athletics, he certainly didn't drive it there with his much younger, much prettier second wife sitting next to him. My dear mother, bless her pious, proper soul,

refused even to sleep in the same room the Old Man had shared with
that *other woman*, the first Mrs. Richard Askew—Paul's mother.

I learned this fact not from Paul but rather from the Old Man
himself. He had a terrible habit of launching into incontinent
monologues in front of his elementary-school-age son the way he
might in speaking to some random stranger passing a boozy hour
or two on a layover at an airport bar. Inevitably he'd catch himself and remember whom he was talking to. "If you ever tell your
mother," he would say, to which I would nod solemnly, proud as I
was to be considered worthy of keeping his secrets.

My mother was young enough to be the Old Man's daughter;
hence he sometimes spoiled her as if she were. To spare her from
having to sleep in his ex-wife's bedroom, the Old Man had a large
addition built behind his study with a vaulted ceiling and a great
stone fireplace. The Royal Chamber, Paul called it.

Though he'd been offered any room on the second floor, Paul
kept the one he'd always had. It was the smallest of the four rooms,
but it had the best light—a kind of fishbowl effect that made it
feel somehow separate from the rest of the house. From as early
as I could remember, I would join him there whenever he would
let me. Together we would stretch across the width of his bed,
gazing out his windows across the yard to a broad, grassy knoll in
the distance, atop which sat the old white-columned estate house
known as Twin Oaks.

Twin Oaks had been vacant for many years. The house stood in
a clearing on the horizon, under the two southern red oak trees for
which it was named. The two trees must have been considerably
smaller when the house was built, but by the time we came along,
they were both giants, a hundred feet tall, as thick at the base of
their trunks as the columns of an ancient temple built to honor an
exalted god.

"It's haunted, you know," Paul told me.

He was sixteen then. I was almost eight.

"No, it isn't," I said.

"Sure it is," Paul said.

In a low, theatrical voice, Paul explained how Twin Oaks had once been the country home of Frank Spencer Cherry, a descendant of the founder of Spencerville and heir to the large fortune his ancestors accumulated in the tobacco trade. Cherry was no farmer, nor did he do much of anything, according to Paul—his first cousin ran the family business.

"What did he keep on his farm?" I asked.

"Liquor, poker, and whores," Paul said.

Paul sat up on the bed and lit a cigarette. In 1977 you could still buy cigarettes at sixteen. They didn't even shut down the smoking pavilions at the public high schools until more than a decade later. In a town built on tobacco money, people were willing to plead ignorance as long as the world would let them.

Still, it baffles me now that my parents let Paul smoke, especially in the house. My mother swears she never smoked in her life, not even in college. I've seen sepia-toned photographs of the Old Man holding a pipe, but he had given that up long before I was born. Years later, when I asked my mother what they were thinking, she made no apologies.

"In this life," she said, "you choose your battles."

Since I didn't know any different, Paul's smoking seemed perfectly normal to me. I loved to watch him tamp the filter against his knuckle and flip his Zippo open with a kind of showy flourish, the way I imagined Fonzie would have fired up his Camel if the networks allowed smoking on sitcoms. Paul didn't have a leather jacket or ride a motorcycle, but I already sensed that he was cooler than the Fonz. After all, Paul could smoke in his bedroom; Fonzie couldn't even smoke in the men's room at Al's.

Paul reclined against the headboard, holding his cigarette aloft.

"Whores?" I asked.

"Yeah," Paul said.

I didn't need him to explain. His crooked smile and breezy air of matter-of-factness made clear exactly what a whore was.

The room was shadowy and blue in the dusk. The only light came from the pulsing flame at the end of Paul's cigarette and the glow-in-the dark poster on the wall behind us—the cover of Pink Floyd's *Dark Side of the Moon*.

Outside in the distance, the sun sank below the horizon behind Twin Oaks. A pale orange glow filtered through where the front and rear windows of the large upstairs rooms aligned. I studied the windows, looking for the movement of ghostly shapes.

"Liquor, gambling, and whores," Paul continued. "Every moonshine runner in the state stopped off at that house at one point or another."

He puffed thoughtfully on his Camel—a short, dramatic pause to let the tension rise.

"Back home," he explained, "Frank Cherry's poor wife suffered alone while he ditched her and the kids for days at a time to come out here. All the leading men of the town felt sorry for her that she had married such a son of a bitch, but the same men were at ole Frank Cherry's card table on Friday and Saturday nights. No one said shit to him or tried to do a thing about it."

I don't know how Paul presumed to know all these details. He was certainly no scholar. He must have heard it from the Old Man, a compulsive storyteller prone to embellishment. I've since done my own research and learned that the bare facts, at least, are accurate. Frank Cherry still has descendants in Spencerville: a fairly wretched lot, penniless and uneducated, deferentially tolerated by the aged few who know or remember that theirs was once among the town's most affluent and influential families. Unsurprisingly I could find no evidence of any epic debauches at Twin Oaks involving the town's "leading men." But Paul told the story with authority.

"In 1929, the stock market crashed, and Frank Cherry lost everything," he continued. "The party was over. The next day, he rode out here by himself. A few days after, when his horse showed up on Main Street with no rider, the police came out and found him in his rocking chair, with a pistol hanging from his cold, dead fingers. His brains were splattered all over the front porch."

Paul sucked on his cigarette. His eyes were black and ominous in the yellow bloom of light around his face. My own must have looked wide and full of terror.

"No one's lived there since," Paul said. "But that doesn't mean the place is empty, does it, Rocky?"

I was born with a droopy eye and had always had a deep voice and an unruly mop of dark, wavy hair. Everyone else called me Richard or Dickie or (painfully) young Dick or little Dick, after the Old Man. But to Paul I had been Rocky, the Italian Stallion, Rocky Raccoon, for longer than I could remember.

"I've been in that house, you know," Paul said. "One night, Rayner and me broke a window and crawled in."

"What did you see?" I asked.

"A lot of dust and garbage," he said. "Whiskey bottles and beer cans. Some random stuff written on the walls. Plenty of people have snuck in to have a look over the years. Maybe a hobo or two has tried to sleep there. But I doubt too many have made it through the night."

I gazed out the window at the house.

"Rayner was upstairs when I first noticed it," Paul said, his voice low and ominous.

"What?" I asked.

"The sound of a rocking chair, creaking back and forth."

"No way," I gasped.

"Uh-huh," Paul said. "At first I thought Rayner was just messing with me. But the noise was definitely coming from downstairs. As I walked around, it got louder and louder, but I never saw anything. Then it stopped. Swear on my soul, Rocky, the air in that room got colder by about fifty degrees. Rayner felt it too. It took us about a second to think about it before we both ran as fast as we could out of that house. We didn't stop running until we were halfway down the hill. When we stopped to look back, we heard a loud crack like the sound of a pistol shot."

Paul took a last drag and stubbed out his cigarette in the ashtray on the bedside table. The ember flared and sizzled and disappeared.

"You know what else, Rocky?" he said.

"What?"

"I didn't find out until after that about old Frank Cherry and the pistol and the rocking chair out on that front porch. So you know I'm not making it up."

Paul slipped another Camel from the pack he kept in his shirt pocket and lit it. I stared back out the window at the shadow of Twin Oaks.

"Want to go check it out, Rocky?"

Of course I didn't.

"Sure," I said.

MY BROTHER PAUL had a reputation around town as a "bad kid." This wasn't entirely undeserved, although what passed for "bad" in provincial little southern towns like Spencerville probably wouldn't arouse much notice in more cultured, cosmopolitan locales like Richmond or Washington, DC, and its suburbs, up there in the other Virginia, the part of the state the Old Man referred to as "occupied territory." The people of Spencerville, however, were not yet inured to the roving carelessness of the young.

We were coming of age in the late seventies, at the sweaty, nauseous, split-headed peak of the hangover between Watergate and "Morning in America." For nearly a decade, our parents and their peers had watched horrified as the far-flung corners of the world burst into flames on their brand-new, first-ever color TVs. The Old Man and his buddies who had survived World War II and Korea felt like they had beaten back Hitler and Tojo all for the sake of sex, drugs, rock and roll, and Martin Luther King Jr. None of the kids played Vietnam on the playground. Burning cities, race riots, hippies fucking in the mud at rock concerts, cars lined up for a mile just to fill the tank, Commie wackos and disgruntled vets storming the barricades at political conventions—to watch the news was to believe that the country had, in fact, found sympathy for the devil.

But not in Spencerville. In Spencerville, elementary school kids could walk alone or ride their bikes to school. Daughters were safe from the clutches of filthy hippies and horny English rock stars in tight leather britches. Sons worshipped God, loved their mothers, and feared their fathers. In Spencerville, what passed for change was a new strip mall or movie theater or some other minor civic improvement, like recalibrating the traffic lights so that, if you observed the speed limit, you could drive the twelve miles without stopping from First and Main downtown across the bridge over the James River (where Main turns into Riverdale), through Colonial Heights and the Spencer College neighborhood, and on out through the last light before Riverdale turns into Highway 29.

The ways in which the world outside Spencerville was evolving showed up in the form of small, short-lived trends, like disco or laser light shows or key parties—occasional frights, distractions, or subjects of titillating gossip, but nothing really to be afraid of. The bad things happened elsewhere. I do not mean to say that the town was free of any sort of calamity, or that we all lived oblivious to the news of the world. But we could still leave our doors open at night. We were isolated, insulated, largely ignored, and perfectly content.

Hence boys like Paul and his friends must have seemed a lot worse than they actually were. Especially among the good Episcopalians and Presbyterians of the Boone's Ferry neighborhood, Paul and Rayner Newcomb and their crew were symbols of menace, with their muscle cars blasting loud rock out the open windows, with their cigarettes and their unkempt hair and their insouciant contempt for the naive idealism of the "good" kids who played sports, ran for student council, and filled the ranks of scout troops and church youth groups.

They threw beer parties when their parents were out of town. They parked their cars in empty lots and dead-end streets, drawing the less reckless but still hopelessly curious girls and boys to them like sailors to the Sirens' song. They picked fights and pulled pranks. They trespassed anywhere and often, mounting the roofs of tall buildings and dangling perilously from trestle bridges. Invading construction sites and boarded-up houses, they plowed the fertile fields of former vestal virgins, leaving behind their spent condoms and beer cans and cigarette butts like dogs marking trees. And Paul was one of them.

I didn't know any of this when I was five. All I knew was that Paul was effortlessly cool—that even the people who scowled at him plainly desired and envied both his beauty and his indifference.

Naturally I worshipped him. And so, naturally, I would follow him anywhere he'd let me, no matter how terrifying, including up through a broken window and into the dark bowels of a haunted mansion.

WE SLIPPED DOWN the stairs and out the door into the damp cold. My shoes and pant legs quickly became soaked in the tall, wet grass. We stopped once, in the middle of the field, for Paul to flip out his Zippo and light another cigarette. The smell of the smoke mingled with the musty odor of the dormant grass as we trudged forward and up the slope of the hill to the house, dark and ominous beneath the towering oak trees, which flanked the great columns and the wide, sagging porch like impassive sentries.

Paul took a last drag off his cigarette before flicking the still-burning butt onto the wet black leaves in the fountain at the center of the circle.

"Wait here," he said.

He walked around to the right side of the house. Climbing onto the cellar door, he hefted himself up and through the same window he must have used before.

I studied the long front porch, imagining Frank Cherry's blood and brains on the walls and on the floorboards beneath a solitary rocking chair. I listened for the sound of that chair creaking back and forth, back and forth in the lonely wind.

As the minutes stretched on, a powerful sense of dread overcame me. I wanted nothing more than to be home, secure in the fishbowl of Paul's room or, better yet, before the roaring hearth of the Royal Chamber, watching *The Muppet Show* while my mother read her Bible and the Old Man sat at his table in the corner, poring over his legal pads and contracts.

I was about to turn and run home when the shape of a man emerged from behind the house on the side opposite where Paul had climbed in.

Though it was very dark, I could see that the man was dressed in a long, dark coat and black leather boots. He looked old, with gray hair cut close to his skull. As he rounded the corner and stepped onto the porch, I realized that, whoever or whatever he was, I wasn't imagining him—he was there, before my eyes, heading toward the front door. I watched in mute horror as the man simultaneously reached for the doorknob and drew a pistol from the pocket of his coat.

Before I could gather my wits to move or speak, a booming crack and a flash of light exploded from within the house, rattling the loose panes of glass in the frames of the windows.

Over the roaring and ringing in my ears, I heard my brother moaning through the black rectangle of the open front door. At last my voice returned to me.

"Die, Frank Cherry, you whore!" I cried.

I didn't wait to see if "Frank Cherry" had heard me. I just ran. I ran so fast the field seemed to fly beneath me. I ran and ran, heaving and sobbing between breaths, stumbling and falling and climbing back up to my feet again, my legs always moving, my eyes fixed on home. When I reached the steps of our house, I barreled through the front door, tracking wet mud and grass across the carpets and the Persian rugs, back to the Royal Chamber.

My mother looked up with a start from where she sat in her armchair. As the Old Man rose from his seat at the corner table, I ran to him and buried my face in the soft cotton of his red flannel shirt.

"What in the hell," he said.

"Frank Cherry shot Paul," I cried.

My mother warmed me with a throw blanket, fussing all the while about how wet and dirty my pants and shoes had become, how cold I was, how likely I might be to come down with pneumonia on account of having been tramping around outside when the temperatures were still dropping below freezing at night. I babbled about Paul and Twin Oaks and Frank Cherry's ghost and the gun and the brains on the wall beside the rocking chair.

The Old Man disappeared into his closet. A few moments later he emerged wearing his hunting boots and jacket. In one hand he held a large police-style flashlight; in the other, his .38 snub-nosed revolver.

"Dick," my mother said, her voice shrill with alarm.

"Just a precaution," he replied.

"Don't be ridiculous," my mother said.

But he was already off, down the hall and out the front door.

My mother led me upstairs and helped me out of my wet clothes.

"Get ready for bed," she said.

She went into Paul's room to stand vigil at the window, her eyes following the journey of the Old Man's flashlight up the hill toward Twin Oaks.

As I envision her there now, standing before the window with her arms crossed, I remember that my mother was still very beautiful then, and quite young. Except for a bit of lingering post-pregnancy weight in her belly and hips, she was slim and dainty, with delicate, nervous hands. She wore her sandy blond hair in a girlish bob. Her eyes were wide and earnest, as if she was always seeking someone's approval.

I had only just begun to comprehend the abnormality of my parents' marriage. In 1977, my mother was thirty-three years old; the Old Man was nearing sixty. The previous fall, on parents' day at my school, my teacher had mistakenly identified the Old Man as my grandfather. I barely noticed her error and would not have been bothered by it but for her obvious embarrassment and the casual scorn in the Old Man's eyes when he corrected her.

I still can't grasp exactly how they ended up together. My mother couldn't have been without other prospects. The most obvious explanation was the most cynical: that she had married him for his money. The dime-store psychiatrist's explanation would be that she had married a father figure. Both of her parents were killed in an accident when she was very small; she was raised by her grandmother, who was already a widow before my mother was born.

Life with the Old Man couldn't have been easy for my mother. Even when you think you know what you're getting into, some situations can't be adequately prepared for—namely Paul, who was not quite old enough to be her brother but too old to be her son and, in his mind at least, too old to follow her rules.

Years later, my mother told me she'd only once considered leaving the Old Man, before I was born. Paul had done her some horrible insult, the nature of which she would not reveal to me. The Old Man had taken Paul's side, and the argument devolved from there. The next day, when the Old Man came home, he found my mother sitting at the kitchen table, her eyes stained with tears. On the table in front of her were a checkbook and her three credit cards: American Express, MasterCard, an Exxon gas card.

"What are you doing?" he had asked her.

"I was going," she said.

"Where?" the Old Man asked.

"I don't know," she said. "I just knew I wasn't going to come back."

The Old Man sat down next to her and grasped her hand.

"Why did you stay?" he asked.

"Because—" she said, "because I don't have any money of my own. Because I knew you could stop my checks and cancel these cards, and I'd have no one to turn to."

"I would never do that," the Old Man said.

His voice was pained and gentle, she said. Filled with love and guilt.

"But I would use the cards," he said. "I would use them to find you."

She must have thought of that moment and all its implications as she stared out the window into the darkness, her arms still crossed, her face blank and absent, as if she had forgotten I was there. She must have seen that flashlight again, moving faster, coming closer, until she could see the Old Man emerge from the darkness into the glow of the front porch light.

"Dear God," my mother said.

We hurried from the window and down the stairs to open the front door.

"What happened?" my mother asked.

"He's been shot," the Old Man's voice replied.

"By who?"

"Brad Culver, the stupid son of a bitch."

I pushed past the Old Man and out the door. Paul sat on the porch with his back against the railing, his face ashen, clutching his leg with bloody hands.

"Get towels," the Old Man said. "Call the emergency room."

I knelt next to Paul and threw my arms around his neck.

"Don't cry, Rocky," he said. "'Tis but a flesh wound."

"Are you going to die?" I asked.

"No, he's not going to die," the Old Man said, appearing at my side with a stack of worn-out bath towels. The anger in his voice felt strangely reassuring.

A pair of headlights turned into the driveway and drew closer. A silver Mercedes sedan sped up to the house and stopped, sliding a bit in the loose gravel of the driveway. Out from the driver's side door stepped the black-clad man I'd seen at Twin Oaks.

"Frank Cherry!" I cried.

"What did you say?" the Old Man asked.

"Don't let him take Paul, Daddy!" I wailed.

"Shut up!" the Old Man barked.

"Dick," the man said. "Let me drive you."

"You've done quite enough, sir," the Old Man answered.

"I told you it was an accident," the man said. "He just surprised me, that's all."

The Old Man stood and moved toward the man, who, illuminated by the headlights of his car, was still, for all I knew, a ghost. My mother, who had returned from the kitchen phone, grasped my shoulders and held me there.

"Dick," she cried.

The Old Man had pulled his own gun from the pocket of his hunting jacket.

"An accident, you say?" the Old Man repeated.

The man said nothing; he merely stared at the Old Man—or, more accurately, at the gun in the Old Man's hand.

"Would you be surprised," the Old Man said, "if I accidentally blew your goddamned head off?"

The man had no answer for that question. On the steps beside me, Paul observed the scene with bemusement.

"Dick!" my mother cried. "Your son!"

The Old Man turned his head toward my mother, his face constricted in a rictus of fury.

The Old Man slowly put the gun back in his pocket.

"I'd like you to leave," he said to the man.

"All right," the man said. "I'll meet you over at the hospital. You can shoot me there if you'd like."

"Maybe I will," the Old Man said.

The man returned to his car, which was still idling. He made a sharp three-point turn and sped away.

The Old Man marched back up to the porch. His lips parted, peeling back to reveal his gritted teeth. His face seemed weighted with something more obscure and troubling than mere rage. With his free hand, the Old Man reached out to take the keys from my mother. With his other, he presented the gun to her, handle first.

"Here," he said.

"I don't want to touch that," she said.

"Take it," he said. "I don't have time to put it away."

My mother grasped the handle of the pistol with her thumb and index finger and held the gun out, dangling from her hand like a dead mouse hanging from its tail.

The Old Man stripped off his hunting coat, revealing where the strain of his efforts and his worry had seeped out of him, staining the armpits of his red plaid flannel shirt. He stooped and draped the coat around Paul's shoulders.

"All right, son," he said. "I'm going to get the car."

He turned and walked briskly toward the garage.

"Yo, Rocky," Paul said. "Could you do me a quick favor?"

He took one hand away from his leg for a moment and tapped the breast pocket of his shirt.

My mother looked on helplessly as I knelt and removed the pack of Camels. I placed a cigarette between Paul's lips, flipped open his Zippo, and sparked the wheel into flame as if I'd done it a thousand times.

2

PAUL DIDN'T DIE. When I came home from school the next day he was there in his room, his leg heavily bandaged and propped up on pillows. Leigh Bowman, Paul's girlfriend, sat on the bed beside him. Across the room by the window, Rayner Newcomb slouched in the desk chair. All three of them were smoking cigarettes and laughing the careless laughter of impudent youth.

"Here's Rocky," Leigh said.

"*Die, Frank Cherry, you whore!*" Rayner squealed.

Again, they laughed, even Paul—perhaps Paul most of all. My whole head went purple.

"Aw, come on, Rocky," Paul said.

"It's not funny," I said.

"I think it's pretty funny," Paul said.

My eyes brimmed at this small betrayal.

"Well, it's not," I said. "You scared me!"

"I know," Paul said. "I'm sorry. But I didn't shoot myself, you know."

My mother appeared in the doorway.

"Hey, Alice," Paul said.

"Are you feeling any better?" my mother asked.

Paul shrugged.

"It hurts," he said.

"Do you need anything?"

"Nope," he said. "Thanks for asking."

"Rayner, would you mind opening that window?" my mother said. "Paul could probably use some fresh air."

Rayner sat up to lift the window sash closest to the desk. He slouched back into his chair without looking up or uttering a word.

"Thank you," my mother said. "Richard, I left your snack on the breakfast table."

The moment she turned and drew the door shut behind her, the three of them dissolved into that same cruel laughter.

"Come here, Rocky," Leigh said, patting the bed beside her.

Leigh pulled me into her arms, her hair draping the back of my head. I breathed in the scent of inexpensive girl's perfume mingled with strawberry shampoo and cigarette smoke.

"I'm sorry Paul scared you, Rocky," she said.

"I wasn't that scared," I lied.

I rested my head on the soft slope of her bosom.

"Say there, little man," Rayner said. "How did it feel to watch your dad point a gun at some dude's head?"

I had to think about it—all of it. Frank Cherry's brains and blood splattered on the walls and porch of Twin Oaks. Paul entering the house, followed by the appearance of the black-clad man. The crack of the gun. Most of all, the image of my brother reclining on the porch—his face drained of all color, his hands covered with dark red blood—and the Old Man, sweating and wild eyed, pointing his gun at the head of a man I had only minutes before believed to be a ghost. I had never seen the Old Man—or anyone else, for that matter—so unhinged. How did that feel?

"Good," I said.

"It felt good, huh?" Rayner said.

Paul scrutinized me with heavy-lidded eyes.

"Yeah," I said. "It felt good."

"What about you, Paul?" Leigh asked. "How did you feel?"

Paul looked away, out the windows up the hill toward Twin Oaks.

"I don't know," he said. "It hurt too much to think."

He reached into his shirt pocket for another cigarette.

"I do remember having one thought the second after I realized I'd been shot."

"What's that?" Rayner asked.

"Oh, hell," Paul said, "my old man's going to kill me."

We all laughed at that.

"My dad probably would have taken the dude's gun and shot me again himself, for good measure," said Rayner. He couldn't contain his envy. Misadventures like breaking into abandoned houses and getting shot were supposed to be his department.

"You know, when I heard the Old Man's voice outside, I expected the worst," Paul said. "But when he came through the door and spotted me with his flashlight, he ran and fell all over me, hugging and kissing me like I was a two-year-old. Culver jabbered on and on about how sorry he was, how it was a big misunderstanding and all. The Old Man didn't even look at him. He just humped me up on his back in the ole fireman's carry and ran down the hill like he was back with MacArthur on the beach in the Philippines, huffing and puffing the whole way home. If I didn't know he was just too out of shape to haul a hundred and fifty pounds on his back at a full run, I would have thought he was crying."

"That's beautiful," Leigh said.

I could feel Rayner rolling his eyes behind us.

"Yeah, I know, right?" Paul said. "Who knew the Old Man could be such a softy."

"Let this be a lesson for you, Rocko," said Rayner. "If you ever feel like your daddy doesn't love you anymore, get somebody to shoot you in the leg."

"Shut up, Rayner," Leigh said.

But Paul laughed.

THE NEXT DAY, Paul's mother arrived from Ohio. The Old Man picked her up from the airport after work. Somehow it had been decided that she was going to stay with us, in the guest bedroom, next to Paul's.

My mother spent the hours before her arrival in a state of keen agitation, her lips pursed, aimlessly pacing the floor between bouts of dusting and vacuuming and straightening of couch pillows and other random objects. Paul lazed in his room, his leg propped up, smoking even more than usual, his eyes drifting back and forth between the ceiling and the windows.

Paul's mother had left Spencerville years earlier, before the Old Man even divorced her, and before the Old Man met my mother. She existed only as a name—Anne—and as a disembodied voice on the telephone, talking to Paul or to one or the other of my parents. No conversation with Anne came or went without discord.

Once, not long before he died, in the throes of dementia, the Old Man pulled me close to him as I sat at his bedside. He fixed his eyes on me, clutching my hands to his chest.

"Son, don't ever marry a Yankee," he wheezed. "She'll ruin your life."

Of all the seemingly endless litanies of fatherly advice he dispensed to me, this little mad kernel seemed somehow fraught with importance.

Still, I know little about the Old Man's marriage to Anne—how they met, whether they were ever happy together. I knew only one fact of consequence: before Paul, there was another child—a girl, Annie Elizabeth, who died of leukemia in 1966, when Paul was five.

To me, Annie Elizabeth could be nothing more than a single photograph: an eight-by-ten black and white in a thin silver frame of a beaming child with Shirley Temple ringlets in a flower-patterned dress with lace trim at the sleeves and the collar, an Add-A-Pearl necklace suspended from her thin, frail neck. Paul claimed he had little memory of her. Whenever she came up, the Old Man described Annie Elizabeth as a vision of winsome beauty and steely courage—a little nine-year-old angel-in-waiting, so certain she was of her place in the paradise we learned about in summer vacation Bible school. When she was gone, the Old Man blocked out the sorrow by pouring himself into his work. Anne poured herself a tall scotch, and another, and another.

One day, as Paul explained it, the Old Man came home from

the office and found Anne packed and dressed to travel, having a last drink and a smoke. Oblivious to what was happening, Paul lay on his belly in front of the television while his mother waited for the taxi to take her to the bus station, where she would board a Greyhound bound for Akron. After that, the Old Man and Paul were on their own, until my mother appeared.

"Were you angry?" I once asked Paul.

"About what?" he replied.

When he was older, two or three times a year, Paul took a bus to Akron for a visit. Once, when his and my mother's difficulties had grown especially intense, he left to live with her. He came back after less than a month.

But Paul never spoke ill of his mother. He knew it was the grief that had done it to her. The Old Man had borne up and gone on with his life. Anne, it seemed, had surrendered.

I SAT WITH PAUL listening to records while we waited for Anne to arrive: side A of *After the Gold Rush*, over and over again.

On the wall above Paul's bed hung a black-and-white image of Neil Young sitting on a bench backstage, legs crossed, an open bottle of beer beside him, eyes downcast and hidden, strumming on his big Martin guitar. His hooded brow and bisected long, dark hair made him look like Geronimo in patched, tattered jeans and an untucked oxford shirt. *Neil Young.* To my ears, the very name was sublimely evocative, like a line of terse, elegantly understated poetry. The exaggerated percussion and practiced sloppiness of the guitars and the barroom piano and that strange, keening, almost childlike voice made the sound seem at once ancient and otherworldly.

The lights of the Old Man's car appeared in the driveway. Paul sighed and lit another cigarette.

"Go on," he said. "Have a look at her."

Downstairs, my mother sat in the living room with her Bible open in her hands—presumably seeking some last-minute spiritual fortification. She stood and smoothed her skirt as the door opened. The Old Man entered, clutching a pea-green suitcase, followed by a small woman in a gray coat.

"I never thought I'd be darkening this doorway again," she muttered.

The Old Man grunted in agreement. When she saw me standing at the bottom of the stairwell, she smiled.

"Hello there," she said.

"Hello," I replied.

"Hello, Anne," my mother said.

To my knowledge, the two women had never met face-to-face before.

"What a healthy-looking boy," she said to my mother.

The Old Man's forced grin looked far too painful to be worthwhile.

"Paul's upstairs," my mother said.

Anne slipped her coat off her shoulders and handed it to my mother.

"Would you mind bringing me a drink, Dick?" Anne asked.

"What'll you have?"

"A rusty nail, if you can manage it."

"I think we're out of Drambuie," the Old Man said.

"Just a scotch on the rocks, then."

"I'll take you to Paul's room," I said. Then I remembered: Anne didn't need me or anyone else to show her the way around our house. I stood by silently as she crept up the stairs. The Old Man hurried to take her coat from my mother's hands and hang it in the hall closet.

"Why don't you come help me in the kitchen, Richard," my mother said.

She was preparing a London broil and a broccoli casserole. The Old Man came in behind me. He took a highball glass from the cabinet and opened the freezer for ice cubes.

"I could use a drink myself," he said.

"Don't you dare," my mother said.

"Christ almighty," the Old Man muttered.

I followed him out to the dining room, where he kept the liquor and wine. He opened the lock on the cabinet and removed a bottle of scotch and poured the glass full to the lip. Glancing back at the kitchen, he slurped down about half the contents. He turned toward me, his brow furrowed.

"If you tell your mother," he said.

I nodded.

The Old Man replenished the glass.

"Here," he said.

He handed me the drink. I wasn't sure what he wanted me to do with it.

"Go on," he said. "I've waited on that woman enough in my life."

I walked away, holding the highball glass out in front of me as if it were the Holy Grail, brimming with the priceless blood of the Savior—so full that it was impossible not to spill.

I tiptoed around the hall to the landing of the staircase. I was still visualizing the blood of Jesus inside it—not the figurative communion wine, but the actual, syrupy stuff, dark and sticky and tasting of iron. This sacred elixir couldn't be squandered, I reasoned. To let it spill to the ground would be a sacrilege. So I decided, in the way children do, that the one solution was to slurp off the top layer.

The whiskey was still lukewarm and almost completely undiluted. Alone at the foot of the stairs, I marveled at the heat in my throat. I felt as if my whole body and brain had been cleansed with fire.

I managed to slide the glass onto the hall table in time to muffle the cough in my elbow. When I recovered my breath, I picked up the glass. Cradling it with both hands, I teetered up the stairs and into Paul's room.

Anne sat across from Paul in the chair next to the open window, smoking a thin white cigarette and tapping her ashes into the sill. Paul was smoking also. He stared off out the window as if he expected someone else to show up. The room felt uncomfortably quiet without Neil Young and Crazy Horse ringing off the walls.

I had never seen a picture of Anne; Paul didn't keep one in his room. What had she looked like before? Had any of Paul's beauty come from her? Had she ever been beautiful at all? She certainly wasn't alluring, as I imagined a "fallen woman" should be. She had an ugly mouth, with thin, angry lips. She wore too much makeup, or maybe not enough. It looked as if it had been applied with the express purpose of appearing careless. That air of indifference was the only way, really, in which Paul resembled her at all.

"Come into my parlor, darling," she said.

I walked toward her and handed her the drink.

"Did you taste it to make sure it isn't poisoned?" she asked.

"No," I stammered. "I just spilled a little."

"I'm teasing you, child," she said.

She held her cigarette aloft with one hand and sipped her drink with the other, taking her measure of me. I rocked back and forth from my heels to the balls of my feet, contemplating the numbness of my lips and the sudden thickness of my tongue.

"So," she asked, "am I as monstrous as you've been led to believe?"

The question confused me.

"I don't think Rocky here has an opinion, Mom," Paul said, his eyes still fixed on the window.

"How would he?" Anne said. She sipped her drink. "You all prefer to behave as if I don't exist."

"He's seven years old, Mom."

"Almost eight," I added.

"When's your birthday?" Anne asked.

"July twenty-ninth," I said.

Anne's mouth fell open. She gaped at me for a moment before turning to address Paul.

"You never told me that," she said with a dry chuckle. "Why didn't you tell me that?"

"Why would I?" Paul said.

"What?" I asked.

She aimed her small, cold eyes at me as she stamped out her cigarette.

"We have the same birthday, young Richard," she said.

"You and me?" I asked.

"That's right," she said. "How could this have escaped me, Paul?"

"Maybe somebody told you and you just forgot," Paul said.

"Maybe," she said, still chuckling. "Maybe. Well, young Richard, I won't forget this time."

"Thank you," I said, assuming she meant to send me a present.

AT DINNER, THE OLD MAN and Anne sat at opposite ends of the dining table. Paul came downstairs for the first time since he'd returned from the hospital. He sat alone on one side of the table, positioned so he could prop his leg up on the chair next to him. My mother and I sat on the other side.

My mother was having trouble keeping her hands still. She pushed the food around on her plate with the dinner fork, but I never saw her take a bite. When she put the fork down, she would either put one arm around me or the opposite hand on the Old Man's forearm.

Like my mother, Anne ate little to nothing. It was as if the two of them were in a hunger contest. Across the table, Paul picked at his food without much interest.

I was hungry, however. I devoured everything in front of me. The Old Man also ate eagerly. We were dutiful plate cleaners at every meal, the Old Man and I. Maybe it was because we didn't smoke. My mother didn't smoke either, nor did she drink much more than the occasional glass of white wine or a small snifter of sherry before bedtime if she was feeling a little wired. "Alcohol ages the skin," she would say.

The Old Man had managed to sneak a few in, however. Who could blame him? And Anne—well, her food was cold on her plate before she started slurring her speech, but otherwise she made no effort to disguise her habit or her condition. My mother's feeble attempts at polite conversation—inquiries about the weather in Akron, the flight, and so forth—were met with curt, dismissive replies. As Anne grew increasingly drunk, she made a point of calling my mother "child," as in "The weather was miserable, child," and "Who wouldn't be exhausted after two hours packed into one of those puddle-jumping sardine cans that pass for planes these days, child."

My mother pretended not to notice her condescension. The Old Man just kept refilling her glass. He must have hoped she would pass out soon. Or maybe he wanted Paul to see her good and drunk so he'd be reminded of what he had to look forward to if he ever decided—as Paul sometimes threatened to do when he and my mother were at odds—to leave and move in with Anne.

"So Paul tells me the historical trust has finally found someone sufficiently pedigreed to buy that old wreck of a house up the hill," Anne said.

"That's right," said the Old Man.

"Sufficiently pedigreed?" my mother asked.

Anne lit a cigarette.

"Hasn't Dick ever told you?" she said to my mother. "He tried to buy that house years ago, but those snobs at the Spencerville Historical Trust refused to sell it to him. What did they say they were going to do with it, Dick?"

"A museum," the Old Man said.

Anne neither asked for nor was offered an ashtray. Instead, as my mother's mouth fell open, she tipped the ashes onto her nearly untouched dinner.

"Yes, that's right," she said. "A museum, like the Quaker Meetinghouse, where the old gals from the DAR put on their Colonial-period costumes once a month and show groups of kindergartners how the settlers used to make candles."

She turned to me.

"Have you been on one of those tours, young Richard?"

I nodded.

"Are they still dipping the candles?"

"Yes, ma'am," I said.

"But this fellow Culver that they've sold the place to," she said, turning back to the Old Man. "He won't turn it into a museum, will he?"

"No," the Old Man said. "He's going to renovate it."

"How long will that take?" my mother asked.

"A year or so. Maybe more, maybe less. We'll see."

"And why," Anne asked, "is this Culver good enough to be allowed to own it and you weren't?"

"He's married to Jane Cabell," the Old Man said.

"Ah," Anne said. "That explains it. Well, you never could buy your way in with the FFV crowd, could you, Dick?"

Paul later explained to me that FFV stood for First Families of Virginia: the kind of people who still thought money mattered less than whether you could trace your ancestry back to the court of King Charles I.

"They just moved back from somewhere abroad," the Old Man said. "Culver was in coal or iron, I think. Made his millions, cashed out, and got into investing. Since you can do that from pretty much anywhere, Jane made him move to Spencerville as payback for dragging her all over the world to keep house while he was off digging mines. I'm sure buying the old Cherry place was her idea."

"And are you going to press charges?" Anne asked.

"For what?"

"For nearly killing my son."

"*Our* son was trespassing on his property at the time," the Old Man said.

"I didn't know anyone had bought the place," Paul said.

"That makes no difference," the Old Man said. "It's still illegal."

"People have been going in that house for years," Paul said. "I bet you've been in it before. Without permission."

The Old Man didn't answer him.

"I think you should press charges," Anne insisted.

"No."

"If you don't, maybe I will."

"Suit yourself," the Old Man said. "But you're not going to have to live next door to the man."

"You weren't too concerned about that when you threatened to kill him, were you?" she said.

"It was the heat of the moment," the Old Man said. "Culver understands that. We've already talked it over and walked away as friends. He feels terrible about all of it."

"I see," Anne said.

She extinguished her cigarette in an especially rare slice of London broil.

"So, Dick," she said. "I find it remarkable that in all of our conversations over the years since this child of yours came along, you never mentioned that he and I share the same birthday."

The Old Man chewed his steak slowly and purposefully before swallowing.

"I'm sure I told you," he said.

"No," she said. "You didn't."

"Sure you did," Paul said. "She just forgot."

"No," Anne said again. "He didn't, Paul. Neither did you, darling."

Anne narrowed her eyes at the Old Man, a faint smile forming on her lips.

"Your birthday is July twenty-ninth?" my mother asked, her voice meek, almost apologetic.

"You never told her either?" Anne said to the Old Man. "Oopsy me, Dick. What a pickle I've put you in."

"I'm sure I must have mentioned it at some point," the Old Man repeated, his face reddening with wrath.

"It must make the date that much easier to remember," Anne said.

"How could I forget?" he said.

Anne turned to me and smiled.

"Do you know who else was born on July twenty-ninth, Richard?" she asked.

"No, ma'am," I said.

"Mussolini," she said.

"Who's Mussolini?"

"That's enough, Anne," the Old Man said.

"It's a fact," she replied. "One he'll hear in school one day. Won't he look smart if he already knows Mussolini's birthday?"

"Who's Mussolini?" I asked again.

"A dead guy," Paul said. "They hanged him from a bridge for killing Jews."

"You're confusing Mussolini with Hitler, dear," Anne said. "Mussolini killed a few Jews, but only because Hitler made him."

"What's a Jew?" I asked.

"Jesus Christ," the Old Man said.

"Maybe you should go to your room, Richard," said my mother.

"Who's Hitler?"

"He isn't Jesus Christ, I promise you," Paul said.

"Go to your room," my mother ordered.

"But we haven't had dessert," I whined.

"*Go to your goddamned room!*" the Old Man bellowed, pounding his fist on the table.

I was too stunned to move or make a sound. My mother gaped at the Old Man, her lips quivering.

"Both of you," said the Old Man.

He slumped back in his chair while Anne sneered at him.

"Come on, Rock," Paul said. "Help me up."

I stood and went for his crutches while Paul shifted out of his chair. He steadied himself on my shoulders and pulled himself to his feet.

"I think me and Rocky here might go listen to some music," Paul said. "Thanks for dinner, Alice."

I followed him out of the dining room and through the hallway to the landing and held his crutches while he hopped up the stairs. When we reached the top step, I handed him the crutches and followed him into his room.

"Shut the door, will you?" he asked.

Paul slumped onto his bed and reached across to the bedside table for his lighter and cigarettes. He lit up and took a long drag.

Downstairs, the shouting ebbed and flowed. In the quiet moments, I could sense the seething through the floor.

"Flip it over," he said.

I turned the disc over to side B and dropped the needle. I crawled up onto the bed next to Paul and looked up at the ceiling and listened. The scotch must have worn me out; I was asleep before the end of "Don't Let It Bring You Down."

I WOKE UP SWEATING and disoriented. I was under the covers in my own bed, still dressed in my school clothes. The Old Man must have put me there. It couldn't have been Paul, with his leg. My mother wouldn't have let me go to sleep without changing and brushing my teeth, regardless of the circumstances.

I slid down off the bed and crept out into the hallway to peer through the open door of Paul's room. Anne was in there, on top of the covers in the bed beside him, muttering or murmuring or singing some dissonant lullaby. Was Paul asleep, I wondered, or just pretending?

The next morning, I noticed that the door to the guest bedroom was open. The bed was already made; the sole remaining trace of Anne was the smell of smoke and a pair of lipstick-stained cigarette butts in an ashtray on the vanity.

3

After a week or so, Paul was up and about. He stayed on the crutches for another month to give the tissue ample time to heal and was prohibited from strenuous athletic activity for another six months or so. This was another perverse stroke of luck for Paul, as it excused him from required participation in afternoon extracurricular activities at Macon Prep, the private school he attended. His afternoons were free for rambling around in his Nova and hanging out at the lunch counter in Pearsall's Drugstore with Leigh and Rayner. Sometimes, Paul and Leigh would take me along to Pearsall's for a hot dog and a milk shake. I would sit in the center of the wide backseat of Paul's car, leaning forward, listening to the music and the laughter, watching their long hair flip in the breezes from the open windows, backlit by the sun.

I was too young to know that Leigh Bowman was already being thought of as a minor tragedy. Her mother had died of breast cancer when Leigh was eleven. Her father—the Honorable Prentiss Powell Bowman III—knew no other way to raise Leigh than to push her to the absolute limits in everything. Leigh had been bred to be a star swimmer and a tennis champion, a blue-ribbon horseback rider and a prima ballerina, a valedictorian and a consummate lady.

To her father's dismay, in the summer before her junior year, Leigh began to be seen riding around in the passenger seat of Paul Askew's big purple car. Before long, she'd given up almost everything for Paul. She still rode her horse, but she refused to compete. She traded tennis and dancing and competitive swimming for lounging in Paul's bedroom, smoking cigarettes and listening to

records. Only in the classroom had she maintained her old standing, probably because she had always made As with little effort.

Her father forbade Leigh to see Paul, which prompted Leigh
to discover quite spontaneously that her father couldn't *forbid* her
to do anything. Something had slipped in her. Judge Bowman
thought it was "the goddamned dope."

Maybe he was right—maybe it was the goddamned dope. Or
maybe it was just a typical case of the good girl falling for the bad
boy who needed to be saved. Maybe, because of her mother and
Annie Elizabeth, Leigh and Paul felt like they understood each
other as no one else could. Maybe Leigh was looking for someone
to help her down off the ceaseless treadmill her father had set her
on. Or maybe Leigh and Paul were star-crossed from the beginning, and she was doomed to love him, come what may.

NOT LONG AFTER Paul retired the crutches, our parents invited
Brad and Jane Culver over for dinner. Paul was not present—off
with Rayner and their friends, "up to no good."

Jane Culver was older than my mother but still seemed much
younger than both her husband and the Old Man. She bent to
meet me at eye level when we were introduced.

"You did such a nice job in *Mame*," she said. "You're very
talented."

Not long before, I had played the role of Young Patrick, the
ward of the flamboyant Auntie Mame, in a local fine arts center
production, having been recruited by the director, Rex LaPage,
who had seen me as Michael Darling in a summer theater production of *Peter Pan*. As the play's one child actor, I had been afforded
the delusion of considering myself a professional.

"You saw that?" I asked.

"When we heard our new neighbor had a speaking part, we had
to attend," she said, smiling and winking at my mother. "I'm so
looking forward to living next door to a rising star!"

I smiled and blushed.

"Come meet Mr. Culver, son," the Old Man said, as if I had
never seen him before.

Even in his pressed slacks and camel-hair blazer, Brad Culver still struck me as a walking cadaver, with sunken eyes and bared teeth.

"Hey there, sport," Culver said, extending his hand.

If I were Paul, I'd have let that hand hang in the air. But I was not Paul, so I shook it, doing my seven-year-old level best to hide my hatred and bewilderment. How could the Old Man court the friendship of the same man who might very well have killed his son—a man he himself had threatened to kill?

Before long, the Old Man and Culver were golfing buddies. Paul remained philosophical about it all.

"Dad would have shot Culver," he reflected, "but he knew they needed someone to fill out his Saturday foursome after Buddy Watkins came down with the gout."

THE FIRST WEEK of June, Anne came back to Spencerville to see Paul graduate from Macon. This time, the Old Man arranged for her to stay at the Hilton out near the new shopping mall by Monacan Mountain. With her was a man named Bill.

Anne's Bill looked as worthless and dilapidated as the suit he wore, which even a second grader could see was cheap and old. His posture was stooped and his hair greasy and in need of a trim. His teeth and fingers were stained with nicotine. I later wondered whether Anne had plucked him off a stool in some skid row dive, or even from beside an oil-drum fire underneath a woebegone Rust Belt overpass.

Anne and Bill smoked and talked throughout the ceremony. Nearby, the Old Man sat with his arms crossed, his balding pate flaming red.

Paul's more illustrious classmates were honored with awards and prizes—Spanish and English and Science medals, scholarships and cash awards named for the school's legendary high achievers and wealthy benefactors, the Headmaster's Award, Best Boy.

"Paul would have had perfect attendance," Anne muttered, "if he hadn't been shot in the leg."

Afterward I rode with my parents to a reception at the home of one of Paul's classmates. Waiters wearing white jackets and black bow ties served flutes of champagne and hors d'oeuvres from silver trays. A keg was provided for the new graduates, who congregated around the pool house in the backyard grotto.

The adults were divided between the families of day and boarding students. For the most part the groups parted naturally, like boys and girls on opposite sides of the gym at a junior high sock hop. Anne and Bill mingled with the out-of-towners while my parents sequestered themselves with their friends in another room.

As soon as I could, I slipped away from my mother and weaved through the legs of tippling grown-ups and out to the backyard, where I found Paul below on the pool deck with his fellow graduates, neckties loosened, nursing red plastic cups. Together they joked and laughed, basking in temporary triumph. Around them were the girls, whose smiling faces betrayed occasional flashes of apprehension, as if they sensed already that, like high school, they were also being graduated from.

Leigh had less reason to fear than the rest. Paul was going no farther than Farmville, only forty-five minutes' drive away, to another all-boys school, famous for the loyalty of its alumni and the epic debauchery of its annual Greek Week. The Old Man wanted him on a short leash, Paul had explained. We'd probably see more of him than we wanted. Nevertheless, Leigh hung on his arm, looking especially young and fragile in her delicate cotton sundress, clinging to Paul like a misbegotten waif.

Behind me I heard the sound of adult voices emerging from the house. I took cover in the hedges so I could spy on the scene unnoticed. Through a gap in the bushes, I saw the casual cheerfulness on Paul's face melt into a more familiar expression.

"There's my darling boy," I heard Anne say.

Her voice had taken on a timbre I recognized from her short visit to our house those months before. She steadied herself on the railing and descended to the pool deck, her Bill in his cheap green suit behind her. An unlit cigarette dangled from her painted red lips.

"Do you have a light, darling?" she asked.

"Sure, Mom," Paul said.

Paul removed his Zippo from its home in his breast pocket.

"Isn't he a handsome boy, Bill?" Anne said between drags. "Didn't I tell you?"

"He sure is," Bill said.

"And what a pretty flower," Anne said, reaching out to stroke Leigh's long hair.

"Exquisite," Bill said.

"She reminds me of Annie Bet," Anne said. "Doesn't she remind you of Annie Bet, Paul?"

"Sure, Mom," Paul said.

I had never heard Annie Elizabeth, the sister who had died before I was born, referred to as Annie Bet.

"She'd have been so proud of you, darling," Anne said.

Perhaps made uncomfortable by being compared to Paul's dead sister, or perhaps by Bill's flagrant ogling, Leigh had lowered her eyes to the ground. She was the first to see the stain spreading down the length of Anne's panty hose and darkening the concrete beneath her feet.

"Oh," she said. "Oh, Paul."

"Shit," Anne hissed.

One of the other boys noticed. A murmur rippled through the navy blazers and neckties. All eyes turned toward the foot of the stairs where Paul Askew's drunk mother had pissed herself.

I felt an unexpected well of sympathy for the woman. It happened, I knew. Sometimes you just get a little excited. Or you forget to go. Or you dream you're in a lake or a pool, where you can feel the peculiarly pleasant warmth in the water, and afterward you wake up in your bed startled, between soaked, clinging sheets.

"Oopsy," Anne said. "I made a boo-boo."

She tossed her lit cigarette into the pool.

"Aw, Mom," Paul said.

He leaned in toward Leigh and whispered something to her. She nodded. They set their red cups on the ground and came around behind Anne, each taking hold of one of her elbows. Paul took the scotch glass from her hand and handed it to Bill without looking at him. Anne tottered up the stairs between them, muttering something I couldn't make out. The wretched Bill followed, admiring Leigh from behind with an appreciative leer.

Paul and Leigh steered Anne off the walk and around the side of the house toward the row of cars parked along the road. Just as they reached the shadows, they stopped. Paul left his mother hanging on to Leigh and hurried back down the hill. He drew up to the hedgerow where I was hidden and knelt to peer in at me, his face almost shaking with indignation. I felt my face redden.

"Don't tell him," he said.

"I won't," I whispered.

"I mean it, Rocky."

"I swear," I said.

"Come out of there and go inside," he said.

I crawled out and stood before him, covered with grime. Paul gripped my arm—firmly, but not painfully. With his free hand, he beat the dust and dirt from my elbows and knees. When he was finished, he released my arm and tousled my hair to clear away a string of cobwebs.

"There," he said. "Now, go."

I trudged up along the moss-flecked bricks to the house, afraid to look back or to search for Leigh and Anne and Bill in the shadowy distance.

"I mean it, Rocky," Paul called. "Don't tell him. Don't tell a soul."

4

WE DID SEE PAUL OFTEN, for the first year at least. He always arrived unannounced, even for the holidays. He might appear a week before Thanksgiving, to my mother's chagrin, loafing around the house, filling the upstairs with the smell of cigarette smoke. Or he might arrive on Christmas Eve, minutes before the Old Man's beloved salt-cured Virginia ham hit the table. Sometimes he just showed up in the middle of the week, to do laundry or switch out some of the records he kept in his dorm room to play on the new portable turntable and cassette player the Old Man had given him as a graduation gift.

The Old Man could never exhibit anything but delight when Paul appeared. When Paul left, the Old Man invariably sank into a mood of quiet longing that might stretch on for days.

"That boy has you on a string," I heard my mother tell him. "He's a born manipulator."

For the longest time, I thought "born manipulator" was a single word.

"He's a man now," the Old Man replied. "I can't force him to do anything."

"A man supports himself," my mother said. "If you live off your father, you're still a boy. And a boy has to follow his father's rules."

"You don't understand, Alice," the Old Man pleaded.

"No, Dick," she said. "It's you who doesn't understand."

"Oh, for Christ's sake," the Old Man moaned.

Almost every conversation they had about Paul ended with the Old Man invoking some holy personage.

Because of what had become or appeared to be becoming of Paul, mine was an excessively governed and supervised childhood.

Mothers like mine—hovering, smothering, overinvolved parents who schedule their children's lives down to the minute—seem now to be the rule rather than the exception. But at the end of the seventies, Spencerville still felt beyond the reach of the looming dread of American life. The worst thing anyone could remember in our neighborhood was Paul's being shot by Brad Culver, an incident considered roughly equivalent to an old crank firing a round of rock salt into the rear ends of teenagers TP'ing the poplars or playing "ring and run."

Nevertheless, I was imprisoned by my mother's anxieties. After school, as my peers piled onto the cacophonous yellow buses or wheeled off on their dirt bikes to do whatever they pleased, I plodded sullenly over to my mother's gigantic, faux-wood-paneled station wagon, ready to drive me off to voice or acting or dance lessons.

My mother could not, however, protect me from the slings and arrows of elementary school—namely, Jimmy Hutter.

We must all recall the incomprehensible spite of the school-yard bully: The random selectivity of his malice, the helpless acquiescence of his prey. Perhaps worst of all, the pathetic betrayal of the victim's so-called friends, who stand aside or perhaps even laugh and jeer, loyalty being a far less powerful instinct than self-preservation. Instead of forming a line of defense, they part and flee, like the herd of wildebeests on *Mutual of Omaha's Wild Kingdom*, blithely trotting away as the lion gorges on the entrails of some unfortunate straggler while Marlin Perkins voices airy platitudes about the circle of life.

Surely Paul had never had to worry about being bullied—or so it seemed when I told him about Jimmy Hutter on one of his quick visits home to do laundry and hit the Old Man up for cash.

"If the kid messes with you," Paul said with a shrug, "just kick him in the balls."

"In the balls?"

"Do it quick," he added. "He won't expect it. Then sock him in the nose, as hard as you can."

Paul explained his plan, which, it turned out, he'd learned from the Old Man, of all people.

"A firm kick in the balls will double a guy over," Paul said. "A hard jab to the nose will make him see stars, which will sort of blind him for a minute or so."

"Then what do you do?" I asked.

Paul admitted that the Old Man had said that after the second blow he should run away. The strategy was designed by the soldiers in the Old Man's unit during the postwar occupation of Japan, for getting out of situations where they might be cornered alone in an unfriendly bar or back alley.

"Should I run?" I asked.

I felt certain that Paul had never run away from a fight himself.

"I don't know," he said. "Just sock him again, I guess."

He stubbed out his cigarette and hopped off the bed.

"Come on," he said. "I'll show you."

On the rug in front of the windows, Paul taught me how to throw a punch.

"Don't swing," Paul said. "Get your dukes up and fire from right beside your head, like this."

I mimicked how he held his fists up below his eyes.

"Plant your feet and get your legs into it," he said. "Same with the kick. Lean forward so you don't fall down."

Paul demonstrated a few quick jab-cross combinations, followed by short, fast knee kicks.

"Here," he said, holding out his palm. "Hit me."

I aimed at his palm and punched it as hard as I could.

"Come on, Rocky," Paul said. "The Italian Stallion can't hit like a girl."

He took out Led Zeppelin's first album and dropped the needle on "Good Times, Bad Times."

"Try again," he said. "And yell when you do it."

"Yell?" I asked.

He turned the knob up on the stereo. The floor buzzed with the heavy bass.

"Yeah. Yell. ARGH!" he bellowed.

"AAAAAAAARGGHHH!" I screamed.

By the end of the album side, I had it down: hard kick to the crotch, cross to the chin, jab to the solar plexus. After Paul left the next day to return to college, I continued my training. Each afternoon, I put on something heavy like Zeppelin or Black Sabbath and practiced, imagining Jimmy Hutter's face floating in the air in front of me, waiting to be pulverized by my furious fists.

A few weeks later, the inevitable moment arrived. As I sat at the lunch table among the other nerds, runts, and oddballs, I felt Jimmy Hutter looming behind me.

"You know what I heard?" Jimmy said, his voice low and menacing.

"No," I said.

"My dad says your dad is one cold-blooded son of a bitch."

The other boys looked on, hushed and alert.

"Is not," I said, my eyes fixed on the table in front of me.

"You callin' me a liar?" Jimmy snarled.

I looked around, trying to spot Mrs. Goode, the lunch lady, who monitored the twittering crowd through the Coke-bottle lenses of her glasses. Mrs. Goode operated the traffic light used to regulate the noise level. If the children were too loud, the light turned red, which meant Silent Lunch, where everyone would be confined to a chair and could only get up with her permission. I prayed vainly that the chatter would rise and Mrs. Goode would turn on the red light, sending Jimmy back to his seat.

"I think you and me need to settle this in the bathroom," Jimmy said.

I remembered something else Paul had told me when I explained Jimmy's intimidation methods.

"How does he get away with pounding kids right there in the cafeteria?" Paul had asked.

"He doesn't," I said. "He always says, 'Let's go settle this in the bathroom,' so the teachers won't see."

"And has anyone ever gone in there with him?"

"No," I replied.

"So you've never really seen this kid beat anyone up."

"No."

"Huh," Paul said.

Paul's inference was clear, even to me. Jimmy Hutter was big and mean, and he acted tough, but it was easy to act tough if no one ever stood up to you. And Jimmy Hutter didn't have training or a strategy. Jimmy Hutter didn't have Paul.

"So are you coming, or are you too pussy?" Jimmy said.

An expansive knowledge of vulgarities was part of Jimmy's special menace.

"No," I said. "Let's do it right here."

The chair screeched on the floor beneath me as I stood and backed away from the table. The din of voices rose around us. But the aging, visually impaired Mrs. Goode, usually so reliably vigilant, made no sound; the traffic light remained green. There would be no rescue, no escape. I took in a deep breath, clenched my fists, reared back, and swung my foot toward Jimmy Hutter's balls with all the force I could muster.

So intent was I on Jimmy's crotch that I didn't notice the steel leg of the red cafeteria chair obstructing the path of the blow. Instead of connecting with Jimmy's scrotum, the kick sent the chair crashing into the table. With my foot twisted in the legs of the chair between us, I tumbled toward Jimmy, who fell to the floor with me, where we lamely slapped and pawed at each other while a cheering throng formed around us.

I felt a pair of powerful hands grasp my arms and lift me from the floor. Byron, the janitor, had stepped through the crowd to snatch the two of us up and scuttle us off to the Main Office. There we sat in front of the desk of Miss Hallenbeck, school secretary and assistant to Principal Powell, while we waited to be summoned, one at a time, for our interrogations.

Jimmy Hutter crossed his arms and stared at the wall, his lips pursed in a sullen scowl, trying to mask his fear. For my own part, I made no effort to disguise my distress. The tears flowed freely.

Jimmy was called in first. I listened intently through the door, hoping to pick up fragments of the conversation, all the while envisioning the stern visage of Mr. Powell, leaning forward with his elbows on the desk. Behind him, hanging on the wall, was the infamous paddle he'd personally constructed: a lean, varnished piece of rosewood with a dozen neat holes bored in two parallel lines across its surface to maximize the speed and force with which it inflicted its discipline. Mr. Powell had even given it a name, etched into its regulation four-inch handle: Swift Justice.

There was more to fear than Swift Justice. Fighting at school generally meant a lengthy suspension. I had never been suspended before; in fact, I'd never been in serious trouble of any kind. Paul was the bad seed—everyone knew this. I had overheard more than a few adults observe how fortunate my parents were that, after Paul, I appeared to be turning out so well.

The silence inside Mr. Powell's office was punctuated by a muffled slap and a sniveling cry—Swift Justice connecting with Jimmy Hutter's rear end.

As I sat there waiting to get hided, I searched my mind frantically to deduce how quickly and easily I had transformed into a "bad kid." I wondered how being bad worked. Was it something that happened accidentally? Did all people start out good? I hadn't invited Jimmy Hutter's torments, but I knew I wasn't innocent either. Was I born bad? I had the same birthday as Anne, after all. She was clearly bad. And Mussolini. Did Mussolini simply wake up one morning and decide to be bad? Surely not. Hitler must have made him that way, like Anne said.

A shape appeared in front of my downcast eyes. I looked up, expecting to see Mr. Powell, ready to take me in for my flogging.

"Hey there, Rocky."

It was Paul, dressed in tan slacks, a navy blazer, and a white shirt and tie. He was clean shaven, and his hair was neatly parted and combed behind his ears. I hadn't seen him in a tie since he graduated from Macon. As far as I knew, he'd never combed his hair in his life.

I was too elated by Paul's sudden appearance at my moment of direst crisis to wonder how he had happened to arrive just when I was about to face Mr. Powell and Swift Justice. Paul must somehow have sensed my need, I assumed, and had come running to my aid.

Ever ready to improvise, Paul behaved from the start as if he'd known he was going to find me there.

"Hey there, Miss Hallenbeck," he said.

He leaned over the desk to give Miss Hallenbeck a peck. Her cheeks flushed pink. As it turned out, even the meanest woman in the Spottswood County Public School System was a sucker for Paul, the "born manipulator."

"So," Paul said, "what has young Richard here gotten himself into?"

"Fighting in the lunchroom," Miss Hallenbeck said, casting a scowl in my direction. Paul sighed and shook his head.

"Kids these days, right, Miss Hallenbeck?"

She giggled girlishly.

"Mrs. Askew didn't mention she'd be sending you, Paul," she said.

"Something came up at the last minute," Paul said. "I'm in town for an alumni thing, so I offered to help out."

A worried look came over Miss Hallenbeck's face.

"Mr. Powell will want to speak with Mrs. Askew," she said. "Or your father."

"One of them will come in tomorrow," Paul said. "They'll call to set up an appointment later on, I'm sure."

"Well, all right," Mrs. Hallenbeck said. "I'll tell him you're here."

She stood and started toward Powell's office. Another loud slap pierced the air on the other side of the door.

"If you don't mind," Paul said, "I'll take the little pugilist here down to the bathroom to clean himself up."

"Make it fast," she said.

As we left the office, Paul winked at Miss Hallenbeck—not a quick, casual wink, but a slow, sensual, flirtatious batting of long, thick eyelashes. For a moment she seemed to lose her breath.

"Come on, slugger," Paul said.

As we reached the end of the hallway, I turned toward the restroom. Paul touched my shoulder.

"Not that way, brother," he said.

He tilted his head toward the entrance to the school, the tall glass doors glowing brightly in the midday sun.

"What about Mr. Powell?" I said.

"Have you ever had a taste of Swift Justice before, Rocky?" Paul asked.

"No."

"I have," he said. "Old Man Powell made me bleed when I was your age."

"He made you bleed?" I whispered.

"That's right," Paul said.

I heard another faint smack and another, louder cry. I envisioned the paddle in Mr. Powell's thick, callused hand, slicing through the air, making me bleed. Who wouldn't run away from that?

We may well have passed Mom's Buick station wagon on the way up the street, but I would have been hidden by the enormous dashboard of the Nova, gazing off to the right at the dogwood blossoms and the magnolia trees that spot the yards along the way to Pearsall's Drugstore.

"So," Paul said, holding the wheel with one hand and lighting a Camel with the other. "What happened?"

"You don't know?" I said.

"How would I?" he said.

"I did what you told me to do," I said. "I kicked him in the balls!"

Smoke spewed from Paul's mouth and billowed over his face as he choked with laughter.

"Shit, Rocky," he said. "What'd you do that for?"

I felt myself start to cry again.

"He said, 'My dad says your dad is one cold-blooded son of a bitch.'"

Paul's laughter dropped off sharply, as if he'd just blown it all out the window like the smoke from his cigarette.

"He said that, huh?" Paul asked.

"Yeah," I answered.

"Well then," Paul said, aiming his eyes at the road. "I guess if somebody says something like that, he deserves to get kicked in the balls."

Paul flipped on the tape deck. We listened to Ted Nugent as Paul drove along Riverdale, past the old boarded-up Zip station and Helms' Market and up to Pearsall's.

"I gotta get some smokes," Paul said.

He stripped off his jacket and tie and tossed them into the back-seat and disappeared into the drugstore. A few minutes later he came ambling out, a fresh Camel Light hanging from his lips, the pack already tucked into the breast pocket of his shirt. In his left arm he cradled a brown paper bag; in his right hand he held a Styrofoam cup.

"Got you a milk shake," he said.

Paul pulled out onto the road and headed back along River-dale toward US 29. He reached behind the front seat and into the brown paper bag he'd brought out of Pearsall's and pulled out a Busch beer. He popped the can open and blew the first little puff of white foam off the rim before taking a healthy swallow.

"Want a sip?" he asked.

"Where are we going?" I asked.

"Well, the commercial says to head for the mountains," he said.

He nodded to the box of cassette tapes he kept on the seat.

"Pick something out," he said.

I chose *Best of the Doobies*. Paul popped it in and turned the knob over. Electric guitar riffs throbbed through the speakers as we whipped past the long, empty hay fields and run-down stables and shacks that line US 29.

I had been to Charlottesville only once before, on a school trip to visit Jefferson's Monticello. I knew that this was where Leigh lived—where she was a student at the university. I gaped at the teeming mass of students hastening to and from classes and in and out of the shops and restaurants that lined University Avenue from St. Paul's Church down to the corner below the trestle bridge at the bottom of the hill, where Paul turned onto Fourteenth Street.

Soon we came to a stop in front of a house surrounded by a high brick wall. Paul stepped out of the car and tossed his cigarette into the street, the last of the smoke slipping from his nostrils like a lost thought.

"Come on," he said. "Let's surprise her."

I followed Paul up onto the sagging porch. Under the window next to the door sat a red velvet couch smelling of mildew. A pair of empty kegs served a dual purpose as improvised end tables and ashtrays. I surveyed a row of beer bottles lining the edge of the porch in front of the bushes while Paul knocked. A few moments later, the door creaked open. A plump girl with long, curly hair appeared.

"Hey," Paul said.

"Oh, hi," the girl said. "Leigh didn't say you were coming."

"It's a surprise," Paul replied.

The girl wore jeans and a faded T-shirt. The boards of the porch groaned under her bare feet.

"Bum a smoke?" the girl asked.

Paul took a pair from the pack in his pocket and flipped his Zippo out. The girl took a hungry drag from the cigarette and tilted her head toward me.

"Who's this?" she said.

"My brother," Paul said.

"Oh, yeah. Rocky," the girl said. "I've seen your school picture."

"Who are you?" I asked.

"I'm Becky," she said to me. "Hasn't she ever told you about me?"

"No," I said.

"Figures," she said. "Shouldn't you be in school?"

"You're not in school," I said.

"He has your manners," she said to Paul.

"Aren't you going to invite us in?" Paul asked.

"Leigh's not here," she said.

"I'll wait."

"Is something wrong?" she asked.

"No. Why do you ask?"

"Leigh's dad called about half an hour ago. Said she needed to call him as soon as she got back. Is somebody dead or something?"

Paul looked down at me and back at the girl.

"Oh," she said. "I get it."

I walked along the edge of the porch and continued inspecting the detritus while the two of them smoked and talked.

"Leigh won't be back for a while," Becky said. "Her class hasn't even started yet. You can wait inside if you like, but you'll have to smoke on the porch."

"Where do you think she might be?"

"You know the amphitheater at the end of the lawn? She studies over there before class sometimes. I think she has a test."

"All right then," Paul said.

Becky tilted her head and squinted at Paul as she sucked on the end of her cigarette. She nodded toward me.

"What's he doing here?" she said.

"I'm babysitting," Paul said.

"Right," Becky said.

Paul dropped his spent cigarette on the porch and ground it under the heel of his shoe.

"Ever heard of an ashtray?" Becky asked.

Paul swept the butt off the porch into the ivy below the bushes. He stuffed his hands into his pockets and spat on the spot where the cigarette had fallen.

"Later," he said.

"Uh-huh," Becky said. "Nice to meet you, Rocky."

"Bye," I said.

We left the squat girl on the porch and walked to the car. Paul drove back in the direction we'd come from. He turned right onto University Avenue and pulled into an empty metered spot across the street from the Rotunda.

"Can I put the coins in?" I asked.

"Sure," he said.

Paul waited impatiently as I carefully slid each coin into the slot and turned the mechanical dial. When I finished, we walked up the stairs and past the bronze statue of Thomas Jefferson, around the great domed edifice and down to the long, sloping lawn, where still more students made their way back and forth beneath the graceful white columns.

At the end of the lawn we turned again and came upon a sunken half circle of large concrete steps in the style of a classical amphitheater. Students were spread out across the steps, reading, talking, and smoking. When I spotted Leigh among them, I ran to her. She was sitting cross-legged, wearing jeans and a halter top, her long hair hanging down past her freckled shoulders. A book was open on her knees. Next to her sat a boy with short blond hair.

"Rocky!" Leigh said.

She rubbed out her cigarette on the pavement next to her and reached up to return my embrace.

"Your dad called," I said. "Somebody died!"

Paul came up behind me, his shadow falling across Leigh and the boy who sat next to her. She closed the book on her knees and stood to embrace Paul, a little less enthusiastically than I expected.

"Hi," she said.

"Hey," Paul said.

"What a surprise," she said.

"I thought you might like it."

"Who died?" she asked.

"Why do you ask?"

"Rocky said my dad called," she said, worry creeping into her voice.

"Don't mind that," Paul said. "It was just some stupid thing Becky said. We just stopped by your place looking for you."

"Oh," she said.

Paul looked down at the blond boy, who hadn't taken his eyes off Leigh since the moment I caught sight of the two of them.

"Who's your friend?" Paul asked.

The boy stood and extended his hand to Paul.

"Hey," he said. "I'm Barton."

"Paul," my brother said.

He took the boy's hand and shook it.

"Barton is my study buddy for econ," Leigh explained. "We have a test."

"A midterm," Barton added.

"I got in a fight at school," I announced.

"Oh, Rocky," Leigh said.

"We need to talk," said Paul.

"Can it wait?" Leigh asked. "It's a really big test."

"Say there, Barton," Paul said. "Would you mind keeping an eye on my little brother for a minute?"

Barton looked at Leigh.

"You don't mind, do you?" she said.

"Not at all," Barton said.

"Stay here, Rocky," Paul said.

I sat down next to Barton. Paul held his hand out and helped Leigh up the steep stairs until they reached the top of the pit and disappeared from sight.

Barton turned back to me, his lips forming a painfully phony smile.

"So," he asked, "what grade are you in?"

"Leigh loves Paul," I said. "They're getting married."

"Is that a fact?" Barton asked. "Are you going to be the best man?"

"Probably," I said. "Or the ring bearer."

"Maybe I'll get invited," Barton said. "Maybe I'll see you there."

"You don't stand a chance," I said.

"Easy there, Rocky," he said.

"Only Paul and Leigh call me that," I said.

"Then what should I call you?" he asked.

"Watch yourself," I said, trying my best to sound as intimidating as Jimmy Hutter. "You might get kicked in the balls."

Barton didn't know what to say to that. I can't imagine he'd had too much experience being threatened by fourth graders.

Barton gave up on the small talk and turned back to his economics book. I wandered away from him down toward the stage, where I ran back and forth, inspecting the doors of the proscenium, glancing back periodically to see if I could spot Paul and Leigh up above along the stone railing that surrounded the amphitheater.

Finally they returned. Leigh's cheeks were streaked with tears.

"He didn't watch me," I told Paul.

"You made it all right," he answered.

"I could have been kidnapped," I said.

"We've got to go," Paul said.

"Are you coming with us?" I asked Leigh.

"No, sweetie," she said. "I have a test, remember?"

She knelt and opened her arms to hug me. I felt the dampness of her cheek against my own as I breathed in that peculiarly enthralling odor of cigarette smoke and strawberry shampoo.

"Think about it," Paul said to Leigh.

"Please, Paul," she said. "Not now."

"You promised," he said.

"You promised too," she said.

Leigh knelt again and faced me. She looked as if she'd walked off with Paul and come back a decade older.

"Go home, Rocky," she said. "Tell him to take you home, OK?"

"I don't want to go home," I said.

I didn't even want to think about home and what was waiting for me there.

"Please," she said. "Promise me, OK?"

"OK," I said.

She stood and embraced Paul again.

"I'm so sorry," she said.

"Go take your test," he said.

"Please, Paul," she said.

"We'll see you around," he said.

I sensed that Paul was suffering a rare defeat. Leigh's eyes followed us as we walked away, to see whether Paul would turn and look back. He didn't, but I did. Leigh waved again and blew a kiss. I turned on my heels to run after Paul.

"She would have come," I said as I came up beside him. "She has a test."

Paul quickened his pace. I had to jog every few paces to keep up with him. When we reached the car, he opened the door and ordered me in.

"Stay here," he said.

In the side mirror, I watched him pace down the block and turn into a convenience store. He emerged a few minutes later with another brown paper sack. He pulled the Nova away from the curb and drove back through the university grounds and across Barracks Road. When we reached the highway, he pulled two beers from the sack and handed one to me.

"Here," he said. "Drink up while it's still cold."

The beer tasted sour and bitter. I drank it fast to be done with it more quickly.

"How about a little Neil?" he said.

"Sure," I answered.

I popped the Doobie Brothers cassette out and slid in *Tonight's the Night*. Paul turned it up loud. Before long, we were both singing along. The wind whipped through the open windows. *Tonight's the night, yes it is.*

We drove a ways before Paul turned off the main highway and up onto a ramp that fed into the Blue Ridge Parkway. We were still singing. I must have had another beer, or maybe I didn't. One was probably enough.

At the top of a ridge, Paul veered the car onto a fire road. We bumped and skidded down a steep, switchbacking slope, over the potholes and around wide bends, little pebbles spinning off the tires and rattling up under the body of the car like machine-gun fire.

At the bottom of the valley, the road became flat and straight. The pace slowed. The rock-strewn path gave way to sand and dirt. An enormous rooster tail of fine grit formed behind us. Paul braked hard. The car slid for a moment and then stopped and was swallowed by the billowing dust.

Paul grabbed the brown paper bag and opened the door.

"Come on," he said.

We walked through the sandy fog and up the bank and through the woods until we reached the base of a stretch of exposed limestone: a giant, bone-yellow slab climbing three hundred yards up to the tree line and a maybe a quarter mile down the ridge. It was essentially as if the trees and earth had been scraped away by a giant trowel, leaving a flat rock face set at what was probably a thirty-five- or forty-degree angle but felt much steeper, particularly when you looked up the length of it from the scree piled at its foot.

Without a word, Paul began edging his way up the face with his feet and right arm while holding the beer with his left. I followed but quickly fell behind. The grade was just gentle enough for us to climb it with relative ease, but steep enough that a slip and a tumble was sure to result in serious injury. I was determined, however, not to be left behind.

Every twenty feet or so, I stopped, panting and heaving, waiting for the burning in my legs to subside. Before long, Paul was just a speck above me, sitting just below the tree line above a rocky hump jutting out of the face, surveying the valley like a jaded emperor.

By the time I reached him, Paul had already finished one cigarette and was preparing to light another. I turned and sat with my head between my knees, catching my breath.

"Want to try one?" he asked.

He held out his pack of cigarettes and shook it gently so that the filter ends slid out toward me.

I'd been watching Paul do it for long enough. I practiced often, with pencils and straws and even Paul's own cigarettes when he left a pack in his room and no one was around to see. I took one out and popped it into the corner of my mouth like a pro.

Paul cupped his hands around the end to light it for me. I took a small puff and blew out the smoke and rested my hand on my bent knee, the cigarette perched between the tips of my right middle and index fingers.

"It doesn't do anything unless you inhale," he said.

He told me to breathe out all the air in my chest and hold the cigarette to my lips and suck in a quick, short toke. I choked and coughed. Instead of laughing, Paul quietly encouraged me. It was almost sweet.

Paul handed me another beer. We sat there together, drinking and smoking as the sun turned the sky pale orange and indigo.

"They call this place John's Gap because a kid named John got lost here back in the seventeen hundreds," Paul said. "His folks were frontier people. One day he was out with his dad, sitting on a stump while his old man cut timber. John's daddy was really into chopping those logs—he was going at it pretty hard. He stopped for a minute and turned around to say something to John, but when he looked at the stump where the boy had been sitting, John was gone."

Paul paused and stared at me, his face blank, emotionless.

"They looked for little John for three days straight and didn't find a stitch of clothing or a hair from his head."

"What happened to him?" I asked.

"Want another cigarette?"

"OK," I said.

Once again he shook one out of the pack for me and cupped his hands to help me light it in the wind. My throat was dry and itchy. I was starting to feel sick. But I lit up anyway and kept on smoking.

"Some folks thought Indians might have crept up behind his old man and snatched him right off the stump without making a sound, covering his mouth so his daddy couldn't hear him scream."

"You're just trying to scare me," I said.

"It's true," Paul said, "as far as I know."

I pictured a hulking, nightmarish Indian warrior with black eyes and long, death-black hair.

"Sometimes at night," Paul said, "they could hear little John in the woods, calling to them. They'd run out and look, but they never found him."

I felt dizzy. When I looked back up the hill at the tree line, the woods seemed darker and closer. Paul flicked his spent cigarette down into the gap, and it went careering off into the falling night, a tiny little hot orange bullet on a field of darkening blue.

The air had grown cold. I dropped my cigarette and let it roll away. Without my asking, Paul pulled out the pack and shook another one loose. I took it and let him help me light it one more time.

My eyes lost focus. I clung to the rock beneath me, yet still felt as if I were tumbling through space.

"Could have been a coyote, I guess," he said.

I dropped my head to the rock and retched. A beery, bilious mess gushed out beneath me, spewing across the sandy surface of the limestone.

I couldn't stop heaving. I choked and gagged and spat, with Paul beside me, still smoking. Except for when he sucked on his cigarette and the ember at the tip fanned out in a little gold bloom over his face, he was invisible.

When I tried to stand up, I felt myself falling forward. I saw myself bouncing down the mountainside, piled up on the rubble, my mangled corpse covered with a layer of soot, as if it had been rolled around in the ashes of a thousand Camel Lights.

I fell sideways and hugged the slope. The rock was cool against my face. When I looked up, Paul was gone.

I whispered his name. I was sure that I had missed him in the darkness, or that he had merely stepped from my field of vision. Lifting my head, I looked up and down and sideways. I howled his name and listened to it echo back to me from across the gap. I cried out again and again until, panting, I put my head back to the rock, listening to the echoes of my cries trickling off into silence.

SOME YEARS LATER, my mother told me a story about how Paul had come to take me out of school and, in one of those odd chance instances, had found me waiting in the principal's office. He might have known what he was going to do all along, or he might just have taken the opportunity as it presented itself. Life happens in moments, she said to me. Sometimes the most thoughtless, accidental, seemingly irrelevant choices seem to ripple on endlessly. Sometimes the weight of the choice is obvious.

That morning Paul had driven home from Ohio. The day before, he had watched Anne, his mother, be lowered into the ground. There was no open casket at the funeral. Anne had passed out drunk in her bed with a lit cigarette in her hand.

Paul had sat there in the church with what was left of his mom's people, looking around for the Old Man, but he wasn't there. Maybe Jimmy Hutter's father was right. There's a strong case to be made that only a cold, arrogant son of a bitch would allow his first son, still essentially a boy, to bury his mother alone. But that's how it went. After that, Paul came for me.

I HAD FALLEN into a fitful sleep plagued by murderous Indians lurking in the woods nearby when I felt Paul pull me up and into his arms. I spat and coughed and rubbed my nose on the sleeve of his oxford shirt. He told me to wrap my legs and arms around his neck and back and he crab-walked down the slope with me clinging to him and trying not to gag from the smell of smoke in his hair.

Paul helped me into the backseat of the car. With my face buried in the crook of my elbow, I listened to the purr of the engine and the pebbles flicking up from beneath the tires until we reached the top of the hill, where Paul hooked a smooth, deliberate left back onto the paved road. As we drove on, I thought of poor little John, wandering around in the hollow, wailing at the night. I imagined a boy about my age, dressed in a frontiersman's knickers and calico shirt and hat, smoking a Camel Light.

After what seemed like a long while, the car came to a stop. I sat up and looked out the window. Paul had parked in front of Twin Oaks. The house was dark, but the exterior was illuminated by a new set of floodlights installed in the flower beds beneath the windows. The remodeling job was nearly finished. The Culvers were set to move in less than a month later, after their return from a vacation in Europe with their college-age daughter, who had been living in England since graduating from a boarding school there.

"Can you walk?" Paul asked me.

"Yes," I said.

He opened the door for me. I climbed out into the cool night air. I still felt a bit ill, but much better. I had no coat—just a pair of dungarees and a long-sleeved rugby-style shirt. I could still taste the bile and the beer and the cigarette smoke. My lips began to tremble.

I followed Paul out to the edge of the driveway and peered down the hill. In front of our house sat a police cruiser.

"I'm sorry, Rocky," Paul said.

"You left me," I said, more as an observation than an accusation.

"I know," he said.

"Why did you do that?"

"I can't say," Paul said.

I looked for his face in the darkness. A whimper broke in my throat.

"Don't cry, Rocky," Paul said.

I felt his hand on my shoulder.

"I want to go home," I said.

"I'm going to have to let you go from here," Paul said.

"I don't want to go alone," I said.

"I know," he said.

Paul kneeled and grabbed my shoulders and pulled me into him. He held me there, unsteady on his knees, his arms shaking.

I could hear his heart rumbling in his chest like the beat of a fast, familiar song.

When I think of that moment, there on that hill, I imagine Paul standing at the edge of a terrible abyss.

"There," Paul whispered. "Just walk toward the porch lights. I'll watch you all the way."

I did as he said. I trudged down the hill whimpering, my stomach still sick, the dew soaking through my tennis shoes and the cuffs of my dungarees in the high grass.

When I reached the bottom of the hill, I turned and looked back. I could just see the faint flicker of Paul's cigarette lighter and the yellow bloom of his face illuminated by the flame in front of the stark, freshly painted white columns of Twin Oaks.

At last I came into the light of our front porch. As I walked up the steps and reached for the door handle, I looked back and saw the Nova's headlights flick on and heard the faint rumble of the engine coming to life. Down deep, I must have understood as I listened to that sound that I was hearing it for the last time.

PART TWO

All That False Instruction

5

THE EVENING AFTER PAUL left me there in front of Twin Oaks, Judge Bowman called our house. His voice was loud and angry enough to be easily overheard through the receiver cupped to the Old Man's ear.

"That bastard son of yours has stolen my daughter," he bellowed.

Once he left me, Paul had raced back to Leigh's house in Charlottesville. After an intense discussion on the porch, Leigh led Paul inside and into her room. The next morning, Becky and the other girls found a note from Leigh on the kitchen table. A neighbor had seen the two of them loading Leigh's backpack and sleeping bag into the trunk of Paul's car.

"You've got to press charges, Dick," Judge Bowman said.

"For what?" the Old Man asked.

"For kidnapping."

"It doesn't sound like he kidnapped her to me," the Old Man said.

"Not her," Bowman snapped. "Your boy."

Judge Bowman knew what Paul had done; by that time, the whole town knew, but Bowman was among the first to hear about it, thanks to my mother, who had asked him to contact Leigh. This was the call Leigh's roommate Becky was referring to when she asked Paul if someone had died.

"He transported your son over sixty miles without consent," Bowman said. "That's a federal crime."

"He brought him back," my father said.

"Don't you see, Askew?" Judge Bowman said. "If you'll press charges, I can get the FBI involved."

"I don't know, Prentiss," the Old Man said.

"You can drop the charges later if you want," Bowman said. "After they're brought home."

"I'm not sure it works that way, Prentiss," the Old Man said.

"Don't tell me about the law, Askew," Bowman thundered. "I'm a goddamned judge, for Christ's sake!"

"I'm sorry, Prentiss," the Old Man said.

"Damn it, man!" Judge Bowman cried. "My daughter!"

Some seven months later, in October, Bowman looked up from the dinner table to find Leigh standing there in jeans and a filthy T-shirt, her hair smelling of woodsmoke, tears streaming down her face.

I heard little about where they had been or what they had done—just that Leigh had come home on a bus ticket that originated in New Mexico. When asked why she had left with him, Leigh offered a simple explanation.

"I failed my econ test," she had said.

What degradations Leigh Bowman might have endured on Paul's behalf became the subject of considerable gossip. We were never able to ask Leigh what really happened or where Paul could be found. Before we even heard she'd returned, her father had already sent her away, "to rest."

The Old Man hired a private investigator to scour the campgrounds and hotels and loitering spots around Albuquerque and Santa Fe, but nothing came of the search. After a while, the glimmer of hope we had felt on Leigh's return faded back to the dull ache we'd lived with in the long months since Paul had disappeared.

I often found the Old Man staring absently out the windows of his study, chin propped on his hand, his eyes cast up to the horizon. Perhaps he was looking at the columns of Twin Oaks and remembering that long-ago night when he picked Paul up from the floor and took him in his arms and carried him across the long, wet field to safety. Or maybe he was still waiting for the purple car to appear at the end of the driveway so that he could run out to meet his son, once dead and now alive again, lost and found.

I WAS NO LONGER "ROCKY." There was no one left to call me that. Paul was gone, and so was Leigh—first, sent off by her father to some undisclosed locale, and then, after a while, back to school somewhere far away. Her father, at least, knew where she was. There seemed to be some understanding that we were not to be told.

After a brief reign as the folk hero of Langhorne Elementary for having escaped Swift Justice by getting kidnapped by my own brother, I went back to being the quiet boy in the back of the room. The summer came, and another year, and another. By the time I passed on to middle school, I had regained my anonymity. Like Annie Elizabeth, Paul became a face in a picture frame, the things he did before he left like the half-true stories about Frank Cherry and Twin Oaks.

Ronald Reagan took office, ushering in a great leap forward for the nouveau riche. Reaganomics might not have worked for most of America, but it was very good to the Old Man—for about seven years anyway. All the wealth enabled by those tax cuts and low interest rates had to be insured, after all. The Old Man managed to get on several boards and committees of small companies and charitable organizations, raising his civic profile and earning him invitations to play golf and cards with some of Spencerville's most prominent snobs.

After a while the Old Man stopped staring out the window hoping to see Paul running down the driveway. Still, he refused to allow my mother to box up Paul's things.

One afternoon when I was thirteen, I overheard my mother and the Old Man arguing. I shook my head in disbelief. Paul could still get between them, even after he'd been missing for four years.

The disposal of Paul's room had become a point of contention. Mother wanted to "redecorate," she said. She thought the house needed another guest bedroom.

"Why?" the Old Man asked. "We never have any guests."

"This is a home, not a memorial, Dick," my mother said.

They were talking in the kitchen while I sat on the other side of the door, doing schoolwork at the dining room table.

"You didn't do this after Annie Elizabeth," my mother said. Even through the door, I could detect a tremor of caution in her voice.

"Annie Bet isn't coming back," the Old Man said.

"What if *he* isn't coming back?" my mother asked.

Nearly half a decade had passed since Paul had disappeared. Still, I didn't want the Old Man to answer the question. Until we learned otherwise, I thought, why should we behave as if he would never return?

"I'll take Paul's room," I said, loudly enough to make the crystal vases vibrate on the sideboard behind me.

I rose from the table and pushed through the swinging door. My mother was leaning against the edge of the sink; the Old Man stood with his arms crossed in front of the stove.

"I'll take Paul's room," I said again, more quietly.

"It's a smaller room, Richard," my mother said.

"I like the windows," I said. "I'm always in there anyway. Listening to records."

The Old Man's eyes drifted off to the window behind my mother's head.

"I'll keep everything the same," I said. "For when he comes back."

The Old Man beamed. My mother sighed.

"All right," she said. "On one condition."

"Name it," I said.

"You must promise me that you will never smoke a cigarette in this house."

"I promise," I said.

She had nothing to worry about. Paul's cruel prank forever purged me of even the most remote desire to put a cigarette in my mouth ever again for as long as I lived.

THUS DID I appoint myself caretaker of Paul's memory. My once burgeoning stardom in the Spencerville Little Theater having been abandoned and forgotten, I cast myself in the lead part for a production with a phantom audience of one. I spent all my allowance adding to what I thought of as "our" collection of what were already being called "classic rock" records. Aloof to Michael Jackson and Prince and Madonna, to new wave and hardcore and hair metal, I cultivated a curator's taste in the likes of Steely Dan, Zeppelin, the Who, Dylan, Rod Stewart, and all the other minor saints in the pantheon beneath the holy trinity of John Lennon, Mick Jagger, and Neil Young.

That fall I entered the ninth grade at Paul's alma mater, Macon Prep. Macon was still all-male then, though the board of trustees was already moving to admit girls as soon as possible as a means of boosting tuition revenues and attracting donations from alums whose philanthropic interest in Macon waned when their children were born without testicles. There were about two hundred boarders and sixty day students in grades seven through twelve. With the exception of a few scholarship students, we were all either children of alumni or miscreants from wealthy families on their second or third stop after getting booted out of Woodberry, Episcopal, or one (or more) of the tonier New England schools. Everyone was a snob, a racist, or both. But the faculty and staff were good people—warm, kind, and idealistic. The rules were a little extreme, but I didn't mind what most of my classmates couldn't stop bitching about—especially the dress code, which enabled me to borrow from Paul's collection of navy blazers, oxford shirts, and regimental ties.

Around this time, the Old Man decided to launch a formal father-son bonding campaign by driving me to school. Unlike most private schools back then, Macon had a bus route that looped through the surrounding neighborhoods, which I rode home in the afternoons. Nevertheless, the Old Man insisted on dropping me off every morning when he wasn't away on business. Sometimes he woke me an hour earlier so that we could "meet up" for breakfast at his favorite coffee shop, where I would consume a plate of sausage and hash browns while he sipped his coffee and lectured me on the art of manhood or told stories about growing up on the farm in Hampton Roads: bird and squirrel hunting with his brothers, fishing in the rivers and marshes, playing baseball in sandy fields, gathering with his family around the fireplace in the days of Saturday evening radio shows. We rarely mentioned Paul. Once, we did discuss the night I mistook Brad Culver for a ghost. I described Paul's account of the life and death of Frank Cherry and asked the Old Man how much of that dubious history lesson was true.

"I'm not sure Cherry was quite the scoundrel your brother made him out to be," the Old Man said. "But otherwise, yes, that's the way it happened."

"Why did you want that house?" I asked.

"I don't know," he admitted. "Probably because the bastards didn't want to sell it to me."

"Why wouldn't they want you to have it?" I asked.

"Some people have everything handed to them and let it all go to shit," the Old Man said. "These people can't stand to see a man who's come from the bottom get ahead of them. They'll take every chance they get to make him feel that he isn't good enough. I've had to deal with people like that all of my life."

He sipped his coffee and glanced out the window with an air of satisfaction.

"Did it make you mad that they sold the place to the Culvers?" I asked.

"Sure," he said. "But not at Brad Culver."

I thought of the look on the Old Man's face that night when he pointed his gun at Culver's head.

"I don't like him," I said.

"I'll tell you a secret," the Old Man said. "I'm about to do a big deal with Culver."

"You are?" I said.

"A real biggie," he said.

"A contract for one of his businesses?"

"Not a contract for a business. An investment. Venture capital," he said. "The big leagues."

I wasn't sure what he meant. I don't think he knew exactly himself.

"Is it some new kind of insurance?" I asked.

"No," he said. "I'm selling the insurance business."

"Oh," I said.

What on earth would lead a man to sell off a profitable business he'd spent more than thirty years building up from nothing to start over from scratch at seventy-three? I suppose he was just too confident, too certain that this "venture capital" scheme was his last chance to make that big, once-in-a-lifetime payday—the one that would make him five times as rich as even the richest of those who had ever looked down their noses at him.

"This is going to be the one, boy," he said.

He leaned forward, his eyes filled with an unnerving exhilaration. You could see through those eyes as if down a narrow tunnel to the past where stood a poor kid from the sticks listening to Huey Long's "Every Man a King" speeches on the radio, gazing out beyond the peanut fields, dreaming. They were the eyes of the eternal optimist. They were also the eyes of a gambler who had just put his whole stake on a sure thing.

6

I OFTEN WONDERED WHAT Paul would have made of the transformation Twin Oaks underwent in the hands of Brad and Jane Culver. Even those big old trees seemed invigorated by the polished surfaces and the bursting fertility of the lawn and gardens beneath the canopy of their limbs. In the dell to the right of the house, hidden from view by a grove of poplar trees, stood a newly raised, air-conditioned stable for the Culvers' horses. A high white picket fence enclosed the breadth of the property. Intentionally or not, this gleaming white border made clear the comparatively diminutive dimensions of the Old Man's parcel of land.

Around the time I started the eighth grade, Patricia, the Culvers' daughter, returned home from England, where I imagined her life had consisted solely of cocktail parties, fox hunting, and polo matches. By the time she showed up in Spencerville for the first time, Patricia was in her late twenties but had yet to marry. She lived at Twin Oaks with her parents during the warm months of the year, when not traveling to competitions, and spent the winter on the equestrian circuit in Florida.

The last night I saw Paul driving away from Twin Oaks, the Culvers had been away with Patricia in Europe, celebrating her graduation from some posh girls' school in southern England—"at the edge of the Cotswolds," Jane Culver had been heard to say. She must have known that the name Cotswolds sounded too regal and timeless for her Spencerville friends to suspect that it merely described a gathering of hills suited for putting sheep out to pasture, very similar to nearby Holcomb Falls or even to the land surrounding Twin Oaks.

Patricia could hardly have been more different from her mother.

Jane Culver had been born in Spencerville, into one of those First Families the Old Man had never been able to impress much. While she carried herself with a distinct air of highborn superiority, Mrs. Culver was thought of as gregarious and gracious, eager to befriend and be befriended. Thin and dainty, she never appeared outside Twin Oaks without looking as if her hair and makeup had been professionally styled. Patricia, on the other hand, appeared to eschew makeup completely and kept her hair pulled back in a utilitarian bun at the base of her scalp. She rarely appeared wearing anything but knee-high boots, riding pants, and a T-shirt or, if the weather was chilly or wet, a forest-green Barbour jacket. Her high cheekbones and small, piercing eyes seemed perpetually filled with boredom and distaste. She had a curvy, athletic build that struck me as being almost spitefully alluring, as if those breasts and hips had been designed for the purpose of attracting attention so that Patricia could then rebuff it with her particular brand of dry contempt.

Not much was known about Patricia. People assumed she'd been sent to an English boarding school because that was just the sort of thing people like the Culvers did with their children. Supposedly she was a brilliant student who—with her parents' encouragement—had turned down an acceptance to Cambridge or Oxford or both in order to pursue a berth on the Olympic equestrian team, but had been thwarted first by President Carter's decision to boycott the Moscow Games and later by a mysterious back injury. Her mother had made attempts to connect her with people her age in Spencerville, but from what I gathered, Patricia left everyone she met with the impression that she'd prefer not to be bothered.

Many days, Brad, Jane, and Patricia rode together, cantering along the edge of the field, their backs rigid and erect. Sometimes Patricia rode alone, her eyes fixed on the ground ahead of her, oblivious to everything else, including the boy walking along the other side of the fence, watching her.

Not long before my fifteenth birthday, Patricia was joined by another woman about her age. Every afternoon for weeks I saw the two of them riding around the pasture together. One day, as I walked home after being dropped off at the end of the driveway after school, they rode past along the fence. As they came up beside me, the woman riding behind Patricia glanced down and back. When for a moment our eyes met, my mouth fell open. It was Leigh Bowman.

I ran to the fence and cried out her name. Had she been alone, I think Leigh might have spurred the horse to a gallop and never looked back. Instead, together, Leigh and Patricia both turned and trotted their horses up to the fence where I stood.

"Hi," I said, gasping to catch my breath.

"Hi, Rocky," Leigh said.

"How long have you been in town?" I asked.

"Awhile," she said.

Of course she'd been back awhile. How had I not recognized her before? How many times had she ridden that horse right across from Paul's house, looking up at the window to the room in which she had spent so many careless hours?

"I didn't know," I said.

"I'm sorry," she said.

"What for?" I asked.

The plain falseness of her smile crushed me.

"How do you two know each other?" Patricia Culver asked.

I had never been formally introduced to Patricia Culver. My parents knew her from cocktail and dinner parties at Twin Oaks. "Horsey," my mom called her. The Old Man referred to her as "the ice princess."

"His brother and I grew up together," Leigh said.

"I didn't know you had a brother," said Patricia Culver.

This seemed a dubious claim, given the fact that every time she walked through the front door of her parents' house, she stepped over the spot where her father had shot Paul in the leg.

But maybe she didn't know. She had been away at school then, after all. I understood why no one would have mentioned it. And yet, it was also possible that Patricia knew every detail and chose to behave as if she didn't. With her pursed lips, her aquiline nose, and the haughty, elevated inflection of her speech, she struck me as precisely the sort of person who took private pleasure in making people squirm with discomfort.

"We were sweethearts," Leigh said. "In high school," she added.

"Charles would be very jealous if he knew your first love lived right next to Mummy and Daddy," Patricia said.

"Who is Charles?" I asked.

"My brother," she said. "I don't think *we've* kept *him* a secret."

"Oh, right," I said. "Charles."

Charles was Brad Culver's son from a previous marriage. My parents had met him also and had socialized with him several times over the years at various events. He was older—forty, maybe. He lived in New York and traveled the world on some sort of business.

"Would you like to tell him the big news or shall I?" Patricia said.

"Big news?" I asked.

Leigh shot Patricia an anxious look.

"Charles and Leigh are engaged to be married," Patricia said.

Momentarily stunned, I gaped up at Leigh.

"When's the wedding?" I asked.

"In October," Leigh said.

She glanced down and away. The bafflement on my face must have upset her—or maybe it was a glimmer of familiarity: the clothes; my lengthening, disheveled hair. I wasn't much like Paul, I know. But we both had the Old Man's eyes.

"Would you like to come?" she asked.

"Yes," I said. "Very much."

"I'll make sure to add your name to your parents' invitation," Leigh said.

A discomfiting silence followed. I wanted Leigh to climb off that horse so that I could embrace her and once again take in the scent of cigarette smoke and strawberry shampoo. But that lustrous long hair was gone now, replaced by the kind of blow-dried, feathered bob hairstyle worn by women my mother's age.

"It's good to see you, Rocky," she said.

"Nobody calls me that anymore," I said.

"I like it," Patricia said. "I can't believe this is the first time we've spoken. We're neighbors after all. I hope we'll see each other more often."

"Me too," I said.

"Good-bye, Rocky," Leigh said.

"Bye," I replied.

Together they turned and were off, riding the green wave of the grass up to the crest of the hill and disappearing into the dell below.

THAT NIGHT AT dinner, I waited until the Old Man was on his second drink before I raised the subject.

"You're never going to guess who I saw this afternoon," I said.

"Who?" my mother asked.

"Leigh Bowman."

The Old Man removed his glasses to rub the bridge of his nose.

"And guess what else," I said. "She's getting married. To the Culvers' son."

"How did you hear this news?" the Old Man asked.

"She told me herself," I said. "Well, Patricia told me, but still."

"Patricia Culver?" my mother asked. "How do you know her?"

"Did you hear me?" I said. "*Leigh Bowman* is getting *married!*"

The two of them looked at each other and then back at me with dour faces, as if I'd caught them in some terrible lie.

"How long have you known?" I asked.

"Awhile," my mother replied.

"Why didn't you tell me?"

"It never came up," said the Old Man.

He picked up his knife and fork and cut into his chicken as if we were discussing the weather. I felt like flinging my dinner plate against the wall.

"May I be excused?" I asked.

My mother nodded.

"Take your plate to the sink," the Old Man said.

Upstairs, in Paul's room, I threw myself onto the bed and buried my face in the bedcovers, wailing all my pent-up rage and confusion into the pillowcases. When I turned over to breathe the cool air, I looked up to find Neil Young staring down at me, strumming his guitar, eyes hidden in shadow, face serene and detached. *Tell me why*, he seemed to say. *Tell me why, tell me why.*

A FEW DAYS later, I watched Twin Oaks from my bedroom window until I saw Patricia emerge from the front door and stroll alone down the path that led to the stable. I went outside, hopped the fence, and strode over the hill and down into the dell. As I drew closer, I noticed Patricia leaning against the frame of the open stable door with her arms crossed.

"Hello there, Rocky," she said. "Richard, I mean."

"Hi," I said.

"Leigh won't be coming today, I'm afraid. She's visiting Charles in New York."

"Actually," I said, "I came to see you."

She stopped and made her measure of me.

"Whatever for?" she said.

"I was wondering if you needed any help around here."

"What sort of help?"

I gestured to the stalls.

"Cleaning up," I said. "Mowing. That sort of thing."

Patricia looked over her shoulder and then back at me.

"It's very dirty work," she said.

"I do all the yard work for my old man," I said.

"Yes, I've noticed you working outside before," she said. "Well, as a matter of fact, Daddy has been looking for a part-time hand around the stable and the fields."

"Then I'm your man," I said.

Patricia stifled a giggle.

"Is something funny?" I asked.

"Not at all," she said, resuming her air of cultivated civility. "As you say, you seem right for the job. What would you want to be paid?"

"My old man pays me five an hour," I said.

"That sounds reasonable."

"I can get started now."

"All right," she said. "Come along, then."

She led me into the stable. There were six stalls—three on each side. The Culvers kept three horses: Reggie, Patricia's competition thoroughbred; Velma, Brad Culver's chestnut mare; and Oberon, Jane Culver's sorrel gelding. A tack room lay just inside the door to the right. At the far end was the feed room; on the wall opposite were a rack of tools, a closet for cleaning supplies, and a hook holding a long hose connected to a pipe with a pump handle. At the entrance where we stood, opposite the tack room, a narrow two-flight staircase led up to the hayloft.

Patricia removed two brushes and combs from the closet.

"Have you used a currycomb before?" she asked.

I shook my head.

"Here," she said.

She handed me the comb and demonstrated how to use it to raise the grime and dirt from beneath the coat of the horse, running along the spine and flank and withers.

"There," she said. "Now, let's see you do it."

Velma eyed me with what seemed like a mixture of suspicion and distaste. I ran the comb across her flank, taking a step back at the end of the stroke.

"You're afraid, aren't you?" she said.

"No," I lied.

"You are," she said, smiling at my discomfort.

"What makes you say that?"

"Velma," she said. "She can sense it."

"I guess she doesn't like me," I said.

"Give her time, Rocky," Patricia answered. "She'll warm up."

She never did, exactly, nor did the others. I didn't care much for them either, though I grew to admire them—especially Reggie, with his magnificent, rippling physique and the shine of his chestnut coat, which I learned to polish to perfection.

All the same, I preferred working in the stables while the horses were out in the paddock or being ridden by Patricia and her parents or, once or twice a week, Leigh. It must have been the peasant blood in me. I didn't enjoy shoveling dung per se, but I took pleasure in the cleaning of a stall and the proper preparation of clean bedding. I liked looking back after sweeping out and rinsing down the floors to see a neat, well-appointed space. For a boy who had always thought of himself as a bit cosseted, I took considerable pride in breaking a sweat and being paid for manual labor.

My main purpose in coming to the barn to ask for a job had been to wedge myself back into Leigh's life—to be where I could see her and where she would have to see me, forcing her to remember things she was clearly hoping to put behind her. As I spent more time around Patricia, however, she began to eclipse my interest in Leigh. I often watched Patricia in the ring, working Reggie through the complex motions of their routine. It was like listening to a torch song performed in a foreign tongue—not being able to understand a word, but nevertheless entranced, and quite certain that the words I wasn't comprehending meant something rich and sensual.

I rarely saw Brad or Jane Culver, though I knew it was his money and not Patricia's I was being handed in a crisp white envelope at the end of each week. Culver rode almost every day, but not often in the afternoons. When I saw him, he was at the fence observing Patricia with Reggie, or checking into some matter pertaining to equipment or supplies. He treated me cordially enough—asking after my father or mentioning some little anecdote from one of their golfing ventures. Nevertheless, in his presence, I always worked with my head down, hoping he wouldn't speak to me.

Maybe a week or two after I started working at the Culvers' stable, I finally met Charles Culver. I was in the midst of running a Weedwacker over the grass beneath the fence surrounding the ring when I saw him walking down the path from the house, escorting Leigh to her afternoon ride with Patricia.

Charles seemed at once older and younger than his actual age. His dark hair was thinning on the top. In contrast with his father—who, even in his sixties, had the lean, compact build of a middleweight boxer and the ruddy complexion of a cowboy—Charles was pale and soft, almost pear-shaped. He wore glasses with cat-eye frames that appeared overly large on his head. He was considerably shorter than Leigh in her riding boots. The thought of him on top of her, naked, struck me as comically absurd.

"Charles, you must meet Rocky," Patricia said. "Mr. Askew's son."

Charles shook my hand and smiled.

"I've met your father," Charles said.

"I know," I said.

"Charles," Patricia said, "did you know Rocky's brother was Leigh's high school sweetheart?"

Still holding my hand, Charles turned and offered Leigh a half-smiling, curious glance.

"The same brother Dad shot in the leg?" he asked.

"That's right," I said.

"My God," Patricia said. "I never heard that story."

Leigh's eyes moved back and forth between Patricia and me, as if to accuse us of some sort of conspiracy.

"That was years ago," I said.

"You were in England, Patricia," said Charles.

He turned his soft face back to me and released my hand from his moist grip.

"Pop told me about it ages ago. Your brother was playing some sort of prank, right?"

"Something like that," I said. "The house was empty for a long time before your parents bought it. It was kind of a dare to go inside. Like touching Boo Radley's porch. Your dad surprised him, I think."

"I should say," Charles remarked.

"Hard to imagine Twin Oaks like that now," Patricia said. "It's so cozy."

"I remember Pop saying it was a rather uncomfortable way to get to know the neighbors," Charles said. "But it seems like he and your father have mended fences."

"There was no fence at all before," I said. "Your pop built it."

"Oh, yes. He did, didn't he," Charles said, chuckling dryly while Leigh looked on in agony.

"And what's become of your brother?" Charles asked. "What does he do?"

"He died," Leigh said.

A wave of panic passed over me like an electrical charge.

"I'm very sorry to hear that," Charles said.

I stared at Leigh pleadingly, but she refused to look at me.

Could Paul really be dead? In a sense, he had already been dead to us for years—as much a ghost as Frank Cherry or Annie Elizabeth. But *really* dead? I was completely unprepared to be faced with such a possibility.

At last, Leigh tilted her eyes toward mine. What I saw was not sadness or sympathy or even nostalgia, but fear. Just drop it, her face seemed to say.

In an instant, the dread I had felt gave way to something else— a rancid bitterness I could never have imagined feeling toward Leigh, whom I had always so adored. Why would she say such a thing? It was like Peter denying Jesus. I wanted to slap her face and call her names. I felt as if all the heartsick love I'd nursed for her since the first time I held her and breathed in the smell of strawberries and smoke had vanished like the butt of a cigarette flung out the open window of a speeding car.

"We better get on, then," Patricia said.

They mounted up and cantered out toward the field. After he waved them off, Charles turned and offered his hand to me once more.

"I've enjoyed getting to know your father, Richard," he said.

"I'm just in town for a quick visit, but I'm sure we'll be seeing more of each other."

"I hope so," I said.

I was quite certain that should Paul materialize at any moment before or even after Charles and Leigh's wedding, Leigh would bolt from Charles Culver's side just like Katharine Ross abandoned that sneering frat boy for Dustin Hoffman at the end of *The Graduate*. I might even be waiting outside behind the wheel of the getaway car—the old purple Nova, rumbling on the curb, ready to blast some triumphant rock anthem like "We Are the Champions" or "Won't Get Fooled Again" out the windows as we sped off toward the horizon.

I was still there mucking out the stalls when the two of them returned to the barn. I dropped my shovel and walked out to meet them as they dismounted.

"Here," Patricia said, reaching for Velma's halter. "I'll take her in."

Leigh was left to face my wounded wrath. I had no intention of making it easy on her.

"I'm sorry, Rocky," she said. "It just came out."

"But it's not true," I said, refusing to look at her. "You just made it up, right? You were lying."

"I don't know," she said. "I mean, I don't know what's happened to him. I hope he's alive, and that he's happy, wherever he is."

"But it would be easier for you if he was dead, wouldn't it?"

"Honestly?" she said. "Yes."

"How can you say that?"

"Time passes," she said. "People outgrow each other and go on with their lives. Don't you see, Rocky? I'm ready to get on with my life."

"It seems a little unfair that Paul has to be dead in order for you to move on," I said.

She paused for a moment before continuing.

"There are some things I just don't want to discuss," she said. "With anyone. Even Charles. What I said—it was just the easiest way to end the conversation."

My throat ached with sorrow and anger. I felt like I was going to cry.

"I know this is hard for you," Leigh said. "But can't you just try to be happy for me?"

I jammed my hands into the pockets of my jeans and kicked at the dirt, fighting back the tears.

"Sure," I said. "I'll try."

"OK then," she said. "Thank you."

I lingered in the doorway as Leigh walked up the path toward the house. Patricia came up beside me.

"What happened to your brother, Rocky?"

I was afraid if I tried to answer, my voice would break and I'd end up a blubbering mess.

"He isn't dead, is he?" she asked.

I shook my head.

"Would you like a drink?" she asked. "You look like you could use one."

Patricia was almost thirty—not much older than Paul and Leigh—but given the way she spoke and her generally dour demeanor, I had always thought of her as being much older, like a teacher. When she walked out toward me, however, her face seemed somehow softer. The usual air of indifference appeared to have been replaced by something approaching compassion. A drink? I thought. Why not? Leigh had definitely put me in the mood to rebel against something.

On one side of the tack room was an old aluminum desk flanked by a pair of captain's chairs, an old filing cabinet, and a minifridge. On the opposite wall hung the saddles and bridles, a length of braided rope, and a shelf for helmets and gloves.

"Have a seat," Patricia said, reaching into the cabinet for a bottle of scotch.

"How do you take it?" she asked.

I thought of what the Old Man usually ordered.

"Old-fashioned," I said.

She laughed.

"We've got a bit of sugar for the horses," she said. "But I left the muddler and the bitters up at the house."

She pulled a tray of ice cubes from the minifridge and a pair of coffee mugs from atop the file cabinet.

"On the rocks, then," she said.

She poured the drinks and handed one of the mugs to me.

"Cheers," she said.

I quickly discovered why people said they "needed" a drink. Almost instantly my anger and confusion were replaced with a mellow calm and a not unpleasant thrumming in the extremities.

The scotch seemed to have the same ameliorative effect on Patricia. A bit of color came into her face. Her lips curled into a crooked smile. In the small, dry room, I could smell the sweat from her back and her nape and the scent of the horsehide from between her thighs where they had clutched the horse's flanks in the saddle.

"Would you like to talk about it?" she asked.

"There's not much to talk about," I said. "Leigh was my brother's girl a long time ago. I had a bit of a crush on her, but I'm over it."

"I don't think we ever get over first love," she said, her voice uncharacteristically soft and wistful.

"It wasn't love," I said. "Just a crush."

"But your brother was her first," Patricia said.

"Yes," I said. I wasn't sure whether she meant to confirm that Paul was Leigh's first love or her "first," but I presumed the answer to both questions was the same.

I drew in a deep breath of the hot, dry air. On the other side of the wall, the horses stirred in their stalls. A gentle breeze lifted the flimsy curtains. The sweat on my nape cooled. I raised the mug and drank until the ice cubes clicked against my teeth.

"Would you like another drink?" Patricia asked.

"Yes," I said.

She took the bottle and filled the mug to the brim.

"So," she asked. "Do you have a girlfriend?"

"No," I said.

"Why not?" she asked. "I bet the girls think you're cute."

"I go to a boys' school."

"I see," she said. "Are you gay?"

I was too startled by the question to take offense.

"Why would you think that?" I stammered.

"I'm sorry," she said. "I didn't mean to upset you."

"I'm not *gay*," I said.

"It wouldn't bother me at all if you were," Patricia said. "Americans are awfully uptight about that sort of thing, especially in the South."

Patricia was always going on about how Americans were this or that, as if she weren't one herself.

"Well," I said, "I'm *not*."

"I just thought—you know. Since you don't have any girlfriends."

"Just because I don't have a girlfriend doesn't mean I lie around dreaming about guys."

This wasn't completely true. I did daydream about guys—the ones on the walls of Paul's room: Neil Young; the Beatles; Mick Jagger in skintight pants, doing his rooster act, preening, his gleaming chest stuck out, hand perched on his ass; Jim Morrison, shirtless, glowering at the camera. What did that say about me?

Patricia leaned forward, her elbow propped on the desk in front of her. I could hear the ice in her drink tinkle against the edges of the coffee mug as she shifted her weight.

"What *do* you . . . dream about?" she asked.

She didn't appear to be teasing me. Still, it seemed clear what she meant by *dreaming*. How on earth did she expect me to respond to that?

I took another sip from my mug.

I had drunk liquor only once before, the time I slurped scotch off the top of Anne's glass on that awful night she spent with us when I was seven. As I considered how best to answer Patricia's question, I began to notice the numbness in my lips and tongue.

My heart had begun to race, and I could feel my pulse echoing in my skull. My gaze drifted down from Patricia's face to the damp spot where her dark green V-neck T-shirt had slipped to reveal a sliver of creamy flesh between where her tan line ended and the bra cup covering her left breast began. Patricia shifted in her chair, prompting me to notice that I was quite guilelessly staring at her breasts. As my eyes darted back up to meet hers, I realized, to my dismay, that I had become aroused.

Patricia stared back at me, a coy smile on her lips, waiting—waiting for what?

"I don't know," I stammered.

If I had been a bit more worldly, I might have noticed that I was in the midst of what most people would think of as an opportune moment. But I was a child, still naive and, for the most part, innocent. I couldn't yet conceive the possibility of anything happening between me and Patricia Culver, regardless of the circumstances.

"I'm sorry," she said. "I didn't mean to embarrass you. You're very mature for your age. I forget you're still so young."

To my relief, my erection began to fade.

"I'm not embarrassed," I lied.

"I hope not," she said. "I'd like to be your friend."

"Me too," I said. "I really don't have anyone I can talk to about this kind of stuff."

"We all need someone to confide in."

"You've got your brother," I said. "And Leigh."

"My brother?" Patricia said, leaning back and rolling her eyes in contempt. "Please. If I told him I needed to go to the bathroom, he'd run straight to Daddy and whisper what I'd said in his ear."

"That's what my mother says about Spencerville."

"What?"

"That you can't go to the bathroom without someone telling the whole town whether you went number one or number two."

Patricia laughed into her coffee mug.

"Charles fits right in, then," she said. "Besides, he's ten years older than me. By the time I was old enough to talk, he was off to university, and by the time he came home, I was off at school in England.

Since then, we've never been under the same roof for more than three weeks at a time. He's more like a young uncle than a brother."

"We've got that in common, then," I said.

"What's that?"

"Older half brothers. You barely know yours. I don't even know if mine's alive or dead."

"Tell me about him," she said.

I thought about Paul. What would he think of Patricia? What would she think of him?

"You should ask Leigh," I replied. "The last time I saw him I was nine years old."

"I don't get the sense she wants to discuss it. We're not the closest of friends."

"You've sure been spending a lot of time with her."

"We've been thrown together by the whirlwind courtship," Patricia said.

"How did that happen, anyway?" I asked.

"Our parents. Charles was always too busy traveling to settle down with anyone. He's very driven. Mummy's been after him to find a wife for years. When the Honorable Prentiss Bowman found out about my brother, he practically flung poor Leigh at him. One thing led to another, and here we are. My parents couldn't be more delighted. Mummy and Daddy want grandchildren. I think they've given up on me. Daddy says I'd rather marry a horse than a man."

"That's kind of a mean thing to say."

"Oh, he was just having a laugh," she said. "But it's true I'm in no hurry to start *breeding*."

"And what do you think of Leigh?" I asked.

"She seems awfully—how should I say it?—anxious. She's quite a bit younger than Charles, and much better looking, as I'm sure you observed. But he can offer her security, if that's what she's after."

"Is that what you think?" I asked.

"It's an important thing to think about," she said. "Even more so if you're accustomed to a certain lifestyle."

"I thought people married for love," I said.

"Only in novels and plays," she said. "That's why they call it romance, no?"

"I don't know what you mean."

"That's where the word comes from. A romance, by definition, is a fictional story."

She was starting to resume her dictatorial air. I was already beginning to gather that Patricia enjoyed delivering lectures.

"Is that how you feel?" I asked. "That love is fictional?"

"That depends on your definition of love. There are different ways of loving someone, Rocky. Try to see it from Leigh's perspective. Around here, it seems, a girl's an old maid if she turns twenty-five without a ring on her finger."

I could see what she was getting at. She'd met my parents. Patricia Culver was not the first to conclude that in marrying the Old Man, my mother had made precisely the sort of compromise Patricia was accusing Leigh of making.

"Don't misunderstand me," she said, her voice softening. "I'm not cynical. I expect the love you remember between Leigh and your brother was like Romeo and Juliet's."

"They both die in the end," I said.

"If they hadn't, it wouldn't have been a tragedy. There are similar stories with happier endings. They just don't make for good entertainment."

She splashed a finger of scotch into her mug and offered me the bottle. I shook my head. I had just considered the fact that I'd soon have to go home and face my parents.

"One thing I am certain of," she said. "You only get one great love. If Leigh's was your brother, then she'll never have another. And anyhow, I can tell you from experience that Spencerville isn't exactly crawling with eligible bachelors who are up to Prentiss Bowman's standards."

"My old man says Prentiss Bowman acts as if his shit smells like a bouquet of roses."

We both laughed. I was surprised at how much I enjoyed gossiping with Patricia Culver. We were thick as thieves now, I thought. In cahoots.

"You're a clever boy, Richard," she said. "I'm glad we're going to be friends."

"Me too," I said.

"Well then," she said. She held her drink aloft. "To friendship."

I STARTED FOR HOME quickly until I began to realize that I'd become short of breath and had begun to list leftward as I made my way up the hill. I staggered slowly downward, breathing deeply, trying to calm the thrumming in my limbs and the blur of sensations in my brain.

I managed to slip into the house undetected. I stole upstairs and into Paul's room, hoping I could sober up enough to get through the rest of the evening without my parents' discovering what I'd been up to that afternoon.

I put on the Beatles' *White Album*. I remembered how once, when we were listening to it together, Paul had leaped up off the bed after the gibberish between "I'm So Tired" and "Blackbird" to stop the needle on the vinyl.

"Listen to this," he had said.

He turned the record counterclockwise with his finger. In reverse, we heard the distorted voice of John Lennon:

Paul is dead, man, miss him, miss him.

"Far out, right?" Paul said.

Far out, I thought.

I lifted my head and peered out the window up at the glowing windows of Twin Oaks. I thought of Patricia in her tight tan pants and knee-high leather boots. How her eyes warmed when she was a little drunk. How the sweat of her nape had dampened and darkened her green T-shirt, drawing a faint inverted triangle descending toward her lovely breasts.

Remembering all of this, I turned over onto my back and dreamed about Patricia Culver for the first of many times.

7

I WAS MOSTLY ALONE when I worked at Twin Oaks, trimming the grass around the fences, steering the zero-turn lawn mower up and down the pasture, cleaning the stalls and hauling hay bales in and out of the loft. Whenever I could, however, I watched Patricia with Reggie in the ring, practicing jumping and dressage. *Dressage!* It was one of those terms, like *cotillion* or *noblesse oblige*, that seemed drenched with privilege.

When we crossed paths at the stables, Leigh Bowman made no effort to mask her discomfort with my presence. I returned her awkwardness with a sneering, almost taunting surliness. After Leigh left, Patricia and I would gossip about her over drinks in the tack room. I sensed that Patricia understood what I was up to. In all likelihood, she grasped my motives better than I did.

"Do you know what Leigh said to me?" Patricia asked one afternoon.

"What?" I asked.

"She told me I should stop toying with you. Do you think I'm toying with you, Richard?"

"No," I said.

Not nearly enough, I thought.

One afternoon while I was alone mucking out the stalls, I heard a car approach and come to a halt, followed by the opening and closing of the driver's side door. A moment later, Leigh appeared in the barn, dressed in slacks and open-toed pumps and a pressed linen blouse.

"Hi," she said.

"You planning to ride dressed like that?" I asked.

"I'm not here to ride," she said. "I came to see you."

I leaned the shovel against the wall and turned to face her, trying to act the way I remembered Paul behaving toward my mother.

Leigh's face looked troubled. I noticed a slight tremor in her hands as they hung at her side. Again, I thought of my mother, with her bird-like hands, fluttering about when she was upset.

"Say," I said, "whatever became of ole Barton?"

"Who?"

"Barton," I repeated. "The guy you were studying with when Paul and I showed up that day in Charlottesville."

For a moment she looked lost, as if she'd forgotten where she was or why she'd come there.

"I don't know," she said.

"Did he tell you what I said to him?"

"I don't remember," she said.

"I told him he didn't stand a chance."

"You were right about that."

We stared tensely at each other, as if we were on the verge of drawing pistols at twenty paces.

"Do you remember what I made Paul promise me that day?" she asked. "I made him promise to take you home."

"He didn't mention it," I said.

"I told him that if he took you home," she said, "I would go with him."

"That was awful good of you," I said.

I didn't grasp what this recollection was designed to convey. What did she want me to say? Was she looking for a thank-you?

"Well," I said, "he took me home, all right. Eventually."

"I know," she said. "I was so angry at him when he told me what he had done. But I loved him. And I loved you too. I still do."

"That's nice," I said.

"I want you to be happy."

"Thanks," I said.

"And I want you to be happy for me."

"I know. You told me. And I am so very happy for you, Leigh," I said, with as much sarcasm as I could manage to convey.

Again we were left staring at each other, Leigh standing there in her grown-up costume, her arms folded across her chest, trying to settle those fluttering hands.

"Was there something you wanted to say to me?" I asked. "I've got work to do, you know."

I gestured to the pile of muck and the shovel I'd left leaning against the wall.

She bit her lip. She wasn't crying yet, but I sensed I wouldn't need to push her much further. It felt oddly thrilling to be so cruel.

"This was a mistake," she said.

She turned to leave. Too late, the remorse overcame me.

"I'm sorry," I called out.

She stopped, her silhouette framed in the open door of the stable.

"What did you want to say to me, Leigh?" I asked, in a tone I hoped she would recognize as sincere.

"I changed my mind," she said.

I CAME HOME to a quiet house. My mother was back in the Royal Chamber, decked out in her spandex, burning her buns with Jane Fonda. The Old Man was in his study with the afternoon edition of the *Wall Street Journal* open on his lap to the stock pages, staring at the television news in disbelief. The date was October 19, 1987. The market had just closed, and the talking heads were already calling it Black Monday.

We had been due for a hard dose of comeuppance, I suppose, ever since the ascension of Reagan, the kindly old grandfather, who had spoiled us with federal deregulation and unsustainably low tax and interest rates. There we were in Boone's Ferry, the prettiest, safest part of the prettiest, safest little town in the world, living our lives of unspoiled comfort. We were willing to go along with anything so long as we still had our German luxury cars, our country clubs, our private schools, and our ballooning stock portfolios. So we deserved what we got on Black Monday, when the market plummeted while everyone stood by helplessly as $500 billion vanished before our eyes.

If I'd been less absorbed with my own affairs, I might have noticed the horror and disbelief on the Old Man's face—an expression of incredulous panic that couldn't have looked much different from the one Frank Cherry wore before he went out with that pistol to his front porch rocking chair at Twin Oaks back in 1929. But it meant very little to me at the time. Nothing was the end of the world, until it was.

I would have to wait to discover the depth of the catastrophe that befell the Old Man that day. I left the room oblivious to his anguish and went upstairs, where I put on Joni Mitchell's *Blue* and fell on the bed to daydream. I wondered what Patricia was doing—whether she thought about me as often as I thought about her, in the way I thought about her. I imagined myself and Patricia as a conspiracy of romantic resistance against the cynicism of Leigh's impending marriage to Charles Culver.

I'm not sure when I fell asleep—somewhere after the beginning of "River." I woke up in darkness. It wasn't like my mother to let me miss dinner. Maybe she thought I was tired because I had been working so hard.

I turned to look out the window. The lights were still on at Twin Oaks. The digital alarm clock on my bedside table read 1:34 a.m.

Paul used to sneak out all the time; it was easy to do with our parents asleep way back in the Royal Chamber. Why not? I thought. So I slipped down the stairs and out the door and across the lawn to Brad Culver's fence, the white paint of which seemed almost to glow in the blue moonlight.

As I reached the crest of the hill, I saw the small gold rectangle of the tack room window at the center of the stable's black shadow. I clutched my jacket around my waist and treaded toward the light, slowing my pace as I drew closer. Inside the stable, the horses snorted restlessly. I moved to the window. Before I could peer in, I was startled by the sound of a voice behind me.

"Trespassing must run in your blood, boy," the voice said.

I started and spun around, my back against the stable wall. Before me stood Brad Culver, teetering on his feet, dressed not unlike he had been all those years before, when I mistook him for a ghost.

Even from ten feet off, I could smell the booze on his breath. He peered at me through heavy-lidded eyes and made a soft grunting noise before lurching and weaving his way over to the open stable door. His whole back, from the close-cropped silver of his skull to the heels of his boots, was covered with a thin layer of wet sand.

As he reached the stable door, Culver grasped its handle and, misjudging its weight, pitched forward. He appeared to lack the strength even to get up from the ground. There he remained, facedown, mumbling into the ground as the horses stamped and snorted.

I stood over Culver for what seemed like a long time, contemplating what I might do to him. How hard would it be, I wondered, to press his face into the soft, sandy dirt until he stopped breathing?

As far as anyone else knew, I was asleep in my bed. I could get away with it, I thought. I could kill this man. Later I would often wonder how different all our lives might have been if I had.

"Come on, Mr. Culver," I said.

"Putrid fuck," he muttered.

I helped him up onto his feet and pulled his arm around my shoulder. The path up to the house was long and steep. We had to stop several times along the way when Culver's knees buckled beneath him. I would wait a moment for him to catch his breath before resuming our slow, staggering walk up toward Twin Oaks.

When we reached the house, I sat down beside him and eased him back onto that old porch where long ago Frank Cherry had ended his own life. Was the blood still there, I wondered, beneath layer after layer of paint, soaked into the grain of the aging wood?

I stepped over Culver and up to the door and rang the bell. I heard a soft peal ring out within. A shadow passed across a window. I took off running back down the hill from where we'd come, slowing as I reached the stable, heaving cold, wet breaths that shot out in visible bursts of steam before me. Patricia appeared in the faint light of the glowing window to the tack room.

"That was kind of you, Rocky," she said.

"I thought you might be here," I said.

She leaned up against the doorframe with her hands behind her back. Instead of boots and riding pants and a T-shirt, she wore jeans and a black crewneck sweater, her brown hair hanging down around her shoulders. I'd never seen her without her hair pinned up before. It was longer than I expected and made her seem younger and more feminine. She looked at once familiar and startlingly changed, as if I were seeing her for the first time after she'd returned from a long journey.

"I should have come out," she said, "but I prefer not to deal with him when he's like that."

"I'm glad you didn't," I said.

Again I felt my heart quicken. This time, however, I wasn't drunk. And this time, I understood what was happening—what I wanted, what I had come out to the barn for. I didn't bother asking what she was doing there at that time of night. It seemed she was exactly where she was supposed to be.

"Don't you want to know why I'm here?" I asked.

"I know why you're here," she said.

She held out her hand.

"Come along," she said.

8

TO THE FEW people I've told about Patricia over the years, I have described her as a mysterious older woman who, through chance and circumstance, took me to bed and stole my innocence. To men, I would treat the whole experience as a naughty little conquest. To women, I would relate it as a dark secret that had marked me with a lingering, melancholy vulnerability. The truth was something more complicated.

Up in the hayloft, Patricia spread out a couple of quilted plaid horse blankets across a square of hay bales. Given my complete lack of experience, I had no expectations or plans for what was about to happen. I assumed at least that she'd make me work my way around the bases. Instead, Patricia simply pulled her sweater over her head, unfastened her bra, and unbuttoned the top of her jeans while I looked on, agape. In a series of deft movements, she stepped out of her slip-on ankle boots, pushed her jeans and panties to the floor, and spread herself out on the blankets. The skin of Patricia's face and arms and neck was darkened somewhat by the amount of time she spent in the sun, but the rest of her flesh was almost alarmingly pale. In the faint light from the open window, her skin seemed blue, like the color of a robin's egg. My eyes traveled up along her legs and past her knees, pausing at the predictable places. She let me study her there for a moment before pulling one of the blankets up to her chin.

"I hate my breasts," she said, in a surprisingly coy and vulnerable tone.

"I think your breasts are perfect," I said. It was true—I did.

"Come along, darling," she said.

Darling! My heart swelled with ardor. I undressed hurriedly, afraid that, if I hesitated any further, she might change her mind.

When I was ready, she lifted the blanket so I could crawl underneath with her. She let me kiss her, whispering instructions on how she preferred the movement of tongues. I grasped at her breasts clumsily but with a fervor she must have found touching, if not flattering.

"You brought something, didn't you?" she asked.

"What do you mean?"

"A condom," she said. "You brought one, didn't you?"

Of course I hadn't brought one. The idea that I might need one had never occurred to me. My fantasies about riding the waves of bliss with Patricia had never included the practical step of unwrapping and applying a prophylactic. The irony was, back in Paul's room, at home, I had a whole box of them: a twenty-four-pack the Old Man had unceremoniously dumped on my desk not long after I started at Macon.

"What do you expect me to do with these?" I had said to the Old Man, holding the box as if it contained radioactive material. I couldn't remember whether I was aware of Paul's having needed rubbers at the beginning of the ninth grade. Perhaps he had.

"If you need any more," he said, "just ask."

A year later, when I might actually have made use of one of those rubbers, they were back across the field in my closet, stashed away under a stack of baseball cards in an old shoe box.

"I can go get one," I said. "It'll take me five minutes. Ten tops."

"Oh, Rocky," she said, with a greater measure of whimsy than exasperation.

"Please," I said, almost whining, my unrelenting hard-on throbbing against her leg.

"There will be another time," she said. "For now, we'll just have to make do."

Before I could speak, she had me in her hand, and then her mouth. I had just long enough to be astonished. Patricia was surpassingly gracious.

"Control comes with practice," she said.

Rolling on to her back, she took my hand and guided my fingers into her, helping me to find her rhythm.

"There," she said.

Her movements quickened; she threw her head back onto the blanket and bucked her hips into the air, holding them there trembling for a moment before she gasped and fell back to the bed of blankets beneath her.

"Oh, my," she said with a sigh.

The next time, I didn't forget the rubbers.

The weeks that followed were a prolonged, exquisite torture. Even before we started sleeping with each other, I had felt both the pull of deep longing and a not-so-subtle uneasiness toward Patricia. Quite abruptly I had gone from having never so much as kissed a girl to doing *everything*, and with an older, experienced partner—every adolescent male's fantasy fulfilled. But I also knew how horrified my mother would be by what I was doing in that barn when I snuck out at night or, sometimes, in the middle of the afternoon, when Patricia felt confident we wouldn't be interrupted or was tipsy enough to be a little reckless. I vacillated between regarding the whole business as a secret stain on my soul and thinking it was the greatest, most thrilling thing that would ever happen to me.

It wasn't just the sex either. Patricia listened to me in a way no one ever had. She confessed her own vulnerabilities in a manner I took to be truthful and sincere. I began to believe that we were in love: that we were soul mates, destined for each other, even if only for a short while. Some of these delusions were due to Patricia's constant talk of tragic literary love stories from the likes of Shakespeare and the Brontë sisters and D. H. Lawrence and Kate Chopin. Quite a bit of it came from the notion that she was herself wounded and thwarted by her circumstances—namely, the misfortune of being Brad Culver's daughter.

Indeed, our pillow talk consisted almost exclusively of complaints against the people who were supposed to love us most. Through Patricia, I discovered a theretofore untapped contempt for my parents: The Old Man's mindless pursuit of money and his constant sucking up to those who had it, the way he never stopped grinding for the next big deal, the way he loved Paul more than he did me. My mother's prudery and moral hypocrisy. Who was she to act so righteous, I thought, marrying an old man for his money and driving off his first son? And what about Paul? He'd ditched us, after all—didn't I deserve to hate him too?

Would I ever have felt this way about my family without Patricia's encouragement? Probably. But a shared sense of indignation seemed to be the one thing Patricia and I truly had in common.

Compared to Patricia's, my own childhood seemed mundane. She had lived all over the world—Venezuela, Austria, France, Singapore, Guam. When Patricia came of schooling age, the Culvers were living in western Africa, where her father was supervising the construction of a mining facility. There was considerable labor unrest in the area, and threats of violence had been made against the company executives. This gave the Culvers the excuse to send Patricia off to England, rather than to one of the nearby English or American schools, which the Culvers considered substandard.

"Both of my parents are insufferable Anglophiles," Patricia explained. The peculiar English accent she clung to despite having lived elsewhere most of her life seemed calculated to appeal to her parents' pretentions.

Patricia was sent to the Blaine School for Young Women in Cheltenham for the express purpose of gaining admission to Cambridge or Oxford. The trouble was that, unlike in the United States, where most students are free to major in whatever subject they choose upon being admitted to a university's college of arts and sciences, British applicants must select a major in advance and sit for a series of related subject tests called A levels.

"My father wanted me to be an engineer, like he was," Patricia explained. "He thought it was the only worthy subject. But I didn't care a whit about engineering, then or now. I wanted to study literature. 'What are you going to do with a degree in *literature?*' he said. '*Teach?*'"

I thought Patricia would have made a very good teacher—assuming that she wouldn't have slept with her students.

Patricia felt she could have earned perfect scores in history, literature, and French. Instead, at her father's insistence, she sat for exams in engineering, mathematics, and geology. She managed Bs in math and engineering but earned a dismal C in geology.

"Geology. I was undone by the earth itself," Patricia lamented. "Only the Prince of Wales could get into Cambridge with a pair of Bs and a C on A levels. And for my father, the difference between Oxford and, say, the University of Edinburgh is like the difference between Harvard and Harvard on the Hill."

Harvard on the Hill was the nickname for the local community college.

With Oxford and Cambridge out of the question, her mother suggested she throw herself into a bid for the Olympic equestrian team. Hence they'd be able to tell their friends Patricia had reluctantly declined admission to the world's most elite universities to pursue her true passion.

She lived like that for most of a decade, long after it became obvious that she had neither the skill nor the quality of horse necessary to make the Olympic team. Her parents never complained—on the contrary. If Patricia was never going to do something *worthwhile*, Jane Culver argued, supporting her lifestyle on the horse-show circuit was, at least, preferable to seeing her graduate from a *second-rate* college to become a *teacher*.

"That way, Mummy reasoned," Patricia said, borrowing a phrase from Jane Austen, "I would be thrown 'in the way of other rich men.'"

But Patricia had no interest in Europe's most eligible bachelors. Not that she was a stranger to the company of men—or women, for that matter—nor was she shy about sharing details, real or imagined.

She refused to identify herself as bisexual; instead she characterized her sapphic adventures as a "natural phase." Temporary lesbianism, according to Patricia, was "an ordinary by-product" of the all-girls boarding environment, as was "buggery," as she referred to it, in the all-male schools. I'd seen no evidence of similar conditions at Macon Prep—on the contrary, Macon seemed to be as hypermasculine an environment as one could conceive. My classmates bartered issues of *Playboy* and *Penthouse* and *Hustler* the way kids of the Old Man's generation traded marbles and baseball cards. All anyone ever seemed to talk about was "getting pussy," though as far as I could tell, I was one of a scant few who had seen or touched a flesh-and-blood vagina.

Given the staggering ubiquity of every variety of pornography that has overtaken American culture since then, the extent to which Patricia's erotic fantasies astonished me when I was fifteen seems almost comical now.

"Do you want to watch me with a woman?" she might ask.

"Yes," I'd reply without much hesitation.

Once, when I was behind her, she reached back and, withdrawing me from the familiar place, guided me into the little aperture above it. "Pretend I'm a boy," she said; I trembled and swooned.

Another time, with her legs resting high across my shoulders, she reached up and around and plunged an unwelcome finger into my own little orifice.

"What are you doing?" I asked.

"What you want me to do," she said.

I didn't agree at all. But I didn't stop her either.

It's difficult to comprehend even now the power Patricia had over me in those weeks when we were making regular trips up to the hayloft. I couldn't concentrate on anything at school. I spent most of my classes daydreaming about Patricia or napping, exhausted as I was from all the sleep I was losing. I avoided my parents as much as possible. I gave up caring about Leigh. If I thought of Paul, it was to assure myself of how impressed he'd be that I was carrying on an affair with a sexy older woman. Nothing mattered but getting over to the barn, where, after finishing my work, I could follow Patricia into the tack room to make out and arrange a midnight tryst or even do it right then and there, while the horses snorted and stamped on the other side of the wall.

SEPTEMBER PASSED INTO October, and the week of Charles and Leigh's wedding was upon us. The house and the stable became overrun with guests and visitors, drawing Patricia into a whirl of cocktail parties, champagne brunches, and group outings. I saw her in the afternoons when I came over to work, but there were too many people coming and going for us to spend any time alone. Afterward I retreated in misery to Paul's room, from which I could see the swirl of activity around Twin Oaks from the windows, having nothing to distract myself with but piles of neglected homework assignments and the consolation of old love songs on vinyl. Two weeks from Saturday, Patricia would be leaving for Florida with Reggie to prepare for the winter equestrian circuit. What would I do with myself then?

On Thursday afternoon, Patricia made the rather daring gesture of calling me at my house. My mother was out running errands; the Old Man, as usual, was at the office.

"They're all gone," Patricia said.

The wedding party was at yet another reception, this time at some lake house just out of town. Patricia had begged off because of the horses.

"I'll be right there," I said.

Reclined on the blankets up in the hayloft, I studied the part in the center of Patricia's scalp as she drifted down to perform her delicate ministrations. I closed my eyes and wished that it could go on forever—that life could be a perpetual blow job from Patricia Culver, naked and musky on a bed of hay in the warm glow of early fall.

To my vexation, Patricia abruptly sat up, cocking her head toward the partially opened hayloft door.

"What is it?" I asked.

As soon as I spoke, I could hear it too—the sound of a car drawing closer to the stable.

"Get dressed," she said.

Patricia leaped up and reached for her clothes. I kicked into my jeans, imagining Brad Culver coming for me with his pistol.

"Rocky," a voice called. "Are you in here?"

It was Leigh Bowman, of all people.

I looked to Patricia. She shook her head.

"Rocky," Leigh called again. "I'm coming up."

I scrambled to the hatch and descended the ladder, almost falling from the ceiling to the floor right on top of Leigh Bowman, who was preparing to climb up in a russet cocktail dress and black patent heels.

"Hi," I said, smoothing my disheveled clothes. "How's it going?"

Leigh looked up at the wooden slats of the ceiling and the hatch to the hayloft.

"I thought you were out at the lake," I said.

"I wasn't feeling well," she said, still studying the ceiling. "Charles understood."

"Oh," I stammered.

Her eyes dropped from the hatch back to me.

"Let's go for a ride," she said.

"On horseback?" I asked.

"In the car."

"I'm not finished with my work," I said.

"Yes, you are," Leigh replied.

She grasped my elbow and pulled me toward the door.

"Come on," she said.

As we walked out of the barn, I glanced back, wondering what Patricia was thinking as I left with Leigh. When we reached the car, I opened the passenger side door and slipped into the seat with the resignation of a condemned man.

9

IN HIGH SCHOOL, Leigh drove a Volkswagen Dasher with a tan interior and a four-speed manual transmission. I remember once seeing her work the stick and level her feet up and down on the clutch and gas pedals while simultaneously lighting a cigarette and balancing a beer between her knees. But the Dasher had been replaced by her father's old BMW.

I listened to the quiet hum of the engine as Leigh steered the car along the rolling hills out toward the intersection with the highway that led up to the Blue Ridge Parkway. As she drove, she studied the road with a strained, purse-lipped concentration that suggested she was working up to some sort of big speech. It was all at once comfortingly familiar and unbearably weird.

When we reached the end of Boone's Ferry, she began.

"I have a real weakness, you see, Rocky?" she said. "I have a terrible time letting go of the past. Every time I think of even the slightest, most insignificant mistakes I've made, the shame hurts so badly I can hardly bear it. Can you understand that, Rocky?"

"Yes," I said.

"Well, I'm not going to be that way anymore," she said. "On Saturday, I'm marrying Charles. After that, I'm going to file the past away and forget it ever happened. So if you're going to know any of it, you're going to have to hear it now."

She paused for a breath and smoothed her hair behind her ears, keeping one hand on the wheel. In my mind, I tried to replace this staid, proper-looking woman in the cocktail dress and pearls with the old Leigh, sunny and lithe, her hair hanging long and free well below the shoulders of her Mickey Mouse baseball shirt with the navy-blue three-quarter-length sleeves.

"Paul," she said with a sigh. "He could have made a fool of so many girls. But he did it to me. And what a fool I was. A stupid little girl. But I loved him. What girl wouldn't? Daddy could just tell that Paul was going to ruin me. You know what I mean, don't you?"

I did. Paul hadn't just done it to Leigh. He did it to the Old Man and me too.

"Before that day the two of you showed up in Charlottesville," Leigh said, "I was almost ready to break it off with him. It wasn't Barton, or any other boy. I can't deny that getting attention from boys who were so different from Paul got me thinking about what else might be out there, but really I felt like sooner or later Paul was going to be the one to leave *me* behind. I was just preparing for that."

She touched my knee.

"You were such a precious little boy, Rocky," she said. "You used to look at Paul like he was floating two feet off the ground. Do you remember that?"

"I remember," I said.

A smile flickered across her face.

"I knew as soon as I saw you together that something was wrong," she said. "Your mother would never in a million years have let Paul take you any farther than Pearsall's Drugstore."

By then, Leigh had driven out past the foothills toward the mountains, brilliant with fall color. I stared out the window at the peaks above the glistening James River as I listened to Leigh recount what took place in the days before I last saw my brother.

Someone in Akron had called the college, and an associate dean was appointed to notify Paul about his mother's death. When Paul called home, he discovered that the Old Man already knew; in fact, he had already cut a check to pay for the funeral arrangements. When Paul offered to drive over so they could go up to Ohio together, the Old Man told him that he wasn't going and that Paul shouldn't feel he had to go either.

"It seemed horrible and ugly at the time that your father would say something like that," Leigh said. "But I understand now what he felt like. When it hurts so much to remember that you just want to forget."

I thought about Anne and wondered what she was like when she met the Old Man. She must once have been someone worthy of his love.

Paul didn't bother to call Leigh, or Rayner, or anyone else. He went to Ohio alone. No one came to the service save for an elderly aunt and a cousin he'd never met. After burying his mother, Paul went to a lonely, forlorn Morrison's Cafeteria with these people he'd never met before in his life. Paul told Leigh he thought they had only shown up because they figured they'd get a free lunch out of it—which they did: Paul paid the tab at the register.

I thought of Paul with these two strangers at a corner table in a noisy room filled with the scent of Salisbury steaks drying up under heat lamps next to the little molded Jell-O cups and plastic ramekins filled with chalky chocolate pudding. After they'd eaten, the three of them lit up together. According to Leigh, smoking that cigarette was as close as they came to anything resembling a family moment. I imagined Paul flipping that Zippo of his and holding it out for those two old women to lean over and tip their Pall Malls into the flame.

When they were finished and had run out of things to say to each other, Paul stood up and hugged both of them because it was less awkward than shaking their hands. After that, he drove straight to Spencerville, stopping only for gas, on his way to me.

"He was out of his mind, you see?" Leigh said, a tremor edging into her voice. "But I don't think he wanted to hurt you. I think he thought you needed to be saved."

"From what?" I asked. I wasn't sure I could believe a word she was saying. But I wanted to hear it all. Truth or fiction, I needed a story.

"From ugliness," she said. "From your father. From Spencerville."
She shook her head and let out a bitter sigh.

"You have no idea how ready I am to put this town in the rear-view mirror and never look back," she said.

"You won't stay away forever," I said.

"Watch me," she said. "You'll leave too, when you have the chance."

"If you hate it so much," I said, "why'd you come back to begin with?"

"Rocky," she said, "the story isn't over."

She reached back between us to her purse, which sat on the floor behind the console. She fumbled for an orange prescription bottle. With a trembling hand, she shook one of the pills into her mouth and swallowed it dry.

The way Leigh remembered it, we were all going to go out west and start over, like Robert Redford in *Jeremiah Johnson*.

"I told Paul he was too upset and that he needed to calm down and think about what he was doing," Leigh said. "I told him how sorry I was about his mother but that he needed to take you back home right away."

"What did he say?" I asked.

"He said you'd be better off dead."

Better off dead. Was that what Paul had in mind, I wondered, when he took me up on that bluff and started plying me with beer and cigarettes?

"If I'd thought for a second that he would hurt you, I would have come with him, like he asked," she said. "But I told him that I couldn't leave, because I had a midterm. Can you believe that?"

After we left, Leigh went into Maury Hall with her study buddy Barton and sat down to take her test. She tried to answer the questions, but all she could think about was Paul—how alone he must have felt—and me, so young and small and trusting, utterly oblivious to what Paul was going through. When she couldn't bear it any longer, she walked out, stepping over a confused Barton as she made her way to the aisle. She went straight to the house and sat on the porch chain-smoking, waiting for the phone to ring.

In the early morning hours, Paul returned. He told her what he had done and that he was leaving right then; she could either come along or say good-bye to him forever.

"He was so broken," she said. "I couldn't let him leave alone. Besides, I'd never walked out on a test before. In the moment, running away seemed easier than explaining that decision to my father."

Within a few hours, they were off, heading west with the rising sun at their backs. Paul had pawned what was left of his mother's jewelry, so he had enough money to keep them going for a while, drifting from campground to campground.

Somewhere along the way, they heard about a commune nestled into a little green alpine valley outside Taos, New Mexico, called New Nazareth. The people there weren't normal hippies. They were Christians—"Jesus freaks," they called themselves.

"I thought Paul just wanted to gawk at the Bible thumpers," Leigh said. "I figured, why not? Paul was going to do what he wanted regardless of what I had to say about it."

In New Nazareth, there were no crusty hippies sleeping in tepees or dilapidated dome houses. Maybe forty or fifty people lived there full-time, but on any given day there might be two hundred people or more hanging around. They all looked like hippies, but there was something different about the blissed-out expressions on their faces. It wasn't just acid and pot, as it turned out. Their trip was something else entirely.

The New Nazarenes greeted Paul and Leigh with predictable warmth—"brother" and "sister" and so forth—and led them down to a large tin-roofed building with a covered porch at the center of the commune's grounds. "You've got to meet Stephen," they said. Who was Stephen?

"He's the prophet, brother," they said.

Almost as soon as they said it, a springy, reedy man with a beard down to his chest and a mass of kinky black curls appeared at the head of the stairs to the meeting hall. While Leigh and the New Nazarenes looked on, the bearded man approached Paul, his mouth parted in a toothy smile. Without saying a word, he put his hands on Paul's shoulders and pulled him into a tight embrace.

Then—as Leigh told it—the New Nazarenes all fell into a hush. A few of the women dropped to their knees in postures of prayer. At first, Paul just stood there, his face buried in the soft fabric of the man's shirt. He tried to pull away, but the man held him steady and whispered something in his ear. Paul started to struggle, but he couldn't break free of the man's grasp. His arms and knees went limp; he started to collapse, but the man held him up. Paul's shoulders started to shake. He cried out in wild, animal sounds. Still holding him, the man sank to the ground and held Paul there as he wept. He whispered something else to him, and within seconds, they were both laughing. Moments later, the whole crowd was weeping and laughing along with them.

This, Leigh said, was Stephen Prophet.

"Later, I asked Paul what Stephen had said to him," Leigh said. "It was a passage of scripture, from Psalm 55: 'Oh, that I had the wings of a dove! I would fly away and be at rest. I would hurry to my place of shelter, far from the tempest and the storm.' Stephen told him, 'Your mother has found peace and rest. This is your place of shelter. Cast your cares on the Lord and he will sustain you.' That was all it took. Paul was a disciple after then."

"That's crazy," I said.

"It seemed like a miracle at the time," Leigh said. "For years, I've been asking myself how Stephen could have known those things."

"Maybe he didn't," I said. "Maybe you're misremembering."

She reached for her purse. I thought she might take another pill from the bottle I assumed contained some sort of antianxiety medication for frail little southern girls, to help them survive the ordeal of getting married. Instead she removed a lighter and a pack of cigarettes.

"I thought you quit smoking," I said.

"Do you mind?" she asked.

"Not at all," I said. In some peculiar way, seeing her smoke again made her more recognizable to me.

She lit up and cracked the window.

"So," Leigh said, "we became Jesus freaks."

I couldn't quite fathom Paul according to the image Leigh described. Without reservation, he threw himself into life at New Nazareth, joining in on building projects and farm work and singing with the house band, which would perform Christianized country rock at evening services in the meeting hall. Leigh joined in with as much enthusiasm as she could muster, taking a place among the women, who cooked, cleaned, and looked after the children.

"I didn't know what to think about it all," Leigh said. "At first I was just happy to see Paul so committed to something. Everyone was so nice to us. I'd never been around people like that before. They were all so . . . joyful. So different from anything I'd ever experienced before. All my friends at home and at school were so cynical about everything. And my father—well, you know my father."

I nodded.

"It seemed like a lovely little utopia," Leigh said.

Along with the meeting hall, there were bunkhouses and a handful of adobes already built for family homes, with others in the works. A mile or so up into the hills, a natural spring fed a blue alpine lake. The New Nazarenes had built an aqueduct from the spring, so there was fresh water for bathing and cleaning, along with a well pump drawn from an underground river.

In New Nazareth, there were just enough rules to make the place feel like a legitimate church community, and just enough freedom to keep everyone happy and confident that they were part of something more beautiful and redeeming than the corrupted world of their parents. Aside from communion wine, booze was frowned on, but pot and psychedelics were, according to Stephen, "A-OK with JC." Free love was practiced, well, freely. It was like a summer camp with drugs and coed bunks.

All the anger and bitterness went out of Paul. He was unburdened, ecstatic with the rapture of redemption. Before long, Paul was leading prayers and giving testimonials at evening worship.

Gradually, Leigh felt her initial happiness for Paul being overtaken by quiet resentment. Back home in Spencerville, she was the exceptional one with all the talent and expectations. Paul was the slacker who wasn't supposed to be good enough for her. In New Nazareth, she was just Paul's girlfriend.

Furthermore, while Leigh had yet to join in on the whole "free love" thing, Paul had become—in Leigh's words—"pretty popular" with the girls.

"Were you OK with that?" I asked.

"Not at all," she said. "But who was I to stop him? For everyone else, that part of life was as normal as evening worship. There was no guilt about it, and no sneaking around. I didn't want to be a square."

One night after worship, Stephen Prophet took Leigh for a long walk in the orchard. Desperate as she was to be special, she gushed to him about all the traumas of her own life: her mother's ordeal with cancer, her father's relentless pressures, the guilt she felt about running away and leaving him alone. When she was finished, Stephen smiled and asked her if she wanted to be baptized. She said yes. After he held her hands and prayed, he laid her down in the grass and took off her clothes.

"I cried the whole time," Leigh said.

"Because of Paul?" I asked.

"Sure," she said. "But I was mostly crying because I wanted my own conversion experience. I had no idea then what that was supposed to feel like. I just knew I wasn't having one."

The next day, Stephen baptized Paul and Leigh together in the spring in the hills above the compound. A few days later—a week, maybe—with Stephen officiating, they were married.

I was dumbstruck.

"You and Paul got married?" I said.

"Not really. I mean, yes and no," Leigh said. She sighed. "It wasn't legal, you know? We didn't have a license. But yeah, I mean, yeah, we were married."

I was speechless. Leigh drove on, sucking long drags from her cigarette, exhaling in thick plumes that seemed to hang in the air before being swept out of the crack in the driver's side window.

"It was all just play, Rocky," she said. "Like third graders staging a pretend wedding on the playground at recess. Everything about New Nazareth seemed like a whole bunch of kids caught up in a big game. The whole time, I felt like sooner or later someone was going to blow a whistle and we'd all go back to our real lives. Do you know what I mean?"

"No," I said. "I don't."

All I could think of was Leigh and Paul placing cheap silver rings on each other's fingers and saying "I do" in front of the same leering hippie who, a few days before, had been off in the woods thrusting between Leigh's thighs.

"The married couples seemed a little more exclusive," she said, "so I thought maybe the wedding would bring Paul back to me a little. But it didn't."

That part I understood.

"Did Paul know about Stephen?" I asked.

"I don't see how he couldn't have known. I mostly did it to make him jealous," she said. "Can you believe how stupid I was?"

She looked at me with wide, pleading eyes. Her pupils were the size of pinpricks. She didn't seem to be looking at the road. Nevertheless, we kept moving at a brisk, even pace up along the shadowy, sidewinding asphalt path of the parkway.

The gaps of light crept through the trees as the forest thinned and the bright blue field of the sky pierced the canopy of yellow and orange leaves. Remembering Leigh as she was back then, my stomach churned with hatred for this blue-eyed hippie charlatan.

The car rounded a wide bend that led up to an overlook. Leigh pulled in and parked in front of a low stone wall facing the broad valley and the distant, narrow line of the James glittering at the edge of the horizon.

"What made you leave?" I asked. "Why did you decide to come back home?"

She cut the engine and lit another cigarette, taking a sharp drag and exhaling out the open window.

"My heart's beating so fast," she said. "I can hardly feel my hands."

"Are you all right?" I asked. "Do you need me to drive you home?"

"Just give me a minute," she said.

She climbed out of the car and walked toward the overlook, pacing back and forth along the sidewalk. I followed her, hovering nearby, close enough to catch her if she fell.

"I'm all right," she said. "I've been through this before."

As the sun began to drop behind Otter Peak, the air turned chilly. Leigh hugged herself, picking nervously with her fingernails at the fabric of her sweater.

"Maybe you should sit down," I said.

"All right," she said.

I grasped her shoulders to help her sit down on the curb. I could feel that she was shivering; I sat down next to her and wrapped my arm around her back.

"Maybe I'll feel better once I just get it out," she said.

"Let's try that," I said as gently as I could. "What happened, Leigh?"

"Oh, Rocky," she said. "You're still so innocent, aren't you?"

I couldn't believe how clueless I had been. But I was just nine when they ran away. I still thought of that whole part of our lives the way I had when I was in the fourth grade. Back then, I thought that babies came out of a woman's belly button and that getting pregnant was as simple and governable as ordering the Sea-Monkeys from the ads in the back of my *Spider-Man* comics.

"When I was finally able to admit to myself what was happening," she said, "I stayed up at night wondering how long it would be before I could tell whether or not it was Paul's."

Once she knew she was pregnant, Leigh stopped smoking or

taking anything. Like most people who abruptly sober up after a long period of foggy indulgence, she started noticing things that would have seemed obvious if not for the reefer haze. For instance, the fact that almost all the married women had at least one child with those dark, kinky curls and disarmingly pale blue eyes—all little Stephens.

"One day, I was with the women in the kitchen. I was chopping cilantro—I remember that very well because I always hated cilantro. When you're pregnant, everything smells so much stronger," she said. "I ran out of the kitchen and into the woods to throw up. I just started crying and couldn't stop. I told myself it was just hormones and decided a walk in the woods would help me calm down.

"I'd been walking for a while before I saw them," she said. "It was Stephen and one of the children with the curly black hair and the pale blue eyes. They were both naked. The boy was on his knees in front of Stephen. I think he must have been nine, maybe ten years old."

Neither the boy nor the prophet noticed her. She just stood there flabbergasted, searching vainly for an explanation that didn't add up to something too profane and horrible even to be imagined. She slowly crept back until she was sure they wouldn't see or hear her. When she felt she was out of their range of vision, she ran back to the compound, hysterical.

It took me a while to process this information. I was old enough to know such things happened, but to hear it described so matter-of-factly, particularly amid everything else I was hearing—I was nearly numb with shock.

"Why didn't you stop him?" I asked.

"I don't know," she said. Tears streamed from her eyes. "I suppose I was just too stunned to react. But that's not good enough, is it?"

I didn't have an answer for her.

When Leigh told Paul what she had seen, they had a long, angry fight. Stephen's a fraud and a pervert, she said. A pedophile. Incest and pedophilia—not even a bunch of stoned hippies could pretend that was "A-OK with JC." Paul said that she must have made a mistake, that she must not have seen what she thought she saw. They were probably just praying, he said.

"But I knew what I had seen," Leigh said, "and it was no mistake."

That night, Leigh lay awake in bed, wondering whether the baby growing inside her would be another little boy with dark, curly hair and pale blue eyes. She wondered how long it would be before Stephen took her own little boy off into the woods to *pray*.

"Ever since I had sobered up, I'd been reconsidering every decision I'd made from the moment you and Paul surprised me in the amphitheater. How long were we going to stay in that place? What was the rest of my life going to be like? Were we going to live like this forever? What would become of the baby inside me? After what I had seen in the woods, I couldn't imagine staying at New Nazareth another day. But where would I go, and if I left, would Paul come with me?"

The next morning, when she woke, Paul was gone. Left alone with her terrible secret, Leigh began to feel afraid. Had Paul gone to report what she had said to Stephen and the others? How would they react? The New Nazarenes worshipped Stephen like, well, like a prophet—like *the* prophet. Leigh knew what people had been willing to do for, say, Charles Manson or Jim Jones.

She put on her shoes and stuffed a few things in a shoulder bag and went outside and started walking off through the hills until she reached a road. She wasn't thinking about anything—she wasn't thinking at all. She just wanted to go home.

"You didn't even say good-bye?" I asked.

"No," she said.

"Why not?"

"I was afraid."

"Of what?"

"Everything," she said.

Before long, an old rancher in a pickup truck pulled up beside her. He could see that she was crying. He knew where she had come from. He drove Leigh to the Greyhound station in Santa Fe, took her out to breakfast, and bought her a bus ticket back to Virginia. It must have made the old man's year to save some stranger's long-lost daughter from the clutches of the longhairs. Two days later she was standing in front of her father.

As she told me all of this, I imagined Leigh in the back of some forlorn bus, frightened and filthy from her trek through the woods. I thought of a clean-shaven old man in a Western shirt and a crisp straw cowboy hat, waving her off as the bus pulled away to take her back home to her father. I wondered whether the old rancher would have felt so proud of himself if he knew the kind of man he was sending that poor girl home to.

Leigh shook her hands as if she were trying to dry them. Behind us, a car cruised past on the parkway. After it passed, the air fell into a still silence.

"Will you get me a cigarette, Rocky?" she said.

I retrieved her lighter and cigarettes from the console. Her hands were still shaking, so I removed a cigarette from the pack and held it to her lips. She managed to keep the tip steady while I lit it for her.

"What happened to your baby, Leigh?" I asked.

She took a long drag and pushed the smoke out into the air above her.

"I've really got to stop these," she said. "I must be turning green."

Her hands still trembled, but she seemed somehow sanguine— as if the act of confession was its own sort of penance, and she was nearing atonement.

"Well, Daddy was happy to have me home," she said. "But he wasn't happy about what I'd brought back with me."

The Honorable Prentiss Bowman III couldn't bear the idea that people might soon learn how his daughter, once the top student in her class and a nationally ranked athlete in two sports, had been knocked up with Paul Askew's bastard.

Even after *Roe v. Wade*, you couldn't just walk down the street in

Spencerville and schedule an abortion like you were ordering up a milk shake at Pearsall's. But there have always been places where things like that could be taken care of. One such place was the Monacan Mountain Rehabilitation Center, which had once been called the Middle Virginia Hospital for the Epileptic and Feeble-minded. For many years, the so-called 'rehabilitation center' was also the place for Virginians of means to discreetly take care of a little "family problem." All that was required was someone to declare the poor patient mentally unfit. Leigh was neither the first nor the last daughter of privilege who had secretly been temporarily declared mad under the same circumstances.

"Have you ever heard of a saline abortion?" she asked. "It's actually a method for inducing labor. Wonderfully humane, if you want to know the truth."

They laid her out on a table, pumped her uterus full of saltwater, and told her to wait for the dam to break, so to speak. She stayed like that for three days, surrounded by raving lunatics strapped to their beds while that tiny cherub floated in the ocean inside her.

On the third day, Leigh felt a tremor in her loins and a sharp pain in her abdomen. She cried out for help. The orderlies came and held her arms while she crouched at the edge of the table and screamed in desperate agony as her little ocean spilled out of her onto the floor.

When she was well enough to travel, Bowman came for her. They never spoke a word about any of it, as if they were honoring some implicit contract to behave as if nothing from the moment Leigh had fallen for Paul Askew to the present had ever happened.

"Daddy had an old friend from prep school who worked in the embassy in Paris," she said. "He helped me get into a study-abroad program there, and later into university. I would have stayed after I graduated, but Daddy insisted that I come home."

Her eyes drifted away from me, off to the horizon and the blue valley below it.

"I like to think that if I'd known for sure it was Paul's, I would have fought to keep it, or at least to carry it to term and give it up for adoption," she said. "But my father never asked me what I wanted, and I never argued with him. It was easier to let him decide. That way, I thought, I wasn't responsible. How's that for cold reasoning?"

"You were young," I said.

She dropped her cigarette to the ground and stamped it out. I reached down to collect the butt and tucked it into my pocket.

"A few years ago," she said, "while I was waiting in a salon for a hair appointment, I picked up a copy of *Rolling Stone*. Inside was an article called 'Prophet: Rise and Fall of a Hippie Preacher.'"

According to the article, one of the other women had found the courage to turn Stephen in. On the night he learned he was going to be arrested, Stephen went out to the orchard to pray. When he wasn't back by morning, they went out after him and found him hanging by his neck from a tree.

Later, I went to the public library and found the article myself. There were pictures of Stephen and some of the others, but no sign or mention of Paul. He must already have left—perhaps, I hoped, because he had come to accept that Leigh was telling the truth about Stephen. Maybe he had gone after her. But that couldn't have been the case; he would have known where she was going.

"When I read that story, it was like I was going through it all over again," she said. "I had to get up and walk out of the salon. I thought I was going to have another one of my episodes right there."

Episodes? I wondered.

"Anyway, New Nazareth dissolved. I don't know what became of the property. I imagine it's still there, rusted over and deserted."

I tried to imagine where Paul would have gone; how long he stayed; how long it had taken him to believe Leigh; whether he'd had to see it himself; whether he left out of horror, or revulsion, or just because.

She held her hand out to me, motioning for the pack of cigarettes and the lighter. I gave them to her, and this time, she pulled out another and lit it on her own.

"Anyway," she said, "I thought you deserved to know."

And here's the rub. In spite of how I pitied her—who wouldn't pity the poor girl after hearing such a woeful tale?—when Leigh told me she thought I deserved to know, I agreed with her. I felt entitled to the information.

She sat silently smoking for a while, her mind still adrift, presumably back in New Mexico, or in Paris, or perhaps on her back on a table in the Monacan Mountain Rehabilitation Center, her legs aloft, waiting for her belly to burst.

Then she was back. She turned toward me, her eyes narrowed.

"I understand why you would want to hurt me," she said. "I deserved that. But what she's doing—it isn't what you think it is, Rocky."

"Who?" I asked.

"Don't be ridiculous," she said. "Once she found out about Paul, that was it. From the moment she saw how I reacted when you ran out to meet us at the fence, I could hear the wheels spinning in her vicious little head."

"I don't know what you mean," I said.

"You're not the only one, you know," she said, a hint of taunting in her voice. "Quite a few others have seen the inside of her hayloft."

"You're making that up," I said. "Why is it any of your business anyway?"

"Maybe it's not," she said. "It never seems to help anything, does it?"

"What?"

"Tampering in the lives of others."

I had forgotten that, before I had fallen for Patricia, the whole point of coming to work for the Culvers had been to meddle in *Leigh's* life.

"I better get home," she said. "People might be wondering if I've turned into a runaway bride."

"Me too," I said. "It's almost dinnertime."

"Rocky?" she asked, her voice plaintive and tremulous.

"It's OK," I said. "Your secret's safe with me."

But was her secret safe with me? I knew even then that it wasn't. Even if I had meant it when I said it—and I don't think I ever truly did—Patricia had no trouble getting whatever she wanted out of me.

We fell into gloomy silence as Leigh guided the car down through the mountains. At one point she turned on the radio. A Whitney Houston song came on—"I Wanna Dance with Somebody." Leigh turned it off and lit a cigarette.

It was completely dark when Leigh pulled her car to a stop at the end of my driveway. Without a word I opened the door and stepped out. I peered back in at her.

"Tell your mom and dad I'm sorry," she said.

"For what?" I asked.

"Making you late for dinner."

"Oh," I said. "OK."

"Good-bye, Rocky."

I felt a sense of permanence in the words, as if she meant for this to be the last time we spoke or even saw each other. Still, I could muster nothing more than the feeblest of replies.

"Bye," I said.

I shut the door. She drove away, her car rising and falling across the rolling line of the road until it disappeared from sight. I glanced across the field toward the dell and the stables, wondering whether Patricia was still there, waiting for me. But there was no time—I would have to wait to see her again.

That night after dinner, I dropped the needle on an old, familiar record—*Tonight's the Night*. I lay across the bed and thought about Paul out west on an alpine desert dressed in coarse linen robes, his hair and beard long and full, grooving to the music in front of a smoking, burning bush.

10

I CAN'T HELP THINKING that Leigh knew I wouldn't keep her secret. At the least, she should have expected me to tell the Old Man, on the off chance that the story might help lead him to Paul. Given her opinion of Patricia and her conviction that I was being toyed with, she could hardly have chosen anyone less trustworthy to confide in. But maybe that was the point; maybe Leigh was using me to expose herself so that, once she was officially revealed as damaged goods, Charles would call the whole thing off and spare her direct responsibility for disappointing her father yet again. Still, I cringe every time I think of how carelessly and eagerly I betrayed Leigh Bowman, the first girl I had ever loved.

"My God," Patricia said. "That poor girl."

"I know," I said.

She stood and walked toward the open door of the hayloft and peered out into the darkness.

"It's a pity that this had to happen now," she said.

"What do you mean?" I asked.

"You know what I mean, Rocky."

She came back and sat down next to me on the blanket. She inched her body closer, drawing the tips of her fingers across my bare chest. I pulled the blanket back over us, and we lay there huddled together in our woolen cocoon, starting at the occasional noise from the horses.

"It means we're going to have to put an end to this part of our friendship," she said.

"Why?" I asked.

"You know why, Rocky," she said wearily.

"What could they do to us?" I asked.

"To you? Nothing. To me, on the other hand—people go to prison for this sort of thing, you know."

I thought about how my mother would react if she found out about me and Patricia. I thought about how the blathering gossip-mongers of Spencerville would salivate over every detail, true or not. Naturally these reflections completely disregarded my hypocrisy on the subject of gossip.

"You knew this time was coming," Patricia said. "It just seems to have arrived a little sooner than we had hoped."

I laughed bitterly.

"What is it?" she asked.

"I've never been dumped before," I said.

"Don't think of it that way," she said.

"How should I think of it?"

"As part of your education," she said.

I could object no further, already stiff in her hand as I was.

"Now," she said. "Once more, with feeling."

THE NEXT DAY, it was my mother's turn to host the weekly Bible study led by Miss Anita Holt. The group met every Friday, rotating from home to home. The hostess served an afternoon tea, which often included a bottle or two of chardonnay. It was a wonderful thing for my mother. She'd never had many friends.

Miss Anita Holt came from an old Spencerville family that had made a fortune in the furniture business. The widow of a prominent attorney and former city councilman, she was regarded as a personage of near saintly authority in the halls of Holy Comforter, not least because she was known to have "visions"—dreams, apprehensions, and instinctive knowledge of things that had not yet come to pass. Miss Anita's visions were rarely concrete; rather, they were just images or feelings about something or someone. A man at church might be out of work, for instance. On Sunday, Miss Anita would approach him and engage him in conversation after the service. "I had a dream about you," she might say. She'd tell him about how she had seen him in a peculiar building, or show him a drawing of some image that had lingered in her mind when she thought of him: a triangular design, say, and a picture of a hillside decorated with three narrow pylon-shaped objects. The next week, the man might be offered a job in a building like the one Miss Anita had described, for a company with a triangular logo, on a construction or engineering project involving a trio of plant or reactor buildings set on a green hillside.

Sometimes, Miss Anita's premonitions related to people she didn't know. A few years prior, the disappearance of a fifteen-year-old girl had made the national news. The girl had vanished from her family home while her parents were out at the movies. The night her disappearance was reported on television, my mother received a call from Miss Anita Holt.

"Alice," Miss Anita said breathlessly, "the moment her picture came on the screen, I saw that girl's body buried under a pile of dirt and leaves."

A few days later, the girl was found as Miss Anita had described, less than a mile from her parents' home. But Miss Anita couldn't see what had happened to her, or who had put her there. There were apparent limitations to her gift.

Nevertheless, her legendary spiritual prowess had earned Miss Anita a discipleship. The weekly Bible study group was a mixed bag of odd ducks, ranging from the elderly dowagers to middle-aged moms like mine to virtuous young protégés. There was a scripture lesson, typically led by Miss Anita, followed by an open discussion of "prayer needs," which devolved rather directly into the primary purpose of these kinds of gatherings. Apparently it's not sinful to gossip about people so long as you are praying for them.

They were already in conference when I arrived home from school, dropped off, as always, at the head of the driveway by Macon's day-student bus. I crept in the front door and tried to make my way to the kitchen unnoticed, but Miss Anita Holt's holy radar must have been up.

"Richard," she called.

Miss Anita had one of those lovely old Virginia Piedmont

accents—the kind where "Richard" is "Rich-*uhd*" and "water" is "*war*-ter."

"Rich-*uhd*," Miss Anita called again, "come *he-ah* so I can see you."

I walked into the living room to find them gathered in a circle around the coffee table. At the center of the cream-colored couch sat Miss Anita, flanked by my mother and Kiki Baumberger, Anita's closest friend and rival; Rosa Lee Baldwin and Lottie Honig, a pair of old spinsters who had managed to be "roommates" for longer than I'd been alive without drawing any suspicion; Laura Hearne and Eleanor Sanders, two of the younger women; and, to my surprise, a rather pale and unsettled-looking Jane Culver.

"Come here, sweetie," Miss Anita said.

I walked over and bent to her upraised arms, returning her gentle hug and cheek kiss and exchanging another with my mother.

"How are you, Miss Anita?" I asked.

"Fine, darling, fine," she said.

She asked me the typical questions an old woman asks a teenage boy. The other women smiled and nodded as if they were interested—all except my mother and Jane Culver. I could sense the tension in the room. Jane Culver stared at the wall behind Miss Anita's head as if she could see through the plaster to something grave and alarming on the other side of it.

To my knowledge, Jane Culver had never attended the Bible study before. I could recall seeing her at church two or three times at the most, and always without her husband or daughter. "Daddy thinks that any decent God would rather that we didn't waste two hours of a good Sunday morning keeping up appearances," Patricia had explained.

Jane Culver looked exceedingly uncomfortable. What on earth was she doing at a Bible study just a few hours before her stepson's wedding rehearsal dinner?

I answered Miss Anita's questions as casually and politely as I could, trying to stifle my creeping panic. Jane Culver had somehow discovered what had been going on in her hayloft for the past few weeks, I thought. Miss Anita had called me into the room so that I could be forced to come clean and allow them all to lay on hands and speak in tongues as they prayed for the healing of my debauched, corrupted soul.

"It's wonderful to see you, dear," Miss Anita said. "You're becoming such a handsome young man."

"Thank you," I said.

I waited, gazing back at Miss Anita so as to avoid making eye contact with my mother or Jane Culver. The other women—including my mother—remained silent. I shrank from the room and made a show of loudly tramping upstairs. I took my shoes off, and after as long a pause as I could stand, I crept back down on tiptoes, drew up to the closed door of the living room, and pressed my ear against the door.

"What do you plan to do, dear?" I heard Miss Anita ask.

"We'll have to go on with it," Jane Culver said. "Too many people have gone to too much trouble. Besides, we don't even know for certain that any of it is true."

"If she is already married, you can't just go through with it," said one of them—Kiki Baumberger, I think.

"I don't see why not," Jane Culver said. "They can just get an annulment afterward, if that's what they decide."

"You can't do that," Kiki Baumberger protested.

"Hush, Kiki," Miss Anita said.

"I'm just thinking about the church, Anita," she said.

"Think about the child," Miss Anita said. "What she's suffered."

"Why doesn't someone just ask her?" Laura Hearne asked.

"Great idea," Kiki Baumberger dryly remarked. "Why, Leigh, honey, don't you look beautiful in that white dress? And what an exquisite bouquet! By the way, is it true that you had a hippie marriage eight years ago to your old high school boyfriend and a secret abortion in the nuthouse?"

"I didn't mean it like that," Laura Hearne murmured.

"We know that, honey," Miss Anita said. "You were trying to be helpful."

Once, about a year or two back, while sitting next to me in the pew during Sunday service at Holy Comforter, the Old Man suffered a bout of vertigo. He'd been dealing for some time with inner ear problems resulting from hearing damage he'd suffered during his war service, so he knew what was happening to him, but he was still powerless to stop it. His knees twisted beneath him; his face blanching with terror, he clutched my shoulder and the edge of the pew, trying to regain his bearings as his vision whirled and the floor seemed to drop away. I could never comprehend how that spinning sensation must have felt to him until that moment outside the living room door. Panic, dread, guilt, fear—all the demons set upon me with crippling velocity. I clenched my fists and waited, listening.

"I'm sorry, Jane," someone said.

It was my mother. I almost didn't recognize her voice, so low and cold and resigned did it seem to be.

"What have you got to be sorry for, Alice?" Jane Culver asked.

"It was Paul, don't you see?" my mother said. "This would never have happened if it weren't for Paul, that stupid, stupid, selfish boy."

Paul! Old or young, here or gone, dead or alive, Paul would always be available for my mother to blame.

"Please, Alice," Miss Anita said. "That's all in the past now."

"The past is never really behind us, is it, Miss Anita?" my mother asked.

"Not entirely," Miss Anita answered. "But we can be free of it."

"We knew Leigh had a bit of a history, but she just seemed so lovely," Jane Culver said.

"A bit of a history?" my mother said incredulously.

"I never dreamed anything like this might have happened," Jane Culver protested.

"Oh, please," my mother said. It was one of her classic retorts, along with "Buck up" and "Choose your battles."

"What have I done to make you so angry, Alice?" Jane Culver said.

"I just find it hard to believe that you, of all people, could be so naive."

"Is that an accusation?" Jane Culver asked, a hint of ire creeping into her voice.

"Alice, honey," Miss Anita said. "This isn't helping."

A tense moment of silence followed.

"I'm sorry, Jane," my mother said, without much more sincerity than an impish brat being ordered to apologize for kicking his sister.

"I just don't know what to do," Jane Culver said.

"You don't have to do anything," Miss Anita said. "Come on, now. Let's pray for Leigh Bowman, and for Charles, and for Jane."

There was a rustling of movement. I pictured the women reaching to clasp hands in a circle.

"Heavenly Father," Miss Anita began.

I cast my own silent plea up with theirs. Dear God, I prayed, please don't let me get caught.

The doorbell rang. I felt as if God were answering my request instantly, in the negative.

Though I feared what might await me at the front door, I knew if I didn't answer it, my mother would. So I darted from my hiding place outside the living room and out to the front hall. When I opened the door, I almost gasped at the sight of Brad Culver, dressed in sharply creased black slacks, a herringbone sport coat, and a pressed white shirt and reeking of scotch.

"Hello, there, young Richard," Culver said.

I had never been capable of greeting the man without a shudder. He would always be at the edge of every nightmare I would ever have.

"Hello, sir," I said.

His eyes swam up and down, as if he'd forgotten what he'd come for.

"Would you mind if I came in?" he asked.

I was afraid to answer. It felt like inviting a vampire into the house.

"Is Mrs. Culver around?" he asked.

"Yes, sir," I said.

Culver stepped past me into the entrance hall. No magic prevented him from entering without invitation.

"So," he said. "Where's Mrs. Culver, son?"

"In there," I said, pointing in the direction of the living room. He started toward the door.

"They're praying," I said.

"I'm sure the Good Lord will pardon the interruption," Culver replied.

When we entered the room, we found the women in a circle of clasped hands around the glass-top coffee table. Miss Anita, it seemed, was receiving the "gift of tongues." The sounds were soft and labial—almost musical. Miss Anita swayed back and forth in her position on the couch, her lips parted in a thin smile, her head tilted back. The other women held on to each other, heads bowed, brows furrowed in deep concentration.

I had seen Miss Anita receive the gift before and so was not alarmed; in fact, I had never been particularly stirred by these scenes, having been instructed years before by Paul that Miss Anita was a "kook" who put on a "carny fortune-teller's act" to satisfy what he called her "guru complex." Brad Culver, on the other hand, was clearly unprepared for what he was walking in on, and was a little too loosened by the scotch to contain himself.

"What in blazes are you people doing?" he barked.

Miss Anita's eyes opened with a start. The murmuring ceased; all at once the women came back to awareness, squinting and blinking as if they were waking from a deep sleep.

"Brad!" Jane Culver exclaimed, wiping the stains of her tears from her dampened cheeks.

"Hello," Miss Anita said. "I don't believe we've met."

"I'm so sorry," my mother said, rising to her feet. "Brad, this is Miss Anita Holt."

"Pleased to meet you," Miss Anita said, extending her hand.

"Likewise," Culver said, recovering himself. "Please excuse me. I've just never seen anything like that before."

When Brad Culver took her hand, a flicker of panic came across Miss Anita's eyes. The color drained out of her face. Her warm society matron's smile went slack. Her whole body seemed to tremble slightly, as if she were being charged with electricity. She was *seeing* something.

Brad Culver stared at her, flummoxed. I wondered whether Miss Anita had fallen into a trance. Abruptly her eyes lifted to meet Brad Culver's. She pulled her hand back as if she had been bitten by a snake.

"I beg your pardon," Miss Anita whispered.

"Are you OK, Miss Anita?" my mother asked.

"I'm feeling a bit faint, honey," she said. "Do you mind if I sit?"

"Please," Culver said. "Let me help you."

"I'll be fine," she said, retreating from Culver to my mother, who helped her back to the couch.

"That must have been a bit of an aftershock," Miss Anita said.

Mrs. Culver scowled at her husband. The other women looked on, fidgeting with discomfort. Whether they felt more embarrassed for Brad Culver or for themselves I could not say.

"I'm sorry if I upset you," Brad Culver said.

"No, no, dear," Miss Anita said. "Forgive me. I'm just an old woman, prone to spells."

Culver stared around the room, shamefaced. The vehemence in his wife's eyes had drained the vinegar right out of him.

"I thought you'd be home by now, honey," he said. "We've got a lot to take care of."

"I needed some advice," Mrs. Culver curtly replied.

"I thought we agreed we wouldn't discuss this with anyone," Culver said.

"You decided," she said. "We didn't agree."

The other women looked around at each other, smiling the way polite women smile when confronted with two people making a scene of themselves.

"I think we've troubled these nice ladies enough with our problems," Culver said.

"It's no trouble," Miss Anita said. "No trouble at all."

Culver shot an angry look at Miss Anita. His face darkened. For a moment I thought he was going to tell her to shut the hell up, or something of the sort.

"Brad's right," Mrs. Culver said. "There are a million things left to do before tonight. Alice, Miss Anita, I'm very, very sorry."

"You've nothing to apologize for, darling," Miss Anita murmured.

"Richard, will you please see Mr. and Mrs. Culver out?" my mother said.

"Yes, ma'am," I said.

I led them out into the hallway and held the door for them as they passed. I heard the living room door close behind me.

"Good afternoon, Richard," Mrs. Culver said.

"See you around the barn, sport," said Brad Culver.

"Bye," I replied.

The Culvers walked out to their cars. They stopped for a moment and exchanged some tense words before parting and hurrying to their matching Mercedes sedans. Just as hastily they sped off down the driveway. When they were gone, I crept back and resumed my position by the door to the living room.

"Was it clear?" Kiki Baumberger asked. "Can you describe it?"

"Did it happen when you touched his hand, or before?" Rosa Lee Baldwin asked.

"Will it happen soon?" asked Laura Hearne.

"Hush," I heard my mother say. "Can't you see she's feeling faint?"

There was a pause, followed by the sound of Miss Anita's voice.

"I will never speak of what I saw," she said, "unless it comes to pass."

11

BY THE TIME WE all sat down at the dinner table, the Old Man had heard all about Jane Culver's visit to the Bible study, Brad Culver's intrusion, and Miss Anita's bizarre reaction to him. The Old Man's immediate thought, naturally, was of Paul.

"New Mexico, you say? What part? We tried there, years ago. Maybe I should try again."

"Paul is not the main concern at the moment, Dick," my mother said.

"He is for me," the Old Man said.

"Stop thinking of yourself," my mother said, "and think about that poor girl."

"Where is this story coming from anyway?" the Old Man asked.

"Jane wouldn't say," my mother said. "A 'reliable source' was all she would admit to. It must be that Patricia. She's been buttering poor Leigh up for months, but I always felt there was something cold in her."

I concentrated on my dinner plate, wondering whether I looked as guilty as I felt.

"Paul and Leigh," my mother said. "Married! Can you believe it?"

"It doesn't sound like anything legally binding," the Old Man said.

"I know. It's just the thought of it. And what happened after! Poor child. That Prentiss Bowman really is a monster, isn't he?"

"You don't know any of that is true," the Old Man said sharply. "Don't you dare pass it around any further than you already have."

"I'm just telling you what I was told, right here in your own house by your new business partner's wife."

"Obviously that's why he came here," the Old Man said. "To tell her the same thing I'm telling you—to keep her goddamned mouth shut about it!"

His voice had risen in pitch. My mother sat silent for a moment, furious but also chastened.

"What if it is true?" she asked. "Could you have done something like that to your child? To your daughter?"

My eyes rose from the plate to find the Old Man staring at me.

"I don't know," he said. "Love can make people do terrible things."

I COULDN'T REACH PATRICIA. She was off at the rehearsal dinner, and then at the after-party, held under an illuminated tent on the front lawn at Twin Oaks. I snuck out into the field, hoping Patricia might anticipate that I was waiting for her and slip away to meet me there. The party went on into the late hours of the evening; eventually I gave up and went back inside to bed.

It was almost noon before I woke. I spent the day in Paul's room, pretending to be sick, hoping my parents would spare me the ordeal of having to watch Leigh walk down the aisle, knowing that, thanks to me, many if not all of the people there would know her dark secret. Bless her heart, they might say, which was just the southern way of excusing oneself for making a trivial diversion out of another person's misery.

I was beginning to think I might escape when, around four thirty, I rolled over to find my father standing in the frame of the door.

"Time to get up," he said.

"I'm not feeling any better," I said.

"I paid sixty bucks to rent that tuxedo," he said, gesturing to the black plastic suit bag hanging from the knob on the closet door.

"I honestly don't think I can."

He crossed his arms over his chest.

"I think there's a rule," he slowly said, "that if you invite yourself to a wedding, you have to show up."

Truth be told, even before I potentially wrecked the whole thing with my incontinent mouth, I had never really wanted to go; I was just trying to get a rise out of Leigh. I never considered actually having to attend.

"I can't," I said. "I just feel too sick."

"We all feel a little sick today," he said. "Now get up."

"But Dad," I pleaded, "I've got a headache!"

He stepped into the room and leaned down toward me, so that I could smell his breath, which was soured with whiskey.

"You're going," he said. "You're going if I have to drag you by your ear."

BLACK WAS THE COLOR of the season: the men in tuxedos, the women an army of black dresses—A-line, scoop-neck, spaghetti-strap, full-length, cut at the knee, tastefully slit or sequined, with touches of white and red and orange and blue and a few striped or earth-toned deviants. They lined up in their blackness, a coven with pearls and brooches, diamond earrings and charm bracelets, frosted hair and face-lifts, pink lips and designer bags.

The setting sun backlit the lingering swaths of fall color in the oaks and dogwoods bordering the long, quiet avenue of stucco, brick, and Tudor paneling. The air was still unseasonably warm. Tiki torches lined the sidewalk path from the sign that read EPIS-COPAL CHURCH OF THE HOLY COMFORTER, EST. 1803, past the boxwood hedges and over a hopscotch game scrawled onto the sidewalk in pink chalk, down to the enormous white tent in front of the Bowman residence, just a block away from the church.

When we reached the doors to the sanctuary, one of the groomsmen extended his arm to my mother.

"Bride's side or groom's?" he asked.

My mother looked back at us. The Old Man shrugged.

"Groom's," my mother said.

The sanctuary was full by the time the bridesmaids appeared at the back of the hall in moss-green sleeveless satin gowns with black sashes tied in the back into rather funereal-looking bows.

Jane Culver was escorted to her seat, wearing a peach Chanel suit and a mask of polite restraint. The groomsmen marched out of step down to the foot of the altar, arms swinging. The organ murmured "Jesu, Joy of Man's Desiring." Father Cannon emerged from his chambers.

I became acutely aware of the heat enveloping and emanating from hundreds of bodies in layers of black wool, cotton, and starch. Handkerchiefs dabbed brows; dry throats swallowed. The peals of the organ lingered in the stifling air.

Charles and Brad Culver emerged from the choir room door. The groomsmen lined up beside them, shoulders back, arms hanging at the side. Maybe the whole business had blown over harmlessly, I thought. Everything seemed to be proceeding as if nothing was out of the ordinary.

The bridesmaids rustled down the aisle in their stiff dresses, each of them wearing an awkward smile. The last of them was Patricia—the maid of honor. How had this escaped me? The irony was too cruel to be believed.

I had never even seen Patricia in a dress before. She never wore heels—only boots or tennis shoes. In the green dress, her athletic body looked ungainly; her shoulders seemed milky and thick, thanks to the visible tan lines at her neck and above her elbows. Her face was heavily made up and her hair styled into a French braid that might have seemed beautiful were it not so disarming to see her wearing any sort of makeup other than pale lip gloss. As she drew closer to us, I looked down at the floor.

When Patricia reached the foot of the steps below the altar, the music ceased. A hush fell over the congregation. A moment later, the organ exploded in a cacophony of notes at once sonorous and dissonant. From the balcony, a trumpeter blew the melody of "Ode to Joy."

Leigh appeared at the sanctuary door in her mother's wedding gown. Next to her stood Prentiss Bowman, tall and lean in his white tie and tailcoat, smiling in such a way that he seemed to be scowling instead. Leigh's eyes took in the stares. I noticed a faint twitching in her jaw at the edge of her lovely mouth. The music bounced around the hall in rolling torrents. A little girl in a pink dress standing on a pew next to us clapped her hands over her ears.

Leigh and Judge Bowman reached the altar precisely as the organist played the last note of the song. Its echo mingled with the sound of shifting bodies reaching for the Book of Common Prayer.

"Who gives this woman . . . ?" asked Father Cannon.

"I do," Judge Bowman replied.

He gave Leigh a brusque kiss on the cheek and retreated to his place on the first pew. Father Cannon looked out to the congregation.

"Into this holy union Leigh and Charles now come to be joined. If any of you can show just cause why they may not lawfully be married, speak now; or else for ever hold your peace."

An excruciating silence followed. Glancing around, I realized that a number of people in the congregation were staring at me and my mother and the Old Man. I wondered whether they were hoping, as I still was, that this would be the moment when Paul returned.

A voice from near the rear of the sanctuary broke the silence. Heads swiveled; a few people even gasped.

"Mommy," the voice said, "is that God?"

Leigh and Charles looked back. Again, the voice came, louder this time—a deep little boy's voice, almost raspy, like a smoker's.

"You told me God was going to be here," said the child. "That's not God. God has a BEARD."

Laughter rippled across the sanctuary. The mother snatched up the young theologian and whisked him out the door into the narthex. As the white door slowly closed and came to a rest behind her, the laughter rose in pitch and intensity. People grinned with naked relief, as if everyone in the room had awoken simultaneously from a terrible dream.

"Let us pray," said the priest.

The room quieted. Heads bowed, we listened as Father Cannon recited the words, so familiar as to be almost meaningless. No one was thinking about the prayer—we were all basking in the euphoria of disaster averted. In retrospect, it was the kind of relief that begs for swift and vicious comeuppance.

Moments later, a loud thud near the altar interrupted the priest's recitation. We all opened our eyes and looked around to see who had fainted.

Then the screaming began.

It was an ungodly sound: hell-bent, bellowing shrieks, higher and higher, bouncing off the walls, off the Tiffany windows, off Moses and Isaiah and Jesus with his hand over his heart, louder and louder, "My God why are you doing this why is this happening God help me stop it stop it stop it . . ."

Dumbstruck, Father Cannon could do nothing but gape at what was happening in front of him, his hands limply clutching his prayer book. Another thud echoed through the hall. One of the groomsmen, we later learned, had locked his knees and fainted, falling forward onto his face and breaking his nose, crimson torrents billowing onto his starched white tuxedo shirt and about half of the first row of Cabell cousins and aunts and uncles.

A pediatrician near the front raced forward. He motioned to Prentiss Bowman and another man I didn't recognize, sitting behind him. The three of them lifted a seizing, shaking Leigh Bowman, eyes rolled up into her head, flecks of foam pasting strands of blond hair to the corners of her mouth, her two front teeth pinching into her lip, a trace of red on her chin. The mass of them tumbled out a side door at the front of the sanctuary, into the darkness. The door closed silently behind them.

Eyes flashed around the room. The stuffiness of too many bodies pressed into such a small space seemed to give way. We were all suddenly alert and awake, glancing around at each other.

Father Cannon stared feebly out at the openmouthed faces

before him, all of them waiting to be told what to do. The look on
his face suggested that he was hoping for some direction himself.
So, naturally, he did what everyone does when thoroughly bewil-
dered and terrified.

"Let us pray," he said.

The organist began playing a soft, melodic arrangement, punctuated by the click and thud of kneelers dropping to the floor on
the backs of the pews. Shoulders dropped as congregants slid forward off their seats. Without thinking, I lurched forward, elbows
on the pew in front of me, head bowed, eyes clenched shut.

I opened my eyes and looked back at the Old Man. His hands
gripped the seat beneath him. His eyes were open, his wet teeth
clenched between his parted lips. The liver spots forming on the
high crown of his head beneath his thinning hair stood out in dark
relief. Vertigo, I thought. The old inner ear playing tricks on him.
I reached back and placed a hand on his knee. His head jerked
slightly, startled. He stared at me, his eyes red-rimmed and hollow.

I looked back to the altar and the stained glass windows at the
front of the church. The Culvers were all still there: Patricia, her
parents, even Charles. None of them had left with Leigh. She was
alone out there with her asshole father and the doctor and the fool
with the broken nose.

While the rest of us prayed, the Culvers conferred with the priest.
The groomsmen and the bridesmaids exchanged furtive, anxious
words. I stared at the back of Patricia's head, hoping she would
turn so I could see the look on her face. When at last the music
ended, Father Cannon resumed his position before the altar.

"Obviously this is all very out of the ordinary," he said. "But the
best thing we can do is to lend support to the families and share
our best wishes through fellowship. I hope you will all be able to
join them at the reception."

He fumbled through some platitudes about faith and the mys-
teries of God's will and compassionate understanding, whatever
that was supposed to mean under the circumstances. There was a

hymn and a benediction, after which the black-clad crowd poured through the open doors, struggling not to trample each other.

The rumors were already flying as the lot of us shuffled out into the comparatively cool air of early evening: comments about frenzied madness and delirium, whisperings of witchcraft and diabolical forces.

The Old Man walked slowly, my mother's hand on his arm.

"Are you all right, Dick?" she asked.

"Fine," he said unconvincingly.

"It's his ear," I said.

He nodded.

"I can't believe they're still having a reception after *that*," my mother said.

"Would it be better to let fifteen grand go to waste?"

"It might," she said. "Are you sure you're all right, Dick?"

"I'm fine," said the Old Man. "It'll pass."

"We should go home," my mother said, her voice transparently broadcasting her reluctance.

"I just need a drink," he said.

Together we walked out through the parking lot to the sidewalk. The torches along the path seemed sinister and ominous after what we had just witnessed. I remembered a story I'd read in school about a young Puritan man during the time of the Salem witch trials who sneaks out to the forest for a secret rendezvous with the devil, only to find everyone in his life whom he'd ever thought of as pious and moral—including his young wife, the rather bluntly named Faith—congregated at the Black Mass that was to be the young man's infernal baptism. "Now are ye undeceived," the devil cries. "Welcome, my children, to the communion of your race!"

By the time we reached the reception, long lines already stretched back from both bars. Clearly ignorant of what they'd missed, the band—an R & B combo fronted by an elfish, bearded keyboard player and an enormous female vocalist in a metallic orange evening gown—were working hard to win over the understandably restrained crowd. The singers traded verses and blended harmonies on "Ain't Nothing Like the Real Thing," segueing seamlessly into "I Heard It through the Grapevine." The horn section, all wearing wayfarer sunglasses, swayed back and forth in unison.

"There," my mother said, pointing to a table at the corner of the portable parquet dance floor farthest from the bandstand. "Anita and Kiki."

I walked behind them as we approached Miss Anita and Kiki Baumberger, sipping chardonnay and trying to look serene.

"Alice," Miss Anita said.

My mother stooped to receive her one-armed hug and a kiss on the cheek.

"Oh, Anita," she said.

"That poor girl," Anita replied. "We'll pray for her, won't we?"

My mother nodded fervently.

"Did you sense something like this was going to happen?" Kiki asked.

"I wish I had," Miss Anita said. "Not that it would have made any difference."

"You might have stopped it," Kiki said. "You might have spared poor Leigh."

"The sight doesn't work that way," Anita said.

"As soon as it happened," my mother said, "I thought it was what you saw yesterday when Brad Culver came to the house."

"No, dear," Anita said. "That was something else."

"What was it, Anita?" Kiki asked.

"I couldn't bear to tell you," Anita answered. "I haven't any idea what it meant anyhow. Sometimes the things I see are meaningless—just an old woman's crazy notions."

My mother and Kiki Baumberger exchanged a knowing glance.

"Would you like something to drink, honey?" the Old Man asked.

"Please," she said, lifting her face to the Old Man's.

"Come along, Richard," the Old Man said. "Let's get your mother a drink."

I followed him as he shuffled over to the bar, my eyes scanning the crowd for green bridesmaids' dresses.

"White wine and a scotch old-fashioned, please, Oscar," the Old Man said.

"Yessuh," the bartender replied.

"And a ginger ale," the Old Man added.

"Uh-huh," Oscar answered.

The Old Man pulled his money clip from his wallet and peeled out a twenty. He held it in the air in front of his furrowed brow. After a long pause, he laid it on the bar.

"Shoot a little something into that ginger ale, will you, Oscar?"

"Happy to, Mr. Askew."

The Old Man motioned me over to the edge of the tent, his own drink in one hand, my mother's wineglass in the other.

"Thought you might need that," the Old Man said, nodding to my drink.

"Thanks," I said.

For a moment I felt as if the future had arrived. Here we were, Dad and me, two men having a drink together. It was almost enough to make me forget what had brought us there.

"Dad," I said.

"Hold that thought," he said. "Let me deliver this. And son, about that drink—if you say a word to your mother . . ."

"I know," I said.

The bridesmaids emerged from the house and gathered at the front of the bandstand. There appeared to have been some sort of mutual agreement to behave as if nothing unusual had happened. The groomsmen joined them as the band played "Smoke Gets in Your Eyes."

"Hello, Rocky."

Patricia was standing a few feet away, in the shadows at the edge of the tent. A jolt of guilt came over me. I looked back for the Old Man. He had taken a seat at the table next to my mother. I turned back to Patricia.

"It's been quite an evening, hasn't it?" she said.

"How could you?" I said.

She frowned in dismay.

"How could I?" she said. "How could *you*, Rocky? I don't recall twisting your arm for information."

"You said you wouldn't tell."

"So did you."

Patricia crossed her arms, her breasts resting across them, as if she was thrusting her cleavage at me to weaken my resolve.

"If you didn't want me to say anything," she said, "why did you tell me?"

"I shouldn't have," I said.

She sighed.

"Maybe I shouldn't have either," she said. "Then again, maybe it was also for the best."

"How can you say that?"

"Charles was very understanding," Patricia said. "And why should Leigh be ashamed? She was the victim. The victim of men she trusted."

"You don't know what you're talking about," I said.

I thought she was referring to me.

"You're not your brother, Rocky," she said. "Besides, her father's surely the one who's at fault here. What an atrocious thing to do to a young girl! And furthermore, he's known all along about her other problems."

"What other problems?" I asked.

"Leigh is very sick, Rocky," she said. "I suppose we might have noticed the signs. Had he known, Charles might have gone through with it. He might even have loved her. But to accept a proposal of marriage without disclosing such a condition—it's unconscionable, really."

She tilted her head and touched her right hand to her chin, as if lost in thought. Despite lacking its former support, her right breast remained upright, if not quite as well secured as its counterpart.

If the manipulation of her breasts was a calculated distraction, it achieved the desired effect. As incensed as I might have been, I couldn't stay angry at her, busy as I was imagining her naked.

"I expect she'll go off for another rest," Patricia said. "After that, who knows?"

The sanctimoniousness of her tone restored my indignation.

"You act like you care," I said.

"But you see, *I do*," she said. "I care deeply. I honestly want the best for her. She was going to be my sister."

"She never trusted you," I said. "I guess she was right."

"Are you suggesting that *I'm* to blame for what happened in that church? Please, Rocky. You give me too much credit. From what I've heard, this wasn't the first time."

I remembered Leigh's mention of her "episodes." Even all those years ago, there was talk that she was "a little off." People protected her then, I think, because of what had happened to her mother. When I'd seen her just a few days before, popping pills and rambling obsessively about her past, I'd assumed it was all due to the stress of the story she was telling and her impending arranged marriage—not because of some preexisting condition.

"Even so," I said, "it didn't have to happen in front of all those people. You can't deny that you—that *we* had something to do with that."

"Please, Rocky," Patricia protested.

"I wish you'd stop calling me that," I said.

"All right, *Richard*," she said. "But really. Why do you think she told you all those outlandish stories? Did you know that impulsive, self-destructive behavior is a classic symptom of manic depression? Did you know that paranoid delusions are also among those symptoms?"

"No," I said. "I didn't know that."

I hadn't thought of Leigh as depressed. We weren't all into labels just yet. People like Leigh were just thought of as being a little *kooky*.

Patricia gave a long sigh and glanced off over her shoulder.

"I'm frankly a bit hurt," she said, "that after all we've shared, you'd be so quick to accuse me. It's actually quite painful."

"I'm sorry," I said.

I looked back toward where my parents were sitting with Miss Anita and Kiki. The Old Man was watching us, his eyes darkened with suspicion.

"I guess it's just hard for me not to feel responsible," I said.

"It would have happened anyway, Richard," she said.

"We don't know that."

"We can't say it wouldn't have either."

"It was so awful," I said.

"As horrifying as it may seem, I'm told it's not all that bad," Patricia said, taking on her professorial lecturer's tone. "Apparently the brain chemistry involved in an acute psychotic break resembles the effect of a very powerful narcotic or hallucinogen. So while it's very disturbing to observe, to the victim it feels pleasurable—even euphoric."

"Terrific," I said. "I feel so much better now. Come to think of it, she looked like she was having an absolute blast."

She moved closer to me.

"This is very upsetting for me too," she said, more softly. "I wish I could hold you."

"Maybe we could talk again later," I said. Even under the circumstances, I was still thinking about getting between her thighs one last time.

"No, darling," she said. "That's impossible. We'll go to the hospital to check in on Charles. After that, we'll prepare to take the horses to Florida tomorrow."

"Tomorrow?" I asked, my voice keening with incredulity.

"I know it's sudden," she said. "But Mummy and Daddy are too horrified to face anyone. They want to get away for a while. So we're all driving down together, a week earlier than planned."

I shook my head in disbelief.

"This can't be happening," I said.

"It hurts me too," she said. "But we knew this day would come, Richard."

She was right. But knowing something's coming and experiencing it are two different things entirely. Besides, I'd thought I'd have another two weeks to prepare for it, even if, technically, Patricia had already let me go. I was sure she hadn't really meant it—that once Leigh and Charles were off on their honeymoon, we'd be back in the hayloft, for a little while longer. I couldn't have been more floored if I'd woken up that morning to learn she'd died in her sleep.

"I'm sure you'll fall in love with a much more worthy girl before I see you again," she said. "At that point you'll be ready to thank me."

"For what?" I asked.

"Hello, young Richard," a voice said, startling us both.

Brad Culver appeared behind us. He held a drink in one hand, a cigarette in the other. The smoke wrapped around his face like a veil.

"Daddy," Patricia said, sighing. "You're smoking?"

"On a night like this," he said, "you can't begrudge a man one lousy cigarette."

I looked over to where the Old Man had been sitting. He was already on his feet, headed in our direction.

"We'll be leaving soon, Patricia," Culver said. "Your mother's waiting in the car."

"All right," Patricia said.

"Make sure you see whoever you need to see," he said.

Culver wheeled and disappeared, leaving the still-smoldering butt of his cigarette on the grass beside us.

"I can't believe you're leaving," I said.

"I know," Patricia answered. "It's a bit like we're fleeing the scene of a crime, isn't it?"

She lifted the hem of her dress and extended a high-heeled pump to stamp out her father's cigarette. Then she leaned in and gave me a light peck on the cheek.

"Be sweet, won't you?" she said.

I was too dazed to think of anything resembling a witty riposte.

"I'll try," I said.

I stood with slumped shoulders as Patricia trudged off in that ill-fitting dress to intercept my father. She shook the Old Man's hand and nodded and smiled and shuffled over first to my mother and then to the bridesmaids, pecking each of them on the cheek. I touched the spot where I could still feel the faint brush of her lipstick, cool on my face in the dry night air. I clenched my eyes shut. When I opened them again to look for her, the Old Man was standing in front of me, holding a drink in each hand.

"Culver left, didn't he?" he asked.

"Yes, sir," I said.

"That son of a bitch."

The wrinkles around his eyes deepened as he studied the spot on the ground where Culver had dropped his cigarette.

"Doesn't even have the nerve to face me, does he?" he said.

"They're leaving for Florida," I said. "Tomorrow."

"That figures," the Old Man said. "He's just the type to light a house on fire and then skip town while it's still burning."

I had no idea what he was talking about, or why Brad Culver was suddenly a "son of a bitch" again or wouldn't want to face the Old Man. I nodded guiltily, assuming it had something to do with me.

"Here," he said.

He handed me one of the two drinks—another ginger ale spiked with a generous splash of bourbon.

"Dad," I started, ready to make my confession.

"I know," he said, as if he didn't want to be told.

Everyone at the party seemed to have concluded that the most polite thing to do was to get drunk and behave as if nothing un-usual had happened. The band drew the crowd back with a spir-ited medley of "Proud Mary," "Celebration," and "Shout." Old men sated with scotch and shrimp cocktail shed suit jackets and merged into the mass of shambling bodies, their necks straining against tightening collars, grinning and twisting, twirling the arms of younger girls and adventurous wives. Together they threw their arms up toward the taut white canvas skin above them. I wondered whether, at that very moment, Leigh Bowman sat huddling in the corner of some padded cell, dressed in a straitjacket, dosed up to her eyeballs with tranquilizers, swimming toward the receding dream of another life.

The Old Man placed his hand on my shoulder. It warmed me at first, this contact—this rare sign of physical affection. Then the hand grew heavier. I felt myself start to slip. Too late, I realized that the Old Man was not consoling me but rather grabbing for purchase as his knees buckled beneath him and he crumbled to the ground.

I didn't have to call for help; they were already around me, around him: the good men of Spencerville, poised and ready, as if they all sensed we had not yet seen the last of the night's calamities.

Another doctor—Inman Fox, an orthopedic surgeon—knelt over the Old Man, checking his vitals.

"It's his ear," I said. "He gets vertigo."

I can still see the Old Man's stricken face as Dr. Fox loomed over him and began to administer CPR. I remember how his lips parted and remained open; how his head bobbed with each compression; how his eyes rolled up above our faces, staring at the roof of the tent as if he could see something other than a blank field of white.

PART THREE

Blood on Blood

12

OUR TOWN FED ON the corpse of Leigh Bowman's disastrous wedding until only the bones remained. For weeks, it seemed, no one could talk of anything else but the haunted wedding where the bride was diabolically possessed in front of a whole congregation of believers. Being able to say that you were there, that you saw it with your own two eyes, was like having seen Hendrix play "The Star-Spangled Banner" at Woodstock. Rumors flew about witchcraft and hippie thrill-kill death cults in the mountain West. A saline abortion at the Monacan Mountain Rehabilitation Center became a ritual baby sacrifice or a desperate attempt to prevent the birth of the Antichrist. Some went so far as to suggest that the demon bride had telepathically zapped the father of her cruel ex-boyfriend for having the indecency to show up at her daddy's circus-tent wedding reception while she was being tied up in a straitjacket on the fifth floor of the Baptist hospital.

Almost immediately, Charles Culver left to resume his globe-trotting business career. After a few weeks, the Culvers returned and resumed their relatively solitary lives at Twin Oaks. Patricia remained in Florida, "eventing." As she had predicted, Leigh Bowman disappeared, off at some undisclosed "place of rest."

BEFORE THE OLD MAN came home, it was still possible to think that he might experience a full recovery. Even up to and after Thanksgiving, with his daily therapy sessions and his slurred promises that he would soon be back to work, we still believed that he might at least regain a modicum of self-sufficiency. There was no reason for us to feel this way. Call it misplaced faith in the power of positive thinking.

He spent most of his days sitting in an armchair in the Royal Chamber, a pale, shriveled creature with a little tuft of white hair poking up from his liver-spotted scalp. After a week or two, he could feed himself, provided that the food was soft and cut up into very small bites. Discounting the occasional moments of incoherence, his speech returned to normal, though we might have preferred that he'd lost his voice entirely.

"That mother of yours is sleeping around on me," he might say. "She dresses up like a bitch in heat and tramps around all over town."

"Don't say that, Dad," I'd reply.

"You know who she's screwing, don't you?" he'd say. "Brad Culver."

"Come on, Dad," I'd say. "You know that's not true."

"Oh, but it is," he'd say. "She locks me up in this room and flashes the front porch lights to give him the all clear. I can hear them, you know. I can hear the two of them screwing, right through the goddamned door!"

Often I sat with him in his bedroom, watching reruns on television. His two favorite programs were *The Waltons* and *Charlie's Angels*. He couldn't follow the plot of either program, but the bucolic, pastoral life of the Walton family seemed to elicit a gauzy nostalgia for his Depression-era childhood. The appeal of *Charlie's Angels* was understandably less quaint.

One afternoon in his first week home, I left the Old Man with Farrah Fawcett and Jaclyn Smith and crept out of the Royal Chamber. Heading toward the kitchen, I overheard my mother in the dining room speaking with a man whose voice I recognized to be that of Mosby Watts, the Old Man's accountant.

"I warned him, Alice," Watts said, his voice pleading and contrite. "But he wouldn't hear it. He said this First Atlantic deal was a sure thing."

As I listened, I began to realize that it was not my mother but the Old Man whom Brad Culver had screwed. Black Monday had done their big venture-capital plan in. A day or two before Leigh's wedding, Culver had informed the Old Man that their company—First Atlantic Investors LLC—was going to have to declare bankruptcy. They had lost their entire investment—which, for the Old Man, was *everything*.

Ever since Black Monday, the Old Man had privately borne the dizzying fact that he was facing ruin, hoping against hope that something could be done to avert the inevitable. On the night of Leigh's wedding, the skyrocketing pressure of his blood seared off that one, tiny fragment from the walls of his arteries and sent it tumbling into the fragile webbing of his brain.

Perhaps, like Leigh's spectacular breakdown, the stroke would have happened either way. Had the First Atlantic venture-capital group prospered, had Black Monday seen a 20 percent gain instead of a horrific drop, had Leigh's wedding gone off without a hitch, had Paul never left and Annie Elizabeth never died, and on and on, he might very well have ended up in the same exact position at the same exact time. But if all those things had happened, one critical difference would remain: the Old Man wouldn't be flat broke, with a cascade of medical expenses descending just in time for Christmas.

NOT LONG AFTERWARD I went snooping through my mother's rolltop secretary and found where she'd hidden the stack of bills. I flipped through them, my eyes widening over what then seemed like staggering amounts: $5,000 to a medical laboratory for a list of tests I'd never heard of; $14,000 to the hospital for fees uncovered by insurance; $2,000 owed to a contractor for repairs on the roof of the Old Man's office building.

Among the bills, I found a crisp white envelope with the crest of Macon Preparatory Academy in the upper left corner. I slipped out the contents—a kindly phrased letter on Macon stationery with the signature of the head of finance at the bottom, followed by a xeroxed copy of a tuition bill for $18,000.

$18,000! Could a year at Macon really cost that much? I'd never thought about it. I just treated my education as a given—as if it came at no expense.

Studying the bill more closely, I discerned that the past-due amount was not for a year's tuition but rather for three semesters, including unpaid balances for miscellaneous items—meal plan, required athletic apparel, and so forth. The Old Man must have needed every free penny to buy into Brad Culver's venture-capital scheme. He probably assumed that once First Atlantic started bringing in the big returns, he'd pay it all off with a single check.

That evening, I was alone in the kitchen with my mother after dinner, helping her wash and dry the dishes.

"Mom," I said, "I've been thinking. Maybe I could go to Randolph next year."

"Why on earth would you want to do that?" she asked, as if I'd just told her I was running off to join the French Foreign Legion.

"I'm just not really happy at Macon," I said.

"Nonsense," she said.

"I mean it."

"That's ludicrous," she said. "Trust me, you don't want to end up at Randolph."

Randolph High, our district public school, had once been considered a jewel in the crown of the Virginia public system. Leigh Bowman had graduated from Randolph, along with most of the other children of all but the most affluent families in Boone's Ferry. In recent years, however, rezoning and a resurgence of white flight had diminished Randolph's reputation considerably. It was now thought of as "rough" and "rowdy," which was really just a polite way of saying that a large percentage of the student body there was poor and black. For Macon students and their parents, being forced to attend Randolph had become tantamount to being shipped off to a Siberian gulag.

"Randolph High is simply out of the question," my mother said.

"I just feel like I don't fit in at Macon anymore," I said.

It was true; I didn't. No one at the school knew it yet, but I did. We were poor now. Poor kids don't get to go to private school unless they're exceptional. My only exceptional accomplishment since giving up my nascent career as a prepubescent theater prod-

igy was having an illicit affair with an older woman—not exactly
the type of accolade Macon would want mentioned in the alumni
magazine.

"I can't really handle any more big changes right now, Richard,"
my mother said. "Besides, it's important to your father."

If it were that important to him, I thought, he'd have paid the
tuition.

I decided to try another tactic.

"I think—I think I might be happier going to school with girls,"
I said.

My mother set down the dish she was scrubbing into the murky
water and sighed.

"You've been going through the bills, haven't you?"

I shrugged and nodded.

"It's nothing for you to worry about," she said. "I've already spoken to the finance office. This is really not all that unusual. People
make late payments all the time."

"Mom," I started.

"We're working something out," she said. "It's going to be taken
care of."

She smiled in a way meant to seem reassuring. She didn't know
that I'd overheard her conversation with the Old Man's accountant. I didn't want to bring this up, however; it seemed better to
let her preserve the appearance of stability and control. Or maybe
I just thought she'd be angry with me for spying on her. I decided
instead to exploit an old weakness.

"It's just that—well, I think my teachers—they hate me, Mom."

Nothing could be further from the truth. I'd always been
treated with exceeding warmth and generosity from my instruc-
tors, even more so in the weeks since the Old Man fell ill.

I noticed my mother's knuckles whitening as she gripped the
edge of the counter.

"Why do you think that might be?" she asked.

"Probably—"

I had to pause for a breath to finish.

"Probably," I said, "because of Paul."

My mother refused to lift her eyes from the bottom of the sink. For a moment I thought I'd touched the right nerve. Finally she spoke, her voice surprisingly stern.

"You will remain at Macon," she said, "and you will graduate from Macon."

"But Mom," I protested.

"End of discussion," she said.

I understand now why my attending Macon seemed so much more important to my mother than it did to me. It had nothing to do with class sizes or AP courses or even with the aesthetic appeal of tastefully tousled preppies in blazers and ties, ambling along brick sidewalks in front of white-columned neoclassical buildings. Rich people stick together and look out for each other—this was what the Old Man had always believed. Places like Macon existed primarily for the purpose of giving them cloisters in which to cultivate their alliances and ensure that their inferiors were kept in place. If you had children at places like Macon, you were in the club.

It would take me years to grasp the real reason my staying at Macon mattered so much to my mother. I very clearly understood, however, that I'd never persuade her to let me withdraw voluntarily. She was going to do everything in her power to keep me there, no matter what sort of reckless or humiliating steps that decision might require of her. I was expected to remain a spoiled little lord, traipsing off every day to a fancy school we could no longer afford, while what little money we had left dwindled and my mother lay awake at night trying to think of what else she could sell, what needed to be paid for first, what bills could be neglected the longest without being turned over for collection.

I already felt I was at fault for what had happened to Leigh and, consequently, to the Old Man. I couldn't bear the thought of being responsible for yet another burden and degradation for someone whom I loved, and who loved me in turn, more than I felt I deserved. Consequently a course of action became clear to me. The only way I was going to get us out of that tuition bill was to do something drastic. If my mother wasn't going to let me withdraw, I was going to have to get myself kicked out.

In retrospect my reasoning seems specious to the point of absurdity. How could I have thought my mother would take my getting kicked out of school as a relief? Maybe only a spoiled, delusional adolescent is capable of such self-indulgent thinking. Maybe it was Paul again, creeping up in my subconscious, whispering in my ear like a little demon perched on my shoulder: Go on, do it—it's better to be bad than to be good. Maybe I was genuinely traumatized by what was happening to the Old Man, or emotionally scarred by Patricia's manipulations. Or maybe I just couldn't stomach the thought of all the studying I'd have to do to pass exams.

Indeed, flunking out intentionally was the first thought that came to me. That plan, however, wouldn't get me booted until the end of the year and might not work anyway, given how much slack my teachers had been cutting me since the Old Man's stroke. My second idea was to get caught cheating on an exam. But nobody ever got kicked out of Macon for cheating. If the school expelled every boy who cheated on a test or paper, the enrollment—and moreover the tuition revenue—would drop by a third or more. You had to get sent to the honor council at least three, maybe four times to get expelled. I was going to have to come up with a far more heinous offense.

At Macon, in the final weeks of the first semester, classes cease and are replaced by formal review sessions and extended study halls. My study hall assignment was the school library, at a table between a cluster of potted plants and a large display of "recommended reading" atop a chest-high stack filled with reference books. I shared the table with a new boy named Stevie Lanier. Macon was his third stop in as many years—he'd flunked out of Choate and got booted from Woodberry for destroying a library toilet with a cherry bomb. His father was a shipping magnate of some sort. Over the few months we'd known each other, Stevie had distinguished himself only as a simpering misanthrope with a healthy contempt for the preening jocks and striving achievers who overshadowed wallflowers like us. I'd all but ignored him—until the afternoon I discovered that Stevie and I shared a peculiar predilection.

Every boy, it seems, at one point or another scribbles a little phallus on wood, paper, wall, or bathroom stall door. It has been documented to the point of tiresomeness how much time the average teenage boy spends thinking about sex. But what so compels him to draw pictures of genitalia? And why his own, instead of that of the object of his desire? Perhaps it's the fact that he's so much more familiar with his own equipment than the other kind. Freud and Kinsey would probably chalk it up to latent homoerotic impulses. It might come down to mere aesthetics: after all, even the most pathetic reproduction of a penis is somehow luridly amusing, while a bad drawing of a naked woman is just a sad reminder of how little any boy really knows about beauty. In any case, the compulsion to draw a penile rocket ship is a rite of passage as certain and familiar as a wet dream or acne. They say the earliest known cave paintings depict images of the hunt, but long before those deer and bulls and bison went up on the wall, I'm quite certain there was a giant paleoerection lurching out from between a pair of hairy testicles.

My first stabs at the form were the casual, unconscious type, inspired by the hasty versions generally found on public restroom walls next to scrawled phone numbers promising a "good time." At some point, however, my ding-dong doodling escalated from the odd scribble into a sort of creative compulsion. I began to experiment with elaborate variations: actual rocket ships, with swollen thrusters and fins and tiny little smiling astronauts peering out from, yes, cockpits; World War II–era tanks and bombers; the Batmobile.

I was very careful to hide my creations. One day during study hall, however, a series of phallic Russian *matryoshka* dolls slipped out of my binder in full view of Stevie Lanier.

His mouth twisted into a lurid smirk.

"You're quite the artist, Askew," Stevie said. "A regular cocksman, as it were."

My face grew hot. Knowing Stevie, by the afternoon my drawing would be seen by half the school. Boys I didn't even know would point and snicker at me in the hallways. I'd be forever branded Dick Artist Askew.

I lunged for the drawing, but Stevie snatched it away.

"Give it back," I snapped.

"Now, now," Stevie said. "Calm down. Your secret's safe with me, Askew. As a matter of fact, there's something I'd like to show you."

He tucked the drawing into his own binder and shifted in his chair so he could reach the shelf of reference books behind our table.

"Here," he said.

He handed me the *P* volume and opened the front cover to reveal a full-color schlong over the phrase P IS FOR PENIS.

"Flip to the back," he said.

There, I found another enormous, elaborately detailed member over the words P IS ALSO FOR PRICK.

"When did you do this?" I asked.

"I get plenty of time alone in here on the weekends," Stevie said.

Of course he did. Stevie played no sports and refused to involve himself in any nonmandatory activities. I appeared to be the closest thing he had to a friend. His roommate was a loutish lacrosse player—a classic thug jock who was far less likely to befriend a guy like Stevie than dunk his head in a toilet. And anyway, it wasn't like Stevie would have been all that interested in spending his free time in the fitness center with the lacrosse team, lifting weights and practicing stick skills. Instead, Stevie had whiled away the hours alone in the library, vandalizing the reference section.

"Here," he said.

He handed me the *A* volume. In the front cover was a shapely if somewhat androgynous rear end, with another hairy thruster floating above it, poised to take the proverbial plunge. A IS FOR ASS, read the inscription below.

"I've been working my way through the alphabet," Stevie said. "But I'm running out of ideas."

Stevie didn't even have to ask. Before long, I had all but taken over the project. It was just the sort of misdeed that could get me kicked out of school before my mother started selling blood plasma to pay down my tuition bill.

Stevie had the right idea, I thought, but he needed a little more vision. We could do much better than D IS FOR DICK. I began with a full-color naval destroyer with a dozen pink "guns" peeking out from hairy turrets. Other similarly puerile metaphors weren't difficult to come by. By the first day of exams, we'd defiled close to half the volumes of the encyclopedia.

As the days passed, however, I began to worry that the project wouldn't be enough to achieve the goal I had in mind before the end of the semester. Hardly anyone ever looked at the *World Book*, after all, except for a research paper or a history report, and no one would be working on that sort of assignment until after the holidays. There was also the added complication of Stevie Lanier. Stevie thought we were just having a little fun. He talked about the dick-art encyclopedia sitting on the shelves for years to come, a private joke among the few students who stumbled upon it. He had no idea he'd tossed his lot in with the one kid in school who actually wanted rather urgently to get expelled. As resolute as I may have been, I didn't want to take Stevie down with me. I had to make sure both that the project was discovered and that I would be held solely responsible for it.

With three days left before the holidays, I was working on the front cover of the *F* volume, sketching out a map of Florida with a thicker, hairier, more orbicular version of the panhandle and a circumcised peninsula while silently trying to imagine a more reliably effective way of disgracing myself. Maybe a big hairy johnson spray-painted onto the walls of the faculty room?

"Heads up, Askew," said Stevie.

Mrs. Carswell, the new librarian, was making her rounds through the study hall tables. We hastily closed our volumes of the

World Book and pretended to be working on math problems when she peered around the stacks. Mrs. Carswell smiled and waved and floated off to the next set of tables.

"How old do you think she is?" Stevie asked me.

I peered up to get a look at Mrs. Carswell. It was her first year at Macon. I knew nothing about her and didn't have a clue how old she was. Like most of the women at the school, she was purposefully modest in her appearance. She was pretty, but her appearance seemed calculated to deflect rather than attract our attention. She dressed, well, like a librarian: knee-length skirts, buttoned-up blouses, a string of pearls, and so forth. I guessed she was older than Patricia, who was around thirty, but younger than my mother, who had just turned forty-three.

"I don't know," I said. "Thirty-five, maybe?"

"Good guess, Askew," Stevie said. "Did you happen to know that a woman reaches her sexual peak around thirty-five?"

"What does that mean?" I asked.

"It means," Stevie drawled, "that at thirty-five, a woman's body is perfectly ripe. She's nearing the end of her child-bearing years. Her body is screaming for one more chance to procreate. All her hormones are exploding."

"Exploding?"

"Exploding," Stevie said. "When a woman is thirty-five, she's insatiable."

Insatiable, I thought. Patricia wasn't quite thirty-five, but she was close. She had seemed fairly insatiable to me. Maybe it was just hormones.

Pondering the image of demure Mrs. Carswell in a state of orgasmic frenzy, I had an epiphany. As an artist, I was ready for a new motif. It was the beginning, you might say, of my Blue Period.

The sketches didn't require much imagination. At lunch, Mrs. Carswell often sat with Dr. Giffen, the headmaster, who was newly single that year. Everyone knew the embarrassing story behind the end of poor Old Giff's marriage. A student who had gone back to the wrestling room to collect a forgotten textbook had walked in on Old Giff's wife with Coach Cranmer on top of her, performing a move the wrestlers referred to as the Saturday night ride. The word filtered up to Old Giff and the board, and a few days later, Coach Cranmer and Mrs. Giffen were both gone. There were numerous other faculty members whose sex lives were frequent topics of discussion in the dorms and around the lunch tables. Mr. Dewerson, the chemistry teacher, was not yet thirty but already had five kids crammed into his little dorm apartment with his blowsy, buxom young wife. Plenty of jokes about the Dewersons involving minks and rabbits proliferated around the halls of Macon. Then there was Miss Sunday, one of the guidance counselors—a hopeless flirt who was rumored to annually select a second-semester senior for "initiation." Most of us thought this was pure fantasy, but after what I'd been through with Patricia, I had no problem believing it to be true. It didn't matter anyway; I wasn't looking for facts—just inspiration. With my remaining study halls and a little extra time logged in the afternoons, I managed to complete a series of panels I knew would be more than enough to get myself booted, effective immediately. The last step was to ensure that it saw the light of day, sooner rather than later.

On the morning of my history exam, I crept into the library alone. The place was empty; everyone else was in a classroom, including Mrs. Carswell, who was proctoring my own American History exam. One by one, I placed the volumes of the World Book around the library tables, covers open, making sure all the drawings from my new series were—ahem—exposed.

I needed only one added flourish for insurance purposes. With my favorite black Sharpie, beneath the drawing I'd made of Dr. Giffen mounting Mrs. Carswell from behind atop the library checkout desk, I drew my initials—not just RA, but RVA Jr. As far as I knew, I was the only person in school with a middle name that began with the letter V. I'd always hated my middle name— Vernon—but in this case, such a distinct initial came in handy.

I thought it wisest not to show up at the scene of the crime;

hence I didn't witness the look on Mrs. Carswell's face when she saw her image defiled alongside that of Dr. Giffen, or her reaction to the pictures I'd drawn of Mr. and Mrs. Dewerson, Miss Sunday, and several more of their colleagues, depicted in flagrante delicto with students, fellow teachers, and the school mascot, the Red Devil. I winced when I heard she was found with tears streaming down her face as she struggled vainly to hide my work behind her desk while a chorus of guffaws echoed through the library and down the hallways. Stevie Lanier was seen running from the building, cursing my name under his breath.

Within the hour, Mr. McMahan, the dean of students, found me waiting on a bench in the quad outside my classroom building and escorted me to the inquisition. He deposited me in a holding room in Leggett Hall, where I was left to stew for what seemed like a very long time. Eventually, Dean MacMahan opened the door.

"Let's go, Picasso," he said.

The headmaster's office was a warm den of polished wood and leather. When we entered, Dr. Giffen was slumped in his chair, his fingers laced atop his chest. His face was gray and his eyes bleary, like he was fighting off a nasty cold. On the desk before him was the complete set of the *World Book Encyclopedia*. He did not stand when I entered the room.

"Have a seat, Richard," he said.

His voice seemed tired and jaded. I thought of the picture I'd drawn of his ex-wife entangled on the wrestling mat with Coach Cranmer. Old Giff was having a rough year. Only when I was sitting before him did I begin to think of him not as a remote, indomitable embodiment of authority but rather as a human being, with feelings and emotions just like anyone else—just like me. I wished I could apologize, or make it up to him somehow, or even take it back. But it was too late for that. I swallowed hard and silently vowed to finish what I'd started.

Giffen removed his rimless eyeglasses and began wiping the lenses with a paisley-patterned silk handkerchief.

"I'm very sorry about your father, Richard," Dr. Giffen began. "That's a difficult thing for a boy your age to go through. It probably explains a lot."

He replaced his glasses and rose and walked around to take a seat on the edge of his desk in front of me. He took the volume from the top of the stack nearest to him and opened its front cover. There I saw the image I'd drawn of him behind Mrs. Carswell—both clearly identifiable, he by his bow tie and rimless glasses, she by the hairstyle and the string of pearls and the tweed dress bunched up around her hips. Beneath the image were my initials.

"Is this your work, Richard?" he asked.

"Yes, sir."

"Mrs. Carswell is humiliated, young man," Old Giff said.

"I know, sir," I said.

I glanced up at Old Giff. Rather than anger, his expression suggested a sort of calm bewilderment. I think I'd have been less frightened if he'd been red-faced and bellowing, or if he'd gone back to his desk drawer, pulled out a paddle like Mr. Powell's Swift Justice, and ordered me to assume the position.

"So these are your drawings, Richard?" Old Giff asked.

"Yes, sir," I said.

"How many?" Giffen said.

"All of them," I replied.

"And you did this all alone?"

"Yes, sir," I croaked.

"You're quite sure Stevie Lanier had nothing to do with this?"

"Yes, sir," I said. "It was all me."

"That's what he told us," Dr. Giffen said, "though given the trouble he's had in the past, I'm not inclined to believe him."

So Stevie had already been brought in and had thrown the full blame onto me! The bastard! I thought. It was what I wanted, but still—what a little shit!

"It seems far more likely," Giff continued, "that you were drawn into this whole business, and that Mr. Lanier put your initials on this . . . work of art . . . in order to ensure it would be you and not he who bore the brunt of the punishment."

I shook my head slowly.

"No, sir," I said. "It was all me."

Giffen turned the book around and studied the picture.

"Not a bad likeness," he said. "It's a pity you haven't made use of those talents on more appropriate subjects."

Despite the circumstances, I felt a smile begin to creep up at the corners of my mouth. What the hell, I thought.

"I'm only good at drawing one thing, sir," I said.

"Richard," Old Giff said sharply, "this is no laughing matter."

The momentary sense of mirth evaporated.

"I know, sir," I said.

"What do you suppose I'm to do about it, then?"

I tried not to seem too eager.

"If I were you," I said, "I'd expel me."

Old Giff was no fool.

"You've never been in any trouble here, of any kind," he said. "Why would you do such a thing now, of all times?"

"I don't know, sir."

It was mostly an honest answer.

"Could it have anything to do with worries about things at home, son?"

"No, sir," I said.

"I've already spoken to your mother," he said. "She's on her way here now."

Back when I was plotting my own demise, I hadn't completely overlooked the possibility—nay, the certainty—that my plan, once enacted, would cause my mother considerable pain. It hadn't seemed quite so unpleasant, however, when it was only an idea. With the announcement of her imminent arrival, I felt a powerful roiling of remorse and the first glimmering of the tears I had promised myself not to shed.

"I know you know about the money, Richard," Old Giff said. "Is this because of that?"

I didn't answer. Old Giff sighed.

"I think it is, son," he said. "I think you got a damned-fool idea in your head, and now it's come to this."

He held his arms out in the air for a moment—a gesture to the magnitude of my predicament.

"How well do you know Mrs. Carswell, son?"

"Not at all, sir," I said.

"She's a very kind and decent young woman who is trying to move forward with her life in the wake of a painful divorce," Old Giff said. "Did you know that, son?"

I shook my head.

"Would you like to know something else about Mrs. Carswell, Richard?"

I didn't, but I knew he was going to tell me anyway.

"Her father is a very close friend of mine. Mr. Wells Basten," Old Giff said. "Do you know Mr. Wells Basten, son?"

"No, sir."

"You should. He's the chairman of our board of trustees."

My eyes widened. Wells Basten, I thought, as in the Basten Tennis Center and the Basten Alumni House.

"Mr. Basten and his family have long been important supporters of this institution," he said. "In addition to substantial sums to our annual fund and dedicated gifts to development projects, he likes to provide up-to-date reference books to our library's collection. Can you see where this is going, Richard?"

"Yes, sir," I said.

"I have to hand it to you, boy. You've got a knack for self-destruction."

I had to agree with him.

"If it was anything else," Old Giff muttered, "or anyone else . . ."

His voice trailed off into a long sigh.

For a moment we sat together in silence. Miserable as I was, I felt a welling up of sympathy for Dr. Giffen. Even after what I'd done to him, he still wanted to spare me. But I'd left him with only one course of action.

"It's all right, Dr. Giffen," I said. "I deserve it."

He walked back around his desk and slumped into his chair.

"What do you think this is going to do to your mother, boy?"

At last the tears came.

"Please, Dr. Giffen," I said, my voice quivering with despera-
tion. "You don't have to talk to her. Just kick me out already."

Old Giff removed his glasses again and set them on the desk in
front of him. He rubbed his eyes and let out another long sigh. He
must have been thinking what I needed was therapy, or a good ass
kicking, or maybe just an arm around my shoulder from someone
like him. But it didn't matter. I had insulted the headmaster and
traumatized the daughter of the chairman of the board of trustees.
My fate was sealed before I walked through the door.

A light flashed on Old Giff's phone. He lifted the receiver to
his ear.

"Yes?" he said. "All right. Thank you, Marilyn."

He gently set the receiver back in its cradle.

"Your mother's here," Old Giff said.

I could never have prepared for the depth of self-loathing I felt
as I watched my mother wilt while Dr. Giffen explained to her why
I was being dismissed. It would be utterly foolish, then or now, to
suppose that there was any glimmer of relief beneath the shock
and the distress. Nevertheless, I held on to the conviction that I
had spared her a small part of her burden. Besides, she wouldn't
worry about it for long, I thought; we had bigger problems.

"Well then," Dr. Giffen said.

And so it ended for me at Macon Prep. I followed my mother
out of Old Giff's office and down the stairs of Leggett Hall for the
last time as a student. As we drove in silence under the gates and
on toward our uncertain future, I was overcome by an odd sense
of euphoria. At last, I felt at least partially purged. And for a while
anyway, I was free. I wouldn't have to start at Randolph High until
January.

13

MY MOTHER TOOK MY expulsion from Macon rather well, all things considered. She was finding herself suited to the role of martyr. The Bible study women again rallied around her, as they had since the Old Man's stroke. My return to the public school system was the subject of many prayers.

Christmas came and went. My mother made the best of it, doing her usual bit with the decorations: garlands of pine needles wrapping the banisters, tied off with red velvet bows; white Christmas lights in the boxwoods and the dogwood trees lining the driveway; a tasteful tree and an heirloom crèche set on the mantel.

With the Old Man no longer able to work, my mother had to find some kind of employment. She ended up taking a job behind a desk at the furniture company that belonged to Miss Anita Holt's family. Something was better than nothing. The accountant, Mosby Watts, put my mother in touch with a private car dealer, and within a week the Mercedes was gone, the sum of its sale already spent on bills. I was surprised at how sorry I was to see it go.

The Old Man had a regular aide during the daytime—a young black man named William. William wore hospital whites and a pair of Air Jordans. They spent a lot of time watching sports on TV. When dementia made the Old Man forget himself and start referring to him as "boy" or "the nigger," William just ignored him, as if they were an old married couple who had lived with each other's careless words for too long to be bothered by them.

William started inviting me out onto the back porch to keep him company during his smoke breaks. He was full of questions about what it was like to grow up rich.

"I'm sorry he says those things to you," I said.

We were out on the side porch. William smoked one of his Kools, huddling against the cold in his suede jacket.

"Dag, man," he said. "Cold out here. Where your rock at?"

"My rock?"

"Your ball, homes."

He pointed at the basketball hoop on the gable of the garage.

"I don't know," I said.

"Just thought we might shoot a little to stay warm."

"I'm not sure we still have one."

We stamped around a bit, hands stuffed in pockets, William's cigarette dangling from his mouth.

"He's not a racist, you know," I said. "He's just old."

William lifted his cigarette and pointed the smoking end of it out toward Twin Oaks.

"Who lives up there?" he asked.

"The Culvers," I said.

"Ah. 'That son of a bitch Brad Culver,'" William said, imitating the Old Man's angry-codger voice.

"That's the one," I said.

I told William about Twin Oaks and Frank Cherry and Paul's run-in with Culver. William absorbed it all thoughtfully, sucking his cheeks in when he puffed on his Kool.

"It's a nice house," he said.

"Yeah," I said.

It was an abnormally cold winter. The house was always drafty, with its high ceilings and stone and wood floors. To save money, my mother kept the thermostat below sixty. Every morning, I built great, heaping, roaring fires to quiet the Old Man's shivering under his blanket in the armchair in front of the daytime reruns.

One morning, before William arrived, I left the Old Man and, bundled up in gloves, a stocking cap, and a flannel-lined parka, went out into the frosty cold to restock the woodpile next to the fireplace. Grabbing the garden cart from where I had left it a few days before, I trudged out to the big stack of split logs behind a small hedge in the side yard. Off in the distance, I could see the smoke rising from the Culvers' chimneys. Since they had returned, Brad Culver hadn't even bothered to call.

Culver was not the only one of Dad's former business associates or so-called friends who had made little to no effort to comfort him in his decline. I understood this neglect better as I grew older. These men were all over sixty; many of them, like the Old Man, on into their seventies. They had all lived through at least one of three wars, smoked heavily in their younger days, drank hard liquor, and ate plenty of red meat. They exercised little beyond a weekly round of golf and maybe a few minutes a week standing in one of those old belly-fat vibrating machines. None of them wanted to be confronted with what they might themselves soon be facing.

Brad Culver was no different, yet his neglect struck me as unforgivable. As I loaded the garden cart with wood, I visualized Culver in a much warmer room in front of a cheerier fire. I imagined myself clubbing him over the head or whacking him at the knees or, as Paul had instructed me so long ago, right in the balls and then in the nose. I indulged this brutal daydream until I was heaving, the sweat running across my stomach beneath the parka, my breath firing out in white bursts of steam.

I pulled the cart behind me back up to the house, quieting my breath as I went, feeling the sweat go cool beneath my coat. As I reached the side door and opened it, I heard the muffled sound of the Old Man calling to me, his voice high pitched and desperate.

I found him in the bathroom, standing with his back to me, his slippered feet spread awkwardly on the white tile floor. One white-knuckled hand gripped his aluminum walker, while the other splayed out flat against the wall. His pants fly was open, and his flaccid member dangled out, dribbling urine down his leg. Without thinking, I stepped under his outstretched arm so that he could lean on me, grabbed his flank with my right hand to hold him up, pinched his pecker with my left, and aimed it at the toilet bowl.

There I stood in silence, my Dad hanging on to me, his face

clenched in a grimace of effort. I felt the rush of steaming piss pulsing beneath my fingertips, listened to his stream splashing in the water beneath us. This is where you got your start, boy, I thought.

WILLIAM STARTED BRINGING a basketball with him so he could shoot hoops while the Old Man slept. I stood under the goal and tried to catch the rebounds as William tossed the ball up between puffs on his cigarette.

William was as inscrutable as the Sphinx. He liked to talk, but not about anything personal—just sports and cars, mostly. I wanted to know everything about him: what it was like to take care of people like the Old Man, how he'd happened to end up in the job in the first place, how long he expected to be doing it, what his dreams were, what it was like to be black. I never asked him these things. In fact, though I began to think of him as my best friend, I knew next to nothing about him.

The first Friday in January was my mother's turn to host the Bible study. The Old Man had dozed off. William and I were outside playing our little game of shoot, catch, and pass as the cars began to roll in.

William had arrived that day wearing the new pair of Air Jordan 2 basketball shoes he'd received from his mother for Christmas.

"Do your shoes make you fly?" I said, passing back a rebound.

"I can fly over you."

"Prove it."

"When I'm done with my cig."

He set his stance in his new white shoes and rocked forward onto his toes, releasing a smooth, arcing jump shot that bounced off the board and clanged through the rim.

"You didn't call bank," I said.

William ignored me, catching the ball with one hand and dribbling between his legs, spinning around and popping up a fallaway jumper that rasped through the stiff, frozen net. He flicked his cigarette butt into the grass and popped up another jumper.

"Did you know people are being shot over those shoes?" I asked.

"People get shot over a lot less than a pair of Jordans," William said.

"That's true, I guess."

William stopped and tucked the ball under his arm, gazing back toward the house. Behind me stood a woman in a maroon down overcoat and white Tretorns, smiling at me.

"Hello, Rocky," she said.

It was Leigh Bowman, back from the funny farm.

Her hair was much shorter and looked dirty. She wore no makeup. Her eyes were wide and glassy. She looked like someone who had just woken up from a case of the flu and walked outside to check the mailbox before going back to bed.

A wave of guilt overtook me. Since she had been gone, we had all been so consumed with our own problems that I had scarcely thought about what had become of Leigh or what I had done to her. I felt like running away. Instead I stuffed my hands in my pockets and trudged over to her. William followed behind, the basketball tucked under his arm as he lit another cigarette.

"Who's your friend?" she asked.

"This is William," I said. "He takes care of my dad."

"Could I trouble you for a cigarette, William?" Leigh asked.

William removed another cigarette from the pack of Kools in his coat pocket and handed it to Leigh. She leaned forward as he cupped the lighter to her face and back to his own.

"Mmm, menthol," she said. "Perfect on a cold day."

"I didn't know you were home," I said.

"For a few weeks now," she said. "I'm sorry I haven't been by. Daddy's been very protective."

I could sense no irony in her words or in her tranquilized gaze.

"Leigh, are you all right?"

It was Miss Anita, peering out from the side door.

"I'm fine, Miss Anita," Leigh said, furtively hiding the cigarette behind her back. "Just saying hello to Richard here."

"Come inside, dear," Miss Anita said. "It's cold."

"Yes, ma'am," Leigh called back. "In a minute."

"Hello, Richard," Miss Anita said.

"Hi, Miss Anita," I said.

She disappeared back into the house.

"Miss Anita has been my angel," Leigh said. "She's been like a mother to me since I got saved."

"Saved?" I asked.

"Yes," she said. "It's wonderful, isn't it? I finally understand what it means to know the Lord. It's truly incredible, especially after what I've been through. You know what they were saying about me, don't you?"

"No," I lied.

She took a drag from the cigarette.

"That I was *possessed*," she said. "By the *devil!*"

She laughed—a barking sound, like a seal. Little wisps of smoke trickled from her nostrils.

"Leigh," Miss Anita called again from the house.

"I better run," she said. "It's so good to see you."

She opened her arms. Slower than I should have, I returned her embrace. She felt thin and fragile beneath the down overcoat, as if she had the hollow bones of a bird.

"Bye, now," she said. "God bless!"

She ran back to the house, her arms stiff beside her, legs trudging along beneath the overcoat.

"Who was that?" William asked.

"My brother's old girlfriend," I said.

"Judge Bowman's girl?" William asked.

"Yes," I said. "How did you know?"

"Your daddy got some stories to tell."

"Oh," I said. "What did you think of her?"

He shrugged.

"She used to be so beautiful," I said.

"Huh," William replied.

He took a last drag off his cigarette and extinguished it on the ground next to where Leigh had left her butt. He stooped and picked up both butts and tucked them into the pocket of his coat. I turned toward the house, to the window by the door, where I could see the Old Man peering out at us, up from his nap.

14

ALL THE INDUSTRIAL-STRENGTH ANTISEPTIC cleaners in the world can't purge the stench of oily, pimpled, hormone-charged vileness that permeates the halls of public high schools. The funk hangs in the air like a green mist, almost visibly wafting from the vents of the lockers lining the walls. It is an honest odor; human beings are, after all, a fairly wretched lot.

There were plenty of familiar faces in the halls of Randolph High, including my old tormenter, Jimmy Hutter—once the formidable bully, now just another average white boy among the bustling, blended halls of the proletariat, shuffling along with his eyes downcast, hoping to be ignored. Indeed, in classes of thirty-five or more, one could practically disappear. As the new kid, I would stand out for a few days, but soon enough I'd be just another face among the throngs.

When registering for classes, I learned from the guidance counselor that I would need at least two elective credits to graduate on time. My mother suggested that I take a drama class.

"Maybe now's the time to get back into it," she said. "You need an outlet."

An outlet. I imagined myself as some sort of robot, like C-3PO, my penis replaced by a dangling electrical cord plugged into a wall to recharge.

"You'll never guess who's the teacher," my mother said.

"Who?"

Her eyes flashed with an anticipation that could only be called girlish.

"Mr. LaPage," she said.

I remembered Rex LaPage all too well. Years before, when he

was still the drama director at the Spencerville Fine Arts Center, Rex had been the one who approached my mother backstage after the summer performance of *Peter Pan* to recruit me for his forth-coming production of *Mame*.

"One day, honey," I remembered Rex once telling me, "I'll be bragging to people how I was the one who gave you your big start!"

Back then, Rex was new in Spencerville. Like a lot of small-town little theater directors, Rex was a refugee from the New York theater world, where he'd been good enough to earn an MFA at NYU and a slate of off-off-Broadway and touring company credits but never managed to reach the level of not having to wait tables to make rent. Thanks to his advanced degree, Rex had credentials, so he scoured the want ads and found his way to Spencerville, where he was treated like the second coming of Oscar Wilde by the wealthy, culture-starved grandes dames whose fund-raisers kept the fine arts center running. For years, Rex LaPage helmed the theater program at the fine arts center, to varying degrees of success. But money woes had left the center on the verge of clos-ing its doors. When the longtime Randolph drama teacher retired, Rex's advocates persuaded their friends on the school board to fast-track his teaching certification and offer him the position.

We had that in common to start with, Mr. LaPage and I. Rex had a semester's head start getting acclimated to Randolph's indig-nities, but we were essentially the same—strange birds brought to land in a foreign tree.

Drama classes were held not in the theater but rather in the adjacent basement, which doubled as a classroom and green room: a dim but warm space cluttered with old props and scenery. The walls were covered with posters from past productions, auto-graphed by casts and crews. One long, white-painted cinder-block wall was covered with quotations of favorite lines from at least a decade's worth of plays, written with black permanent markers and accompanied by the autographs of the students who'd selected them. Instead of desks, students sat on a motley collection of old couches, recliners, and folding chairs.

There was no escaping the recognition of Rex LaPage, who found me immediately among the slouching wave of sullen indifference that tramped down the stairs for fourth-period Introduction to Theater Arts.

"My Young Patrick," LaPage cried. "Look how you've grown! Not quite the chubby little cherub anymore, are we?"

He seemed much smaller to me, for obvious reasons. Otherwise, with the exception of a few flecks of white in his beard and mustache and rather distinguished-looking patches of silver at his temples, Mr. LaPage was exactly as I remembered him: thin, narrow legs in dark jeans; disproportionately large, powerful hands; thick, long eyebrows that moved wildly above his flashing blue eyes.

"I guess not," I replied.

He held on to my shoulders, beaming at me as if I were a long-lost child instead of a kid he faintly remembered from a few unremarkable weeks' worth of rehearsals and performances nearly seven years before. What can I say? He was a drama teacher.

Finally he released me. I retreated to an empty club chair near the back of the room. I hunched down into the chair and waited for class to begin. Behind me, I heard the sound of voices in the shadows.

"She literally took the brush out of my hand and started painting," a girl said. "On *my* picture. Can you believe it?"

"That woman is the enemy of all creativity," a boy's voice answered.

I peered over the back of the chair. An older-looking boy and girl sat in a collapsing love seat. The girl's face was partially hidden behind a mass of dark hair with streaks of a burnt-orange dye. She wore a black leather biker's jacket and a long skirt that resembled a Mexican rug over a pair of red sixteen-hole Dr. Martens.

I had seen the girl before: she worked as a clerk at the Kroger where we did all our grocery shopping. The way she passed the items over the electric eye and fired the numbers into the cash register gave her an air of apathy beyond her years.

"What have we here?" she asked.

"An interloper, I'd say," the boy replied.

"Sorry," I said. "I didn't know anyone was behind me."

"Well, now you know," the girl said.

I smiled and shrugged.

"OK, buh-bye, now," she said.

She waved her fingers. I sank back into the club chair and turned my attention to Mr. LaPage, who was just preparing to introduce the new student to the class.

"We have a new addition, people, and I know from experience that he's quite the talented performer," he said.

A few snickers followed.

"Stand up, would you, honey?" LaPage said.

I rose without protest, hoping to end my misery quickly.

"Class, this is Richard," LaPage said. "Richard, class."

I offered a meek wave to the blanket of slack, dull faces and then sank back into my chair.

Mercifully, Mr. LaPage did not force me to participate in any of the day's exercises—a typical drama-class improv game, followed by a required "scene" performance in which two white students gave an unintentionally amusing rendition of a scene from *A Raisin in the Sun*. After class, I managed to slip away without having to face LaPage again, lurching up the stairs and into the light, where I prepared myself to run the gauntlet of the school cafeteria.

By the time I entered, the tables were all flooded. The room rippled with noise and energy. No one seemed to acknowledge my presence at all, and yet I felt a palpable fear, as if at any moment I might be hit with a blindside tackle or a lethal projectile. Lowering my head, I walked straight through the room, pushing through the rear doors out onto the smoking patio, continuing on past the hoodlums in their blue jean jackets and the skate punks with their Mohawks and bangs dangling down to their pouting lips, into the yard and out toward a solitary tree. There, I thought, I might consume my turkey sandwich without being violated.

I leaned up against the tree and removed my sandwich from

the brown paper bag on which my mother had used a Sharpie to write my name with a flourish over a quick sketch of a sailboat. As I chewed, I noticed the smell of cigarette smoke. From the other side of the tree appeared the girl from drama class—the Kroger checkout girl.

"Did your mommy draw that for you?"

I blushed and nodded. She took a long pull on her cigarette, a Marlboro Light—what Paul used to call a slut butt.

"That's so cute," she said. "Does she do that every day?"

"Sure," I said. "I keep every one of them. They're all collector's items. A personal history of sunflowers, sailboats, and daisies."

"That's sweet," she said.

She turned her head and exhaled a long, narrow funnel of smoke.

"Do you like to draw?" I asked.

"Why?"

"I just figured you did," I said. "You were talking about a painting back in class."

"Oh," she said. "Yeah. Well, yes, as a matter of fact, I do like to draw."

"Cool," I said.

"My name's Richard," I said.

"I know," the girl said. "It's written on your lunch sack."

"Oh," I said, looking down at my mother's childish drawing. "Sorry."

"Cinnamon," she said.

She held a hand out to me. I reached up and touched the cold tips of her fingers.

"Like the song," I said.

"What can I say?" Cinammon said. "Hippie parents."

"I'm pretty into Neil Young," I said. "My brother was kind of a hippie."

"You have my sympathies," she said.

She removed another cigarette from her purse and lit it off the dwindling butt end of the first.

"I've seen you around," she said. "At Kroger. Why did you leave Macon?"

"How did you know I went to Macon?" I asked.

"School uniform," she said.

"Oh," I replied.

"It's a little game I play," she said. "Trying to figure out what people are like from their clothes and the things they buy. You sure can imagine some interesting possibilities."

"What did you imagine about me?" I asked.

She ignored the question.

"So, like, for real—why'd you leave Macon?"

"I got booted," I said.

"What for?"

I doubted that an honest account of the circumstances surrounding my expulsion would get me very far with a girl like Cinnamon.

"You don't want to know," I said.

"Ooh," she said. "Mysterious."

I shrugged nonchalantly.

"I would have had to leave after this year anyway," I said. "My old man had a stroke. He lost a lot of money in the stock market."

"That sucks," she said.

"Yeah," I said.

"So you're ex-rich now, is that it?"

"I guess," I said.

Cinnamon struck me as the type of girl who would appreciate the inherent drama of a sudden reversal of fortune.

"To be honest," I added, "we're pretty much broke."

She tilted her head and exhaled another neat funnel of smoke from the corner of her mouth.

"Welcome to the lower class," she said.

She turned her head toward the student parking lot. A black Pontiac Fiero idled at the curb.

"That's my ride," she said.

"Are you ditching?" I asked.

"Senior off-campus lunch," she said.

"Oh," I said.

"I'd invite you along," she said, "but you're not a senior, are you?"

"Sophomore," I admitted.

"You could ditch if you wanted," she said. "I doubt anyone would notice."

"I don't think I'd fit into the car," I said.

"I know," she said. "It's kind of ridiculous, isn't it? He thinks it's so cool."

I didn't bother to ask who *he* was.

"Guess I'll be seeing you around," she said.

She skipped over to the Fiero and slid through the open door onto the passenger seat. I hummed a line from "Cinnamon Girl" in my head. A *dreamer of pictures*, I thought, as the little car rolled over the speed bumps in front of the school and zipped away.

CINNAMON KINTZ APPEARED to subsist on cigarettes, MoonPies, and Doritos. She spoke of exercise as if it ought to be illegal. She had a crooked canine and an overbite and a slight gap between her two front teeth and a tattoo of a butterfly on her wrist, back when tattoos were still rare and edgy. She eschewed bras with scandalous regularity, allowing her breasts to demonstrate their miraculous, gravity-defying firmness and elevation while testing the limits of a dozen different perfectly aged concert T-shirts.

Each day I tried to find something to say to her—some clever quip or non sequitur—or at least to exchange eye rolls as we simultaneously suffered through the indignities of Introduction to Theater Arts with Mr. LaPage.

I wasn't friendless, mind you. Old acquaintances were renewed and new ones made. Regardless of why it had happened, my having been kicked out of Macon gave me a modicum of what passed for street cred in a small-town public high school. By the end of the first week, I didn't *have* to sit alone at lunch. Still, I always made a habit of drifting out to the old dead tree where Cinnamon lurked—sometimes with a gaggle of girls or Marcus Vaughan, the curly-haired boy with the cable-knit sweater from drama class, but more often alone.

After a few weeks, I worked up the courage to make the ultimate adolescent male overture: a mix tape, assembled from my burgeoning collection of cassettes, using a dubbing deck I'd acquired to record vinyl records. I plotted the tape out judiciously, blending a variety of familiar hits with offbeat tracks usually hidden on the bottom half of a B side. There were girl-friendly rockers and melancholy acoustic ballads and obscure gems from lesser known acts like Big Star and Badfinger. I debated giving the mix tape a title—"Cinnamon Songs" or "Songs for a Cinnamon Girl." In the end I concluded that Paul would just act like he happened to be carrying it around. I wrapped it all up with my old friend Neil—not the obvious "Cinnamon Girl" but instead, from *After the Gold Rush*, "Only Love Can Break Your Heart."

Heading out to the bus after seventh period, I saw Cinnamon smoking on the loading dock outside the theater, waiting for her ride.

"Hey, Macon," she said as I approached her.

"I wish you wouldn't call me that," I said.

"Sorry," she answered. "I guess you need another nickname, now that you're working class and all."

"My brother and his friends used to call me Rocky," I said.

"Rocky?" she asked. "Is that a joke?"

"They thought I looked like a little Stallone," I said.

"Not really seeing it," she said. "But whatever. Rocky it is."

"What about you?" I asked. "How'd you get yours?"

"Mine? Oh, that's my real name."

"On your birth certificate?"

"I don't have one," she said. "I wasn't born in a hospital, and my parents never bothered. I do have a Social Security card though. So yeah, on my Social Security card, that's my name—Cinnamon Saffron Soma Kintz."

"Wow," I said.

By then the buses were pulling away.

"Look," Cinnamon said. "You're missing your bus."

"I've got a ride," I lied.

She lit another cigarette. I pulled the cassette out of my pocket.

"Hey," I said. "Maybe you could listen to this while you're drawing your pictures."

She held the tape and examined the track list, which I had written neatly on the case insert.

"Thanks," she said.

"No problem," I replied. "I have another copy at home."

"You make more than one copy of a mix tape?"

Was it stupid to make more than one copy of a mix tape? I wondered.

"I mean, I have another copy of all the songs," I said.

"Right," she said. "Well, I'll give it a try."

We sat on the loading dock, waiting. I was too content in her company to be especially worried about how I was going to get home.

A white Toyota Celica pulled up in front of us, driven by another tall, rangy, long-haired man-boy I didn't recognize. Cinnamon hopped down and ambled toward the car at the curb.

"Thanks again for the tape," she said.

"You're welcome," I replied.

When I was sure they were gone, I walked out to the street to wait for the city bus.

15

WHEN I GOT HOME, Miss Anita's blue Buick was parked in our driveway. The door to the living room was shut. From the other side came the sound of fervent prayer.

Walking back to the Royal Chamber, I heard another familiar voice. On the couch in front of the Old Man's armchair sat Leigh Bowman, a book open on her lap. William sat backward on a side chair, balancing his chin over his arms, observing.

"Where you been at?" he asked.

"I missed the bus," I said. "Thanks for noticing."

"You look cold," Leigh said.

"I'm all right," I said. "I called the house. No one answered."

"Must have been outside," William said. "Your moms and Miss Anita be doing they thing."

"Oh," I said. "What are y'all up to?"

"I'm reading to your father," Leigh said.

"You never read to me," the Old Man said. "You never read shit. You just sit up there listening to that garbage."

"Come now, Mr. Askew," Leigh said soothingly. "Let's get back to the story."

The tension in the Old Man's face relaxed. He crossed his hands in his lap and waited for her to continue.

"Have a seat, Rocky," she said.

"What are we reading?" I asked.

"It's called *This Present Darkness*," Leigh said.

She held up the cover so I could see it: a painting of a ghostly pair of claws descending from the sky upon a tranquil town surrounded by soft, rolling green hills.

"What's it about?" I asked.

"Spiritual warfare," Leigh said matter-of-factly.

"It's good, man," said William. "Angels and demons and shit."

I took a seat on the couch next to Leigh as she resumed her reading. William was right: it was good—a genuine page-turner. Gleaming blond angels with swollen chests and biceps do battle with scaly, horned, and leather-winged demons in the spirit world, while the devout mortal Christians of Ashton work to expose a so-called New Age organization that, unbeknownst to the towns-people, is actually an underground satanic cult making ready for the rise of the Antichrist.

Within minutes, the Old Man was asleep in his familiar pos-ture: head thrown back, mouth agape. Leigh continued reading, however. William and I sat rapt. She might have gone on like that for an hour or more had she not been interrupted by the Old Man's snoring. Leigh smiled queerly and closed the book.

We tiptoed from the room, slipped on our coats, and stepped out the side door. William offered Leigh a Kool. The two of them puffed away while I collected the basketball from beneath the boxwoods.

"That's some book," William said.

"You can keep it if you like," Leigh said. "I have another copy."

"I like listening to you read it," William said.

I stood under the goal to collect rebounds as William shot bas-kets, cigarette perched in the corner of his mouth. Leigh stood off to the side, casting occasional glances back at the house as if afraid of being seen with a cigarette in her hand. Once, I thought I caught her eyes drift across the bleached winter grass up the hill toward Twin Oaks. But she might just as well have been staring at nothing.

"So is this what you're doing now?" I asked her.

"I'm sorry?"

"Reading," I said. "Is that what you're doing these days?"

"Oh. Yes," she said.

William dropped back to three-point range. The ball clanged off the rim. I took two quick steps, snagged it on the first bounce, and tossed it back out to him.

"I tried working at the preschool for a while," Leigh said.

"You were always great with kids," I offered.

"I liked it," she said. "But some of the parents were uncomfortable."

"Why?" I asked.

"Oh, Rocky," Leigh said with a dry chuckle. "I know what people think of me."

Her words were blunt and unaffected, without any hint of anger or bitterness. She seemed completely at ease with herself—or perhaps, too heavily medicated to be self-conscious. William continued with his jump shots, as if he knew the whole story already or simply didn't care.

"Daddy didn't like me working there anyway," she said. "He didn't think it was healthy for me to be at the church every day."

William launched again from three-point range. The shot swished through the net and fell into my waiting hands. I passed the ball back to him. We were in a flow.

"Why not?" I asked.

"Oh, he says he's worried I'll walk by the sanctuary and have some sort of relapse," she said. "That's why we don't go to Sunday services there anymore—or so he says. I think he's just too proud to walk in there and be stared at along with me."

I silently agreed with her.

"I tried to explain to him that I have so many good memories of Holy Comforter to outweigh the one bad time," she said. "I hardly remember it anyway."

"I remember it," I said.

"I'm sure you do," she said. "Your father remembers it, in great detail. Doesn't he, William?"

"Uh-huh," William said.

"Anyway," Leigh continued, "I understand why the parents weren't happy about my being around the children. But I still wanted to do something to contribute to the church community.

So Miss Anita suggested that I spend time visiting with people like your father."

"That's a kind thing to do," I said.

"Old people really appreciate just a little attention," she said. "They're all very lonely. Even the ones who get regular visits. They just want to see a new face every once in a while."

"I can see that," I said.

"It's very fulfilling," Leigh answered.

"Here," William said, bouncing the ball to Leigh. "Take a shot."

Leigh dropped the dying butt of her cigarette to catch the ball. She cocked her arms and shifted her feet into a nimble stance. As she took aim, the glazed eyes seemed to narrow into focus. The addled waif was again the young athlete. She held the pose for a moment, her bare, exposed calf tensed as she crouched. Her front leg straightened when she sprang up, her wrists flipping forward powerfully as she flicked the ball toward the goal in a perfect, spinning arc. It caught the edge of the rim, rolling in and out and careening off toward the bushes.

We went inside and took off our coats. William slipped off to the Royal Chamber to check on the Old Man. I followed Leigh out to the living room. We could hear the muffled voices of my mother and Miss Anita behind the closed door.

"I should go in and join them," Leigh said.

Again, her mouth formed that queer, unnerving smile. My heart welled with longing and remorse. Had she always been like this, and had I just been too callow and young to notice? Was she going to end up this way regardless? Was Paul to blame? Was I?

"Say," Leigh asked, "are you in contact with Patricia?"

"No," I said. "Not since she left."

"I hope you weren't hurt too badly," she said.

That Leigh would even think of whether I had been hurt by what Patricia had done made my chest ache.

"What about Charles?" I asked.

"Oh, Charles," Leigh said wistfully. "He wrote to me while I was away. Since I've been home, I get the occasional call, but it's hard for him with the time zones. Daddy and Mr. Culver aren't speaking these days."

"Why not?" I asked.

"Mr. Culver accused Daddy of trying to sell Charles a bill of goods."

"What does that mean?" I asked.

"It means I would have ended up costing more than I'm worth," she said.

I stared at the floor between us, trying to think of the right thing to say.

"We haven't officially broken it off, you know," she said. "I still have the ring. It doesn't fit anymore since I lost some weight."

She should sell it, I thought, before Charles or his parents asked for it back. But Leigh never needed money. Maybe she could sell it and give the cash to my mother, I thought. That would serve Brad Culver right, the son of a bitch, as the Old Man would say.

"She'll be coming back soon, I suppose," Leigh said. "From Florida."

The thought of Patricia gave me a sharp pang that reminded me what it meant to feel like your heart was breaking. Was that what Leigh wanted? I knew that I deserved no less.

"It was me, you know," I said. "I told her everything."

She took my hand in hers and leaned forward and kissed me on the cheek with her cold, dry lips. I was reminded of Judas and Christ in the garden at Gethsemane—only there, it was the traitor who kissed the martyr, and not the other way around.

16

LEIGH BEGAN MAKING her rounds to read in nursing homes and the houses of shut-ins on an old Schwinn five-speed bike with a basket on the front, a bell on the handlebars, and one of those wide granny seats. Anita begged Leigh not to ride around like that, warning her that she'd "catch her death of cold." But, enthralled by the relative freedom after so many weeks and months of confinement in sterile hospital rooms and somnambulistic "rest" facilities, Leigh insisted. We soon became accustomed to the sight of Leigh merrily riding that old bike down Bonny Lane and all around Boone's Ferry with a stack of books in her basket, cheeks pink from the frigid cold, the tail of her coat flapping in the wind behind her. Before long she was a fixture—another eccentric institution, like the town drunk.

Gradually I stopped thinking of Leigh in terms of who she used to be or might have been if she had never told me her story, or if she'd been properly medicated on her wedding day, or if she hadn't run off with Paul or had never even fallen in love with him to begin with. Her presence ceased to be a rebuke and instead became a source of comfort.

Something about the shamelessness with which Leigh met the condescending scrutiny of Spencerville made her seem almost heroic. However we may have pitied her, the Old Man and William and I still looked forward to her visits. Thanks to Leigh, we all became experts on popular titles for the evangelical set. At times I even felt myself nearing some sort of spiritual enlightenment—until the end of the day's reading, when the sight of Leigh tooling off down the driveway on her bicycle reminded me that she was, in fact, insane.

FEBRUARY CAME, AND with it a half foot of snow and a long night of freezing rain that formed a hard crust almost thick enough to walk on without breaking the surface. The sky stayed gray for days, as if the sun had tired of trying to shine. We lost almost a week of school waiting for the roads to be made safe enough for the buses. I spent the days with the Old Man and William, watching reruns and continuing my education in living with dementia.

The delusions were not always angry or cruel. Sometimes, William and I became Annie Bet and Paul. In the Old Man's eyes, we were small and adoring, present and alive. It was all routine for William—part of the job, no different from ignoring the casual racism or eruptions of rage, which sometimes resulted in teacups flung against walls or glancing blows to the head or shoulders of whoever happened to be nearest to him. For me, however, these moments were like séances, where the disappeared and the dead whom I had never known were conjured and almost tangible.

When the Old Man would draw back into the past, the dementia was almost a gift. I came to know a sallow, shoeless child, raised on scant harvests and poor prospects through the blight of the Depression years. I followed that boy across the Pacific to the killing fields of Bataan and Corregidor and the 39th parallel. I saw him come home and, in a decade's time, turn a sales job taken on a whim into a thriving business that built him a new house bigger than any he'd ever set foot in as a boy. I saw him leveled by the unfathomable loss of a child, with her Shirley Temple ringlets and a well of hope and courage in the face of certain death. I saw him torn between the joy of a new family and the lingering remorse for the one he'd failed to save, made ever present by an impossible son he could neither control nor abandon. I saw every victory and every failure, all up to the final, crushing blow that had left him bound to the prison of his ruined mind. What I saw—what I sensed but could not yet comprehend—was the arc of a life that was not just the rise and fall of a small, forgettable man, but the story of the American Century: its booms and busts, its catastrophes and regenerations, its fortunes built up from sweat and moxie only to be dashed by bad luck and bad choices, its false hopes and promises broken by the plain fact that we are all mere antic clay, bedeviled by the mystery that animates us.

But these moments were rare. Mostly there was snoring, and reruns, and hobbling to the toilet, and cigarettes and basketball in the ice-covered snow.

IT WAS TUESDAY and Leigh was late. The Old Man was asleep.

William was shooting well that day. Again and again the ball rasped through the stiff, half-frozen webbing of the net. My breath spewed out in sharp bursts of white, almost indistinguishable from William's cigarette smoke.

"You don't think she out on that bike today, do you?"

"God, I hope not," I said.

"I be spinnin' tires all the way up that hill," he said. "Even with the chains."

"She'd get off and walk, I guess," I said.

"Too cold to walk that far."

"It's not that far from her house," I said. "Maybe a mile."

The ball slipped through my fingers and rolled across the snow toward the hedges.

"Maybe we should go look for her," I said.

"Can't leave your pops."

I stood under the basket catching my breath, the sweat running cool down my bundled torso.

"I'm worried," I said.

"She just ain't coming today, that's all," William said.

William lit another Kool. He stamped his feet and smoked his cigarette with his hands in his pockets.

"Maybe you ought to read to your daddy for a change," he said.

"What should I read?" I asked.

"Hell if I know."

William abruptly removed a hand from its pocket and flicked the cigarette from his mouth into the ice-glazed bushes.

"Look," he said.

A small red truck crawled toward the house. We trudged through the crust of snow to meet it. As we came closer, we could see Leigh in the front seat, next to a bearded man wearing a heavy wool sweater, a black watch cap, and a pair of wire-rimmed glasses. As the truck slowed to a stop, Leigh waved and smiled and opened the door. She was barefoot. Beneath a giant black down parka, she wore nothing but a cotton nightgown, nearly translucent from wear.

"Damn, girl," William said. "Ain't you cold?"

There was no note of alarm in his voice. William was accustomed to odd behavior from the frail of mind.

Leigh held her arms up as if she were trying to grasp the air in her hands.

"It's invigorating," Leigh said. "I've never felt so alive!"

As she drew near to me, I could see that her eyes were dull and heavy, the pupils widely dilated.

"Christ," I whispered. "How much did you take?"

"Don't take the Lord's name in vain, Rocky," she said.

The black parka clearly belonged to the man in the truck, who had already climbed out and circled around the front. Leigh teetered for a moment, as if her legs were about to give way. The bearded man lurched forward and grasped her shoulders.

"Why don't you let me carry you?" the man asked.

"Over the threshold?" Leigh asked, with a coy giggle.

"If you like," the man said.

"I can't believe you found me," Leigh said, resting her head on the man's shoulder as he lifted her from the ground. "The Lord works in mysterious ways."

"He sure does."

The bearded man tilted his head and fixed his eyes on mine. My heart seized. The flesh had settled and thickened, along with the heavy beard that was once so thin and wispy. But the eyes were unmistakable. I had waited to see those eyes again for longer than I could remember. Still, it was only when he spoke my name in the old, familiar tone that I believed it was really him.

"Hey there, Rocky," he said.

"Hey yourself, Paul," I murmured.

He smiled. I couldn't say another word; I couldn't even move.

Paul swept Leigh up into his arms as if she were as light as a child.

"Would you mind getting the door for me, brother?" he asked.

I trudged falteringly to the top of the porch. Behind me, my brother climbed the steps with Leigh in his arms, stoned and serene, her face ashen and her lips purple. The ends of the cotton nightgown billowed beneath her in the icy wind as they passed by me into the warm light of the waiting house.

PAUL CARRIED HER into the living room, tracking snow onto the white Wilton woven rug.

"I'll get some blankets," I said.

"Maybe we should build a fire," Paul said.

"We got a fire back where your daddy is," William said, addressing Paul as if they'd known each other for years. William may very well have felt that he *did* know him, given how vividly Paul had come to life in the Old Man's delusions.

"All right, then," Paul said, stroking his beard. "Let's take her back there. Would you like that, Leigh? Would you like to warm up by the fire back in my old man's room?"

"He's expecting me," she said.

Again, Paul lifted Leigh into his arms. We followed William back to where the Old Man still sat sleeping, his head thrown back and mouth agape as usual.

Paul set Leigh down on the couch. I took the down comforter folded at the foot of the bed and spread it out over her. William stoked the fire with the brass-handled poker and placed a fresh slab of wood in the flames.

The Old Man awoke because of the commotion, his arms still

crossed over his chest, his eyes sanguine and sleepy. He peered up at Paul, who stood rooted next to the couch, looking a bit dazed and unready.

"Your beard," the Old Man said, clearing his throat. "I like it."

"Thank you," Paul said.

"I never wore a beard myself," the Old Man said, his voice slow and drowsy. "Tried the mustache for a while when I made rank in Korea. Your mother said I looked like Clark Gable in the pictures. I always thought I looked like a greasy wop or a Mexican."

"It's not for everyone," Paul said.

He held his composure, but his eyes rebelled against him. The tears flowed forth into little rivulets that trickled down in glistening beads over the thick mat of his whiskers.

"Maybe I'll try it again," the Old Man said.

He turned to William.

"What do you think, boy?" he said. "How'd you like to get out of shaving me every goddamned morning? I bet you're good and sick of it, aren't you, boy?"

"Don't bother me none either way," William said.

"Well then," the Old Man said. "I'll grow a beard. Like my son."

His eyes closed and he leaned his head back. It became clear to us all that he was still traveling through some manic dream—that he had seen Paul a hundred times before, on my face, or William's, or in the naked air. He had yet to grasp that his son was actually there before him, in the flesh.

Paul knelt and buried his face in his sleeping father's lap. The Old Man's hands fell from his chest and cradled Paul's head, stroking the thick, brown hair, still wild and long and wavy beneath the watch cap, which had fallen away to the floor beside them.

17

IN THE KITCHEN PREPARING TEA, Paul paused for a moment before opening each cabinet or drawer, as if amazed that everything was still kept in the same places. Even the refrigerator—replaced since he left—seemed to surprise Paul by being in the same corner where the old one had been. When he raised the tea to his lips, I caught him staring at me over the brim of the teacup, his eyes filled with boundless wonder.

For my own part, I was too stunned to remember any of the questions I had thought for years about asking him. I could find the words to ask only one—the same question he used to ask me almost every day.

"Want to go upstairs and listen to some records?"

"Sure," he said.

Paul followed me up the stairs and into his old room. I hopped up onto the bed. Paul scanned the room with muted curiosity.

"I tried to keep things the way you left them," I said. "You can have the room back now, if you want."

"That's all right," he said, almost whispering. "You keep it."

"You really should take it. That's why I moved in, you see? So it would be here for you when you came home."

"Home," he said.

He took the chair by the window. I dropped the needle on CSNY's *Déjà Vu*. He reached in through the neck of his sweater to remove his pack of cigarettes from the breast pocket of his flannel shirt.

"What happened to the Nova?" I asked.

"Sold it a few years back," he said.

"I can't believe you ever got rid of that car."

"Can't get through winter in the Bitterroots without a four-wheel-drive," he said. "Plus I needed the bed for tools and supplies and whatnot."

"I get my license this summer," I said.

"Right on," he replied.

Paul finished his cigarette and lit another. He looked up the hill at Twin Oaks, illuminated by floodlights Brad Culver had installed in the hedges.

"I don't guess you see much of those people anymore," he said.

"It's a long story."

"I might know some of it."

Light from the headlights of an approaching car filled the room. It was my mother, home from work. Paul stubbed out his cigarette on the sill beneath the crack he'd opened in the window.

"Think she'll be happy to see me?" he asked.

The front door opened. My mother's heels clicked across the hardwood floor. She started to make her way back to the Royal Chamber but paused as if overcome by some apprehension. Perhaps she sensed his presence—some odd energy, like a visitation of spirits. More likely she smelled the smoke. When her shadow fell across the door, Paul's face was once again a flinty edifice of indifference, even beneath the warm shroud of his yogi's beard.

"Hello, Alice," he said.

For a moment she stood frozen, taking him in, adjusting her eyes to the absence of light.

"Would you turn that off, please, honey?" she said to me.

I slid off the bed and lifted the needle. The room fell into fraught silence. Finally she spoke.

"Have you seen your father yet?" she asked.

"Sort of," Paul answered. "He was resting."

"How did you find him?"

Paul fingered the pack of cigarettes on the secretary next to him but did not remove one.

"Older," he said.

"There isn't any money, if that's what you're here for."

"I know that," Paul said.

"Do you?" my mother said, an uncommon and unseemly venom creeping into her voice. "How, pray tell, would you happen to know that?"

"You remember my old pal Rayner Newcomb, right?"

"How could I forget?" she said.

"Then I guess you heard he's an attorney in town now."

"Rayner? A lawyer?" I blurted out.

"Yeah, I know, right?" Paul said. "Who'd have thought that Rayner would be the one to turn out respectable?"

"Yeah," I said. "Who'd have thought that?"

My mother glared at me with homicidal ferocity.

"So," she said, crossing her arms and fixing her eyes back on Paul. "After all these years and the thousands of dollars your father spent trying to find you—the thousands of hours he spent wondering if you were dead or alive—all that time, you were in contact with your *old pal* Rayner?"

"I'm not proud of all the things I've done," Paul said. "I know I hurt people."

My mother laughed bitterly. Paul held her gaze.

"Your father never stopped hoping you'd come home, Paul," my mother said. "I think if he'd found out that you were dead, I would have felt relieved."

I had to admire my mother for going straight at Paul like that. I felt a twinge of remorse for having welcomed him back so willingly. After all, he had been a perfect shit.

Paul seemed unfazed by her wrath.

"I understand why you'd feel that way, Alice," he said.

"So why now, Paul?" my mother asked. "Did you just need a place to come in from the cold?"

"Rayner got in touch. He told me things weren't going well," he said. "I thought I might lend a hand."

"Hah!" my mother barked again, rolling her eyes. "Just what we need."

"Jeez, Mom," I said.

"Oh, please, Richard," my mother said. "Let's not forget, the last time you saw your dear brother here, he was trying to poison you to death with his goddamned cigarettes!"

I had never heard my mother curse that way before. I couldn't decide whether to be dismayed or enthralled.

"Ma'am?" a voice called from the bottom of the stairs.

It was William, his timing impeccable, as always.

"Yes, William?" my mother said.

"They up now," he said.

"Who's they, William?" my mother asked.

"Mr. Askew and y'all friend Leigh."

THEY WERE CHATTING amiably when the four of us found them. Leigh was still a bit loopy but seemed to have come down a bit. She had done us all the good service of explaining to the Old Man that the bearded, slightly paunchy Paul he'd seen earlier was not a vision but in fact the genuine article.

"Son!" the Old Man cried, pushing himself up from the chair and extending his arms eagerly toward Paul as he entered the room.

"Hey, Dad," Paul said.

They held each other like that for a long time, the Old Man sobbing into the shoulder of Paul's scratchy sweater.

"Praise God," Leigh said.

"Leigh, honey," my mother said. "What on earth are you wearing?"

Pulling away from the Old Man, Paul explained how he had come to find Leigh standing barefoot in the middle of the road.

"Well," my mother said, the bile still boiling within her, "that was doubtless the one time in her life she was fortunate to run into *you*."

"Oh, don't be angry with Paul, Alice," Leigh said drowsily. "I have a chemical imbalance."

Paul knelt next to the Old Man, who had settled back in his armchair. Together the Old Man and Leigh Bowman beamed at Paul as if he were the risen Christ himself.

"I'd better call your father, Leigh," my mother said. "I'm sure he's worried sick."

She disappeared down the hallway.

"I knew you were coming," Leigh said. "Miss Anita saw it weeks ago. She saw me meeting you, barefoot in the snow. She said it was just a crazy dream, but it came true, didn't it?"

"Miss Anita, huh?" Paul said.

"Oh, she's been so wonderful to me," Leigh said.

I waited for Paul to launch in on how Miss Anita was nothing but a quack in a Chanel suit and pearls. Instead he just smiled.

"That's great, Leigh," he said. "Really."

"Tell me, Paul," Leigh said. "Have you come to know the Lord? For real this time, I mean. Are you saved?"

Paul looked at the Old Man. He clapped his palm on the Old Man's forearm.

"Sure," he said.

"That's so wonderful," Leigh said. "Praise God."

"Yes," I said. "Praise God!"

"Son," the Old Man said, "where the hell have you been?"

"It's a long story," Paul said.

We sat there together, the five of us, listening to Paul describing his rambling years as casually as if he'd just come home from summer camp. After New Mexico, he'd gone to California, and then to Oregon, and Nevada, and finally Idaho, where he'd spent the past few years working at a ski resort and doing carpentry in the off-season.

"Just like Jesus," Leigh said.

"Not exactly," Paul replied.

My mother returned, carrying a red wool sweater, gray sweatpants, white cotton socks, and one of her old pairs of Saucony running shoes.

"Can you wear a size nine, Leigh?"

"I couldn't take your shoes, Mrs. Askew!" Leigh said.

"I insist," my mother said. "Your father would never forgive me if I let you out of this house dressed like that."

Still sitting on the couch, Leigh hiked the sweatpants up beneath the nightgown and pulled the sweater over the top of it, so that the nightie hung down beneath it like an oversize T-shirt. She stood and held out her arms.

"How do I look?" she asked.

"Like a runaway from the nuthouse," the Old Man said.

"Dick!" my mother said.

"I might as well look the part," Leigh said.

"Goddamned right," the Old Man said.

Leigh giggled.

"I'll get you home now, Leigh," my mother said.

"I'll take her," Paul said.

"Why don't you stay here," my mother said. "I need to run by the store."

"Give me a list and I'll pick up whatever you need," Paul said.

"I didn't mention your being here to Leigh's father," my mother said. "I don't know how he'd feel about seeing you pulling up to the curb again."

"He won't recognize the truck," Paul said.

My mother's face reddened.

"I think I'd sooner stab myself in the eye," she hissed through clenched teeth, "than have to explain to Prentiss Bowman how I let poor Leigh ride off *again* with *you*."

Paul, Zen teddy bear that he'd become, responded only with a sad smile and a shrug.

"I'll take her, Ma'am," said William.

"Heavens, William!" my mother said. "We've kept you more than an hour past the end of your shift."

"Oh, I don't mind," he said. "I'd be happy to see Miss Leigh home safe."

"All right then," my mother said. "Thank you, William."

We left the Old Man alone in the Royal Chamber and walked out together to the entrance hall. Standing in the doorway, Paul extended his hand to William.

"Thanks, brother," Paul said.

William took his hand and nodded uneasily. He must have been unaccustomed to being called "brother" by a white boy. William didn't know any hippies.

"You ready, Miss Leigh?" William said.

Leigh nodded, casting a wistful glance back at Paul as William helped her down the steps and into his car.

"I'll see you soon, Leigh," Paul called out.

"I know," Leigh said.

We waved as the car disappeared down the driveway.

"So, Alice," Paul said, "what did you need?"

"What?" my mother asked.

"From the store," Paul said.

My mother sighed.

"Nothing, Paul," she said. "Nothing at all."

18

PAUL LAUNCHED HIS REFORM program by presenting my mother with an envelope full of cash.

"It's a little over three thousand dollars," Paul said.

My mother stared at the money peeking out from the envelope.

"How did you get this?" she asked.

"I came by it honestly, if that's what you're worried about," Paul said.

My mother placed the envelope on the table.

"I don't want your money, Paul," she said.

"I know you don't," Paul said. "But we need it."

"We?" my mother said.

With great reluctance, she took the money. Paul was right. *We* needed it.

Against Paul's protests, I moved out of his room and back into my old one. It would take some getting used to, I knew, but I preferred to have him back where he belonged.

Within a few days of his return, Paul found work on a framing crew for a residential construction company. From seven to three, he humped two-by-tens and hammered nails in the freezing cold. It was no big deal, Paul said; he was used to worse. On Fridays, when my mother came home from the office, Paul handed over a folded-up wad of bills—most of his paycheck. Every afternoon he relieved William. Every weekend he took the Old Man out for a drive.

The first Saturday after he got paid, Paul invited me out to lunch. My mother stood watching from the front window as we drove off down the driveway.

"Where are we going?" I asked.

"To the Wahoo," Paul said. "Thought you might like to see Rayner."

The Wahoo Bar and Grill was full of people about Paul's age, drinking draft beer and longnecks. The walls were covered with personalized license plates and felt pennants. We met Rayner Newcomb back behind the pool table in a wooden booth festooned with carved graffiti. Rayner, once the lean, wiry thug par excellence, was now a balding attorney in pressed khakis and a cashmere sweater, with a belly that pushed up against the table when he sat down in the booth.

"Hey, Rocky," he said, his mouth forming a familiar leer. "You *whore*."

"Jeez, Rayner," I said. "How'd you get so fat?"

"A little mouthy, isn't he?" Paul said.

"I wonder where he picked that up," Rayner replied.

We ordered cheeseburgers and fries. Paul and Rayner ordered beers; I had a Mexican Coke. I couldn't stop staring at Rayner. As nasty a piece of work as he had always been, it seemed somehow unjust that the sharp cheekbones and the dark, deep-set eyes and the coiled, aimless aggression had been replaced by the potbelly and the gin blossom and the aw-shucks grin. It seemed equally unfair that while Paul and Leigh's lives had unraveled so spectacularly, Rayner had survived and prospered.

"We all get what's coming to us," Rayner said, "but we don't all get what we deserve."

"What kind of lawyer are you, Rayner?" I asked.

"He's what you call an ambulance chaser," Paul said.

"I admit," Rayner said, "my heart quickens with delight at the sound of sirens."

He removed his wallet to show us pictures of three cherubic little girls with pale blue eyes and faces framed by garlands of blond ringlets.

"Serves you right, having girls," Paul said.

"I am well aware of the torments that await me," Rayner said. "And I've prepared for them. In recent years I've been collecting assorted firearms and military weaponry. When the young scoundrels come a-courting, I plan to show them my collection of bayonets and demonstrate how I sharpen them on my custom-built grindstone."

"Come on, Rayner," Paul said. "You of all people should know that not even the threat of being sliced off by a razor-sharp Confederate bayonet can hold a teenage hard-on at bay."

I felt a tap on my shoulder. I looked up from the table.

"Cinnamon Girl," I said.

"Hey," she said.

In one hand, she held a cigarette; in the other, a pool cue. Behind her, at the opposite end of the pool table, stood a sullen-looking fellow with auburn hair that hung down onto the shoulders of his black leather motorcycle jacket, smoking absentmindedly as he scanned the arrangement of balls with comical seriousness.

"Thanks for the tape," she said.

"Did you like it?" I asked.

"Most of it," she said.

She puffed on her slut butt and grinned. Smoke piped out from the gap in her two front teeth. Behind her, the reddish-haired fellow glowered at us over the rim of his beer glass.

"Who's that?" I asked.

"That's Yanni," she said.

"Yanni?"

"He prefers John, but his parents call him Yanni, so I call him that too. It's cute, don't you think?"

"I've never seen him at school."

"He's, like, twenty-four. Have you heard of Predatory Nomad?"

"No. What's that?"

"A band," she said.

It sounded like something that should be written on a sign beside a museum diorama of Cro-Magnon man stalking a woolly mammoth.

"What does he play?" I asked, trying to look as unimpressed as possible.

"Bass," she said.

"You seem like more of the drummer type to me," I said.

"Jealous ever?"

"You can do better," I said.

"With who?" she asked. "You?"

"Sure," I said. "Why not?"

"That's cute," she said.

"Is he your boyfriend?"

"I don't like that word, *boyfriend*," she said. "I wouldn't call it that."

I was afraid to ask what she *would* call *it*.

I looked over at Paul. He and Rayner had become engrossed in the basketball game on television. Back in their prime, I thought, Paul and Rayner could dispense with guys like Yanni the Bass Player without even having to extinguish their cigarettes.

"So," Cinnamon said, pausing to puff on her cigarette, "how do you know Rayner?"

"He's my brother's oldest friend," I said.

I elbowed Paul in the rib cage, drawing his attention back from the television.

"This is Paul," I said. "Paul, Cinnamon."

"The long-lost brother," Cinnamon said.

"That's right," Paul said.

"I've heard a lot about you," Cinnamon said.

"You have?" Paul asked.

"No," she replied. "Just that you were gone, like, with the wind."

"Well, I'm back," Paul said.

Paul wrapped his arm around my shoulder. "How do you two know each other?" he asked.

"We're buddies, sort of," Cinnamon said. "From drama class."

"No kidding," Paul said. "Rocky here was once the budding star, you know."

"I heard that," Cinnamon said.

"Cinnamon," Yanni the Predatory Nomad said. "It's your shot."

"Gotta go," she said. "Guess I'll see you at school."

"Right on," I said.

Her Guatemalan wrap skirt swayed as she turned back to the pool table and Yanni the Bass Player.

"*Right on?*" Paul said. "Do people still say that?"

"You say it," I said. "All the time."

"Who might that fey-looking scoundrel be, young Rocky?" Rayner asked, nodding at Yanni.

"That's Yanni," I said. "He's in a band or something."

"If you want to knock him over the head with a barstool, I'll be happy to defend you, free of charge," Rayner said.

"No thanks," I said.

"That little gal has a different Yanni in here every other week or so, if that makes you feel any better, Rocko," Rayner said.

"It doesn't," I said.

"Try not to look so lovesick, brother," Paul said. "Girls don't like guys who act like they care."

"Is that your secret?" I asked.

He shrugged and lit a cigarette.

Their game apparently finished, Yanni grasped Cinnamon by the hand and pulled her behind him, past the pinball machines and out the door. She turned back briefly to wave and smile, cigarette still perched in the corner of her mouth. Her eyes passed over me and rested on Paul, as if she thought he ought to have recognized her from somewhere else.

FOR MONTHS THE Old Man's dementia had been steadily worsening, so that by the time Paul arrived, the lucid moments were increasingly rare. Within weeks of Paul's return, the Old Man's more sentimental delusions were all but gone; more often his eyes rolled madly and the rage spilled forth in gushing torrents aimed at whoever was unfortunate enough to be around—usually Paul, who hurried home after work to take over for William. My mother took some obvious satisfaction from seeing Paul bear the brunt of these attacks. Only William knew how to disregard these rants as meaningless. The rest of us had to wrestle with the suspicion that the dementia was loosening words he'd always believed but would never have uttered before his sense of restraint abandoned him. When it came to finding our rawest insecurities, the Old Man's sickened brain was like a hog rooting up truffles.

One afternoon I came through the front door to the sound of the Old Man's bellowing from all the way down the hall in the Royal Chamber.

"What you've done with yourself," the Old Man said. "What you did to that girl. You ruined her, don't you know that?"

I crept down the hallway and stood outside the door, listening. Growing up as I had, I learned early on the value of eavesdropping, both as a means of discovering truths unintended for my ears and as a strategy for survival.

"Would you like to know the worst mistake I ever made?" the Old Man said.

"Please, Dad," Paul said. "Enlighten me."

"When your sister fell ill, I felt grateful," the Old Man said, his voice shaking with bitterness, "grateful that it was her, and not you. I wanted a son, you see? Did you know that?"

"No, Dad," Paul said. "I didn't know that."

"Think of the pain we'd all have been spared," the Old Man said, "if it had been you."

It was a cruel thing to say. But I doubt Paul had never thought of it himself. As for me, instead of going in to save Paul, as I should have, I stood on the other side of the door and pondered the question, what if it had been Paul who died, and Annie Elizabeth who survived? Would she have lived up to her angelic reputation, or would she have been just as irresponsible and thoughtless as Paul had been? Would we now think of Paul as a blessed holy martyr? Would the Old Man's first marriage have lasted? Would he ever have met my mother? Would I even exist?

"I'm sorry God let you keep the wrong one," Paul said.

"You should be," the Old Man said.

"Wasn't it one of the saints who said that answered prayers

bring more tears than those that go unanswered?" Paul asked. "Which saint was that, Dad?"

"Go to hell," the Old Man said. I imagined him sitting in his chair with his arms crossed, pouting like a petulant child.

"Fortunately for you," Paul replied, "God gave you another son. Maybe he won't be such a disappointment to you."

I felt my breath catch in my throat.

"But you tried to take him from me, didn't you?" the Old Man said. "You'd have done it too, if you hadn't lost your nerve."

"Do you remember that story you used to tell about the old Indian and the blanket?" Paul asked. His voice took on the old, bitter tone I'd not heard since his return. The sound of that voice frightened me. It must have scared the Old Man too—he was suddenly speechless.

"You couldn't possibly have forgotten," Paul said, his words dripping with scorn. "You must have told it to me half a dozen times. Don't you remember? You'd get all solemn going on about the noble Sioux and how when they were no longer useful to the tribe, they went off in the woods alone with a blanket and just sat down to die. Remember what you used to tell me at the end of that story, Dad?"

The Old Man still couldn't answer him.

"Old age is a damned disgrace. That's what you said, Dad. I can still hear you saying it, as clear as day. Well," Paul said, "you've already got the blanket, haven't you?"

I stood on the other side of the door, afraid to move. I pictured the two of them facing each other, all that pain and pride and hatred burning up the air between them. Later I would wonder whether Paul meant what he said, or whether he had just lost his temper. The Old Man had been right, I thought, when he told Paul that story. Old age *is* a damned disgrace. Wasn't that what Neil Young meant when he said, *It's better to burn out*? Wasn't that what Townshend meant when he wrote, *I hope I die before I get old*?

I heard the television being turned on but waited a few more minutes before entering. The Old Man's face had gone slack; his

eyes were dull with weariness. Likewise, Paul wore an expression
of complete exhaustion. I sat down on the couch next to him, and
together the three of us watched *The Andy Griffith Show* in silence.

After my mother came home, Paul and I went upstairs. Paul
put on *Hunky Dory* and sat in his chair, chain-smoking and staring coldly out the window while we listened to Bowie sing about
changes and pretty things and life on Mars. At the end of the side,
when I slid off the bed to flip the disc, Paul spoke.

"Did he ever tell you that story about the Indian with the blanket?" Paul asked.

"Which one?" I asked.

"The one you heard me talking about down there," he said.

I held my breath. Paul lifted his cigarette to his lips and took a
long, slow drag.

"No," I said.

He delicately tamped the edge of his cigarette in the ashtray,
blowing a long plume of smoke out the cracked open window.

"Turn it over, will you?" he said.

Before I could put the needle back on the record, we heard my
mother's voice below us, crying out the Old Man's name.

We hurried back to the Royal Chamber, where we found my
mother standing frozen in front of the Old Man in his armchair.
On his lap, on top of an oily rag, sat his .38 revolver.

"For Christ's sake," the Old Man said. "I'm just cleaning it."

AFTER THAT, MY mother gathered all the guns and brought them
up to Paul's room, where she laid them on the bed.

"I want them gone," she said. "Out of the house."

"Even that one?" Paul said, pointing to the Old Man's shotgun,
a Browning Sweet Sixteen gold-trigger automatic.

"All of them," my mother said.

"You know he bought that gun in Belgium," Paul said. "After
the war. It means a lot to him."

"Maybe your *pal* Rayner will store it for you," she said.

"And what about the others?" Paul asked.

"Just get rid of them," she said.

Paul wrapped up the three guns—the pistol, Dad's Browning, and his own old sixteen-gauge—and took them out to the truck. A few days later, he handed my mother a crumpled wad of bills.

"Here," he said.

"What's this?" she asked.

"Four hundred and fifty bucks," Paul replied.

"What did you do with them?" she asked.

"Rayner knows a guy," he said.

19

BY THE SECOND WEEK of March, the lingering snowdrifts disappeared from the long meadow between our house and Twin Oaks. For the first time in months, we saw Brad Culver again, out in his field pulling a shiny new Bush Hog behind a blue tractor. Back and forth he went across the field, up and down along the fence line. Culver passed our house at close range no less than half a dozen times, his eyes fixed on the air in front of his nose, never turning or even tilting his head to make a sidelong glance.

"Son of a bitch," Paul muttered, rubbing his thigh where Culver's bullet had pierced it.

When I passed the test for my learner's permit, Paul took it upon himself to teach me how to drive stick. We spent a few afternoons in the church parking lot, Paul patiently advising me on how to balance the clutch and the gas pedal. Once I mastered the art of engaging first gear from a stop on an uphill slope, Paul started picking me up and letting me drive home from school while he smoked in the passenger seat. Paul had gathered that I preferred him to show up a little late so that I could linger on the loading dock with Cinnamon as she waited for the latest bass player in his Pontiac Fiero or Mustang 5.0 to pull up and sweep her off, either for her shift at Kroger or, I assumed, to some dingy garage to listen to his stupid band practice.

They developed a curious rapport, Cinnamon and Paul. Whenever he pulled the red truck up to the curb and hopped out to walk around to the passenger side, Cinnamon would wave and grin at him, as if they shared some private joke. Paul always waved back sheepishly, without looking at her.

"Why does she wave at you like that?" I asked.

"I don't know," Paul said. "I guess she thinks we've got something in common."

"Like what?"

"She grew up around the same kind of people I used to be," he said.

"The same people?" I asked.

"Not the *same* people," he said. "The world isn't *that* small. But we have some common experiences. Cinnamon's a pretty cool chick, if you want to know the truth."

"You're on a first-name basis now?"

"We had a conversation."

"When?" I demanded. "Where?"

"At the Wahoo," Paul said. "She came up to me."

"What did you talk about?"

"Relax, Rocky, I'm not interested in your girlfriend."

"She's not my girlfriend," I said.

"Put it into third, bro," he said.

I eased the stick forward and accelerated into the turn onto Boone's Ferry.

"We ought to go up to the parkway one afternoon," I offered.

"When the weather gets better, maybe we will," Paul said. "If your mom's cool with it."

"Maybe we could take Cinnamon with us," I said. "And Leigh."

"Might be a little tight in the cab," Paul said.

"Me and Cinnamon could ride in the back," I said. "I bet she'd like that."

"She probably would," he said.

Paul's face was shrouded beneath his beard, his eyes soft and sad behind the spectacles. I remembered how those eyes had flashed in the glow from the end of his cigarette in the blue darkness up there in John's Gap—how I could feel their muted spite even through the nausea and delirium.

"You used to tell the best stories," I said. "Remember all those stories you used to tell me?"

"It runs in the family," he said.

"The Old Man sure loves a good story, doesn't he?" I asked.

"The Old Man never heard anything sweeter than the sound of his own voice," Paul said.

"He never talked to me the way he talked to you," I said.

"That's because when I was a kid he didn't have anyone else to talk to," Paul said.

"I guess."

I took a deep breath.

"Say, Paul," I said, "why don't you tell me a story?"

"What kind of story?" he asked.

"A true story," I said.

He looked down. In one hand he palmed his old Zippo, burnished from years of riding around in his pockets. In the other he held his cigarette, the trail of smoke that trickled off its end fingering its way up and out the open window.

"I don't remember any true stories," he said.

When we reached the house, William was outside, shooting baskets. It was to be his last week with us. He had seen it coming when Paul started taking his hours in the afternoons. William tried to be cool about it, but you could tell he felt burned. I hadn't thought it would be that hard to find another sick person who needed to be looked after, but apparently we weren't the only people having a hard time affording home health care that year.

Ironically, after months of abusing William with abandon, the Old Man began to regard him as a saintly personage. He grew prone to fits of weeping over how helpless he'd be without William, with no one but the selfish, inept Paul to look after him while his faithless wife was off giving blow jobs to the neighbors. William clearly agreed with the Old Man (about Paul, not the blow jobs).

We met him at the edge of the side yard by the basketball goal. He tucked the ball under his arm and took out a cigarette. Paul lit one of his own and offered his lighter. William grudgingly tipped his Kool into the flame.

"How's the Old Man?" Paul asked.

"Ah-ight," William said. "He sleeping."

"Good," Paul replied. "Is Leigh still here?"

"Uh-huh," William said. "She visiting with a friend."

"A friend?" I asked.

"Yeah," William said. "Her friend from up on the hill."

William pointed his cigarette past us, down to the fence, where we saw the Culvers' Velma, saddled and bridled and tied to the fence.

Paul couldn't have failed to notice the shock on my face, but he didn't say a word. He knew about me and Patricia—I'd told him everything. He'd said it seemed like a good experience for me to have had. He was a bit angry at me for selling Leigh out, until I pointed out that if I hadn't, Leigh might well have ended up living in a gilded Manhattan penthouse as Mrs. Charles Culver. Still, we'd all been a bit too preoccupied with surviving the winter to wonder what might happen when Patricia came back.

Paul dropped his cigarette to the ground and clapped his hand on my shoulder.

"Well, come on then," he said. "I'd like to meet Leigh's friend."

We found them in the living room. On the coffee table was a silver tray bearing a pair of teacups and saucers, cream and sugar, and a plate of the kind of cookies Patricia would refer to as "biscuits."

"Oh, hello, boys," Leigh said. "Look who's here."

They stood from their seats on the couch in front of the tea tray. I must have been staring quite helplessly at Patricia. She looked fit in her weathered jeans and black turtleneck. Her cheeks were freckled and still rosy from the Florida sun. She wouldn't look at me; instead she stared at Paul, who regarded her with a like measure of bemused curiosity.

"I went out with William to have a cigarette after your father went down for his nap," Leigh said. "Lo and behold, there was Patricia, trotting along on Velma. We had so much to talk about, so I thought we might come in and have a little tea party. I hope you don't mind."

"I'm glad you did," Paul said. "I'm Paul, by the way."

"I know," Patricia said, extending her hand to him. "Patricia."

"Nice to meet you," Paul said.

"And you," Patricia said. "You're quite the legend around here."

"I hope you're not disappointed," Paul said.

"How was Florida?" I asked.

"Oh, fine, I suppose," she said, her eyes still fixed on Paul. "Humid. Warm. A bit dull. I always find the place disorienting. Winter should be cold. Sunny and eighty-five degrees makes the Christmas tree look a tad out of place. But it's good for the horses."

We heard the Old Man's voice from down the hall. William disappeared back through the living room door while Patricia continued to scrutinize Paul—mostly, I thought, so she wouldn't have to look at me.

"And how is Charles?" I asked. "Have you seen him?"

"He flew in for Christmas and spent the day with us," she said. "Then back off to New York, and then back to Venezuela. His company has business there. Very serious and important, I'm told. Normal stuff for Charles, you know—spreading capitalism round the globe."

"Charles got married," Leigh blurted out.

"You're kidding," I said.

"I'm afraid so," Patricia said, in that exasperatingly disingenuous tone of polite sympathy I had found so pretentious before she won me over with booze and sex. "Mummy and Daddy were quite shocked. It all happened very fast. They met in Caracas. She's the daughter of some significant personage in the government down there. Daddy claims the marriage was part of a business agreement—like Charles's company gets a break on barrels of oil in exchange for his marrying the daughter of the local *jefe*."

Patricia grasped Leigh's hand.

"It was my understanding that Charles had spoken to Leigh beforehand," Patricia said. "It would have been the gentlemanly thing to do."

"I'm very happy for him," Leigh murmured.

With her free hand, Patricia touched Leigh on the shoulder as if she were comforting a gurgling half-wit.

"Are you back for good, Patricia?" Paul asked.

"Actually I've found a place just outside Charlottesville," she said. "I think Mummy and Daddy were ready for me to move along, and I've loads of friends in the area."

Loads of friends? I thought. She'd never mentioned anyone in Charlottesville to me.

"She's found someone," Leigh said in a comically hoarse stage whisper.

"Please, Leigh," Patricia said.

Patricia blushed. I felt my own face getting hot. I hoped I didn't look as stung as I felt.

"Who?" I asked.

"Just a friend from the circuit," Patricia said.

"I'd like to meet him," I said.

"Maybe I'll bring him around for a visit," she said. She smiled at me—exasperatingly, I thought. Despite my attentions having shifted elsewhere, I still felt more jealousy than relief.

"I'm just glad I got to see Leigh before I left," she said.

"I hope it won't be the last time," Leigh said.

"I'm sure we have many more little tea parties in our future," Patricia said.

She sighed and stretched her back like a sleepy cat.

"Well," she said, "I must be off. Can't leave poor Velma tied to the fence all afternoon. I hope I didn't impose."

"Tell your father I said hello," Paul said with no discernible trace of irony.

"I most certainly will," Patricia said.

"It's so good to see you," Leigh said.

"I'll be in touch," Patricia said.

"I'll walk you out," I said.

I held the door open for her and followed her down toward the fence where Velma stood waiting.

"I'm very sorry about your father, Rocky," she said. "What an unkind twist of fate, especially after his and Daddy's unfortunate dealings."

"We're getting along all right," I lied.

"Leigh told me about what happened at your school."

"Yeah, I guess I blew it."

"It sounded a bit out of character for you."

"Maybe you don't know me that well. So," I said, "Charles ran off and got married."

"That's right," she said.

"He might have told her himself, at least."

"Maybe Leigh forgot the conversation. Given her state, she might prefer to block out such painful memories. Then again, Charles can be rather cruel and remorseless."

"He's not the only one," I said.

"Don't be that way, Rocky," she said. "It's so childish, really."

Her jaw hardened and her eyes turned cold with spite. I glanced down at the ground. When I looked up, her face had relaxed into the old, intimate air of September.

"Have you found a girlfriend?"

"Yes," I lied, again.

"Tell me about her."

"She's nothing like you."

"Goodness, Rocky," she said. "I feel a bit wounded."

"Why?" I said. "It's what you said you wanted."

"Come again?"

"For me to find someone more—how did you put it?—worthy."

"Now you're just being spiteful," she said.

"What about your new friend?" I asked.

"Oh, Nelson?" she said. "It's nothing serious. Just someone to pass the time with. A little fling, you might say."

"That's what you used to say about me," I said.

"If I did," she said, "I meant it differently."

Velma snorted and tossed her tail.

"What happened between us was very special to me, Rocky,"

she said. "I mean that, more than I expect you will ever know. But you must have realized it couldn't last. It was terribly dangerous, more for me than for you. Quite frankly, it still is. If you were to tell anyone . . ."

"I would never do that," I said.

"What about Leigh? She knows."

"Not for sure. I mean, she knows, but I never actually *told* her."

"And Paul?"

I shrugged.

"Do you see, Rocky?" she said. "Do you understand why I just couldn't carry it on any longer?"

"Paul would never get you in trouble," I said. "He thinks it's cool."

"I'm sure he does," she said dryly.

She crossed her arms and smiled softly at me.

"I know you don't believe me," she said, "but it was just as painful for me to leave you behind as it must have been for you to let me go."

I didn't bother to summon a response. I knew Patricia well enough to know that she couldn't be made to feel chastened by how much more favorably things had turned out for her than for me or anyone else.

Patricia mounted the fence and stepped over and pulled herself up onto Velma's back.

"I hope I'll see you again, Rocky," she said. "I'm sure I will."

20

ON APRIL 1, THE OLD MAN had another stroke—a transient ischemic attack, or ministroke, the doctor called it.

"Transient attack," Paul said. "Sounds like he got mugged by a vagrant."

Even my mother laughed at that one.

It had been a long time since any of us had held out much hope that the Old Man's health would improve, but as he grew weaker and less easy to manage, it became more and more difficult to hide from each other that we were all privately praying for his death.

Sometimes, when the Old Man slept, Paul and I would sit on the floor in his room and play chess or backgammon while we listened to records. Most kids my age were into Nintendo by then, but Paul thought video games were for dorks.

One such afternoon, we were surprised to hear the doorbell ring. We thought it must have been Leigh, making a surprise visit. When we opened the door, we found the Old Man standing there, naked but for his diaper, covered in fresh-cut grass. Next to him stood William, dressed in work clothes, clutching the Old Man's arm with one hand and a carving knife in the other.

"Your daddy came calling for Mr. Culver," William said.

"I'm gonna kill that son of a bitch," the Old Man muttered.

We brought him inside and helped him to sit down at the foot of the stairs. I went back to the Royal Chamber to get his clothes. When I returned, Paul was awkwardly brushing him off with a hand towel from the kitchen. The Old Man had begun to shiver and moan.

"Here," William said angrily.

He handed Paul the knife and snatched away the towel. Paul looked on mutely as William cleaned the Old Man with quick, practiced hands, murmuring reassurances as he helped him into his undershirt and flannel button-down and his favorite red cardigan and chinos.

"Jeez, William," I said. "How did you find him?"

"Been helping out at Culver's stable," William said.

William, in my old job! I didn't think Culver would be shoveling his own horse manure for long. I wondered whether Patricia had invited William in for cocktail hour yet. But she couldn't have—she was up in Charlottesville, with her new fling.

"Working for Culver?" Paul asked. "How'd you hook that up?"

"Needed a job," William said curtly. "So I went over and asked. Lucky it was me that found him, huh?"

"I don't know how he got outside without our noticing," Paul said.

"Can't hear him over y'all records."

"He was asleep," I said. "He always sleeps almost until dinner."

"Not always," William said.

"I can't believe he got that far without his walker," Paul said.

William put his arm around the Old Man.

"Guess they a lot you don't know 'bout your pops," William said. "You mind if I get him settled?"

"Sure," Paul said. "I mean, yeah, thanks."

Paul and I lurked in the hallway while William took the Old Man back to his armchair. Paul picked up the kitchen knife from where he had set it on the front hall table and held it up in front of his face. We were both embarrassed, I think, but also a bit amazed—even impressed—that the Old Man's demented fury could get him all the way across the field and up the hill to Twin Oaks.

"Son of a bitch," Paul said, almost admiringly.

A few minutes later, William emerged from the Royal Chamber.

"He in bed now," he said.

William walked past Paul and out the door without a word. I

followed him to his car. He pulled out his pack of Kools and lit one up.

"He don't look too good," William said.

"He had another stroke," I said.

"He need someone to take care of him," William said. "Someone who know how."

"I know," I said. "We just can't afford it."

William looked past me, over my shoulder, at the house. I knew I couldn't explain to him what it meant to be "house poor." Any way I tried to lay it out, we still just sounded cheap.

"I can't believe you're working for Culver," I said.

"Gotta eat, Rock," he said.

"Hey," I said, "since you're around, maybe you could come by and shoot hoops sometime. Or come by when Leigh's here. I bet she would like to see you."

He sucked on his cigarette and exhaled slowly, looking me up and down cooly.

"Keep an eye on your daddy," he said. "And your brother."

NOT LONG AFTER that day with William, Paul didn't show up to take me home from school. Cinnamon had been gone for at least half an hour before I gave up and went into the office to call home. No one answered, so I took the city bus and walked the mile from the end of the bus line at the intersection of Riverdale and Boone's Ferry back to the house, as I had done before.

When I got home, I went back to the Royal Chamber to find the Old Man asleep in his chair with his head tilted forward, a slight, almost invisible string of drool dangling from his lip. In front of him stood Paul, still and solemn. In his hands he clutched a throw-pillow embroidered with a cross-stitch of Noah's Ark.

Paul looked up at me, startled. There was something odd about the look in his eyes. When he glanced back down, the Old Man's eyes were open, watching—pleading, I thought.

Without a word, Paul grasped the Old Man's shoulder and gently lifted him forward and bent to kiss him on the forehead. The

Old Man's eyes slowly closed as he drifted back off to sleep. Paul silently walked past me, out of the room, all the way out through the front door.

I followed him to the edge of the yard, where he stood with his arms resting on Culver's white picket fence. Paul pulled his smokes from his pocket and flipped open his Zippo. We stared at the field as Paul dragged on his cigarette and exhaled through his nostrils like a pissed-off dragon.

"Where is Leigh?" I asked.

"Something happened," Paul said.

Earlier that day, Miss Anita Holt had shown up at the job site where Paul was working, honking the horn and calling his name through the open window. When he reached the blue Buick, Miss Anita had moved over to the passenger seat.

"You drive, honey," she said.

"Where are we going?" Paul asked.

"To the Culvers'," Miss Anita said. "And put your foot down."

Along the way, Miss Anita explained to Paul how Jane Culver had come out of her house that morning to find Leigh Bowman standing on the hood of her Mercedes dressed in her thin cotton nightgown, carrying on a murmured conversation with the air above her. Mrs. Culver ran back into the house. She tried but was unable to reach Prentiss Bowman. When Jane came back to the window, Leigh was gone. She waited a few minutes before she crept outside, peered around, and ran to her car. Just as she was about to escape, she heard a reedy, high-pitched wail behind her. Leigh was perched on the roof of Twin Oaks at the peak of the highest gable, her arms uplifted as if someone was reaching down for her.

Mrs. Culver ran back inside and called her husband first and then Miss Anita, who went straight for Paul. When they arrived, they found Brad and Jane Culver and our old friend William, who was trying unsuccessfully to coax Leigh down from the roof.

"I don't know how she got up on the roof of that house," Paul said. "It was like she flew up there."

Miss Anita and Paul spoke soothingly to Leigh until finally she sat down on her rear end and slid down the slate tiles to the gutter, where Paul waited for her at the top of a ladder William had brought up from the barn.

"I asked her what she was doing," Paul said. "She said she'd seen the angels calling to her."

Paul lit another cigarette off the end of the first one and tossed the butt into the field before him.

"Maybe she shimmied up the columns and swung up from the gutters," he said. "She's light enough not to pull them out or bend them."

"That sounds a little—I don't know—acrobatic," I said.

"People with Leigh's kind of problems have been known to pull off extraordinary feats," he said.

I imagined Leigh in her nightgown, scrambling up the columns like Spider-Man.

"Maybe she is possessed," I said.

Paul shot me a withering glare.

"What was she doing over at the Culvers' anyway?" I asked.

"She said she was going over to return Charles's ring. I thought she was over the whole Charles business," he said, "but I guess it's natural for her to get a little upset when she heard the guy went and got married without even telling her."

I nodded.

"What's going to happen to her?" I asked.

"I don't know," he said. "I expect they'll just observe her for a day or two. Change her medications. Then again, that asshole Bowman might decide to ship her back to the nuthouse for good this time."

The sky was overcast. Twin Oaks loomed over the pasture, silent and still. I pictured Leigh on top of it, a silhouette on the pale sky behind her, her arms arching up, grasping at phantom shapes in the empty air.

"This is all their fault," I said.

"Who?" Paul asked.

"The Culvers," I said. "Their hands have been on every bad thing that's happened to us since that first night when you went into their house."

Paul appeared to consider my argument as he finished his cigarette. He dropped the butt to the ground and extinguished it under his heel.

"Don't worry," he said. "The Culvers will get theirs yet."

21

I HAD BEGUN to think I would never find a way to get past Cinnamon's string of bass players and shady-looking older dudes with their leather jackets and motorcycles and tacky little sports cars. Just when I was about to give up and accept that I was destined to be no more than "just a friend" to her, the allure of the spotlight and the persuasive rhetoric of Rex LaPage presented an opportunity too serendipitous not to seem like fate.

I was frankly a little shocked when Cinnamon anxiously informed me that she was planning to audition for LaPage's spring production—a play called *Equus*. She'd yet to show any great promise as an actress and was apparently so cynical about almost everything that I doubted her capable either of the necessary earnestness or of accepting the risk of humiliation inherent in any kind of live performance. When Mr. LaPage approached her outside class, however, flattering her and all but guaranteeing her a part, she'd taken the bait. He'd done the same with me, but I'd begged off, largely because I thought Cinnamon would think it uncool, particularly compared to playing bass in a hard rock band.

"You're really doing it?" I asked.

She shrugged.

"Thought I'd give it a try," she said. "For kicks."

Instantly I visualized hours of rehearsals with Cinnamon, who would have no time for shady-looking bass players with tacky little sports cars. I pictured us running lines together in the dimly lit house of the theater. Or backstage. Alone. At night.

"Me too," I said. "For kicks!"

In retrospect it boggles the mind to think that even Rex LaPage would have been reckless enough to stage a play like *Equus* at little old Randolph High School in Spencerville, Virginia, smack-dab in the cradle of the Moral Majority. A repressed, impotent psychiatrist becomes infatuated with one of his patients: a teenage boy who has blinded a stable full of horses with a hoof-pick. As the play progresses, the psychiatrist unearths the boy's history of psychosexual and religious torment at the hands of his well-meaning but ludicrously inept parents, whose violent arguments over sexuality and religion (the mother is a devoutly puritanical Christian; the father, an atheist) warp their troubled son's mind into forming an erotically charged religious obsession with horses. In a scenario I found eerily familiar, the boy ends up taking a job at a stable, where he is seduced by a fairly aggressive and much more experienced girl, who shortly persuades the boy to join her for a tryst in a hayloft above a stable full of horses.

At this point the story deviates quite significantly from my experience: the boy hears the horses' stamping and snorting beneath and mistakes it for the jealous anger of his self-invented horse-god. In a futile attempt to hide his imagined betrayal, he stabs the horses' eyes with the hoof-pick before going catatonic, subsequently ending up in the psychiatric hospital where the play begins.

All this backstory is revealed in flashbacks, staged on a platform that doubles as the psychiatrist's office. Furthermore, on stage, the horses aren't horses, or even models of horses, or imaginary horses, but rather boys in tight black spandex with horse-head "helmets" designed by students in the art department. This bit of stagecraft lent the whole proceeding a blunt homoeroticism that could be overlooked only by the willfully obtuse—a description that fortunately fit most of the theatergoing audience in little ole Spencerville, Virginia.

It was all astonishingly edgy for a high school where *Jesus Christ Superstar* was considered avant-garde. Hence there was an air of tense excitement around the whole proceeding that one wouldn't find in auditions for *Bye Bye Birdie* or *West Side Story*. The small throng of hopefuls shifted nervously in their chairs, waiting for their names to be called as Mr. LaPage put pairs of aspiring thespians through their paces.

After half a dozen auditions ranging from mediocre to pathetic, LaPage called me and Cinnamon up together.

"Page twenty-three," he said. "Cinnamon, you read Jill; Richard, you read Alan."

"Where should we start?" Cinnamon asked.

"Start at 'You've got super eyes.'"

The scene consisted of a flirtation in a stable between Alan Strang, the boy who blinds the horses, and Jill, the girl who helps him get a job as a stable boy and unwittingly sets in motion the events leading up to his violent breakdown.

"I love horses' eyes," Cinnamon said, throwing her hair and tossing her hip in a gesture meant to look provocative.

I almost forgot Cinnamon was there. In those brief pages, Alan Strang was nothing more than me—a horny boy who'd been a little fucked up by his domineering father and his reserved, hyperreligious mother, being offered the unexpected gift of casual sex and finding himself confused about what to do with it. I had never much liked horses, but I understood very well the power of their presence and the deep, vaguely tyrannical, watery luminescence of their eyes, which seemed at once impassive and full of stern disapproval. The role had practically been written for me. Furthermore, for the first time in years, I felt the urgent need to perform—something that had once come so easily to me but had been filed away and forgotten after Paul had disappeared.

Mr. LaPage posted the cast the following Monday. There, next to "ALAN STRANG," was my name, as I somehow already knew it would be.

The role of Jill had gone to Betsy Mayhew, a curvy, gingerheaded junior. Cinnamon would play Alan's mother, Dora Strang. At least she had a role, I thought. She wasn't much of an actress.

"No more playing it safe," Rex proclaimed at the first readthrough. "We're going to blow the audience away, people!"

Marcus Vaughan, the boy cast to play the psychiatrist, Dysart, was stunned and delighted to learn that Mr. LaPage wanted him to smoke cigarettes during his monologues, as instructed in the stage directions. The love scene between Alan and Jill would have to be censored and some of the more explicit language amended, but otherwise, as LaPage insisted, we were to be "true to the text."

The role of Nugget, the lead horse, was to be performed by Blake Burwell, a tight end on the football team with a terrific build and the kind of technically handsome but still somehow bland good looks of a catalog model. Blake had never acted before; Rex had asked him to come out. Having somehow acquired the false impression that theater girls were desperate to be laid by guys like him, Blake gamely agreed. He spent most of the rehearsals flexing his arms and torso and mugging at Betsy Mayhew.

"Dude," he would say to me between scenes, "is she looking at me?"

"I don't know," I'd say, or "I can't tell."

"Gonna be hittin' that, bro," he'd say, as if it were a prescheduled event, like prom or graduation. "Red up top, fire in the hole."

Several scenes required me to climb onto Blake's back and straddle him, or to stroke his chest and be nuzzled by the horse mask constructed out of wire by Cinnamon and her cohorts from art class. This didn't seem to bother Blake—on the contrary: he thought it would be a real "turn-on" for Betsy Mayhew.

In rehearsals, Mr. LaPage didn't behave like a teacher. He was *touchy*. He used salty language. He balanced explosions of raging temper with tender, beseeching encouragement. He called everyone "honey"—boys and girls alike. We were all terrified of his wrath and desperate for his approval.

Since Marcus was allowed to smoke in the play, everyone else felt entitled to do the same. Mr. LaPage never said a word. Therefore a constant fog of cigarette smoke hovered in the air over the set. Before long, we were all behaving as if we were members of an experimental theater company in Paris or Greenwich Village

instead of small-town southern teenagers with homework and cur-
fews, putting on a school play.

I was surprised at how happy it all made me. Back onstage for
the first time in years, I rediscovered my latent narcissism. The
role was full of the kind of histrionic melodrama high school kids
really buy into. I basked in the admiration and envy of my peers
and the effusive flattery of Mr. LaPage. Moreover, when I wasn't
onstage, I was in the back of the theater or out on the loading dock
with Cinnamon Kintz.

AS OPENING NIGHT neared, rehearsals shifted over from afternoons to evenings. Paul dutifully ferried me back to Randolph and
was waiting for me when we came out.

On the third night, rehearsal ran late. We were scheduled to
finish up at nine; at ten thirty, LaPage showed no sign of abat-
ing. It was typical of him to lose track of time, but that night was
excessive even for Rex. The rehearsal had been a disaster. It was
as if all of us—Mr. LaPage included—had suddenly realized that
before long we were going to be performing this play in front of
our parents. This latent anxiety fed a contagion of mistakes, from
flubbed lines to missed lighting cues to forgotten stage directions.
Rex should simply have given us a pep talk and sent us all home;
instead he blasted every error from his director's table at the center
of the house and made us start over again, from the top of the act.

Finally, at around 11 p.m., one of the horses' mothers stormed
onto the stage. After brusquely informing Mr. LaPage that it was
a Wednesday and therefore a "school night," she led her mortified
child off the stage by the bridle of his steel-wire horse head.

"All right, all right," Rex said, sighing. "Go home, people."

Exhausted, we gathered our things and went outside. All the
cast and crew disappeared until only Cinnamon and I remained.
Paul was nowhere to be seen.

"Do you think he left?" I asked.

"If my ride left," she said, "he isn't coming back."

"Paul would come back," I said.

"What makes you so sure?"

"Nothing," I said. "I'm not, I guess."

She lit a cigarette. We sat down on the edge of the loading dock.

"Your brother told me all about you," she said.

"You and my brother," I said. "Should I be jealous?"

"Maybe I should be jealous of you," she said.

"Because of Paul?" I asked. "You should have known him ten years ago."

I was sure that if Paul were ten years younger, Cinnamon wouldn't trade the chance to ride around in the passenger seat of the old purple Nova for all the bass players in the world, no matter how often Paul left her waiting in the dark after play practice.

"Paul and me," she said, "we're just alike, that's all."

"How's that?" I asked.

"I don't know," she said. "We just are. We've both done the commune thing, for one. My parents spent most of my childhood drifting from one 'intentional community' to the next. They tried four or five different religions and about a million tabs of LSD. You know the type."

Unless Paul and Leigh counted, I didn't know anyone like that, but I nodded anyway.

"And then we ended up here," she said, "in the dullest place on earth."

"It's not so bad," I said.

"You've never been anywhere else."

This was mostly true.

"As soon as I graduate, I'm gone," she said. "My sister lives in California. Runs a tattoo shop on Venice Beach. She's got the most amazing sleeves you ever saw. Do you have any tattoos?"

"No."

"I just have the one," she said.

She pulled up her jacket sleeve to reveal the ornate butterfly above the tiny blue veins at the base of her wrist.

"It's kind of dopey, I know," she said. "I was just fourteen; I wanted a butterfly. So that's what she gave me. What would you get?"

"I don't know," I said. "Nothing, I guess. My mom would kill me."

"When I get to California," she said, "the first thing I'm going to do is start getting some sleeves like my sister's. I'm designing them myself. I'll show you sometime, if you want."

"Yeah," I said. "Cool."

She lit another cigarette.

"You're lucky to have a brother like Paul," she said.

"You're the first person in history to hold that opinion," I said.

A blue fog of smoke funneled out of her nose and drifted up over our heads.

"If you ever met my brother, you'd understand."

"Where does he live?" I asked.

"No clue," she said. "When he turned eighteen, he joined the Marines. People like Paul rebel against their parents by running off to join a hippie commune. People like my brother join the Marines."

"So he's, like, overseas?"

"Oh, no," she said. "Got busted for DUI and dishonorably discharged. Then he was back home, smoking crank, stealing from the house, and bringing home his sketchy friends. Those losers were always trying to fuck me, and he didn't even care. My dad finally got sick of it and kicked him out. He took off, and we haven't seen him since."

"He kidnapped me once, you know," I said. "Paul."

"I know," she said. "He told me."

"I think he was going to leave me to die. Did he tell you that?"

"Not exactly."

"Well, he nearly did it," I said. "But he lost his nerve."

"And you still love him, don't you?" she asked.

"Yeah," I admitted. "I do."

"That's how I feel about my brother," she said.

I looked at my watch. It was almost midnight.

"Jesus," I said. "Where the heck is Paul?"

"I'm pretty sure I've been ditched," Cinnamon said.

"Paul can give you a ride," I said. "If he ever shows up. Man. My mom's gonna kill him."

"Are you sure?" she said. "I live out in Holcomb Falls. Near the parkway."

"Far out," I said.

"Little Rocky, with the hippie lingo," Cinnamon said.

"Quit making fun of me," I said.

"I think it's cute."

I didn't want to be *cute*. Not to her.

About ten minutes later, Paul's red truck pulled into the parking lot and sped up to the curb. We hopped off the loading dock and strolled down to him.

"Jesus," Paul said when I opened the door. "Take your time, why don't you."

He looked haggard.

"What's your big hurry?" I said. "You're an hour and a half late."

"Just get in the fucking truck, brother," he said. "I've got to get you home before Alice calls the cops on me."

"Cinnamon needs a ride," I said.

He peered out at Cinnamon.

"Where do you live?" Paul asked.

"Holcomb Falls," she said. "Look, if it's a problem, I can call my dad."

"It's not a problem," I said. "Is it, Paul?"

"No," he said. "No problem at all. But I'm taking you home first, Rocky."

"No way," I said. "I'll ride with you."

"Just do what I say for once, will ya?" he snapped.

"Jesus, Paul," Cinnamon said. "Fine. Just chill the fuck out already."

We huddled into the cab. Cinnamon sat between us, her knees tucked over toward mine to make room for Paul to work the stick. I let my palm fall onto her thigh just above the knee. She placed her hand over mine. I breathed in the smell of cigarettes on her breath. All my nerve endings seemed to lead from the small, vibrating spot where the soft swell of her breast rested against my arm.

Paul paid no attention. He smoked nonstop, flicking his ashes out the cracked window. The tape deck played *Music from Big Pink*. Paul turned the knob over to full blast on the creepy organ solo at the beginning of "Chest Fever."

"Why are you so late?" I shouted.

"I got held up," he said.

"Where?" I persisted.

"At Rayner's," he said. "Catching up on old times."

"I bet Rayner's wife was thrilled about that," I said.

"What?" Paul said.

Cinnamon reached up and turned the volume down sharply on a hard pop of the snare drum, which seemed to echo in the cab when the music was silenced.

"What's your problem?" Cinnamon said. "Are you drunk?"

"No," Paul said. "Maybe a little. Rayner kept feeding me booze. I lost track of the time."

"Maybe I should drive," Cinnamon said.

"He's fine," I said. I didn't want her to move from where she was, pressed up against me, holding my hand.

"That's right," Paul said. "I'm fine."

We drove on in silence. Cinnamon reached up and turned the knob back over.

When we reached the house, the front porch light was on. I knew my mother would be waiting up for me. As I opened the door to get out, Paul reached across Cinnamon and grabbed my arm.

"Listen, Rocky," he said. "You've got to cover for me."

"What do you mean?" I asked.

"Just tell your mom I was there on time," he said. "Tell her your teacher let you out late. Could you just do that for me?"

"What do you care?" I said. "Mom can't do anything to you."

"For Christ's sake, Rocky!"

"OK, OK," I said. "Sure. Like, no problem."

Cinnamon looked at the floor. I felt her hand slip off mine. As I stepped from the cab and pulled my bag from the bed and turned to wave good-bye, she came to her feet outside the door, facing me. She leaned in and placed a damp, tender kiss on my cheek.

"See ya," she said.

She hopped back into the passenger seat and closed the door. I stood and watched as Paul pulled around and drove away, trying not to grin like an idiot.

I was so caught up in my excitement about breaking through with Cinnamon that I had forgotten about my mother. I found her curled up on the living room couch in her housecoat and slippers, sipping sherry from a small stemmed glass.

"You reek of cigarettes," she said. "I can smell you from here."

"You know I don't smoke, Mom," I said.

She sipped from her glass and set it on the end table beside her. Her face appeared pale and gaunt in the lamplight.

"Where's Paul?" she asked.

"Cinnamon needed a ride," I said. "He brought me home first."

"How thoughtful of him," she said.

"We just ran late tonight. Paul was waiting for a long time," I said.

"I should give Rex a call," she said. "This is absurd."

"He just loses track of time," I said. "He said to tell you hello for him. He told me, 'Give that pretty mother of yours a kiss for me.'"

"How sweet," she said with apparent sincerity.

"I'm sorry for keeping you up," I said.

I leaned over and she rose to meet my kiss.

"Good night," I said.

I turned and started toward the stairs.

"Prentiss Bowman called, about half an hour ago," she said. "He wanted to speak to Paul."

I stopped at the landing, my hand on the banister.

"I told him Paul was over at Randolph, picking his brother up from rehearsal for the school play," my mother continued. "He called me a liar. He said Paul had just dropped Leigh off at the curb. That her hair was all wet and she was wearing strange clothes—men's clothes. He told me the next time Paul decided to take Leigh skinny-dipping in the middle of the night, he was going to get *his* gun and shoot him, and not in the leg, if you know what I mean."

Had Paul's hair been wet? I didn't notice—he was wearing his watch cap.

"You'd think Paul would have enough decency to leave that girl alone after what he did to her, bless her heart," my mother said. "If I were her, I wouldn't want anything to do with him."

I resisted the urge to defend my brother.

"Then again," she said, "Leigh's got no one else now."

"Yes, ma'am," I said quietly.

"Come sit with me," she said. "Just for a minute."

I walked back into the living room and sank into the couch next to her.

"I feel like I never see you anymore," she said. "Like we've become strangers."

"I know," I said. "I'm sorry."

Her face tipped into the harsh white light of the reading lamp as she reached for her sherry.

"There's something I need to tell you," she said.

"What is it?" I asked.

For a fleeting moment, I thought she was going to say that the Old Man was dead.

"It's about the house," she said.

The next Monday, my mother explained, a real estate agent would be coming over to help her prepare our house for sale.

"We need something smaller anyway," she said. "Something closer to school and the office."

I stared at the floor in front of her chair. All the joy I'd walked through the door with after that unexpected peck on the cheek from Cinnamon vaporized, leaving only a faint twinge of disgust with myself for having briefly felt so hopeful.

"I'll quit the play," I said. "I'll get a job after school."

"You'll do no such thing," my mother said. "Rex is depending on you. Besides, honey, a part-time job after school isn't going to save the house."

"I can get a job at Kroger," I said. "Cinnamon works there. She says they're always hiring."

"Cinnamon?" my mother asked. "Oh, yes. Well, that's something to talk about."

She smiled. Her eyes were heavy lidded; her mouth parted almost grotesquely. I noticed something that looked like a piece of spinach stuck in her teeth. In the white light of the reading lamp, I noticed for the first time that her hair was turning gray.

My mother was too young to be lashed to an invalid, I thought—too young to be so tired. If the Old Man had loved her, he wouldn't have doomed her to be left either alone or with the responsibility of tending to a helpless old man. Then again, if my mother hadn't married the Old Man, I would never have been born. What would it mean to believe that my existence was the consequence of a ruinous error in judgment?

"You better go to bed," she said. "I'll wait up for your brother."

I did as she asked, listening for the sound of Paul's truck as I readied myself for bed. I knew it would be some time before he returned—the drive to Holcomb Falls took at least twenty minutes, not counting the return trip. I brushed my teeth and went to my room to undress and crawl into bed. My thoughts moved restlessly from Cinnamon to Paul and Leigh and the accusing phone call from Prentiss Bowman, to the unfathomable notion of leaving the house the Old Man had built for himself—the only home I'd ever known.

Not long afterward the headlights of Paul's truck cast a silhouette of skeletal limbs and window frames across the plaster walls of my room. I listened as he entered and my mother called him into the living room. I couldn't discern what they were saying, but I felt certain that the bitterness I sensed passing between them was real and not just the progeny of my fears. I had heard such conversations before, after all—years before, when their mutual loathing was not tempered by the extremity of the Old Man's circumstances. I prayed that my mother would not provoke Paul to disappear again, just when things seemed to be at their worst.

At last I heard Paul's heavy boots on the steps. When he reached the top of the stairs and entered his room, I slid from beneath my covers and went to him. The room seemed extraordinarily dark. There was no moon or stars or any other ambient light. Paul had eased into his seat by the window.

"Hey," I said.

"Hey yourself," he replied.

I didn't ask Paul about what my mother had said to him or what she'd told me about Leigh and her father and the skinny-dipping.

"I guess you heard about the house," Paul said.

I nodded.

"It has to happen, Rocky," he said. "If she waits any longer, the bank will foreclose and we'll have to leave anyway, with nothing to show for it."

"I understand," I said.

"It should go for a good price," he said.

"Where will we go?" I asked.

"Your mom will find something," he said. "It won't be so bad."

As Paul lit his first cigarette, I realized why everything had seemed so strangely dark.

"Look," I said.

"What?" Paul asked.

I pointed out the window at Twin Oaks. The floodlights that normally illuminated the house at night were extinguished.

"It's not there," I said.

22

SINCE PATRICIA HAD RELOCATED to Charlottesville with her horses, it would not be uncommon for a week to pass without the Culvers seeing or speaking to anyone. There was William, but like me before him, he might go for days without seeing either Brad or Jane Culver, visiting the house only to collect his week's pay. We had noticed the absence of the horses from the field and the darkness of the house in the evening, but they might just have been traveling, off to watch Patricia in some horse show or to visit Charles in his new manse on the coast of Venezuela. Culver usually left the lights on a timer, but he might simply have forgotten before they departed. We paid it little mind. The Culvers weren't our friends anymore. Neither house was much concerned with the welfare of its neighbors. Who knows how long they might have lingered there if not for the preternatural visions of Miss Anita Holt.

Paul and I were, as usual, upstairs listening to records when we noticed the blue Buick coming up our driveway. I assumed she'd left something behind, like a prayer book or a pair of the kid gloves she still wore everywhere she went.

I don't recall hearing the doorbell; it might have been lost underneath Robert Plant caterwauling about Valhalla and the western shore. Or Miss Anita might have barged in without ringing. We did, however, hear her announce herself—not even Zeppelin's howling dogs of doom could have washed out the sound of her shrieking.

"Blood!" she screeched. "Blood, *blood*, BLOOD!!!!!"

DRIVING AWAY FROM a Saturday morning prayer meeting with my mother, Miss Anita had felt an overpowering, extrasensory urge to drop in on the Culvers. She thought "the sense," as she called it, was leading her there on behalf of Leigh. As she soon discovered, she was on a different kind of errand entirely.

When Miss Anita drove up to Twin Oaks, the Culvers' matching Mercedes sedans were parked in the driveway. She went to the door and rang the bell, twice. The silence, she said, was unsettling. When no one answered after she rang the bell a third time, she grasped the doorknob and turned it. Discovering that the door was open, she walked in.

She must have screamed, or perhaps she stood silent, mute with shock. There was so much blood, everywhere—on the floor, on the walls, smeared across the dining room table. Laid out next to each other on the floor in front of the fireplace were Brad and Jane Culver. Someone had pulled the coffee table over to the wall to make room for them both. Their hands and legs were spread out, as if they had been frozen in the midst of making snow angels. They were quite obviously dead—eyes open, mouths agape, covered with wounds, blood everywhere. On the wall above the mantel were the words *pig* and *whore*, written in blood.

One look at that horrible scene—well, that was enough for Miss Anita. She ran outside and to her car, whereupon she sped down the hill, back onto Boone's Ferry, and quickly over to us.

Thus did our little town's innocence end, replaced in mere hours with panic and paranoia, dread and suspicion, recrimination and lurid fascination. Before the sheriff's deputies had even finished wrapping the yellow crime scene tape around those two great oak trees and the house that bore their name, phones all across the Boone's Ferry neighborhood were all but ringing off their hooks, charged as they were with such incendiary astonishment.

For days and weeks afterward, the slightest creak in an old house or the brushing of naked tree limbs against each other in the wind caused people to sit bolt upright in their beds, peering frantically at the darkness until they convinced themselves that there were no knife-wielding murderers lurking in the bushes or beneath the trees or, worse, on the other side of the bedroom door.

The pawn shops and the sporting goods stores sold out of almost every form of firearm. Allegedly, even police officers and sheriff's deputies were sleeping with pistols under their pillows.

Some facts were immediately reported in the newspapers, and others revealed in the weeks and months that followed. Rumors trickled out through the gossip tree. Miss Anita told us everything she saw, but she hadn't exactly stuck around to study the crime scene.

The police believed that the Culvers had been dead for at least a day when she found them. They must have died quickly: Brad Culver had two distinct slashes on his neck, either of which would have done him in, while the slash across Jane Culver's throat was so deep that she was almost decapitated. Both had defensive wounds, especially Brad Culver, whose palms and forearms had deep gouges that suggested he had blocked several blows and tried to grab the knife from his attacker.

The bodies had been moved and arranged on their backs, heads pointing north, legs and arms spread, inside circles painted with their own blood. Around each body, five candles had been placed along the line of the circle, positioned at the head, hands, and feet. The candles had been left burning, so that all that was left of them were little puddles of cream-colored wax dotted with the blackened ashes of the wicks. Aside from the words *pig* and *whore* written on the walls in blood, the killer's other little touch was to paint inverted crucifixes and five-pointed stars enclosed in circles—pentagrams.

There had long been rumors in Spencerville of devil worshippers who lurked around out in the mountains past Holcomb Falls. The name of Squeaky Fromme was still fresh in our minds after her recent prison break in West Virginia. Squeaky's suspiciously easy escape had already led to quite a bit of talk that there might still be a few deranged longhairs out there, ready to pick up right where Charlie Manson left off. To many, the murder of Brad and Jane Culver confirmed these suspicions. Others suggested that some old enemy had emerged from Brad Culver's past to settle a score. Between what I had heard from Patricia and the Old Man's experience, I had no trouble believing there might be a number of people out there who'd like to see Brad Culver dead.

One other detail of the crime, however, would not come to our attention for several more days—one that was more chilling to me than all the buckets of blood and intimations of black magic combined. When the autopsy of Brad Culver's body was conducted, the county coroner discovered among the host of stab wounds and slashes a single gunshot wound—a slug from a .38 revolver, buried in the flesh of Brad Culver's thigh.

THERE WAS NO hiding the news from the Old Man. As poor as his hearing had become, he still heard the screeching yowl of Miss Anita when she came through our door that day, and he was there with us, watching through the windows as the flashing blue and red lights descended on Twin Oaks and the deputies came by to question us all.

"Serves the son of a bitch right," the Old Man muttered. "Son of a bitch, son of a bitch."

"Hush, Dick," my mother said.

"Don't you hush me, woman," he said.

"I mean it," my mother said. "It's not Christian."

"Oh, bullshit," said the Old Man.

Later that evening, we received a visit from an investigator from the sheriff's office. Bobby Carwile had only recently been promoted from deputy to investigator. All of thirty years old, he was barely a month clear of dealing with boat accidents, DUIs, the occasional burglary, and general redneck nonsense when he was handed the most sensational case the town had ever seen.

"How do you do, ma'am," Carwile said to my mother when he arrived at our door, dressed in a navy blazer, khaki pants, Weejuns, and a cheap-looking necktie—the same outfit almost every boy in Spencerville wore to church every Sunday. He seemed a little embarrassed to be bothering us.

"I was wondering if I might ask y'all a few questions," he said.

"Certainly," my mother replied. "Come have a seat."

She gestured toward the living room, where we were all already seated around Miss Anita—all of us except for the Old Man, who sat in the armchair nearest the window, peering up and out across the field toward the flashing lights.

"Is there a place I could talk to each of you alone?" Carwile asked.

"Well, Mr. Carwile, except for Miss Anita, we all saw the same things," my mother said. "And you know what she saw."

"I understand," Carwile said. "But it's just procedure. Just one of those things we have to do."

My mother led him to the Old Man's study, on the opposite side of the entrance hall. Bobby Carwile began with Miss Anita. The rest of us sat out in the living room, anxiously waiting our turns.

After Miss Anita came out and joined us in the living room, Bobby Carwile called my mother in. Miss Anita sat down beside me; I put my arm around her.

"I'm so sorry you had to go through all that, Miss Anita," I said.

"I've seen it before, you know," she said. "Do you remember, young Richard, when Brad Culver came here, to this very room, the day before that dreadful wedding?"

"I remember," I said.

"I saw it then," she whispered. "When he touched my hand, I saw him, just as he was when I found him today."

I looked at Paul, expecting to see his eyes rolling with disdain. Instead he listened intently, without apparent skepticism or contempt.

"Did you see who did this, Miss Anita?" Paul asked.

She stared back at him in thoughtful silence, her mouth slightly agape, as if she were waiting for the spirit to provide her with an answer.

"No," she said. "There was nothing else."

When my mother came out, Paul and I helped the Old Man up and across the hall to the study.

"Just so you know, he's not in his right mind," Paul said. "Stroke."

"I understand," Bobby Carwile said.

"You can't take anything he says too seriously," Paul said. "He can't remember what year it is from one minute to the next. He might even forget who you are."

"Mrs. Askew explained that to me," Carwile said.

I left the Old Man in the armchair and joined Paul at the door.

"It'll be just a minute or two," Carwile said.

"Mind if I go outside to have a smoke?" Paul asked.

"Go right ahead," Carwile said. "I'll join you when I'm done here."

I followed Paul into the hall and out the front door, down the front stoop, and out to the fence. Paul lit up. Across the field, the lights of the patrol cars illuminated the white columns of Twin Oaks.

"Who do you think did it?" I asked.

Paul took a long drag and blew it out and cocked his head toward me.

"Maybe it was Frank Cherry's ghost," he said.

THE NEXT DAY, from Paul's room, we saw a large brown four-door pickup truck pulling a horse trailer coming up the Culvers' driveway, escorted by a patrol car. The truck drove up past the house and down toward the stable.

"That must be Patricia," I said to Paul, who sat by the window, stroking his beard.

She had arrived the night before and was staying with Kiki Baumberger, who had been Jane Culver's closest friend in Spencerville. Charles would arrive the next day. The Culvers couldn't be buried until the coroner concluded his investigation, but a memorial service would be held that Wednesday afternoon at Holy Comforter. What would happen to the Culvers after that was still unsettled, perhaps even for Charles and Patricia. Jane Culver had been born here, but the children had no roots in Spencerville.

Once the state settled the matter of their parents' murder, it was likely that neither Charles nor Patricia would ever return again, even for a casual visit.

"Should we go over there?" I asked.

"What for?" Paul said.

"I don't know," I said. "To pay our respects or something."

"You go if you want," he said.

I didn't.

Because she expected to be showing the house soon, my mother had asked me and Paul to straighten up the yard. The grass had begun to grow again and was rough and uneven. Patches of weeds were scattered through the lawn, and the boxwoods needed trimming. Paul took the riding mower, working his way out from the house in circles. I took the push mower and trimmed the edges and borders of the flower beds and the fences. I was out front near the pasture pushing the mower when Patricia crested the hill atop Velma, her father's chestnut mare. Next to her on Oberon, her mother's sorrel gelding, was a young man I immediately concluded was my replacement.

They broke for the corner of the field and came around to trot along the fence toward me. I cut the motor and stood with my arms along the fence, waiting for the two horses to slow and stop. I looked past Patricia at first, curious as I was to scrutinize her companion.

He was small—less formidable than Patricia in every aspect. He looked down absently. He might merely have been distracted by the discomfort of the situation; nevertheless, I interpreted his blank stare as a deliberate effort to make plain that I was not nearly as significant a personage to him as he was to me. I also noticed that he was young—plainly younger than Patricia, not much older than me.

"I'm so sorry, Patricia," I said.

"Thank you," she said.

She looked a bit dazed, as if she hadn't slept for quite a while; most likely she hadn't. I remembered how she had appeared not

long after I first met her, before we got involved, even as friends—
when I first began to think of her not as aloof, but as isolated;
lonely and alone; not an ice princess, but a princess in a tower.

"I was planning to come see you when I could," I said.

"That's sweet of you," she said. She tilted her head to the boy
beside her. "This is Nelson," she said.

I mounted the fence and extended my hand. The boy nudged
the horse toward me and reached out to meet my grip.

"Nice day for a ride," I said.

"The horses needed to be looked after," Nelson said. "It's not
their fault what's happened, after all. They've been cooped up in
that stable half-starved for three days."

"At least," Patricia added.

Behind me, Paul cut the engine on the riding mower. The sound
of the motor was replaced by the slight breeze and the swishing of
the horses' tails. Paul appeared beside me.

"Hello, Paul," Patricia said.

"I'm so sorry about what happened," Paul said.

"I know," Patricia said.

"Do they have any idea who did it?" Paul asked.

"They don't seem to have a clue," Patricia said. "It seems random. But Daddy had a lot of enemies." She trained her eyes on
Paul. "I don't suppose I need to tell you that," she said.

"All the same," Paul said. "It's really just—well, there really
aren't words for it."

Patricia nodded gravely.

"Have you all taken any precautionary measures?" she asked.

"Nothing special," Paul said. "I wouldn't expect whoever it was
to come back."

"I suspect you're right about that," said Nelson.

Patricia's doleful eyes drifted back up to the house. Her horse
snorted in the heavy, humid air.

"I keep wondering," she said, "what if I had been home with
them?"

For a moment she seemed to float off into some ghastly vision of an alternate reality. Was she picturing herself beside them on the floor, surrounded by a circle drawn with her own blood?

She turned back toward us. Her face resumed a more familiar dispassion, as if she'd exceeded her day's allowance of soul-searching and empathy.

"Rocky," she said, "do you have the number for that boy who came to work for us? The one who used to sit with your father?"

I felt a twinge of offense on William's behalf. Don't call him "boy," I wanted to say. The Old Man had done it a million times, along with much worse, but still.

"His name is William," I said.

"That's right," Patricia said. "William."

"I'm sure my mother has it," I said.

"They won't take me into the house until Charles arrives," she said. "I can't get to Daddy's address book or Rolodex to find William's number."

Daddy's address book. My eyes clouded with an unexpected swell of empathy.

"Would you mind calling him to ask if he will see after the stable? Nelson will be taking the horses back to Charlottesville this afternoon. I want to have everything shipshape before Charles gets to town."

"Why don't you let us take care of it, Patricia?" Paul said.

"I couldn't," she said.

"It's the least we can do," Paul said.

Patricia peered down at Paul warily.

"Maybe I should do it myself," she said.

"Nonsense," said Paul. "You just leave the padlock open when you go this afternoon and we'll take care of it and lock up when we're through."

Patricia took a moment to consider the proposition.

"All right then," Patricia said. "Thank you both for your help."

"It's nothing," Paul said.

"We should go, Patty," said Nelson.

Patty? I thought. Oh, please. It must speak ill of me that even under the circumstances, my jealousy of Nelson overtook any sympathy I might have felt for our murdered neighbors. I'd like to think it had more to do with wishing to comfort Patricia in a way I no longer could than with a lack of pity for her parents.

"I hope I'll see you again," she said. "Before I leave."

"I hope so too," Paul said, as if she were speaking only to him.

AFTER LUNCH WE walked across the field and over to the Culvers' stable. As we looked up at the trees and the stately columns of Twin Oaks, I realized for the first time that I had never actually been inside this house that had loomed in my imagination for so many years. Paul had gone in, at least twice. I wondered whether that, as much as anything else, was the difference between us.

The stable was empty, but the door had been left unlocked, as promised.

"Lead the way," Paul said.

I pulled the door open and stepped over the spot on the sandy dirt where, a few months earlier, I had stood over a drunken Brad Culver, contemplating his murder.

"So," Paul said, "what did you do?"

"I'm sorry?" I asked.

"Where do we start?" he said.

I showed him where the tools were kept. With shovels and pitchforks, we cleared all the stalls of dung and bedding. Afterward we used wire push brushes to scrub the stalls with disinfectant, drained and rinsed the water buckets, and stored and sealed the leftover feed in rubber bins.

When we were finished, I took the tools back and locked the cabinets. When I turned back to the stable door, Paul was on the ladder leading up to the hayloft.

"Want to check it out?" he asked.

He climbed to the top of the ladder and pushed the ceiling door up and over; it landed with a soft thud. I swallowed hard and followed him up.

Paul strode across the room and flung open the loading door, flooding the room with light. On the floor in the old familiar place was the same pair of blankets I had used with Patricia. Perched atop a small nest of hay next to them was a used condom.

"Yours?" Paul asked.

I shook my head weakly.

"I guess they forgot to clean up after themselves," Paul said.

Over his shoulder, through the loading door, I could see the paddock and the ring and the driveway that led up to Twin Oaks.

"Should we get rid of the evidence?" Paul asked.

I couldn't speak.

Paul turned and bent to pick up the blankets. Tucking the blankets under his arm, he kicked a loose clump of straw up and onto the shriveled rubber.

"Come on," he said. "Let's go."

I shut and latched the loading door as Paul descended the ladder. Alone in the darkness, I looked down to where the blankets had flattened the straw. My education, I thought.

Downstairs, Paul had already placed the blankets in one of the cabinets along the wall inside the tack room.

"Anything else?" he said.

I shook my head.

"You do the honors."

I pushed the door shut and took the padlock from the bench beneath the window and closed it in the latch for what I assumed would be the last time. When I turned around, Paul was already making his way up the drive toward Twin Oaks.

"Where are you going?" I asked.

He stopped and looked back at me as if I'd asked the most foolish question imaginable.

"Don't you want to see?" he said.

I followed him, as I always had.

The sun was still well above the horizon; otherwise I'm not sure I could have found the courage to step under the yellow tape.

"We shouldn't be here," I said.

"I just want to have a look in the window," Paul said.

"Don't touch anything," I said.

Paul stepped up to the windows beside the door and peered in. Behind him I anxiously watched the long driveway.

"Come look," he said.

We couldn't see much through the partially drawn curtains, but the gap was just wide enough to reveal the giant dark stain and the outline in white tape of where the bodies had been found at the center of their dark, rusty circles. On the far wall was the bloody writing Miss Anita had described. Observing even the small fragment of the scene visible through the sliver between the curtains, I felt a preternatural apprehension come over me—an almost tangible dread, like a conscious entity, pressing against me with crackling, invisible electric force.

When I turned around, Paul was standing out in the driveway at the edge of the yellow tape, smoking. I stepped off the porch and ran out to meet him.

"What did I tell you?" he said.

"I don't know what you mean," I said.

He flicked the ash off the end of his dwindling cigarette, pinched the end with his callused fingers, and tucked the butt into the pocket of his jeans.

"I told you they were going to get theirs, didn't I?" he said.

23

NEVER BEFORE HAD THE Spottswood County Sheriff's Office dealt with a case of such sensational magnitude. Crime scene investigators from the state police offices in Richmond were invited in to go over the evidence. The FBI had sent an agent, the newspaper rather breathlessly reported, who specialized in profiling serial killers. The Spencerville City Police also offered their dubious expertise. All these various arms of law enforcement coalesced into the auspiciously named Twin Oaks Task Force.

The first task, it seemed, was the pursuit of office space. By the time I arrived at school Monday morning, word had already spread through the halls of Randolph High that the Twin Oaks murder investigation was being conducted right on our own campus, in the field house annex. Bobby Carwile had mentioned to an old pal who happened to be an assistant football coach at Randolph that the sheriff's office didn't have the room to accommodate all the visiting experts. The coach suggested that they use the annex, which had originally been built to house a long-defunct vocational arts program and had since been claimed as office space by the football staff, which essentially meant it wasn't much more than a place for the male coaches to go take a nap or dip snuff during school hours. It was a public building, closer to the crime scene than the Spottswood County Sheriff's Office, with plenty of room—an ideal spot to base a law enforcement task force. Apparently when the city superintendent of schools agreed to the request, he had done so without fully considering the monumental distraction an active murder investigation would be to a thousand high school students.

At lunch, Cinnamon and I took up our usual position beneath

the tree outside the smoking pavilion. Down the hill, clusters of students gathered at the end of the yard against the fence over-looking the track and the field house annex.

"I don't know what they think they're going to see," Cinnamon said.

"Maybe a devil-worshipping hippie maniac being pulled out of the back of a squad car," I said.

Inspired, Cinnamon perched her cigarette in the corner of her mouth and pulled her sketch pad and a box of charcoal sticks and pencils from her shoulder bag. With quick, graceful strokes of charcoal she outlined the shape of a lanky, bearded man with glowering eyes, clutching a dripping knife the size of a machete. Instead of feet, she drew cloven hooves. From between his legs curled a rather phallic forked tail; from beneath his bushy hair, a pair of pointed horns. She held the picture up and grinned.

"Nice," I said. "I think I'll have it framed."

She tossed the smoking butt of her cigarette into the grass at her feet and stamped it out under the soles of her cherry-red sixteen-hole Dr. Martens.

I told her about seeing Patricia and her new boyfriend in the pasture.

"Seems kind of cold," Cinnamon said, "going horseback riding in front of the house where her parents got murdered."

"The horses needed to be exercised," I said. "They'd been stuck in the stalls for a few days. Somebody had to do it."

"What about you?" Cinnamon said. "How did it feel to see her?"

"I don't know," I said. "She wasn't herself. It was weird, seeing her all—I don't know—sentimental."

"What did you think of her boyfriend?" Cinnamon asked.

"He's, like, twelve," I said.

"Seriously?"

"No. But he couldn't be more than nineteen or twenty. My mom heard he was a freshman in college, but he quit and decided to do the horse thing instead. Nelson Waltrip. That's his name. Have you ever heard anything so douchey in all your life?"

I told Cinnamon about the surprise Paul and I had found in the hayloft.

"What a bitch," Cinnamon said.

"I don't know. Paul thought it was as good a way as any to get your mind off things," I said. "They must have forgotten they left it there."

"Bullshit," Cinnamon said.

She lit another cigarette.

"Don't be so sad, Rocky," she said.

"I'm not," I said. "It was over a long time ago."

"You don't look like you're over it," she said.

I looked down at the grass. "Like I said, it's just weird."

"Well, cheer up," she said. "You've still got Mr. LaPage."

"Hilarious," I said.

We stood and shouldered our bags. Cinnamon took a final drag before flipping the butt off into the yard toward the annex building, where a crowd of students still pressed up to the fence, hoping to see something remarkable.

I rode the bus that afternoon; Paul had said he had something to do. When I got home, a white panel van and a pair of police cruisers were parked in front of Twin Oaks. Charles Culver would have arrived by then, I thought. I wondered whether he and Patricia had been allowed to go inside.

I found my mother alone at the kitchen table, staring down into an empty coffee cup. She had taken the afternoon off to meet with the Realtor.

"How did it go?" I asked.

"Well, the good news is, we won't be showing the house for a while," she said.

The reasons were obvious enough. Who would want to go out to pick up the newspaper every morning and have to look up across the field at the murder house?

"So what do we do now?" I asked.

"Something will work out," she said. "It always does."

The doorbell rang.

"You see?" she said. "I'm sure that's the Realtor right now, here to tell us she's had a surprise offer, above the asking price. Salvation is always just a moment away."

I followed her out to the entry hallway to answer the door. It was not the Realtor but rather the sheriff's investigator Bobby Carwile, in his weathered chinos and necktie and the same navy blazer he'd worn when he visited us the day before.

"Hello there," Bobby Carwile said. "Is your mom home?"

Over his shoulder, I could see another white van, just like the one in the driveway at Twin Oaks. Two men wearing navy-blue jackets with the word POLICE emblazoned in yellow across the back were removing a series of what looked like fishing tackle boxes from the open rear doors.

"Hello, ma'am," Carwile said.

"How can I help you?" said my mother.

"I just thought, if you didn't mind, that I might ask you a few more questions."

"Who are they?" my mother asked, pointing at the two men behind the panel van.

"Oh, they're just some boys from Richmond, come to help us out," Carwile said. "I thought if it was OK with you, they might look around some. It's standard procedure."

A look of confusion crept over my mother's face.

"We just want to make sure there aren't any signs that your house has been bothered by the same people who did this," Carwile said.

A car appeared at the end of the driveway—a black BMW M3, speeding toward us. The car skidded to a halt behind the van. Rayner Newcomb stepped out from the driver's side door, dressed in a generously cut gray suit and pink tie, what hair he had left smoothed to his head with some sort of pomade. In the passenger seat was Paul.

"Sorry I'm late," Rayner said.

"Late?" my mother said.

"Come on, now, Carwile," Rayner said. "You weren't planning on interviewing my client without her attorney present, were you?"

Bobby Carwile turned back to my mother.

"Now what would you need an attorney for, ma'am?"

"I don't," my mother said. "Do I?"

"Bobby, really," Rayner said. "I thought you had better manners."

"Now, what are you up to, Ray?" Carwile asked.

"It's like my daddy told me they used to say when he was a kid during the war," Rayner drawled, his mouth widening into an unseemly grin. "*Loose lips sink ships.*"

Carwile smiled uneasily at my mother.

"Don't let Ray here frighten you, ma'am. Like I said, we're here for your benefit," he said. "And for your protection."

My mother glanced at Rayner, who shook his head slowly. Then she looked back at Carwile.

"Can I have a minute, Detective?" she asked.

"Yes, ma'am," said Carwile, a hint of resignation in his voice.

Rayner and Paul approached the stairs and brushed past Carwile and the crime lab boys and into the house.

"How did you know to come here, Rayner?" my mother asked.

"Those rubes from the sheriff's office never had anything this interesting happen to them in their entire lives, Mrs. Askew," Rayner said. "They couldn't keep a secret to stay out of hell."

My mother looked at the door as if she were breaching decorum to leave the genial Bobby Carwile standing too long on the stoop.

"He told me it was for our benefit," my mother said.

"How could it possibly benefit you to have those men handling your belongings, Mrs. Askew?" Rayner asked.

"But we haven't anything to hide," she said. "Have we, Paul?"

"Remember what happened with the Old Man and the kitchen knife, Alice?" Paul said.

"How could I forget?" my mother said.

"They interviewed William this morning," Paul said. "He told them everything."

It would be unfair to condemn William as a traitor for telling the truth. Perhaps he was afraid of being accused himself. Or perhaps he was just naive. I was willing to consider any possibility other than the notion that William might take revenge for the loss of his job by pointing a finger at any of us—least of all the Old Man.

"You don't think they suspect Dick!" my mother said. "That's just foolishness."

"Mrs. Askew, people are scared," Rayner said. "These yokels haven't got a clue who did this. They will grasp at any straw that presents itself to them."

My mother scowled at Paul, as if she were certain that, one way or another, this was all his doing.

"And what if they have a warrant?" she asked Rayner.

"If they had a warrant, ma'am," Rayner said, "they wouldn't be sitting out there waiting for your permission."

My mother sighed.

"All right then," my mother said. "What do we do, Rayner?"

"Are you retaining me as counsel, Mrs. Askew?" Rayner asked.

"I'll warn you, Rayner," my mother said. "We're flat broke."

Rayner couldn't contain his glee.

"I know that, ma'am," he said.

Paul rolled his eyes and sighed.

"So what am I to tell young Mr. Carwile?" my mother asked.

"Leave everything to me," Rayner said.

Rayner opened the front door with a flourish. The crime lab men were back down behind the panel van having a smoke. Bobby Carwile stood on the porch, his hand on the railing, one foot planted on the topmost step, his face darkening with politely restrained fury.

"You're welcome to come in, Investigator," Rayner said. "But you'll have to leave the dogs outside."

Carwile's interview with my mother lasted half an hour. Paul and I were dismissed to the kitchen. Paul prepared coffee while I crept back out to eavesdrop.

Bobby Carwile respectfully questioned my mother, patiently tolerating Rayner's interjections. Many of the questions puzzled me until Rayner was able to clarify them all for us after Bobby Carwile and his posse left. I did not know then, for instance, about the bullet that had been removed from Brad Culver's thigh. So it had seemed strange to me when Carwile asked my mother whether the Old Man had ever owned a .38-caliber pistol and whether it was still in our possession.

My mother answered truthfully that she had given all the guns in the house to Paul to dispose of when she began to worry that the Old Man might accidentally shoot himself or someone else, and that Paul had told her he'd sold them, with Rayner's help. Rayner explained that he himself had purchased the gun as a favor to Paul. Rayner also offered, without being asked, to produce the gun for the police to inspect.

Carwile also surprised me by asking my mother whether it was true that she had given Leigh Bowman a pair of women's size 9 running shoes and whether Leigh had ever returned the shoes. Yes, my mother said, she had given Leigh the shoes, and no, Leigh had not yet returned them. Carwile explained that one of the scant bits of evidence collected from the crime scene was the imprint in mud outside the sliding glass door at the rear of the house of a size 9 running shoe.

"If I showed you a pair of shoes, could you tell me if they were the same ones you gave Leigh Bowman?"

"I don't know," my mother said. "Maybe."

"And the knife your husband had with him when William Nowlin brought him home that afternoon," Carwile asked. "Do you still have that knife?"

William Nowlin, I thought. It was the first time I'd ever heard his last name.

"I don't know which knife it was," my mother said.

"Would you mind if I had a look at your knives, Mrs. Askew?" Carwile asked.

"I don't think that's a good idea," Rayner said.

"Why not?" my mother asked.

Behind me, Paul paced the kitchen floor. I pressed my ear harder against the door, trying not to miss any of the conversation. So absorbed were we all that we had forgotten about the Old Man. None of us heard him rise and steal away down the corridor and through the entrance hall, his shuffling steps and the halting progress of his walker muffled by his thick wool socks and the set of four tennis balls William had thoughtfully sliced open and placed over the four prongs of the walker's legs to soften the impact on the Old Man's arthritic shoulders. I became aware of his presence only when I heard his voice break into the conversation, stunning all of us with his bellowing.

"I killed that son of a bitch," the Old Man boomed. "And I'd do it again!"

24

IT TOOK ALL THREE of us to subdue the Old Man. Paul and I dragged him back to the Royal Chamber, where my mother talked him down while we held him in his armchair. We spoke calmingly to him until the tension in his grip released. I stood and stepped back and worked the ache out of my palm where the Old Man had grasped it. Paul knelt at his side.

"It's all right, Dad," Paul said.

"I did it," the Old Man mumbled.

"No, you didn't, Dad," said Paul.

"Yes, I did," he moaned. "I did them both."

"No, you didn't, Dad," Paul repeated.

The Old Man looked up at Paul with wet, pleading eyes.

"Run, boy," he whispered. "While you still can!"

"I'm staying right here, Dad," Paul said. "Right here with you."

His voice was soothing; his eyes were warm and unworried. He stroked the leathery, liver-spotted skin of the Old Man's hand, which was clutching his own.

RAYNER HAD GOTTEN rid of Bobby Carwile. He handed my mother a business card.

"Here," Rayner said. "If they come back, you call me right away."

My mother held the card out in front of her as if it were stained with bird shit.

"Thank you, Rayner," my mother said.

"Call anytime," Rayner said. "Day or night."

Paul left with Rayner to retrieve his truck, promising he'd be back in time to take me to rehearsal. But I didn't really care. I wouldn't have been angry at him if he'd never come back at all.

Part of me hoped that he wouldn't—that he would run, like the Old Man had begged him to.

Paul returned just in time for supper—boiled cabbage and kielbasa sautéed with onions. Only the Old Man seemed interested at all in food.

Paul pushed his chair back and stood.

"Come on," he said. "You're going to be late."

As usual, I walked around to the driver's side. Wordlessly I started the engine, shifted into first gear, and eased the car down the driveway, turning slowly onto Boone's Ferry. We had turned onto Riverdale before Paul noticed it—or at least before he pointed it out to me.

"Look," he said, pointing at the rearview mirror.

The police cruiser was unmarked but not inconspicuous, thanks to the searchlight mounted above the driver's side-view mirror.

Paul took his pack of cigarettes from the breast pocket of his coat and shook one up into his mouth, then replaced the pack and removed his Zippo and lit up.

"Where were you on Thursday, Paul?" I asked.

"I told you," he said. "Over at Rayner's."

He took a long drag and exhaled slowly.

"And Leigh was with you?" I asked.

"That's right," he said.

"And what about that call from Judge Bowman, Paul?" I asked. "What about the skinny-dipping?"

Paul chuckled dryly. Why was I even bothering to ask him these questions? What did I expect him to tell me?

"Coming over to pick you up, I saw her peddling down the road," he said. "Her clothes and hair were soaking wet. She'd gone out for a ride after dinner on the path down by Hat Creek. She'd steered too close to the edge, she said, and had fallen in. Well, I couldn't take her home all soaked and covered in creek mud. After her little climb up onto the roof at Twin Oaks, I figured old Prentiss was a hair away from having her shipped back to the loony bin. So I took her over to Rayner's so she could clean up and throw her clothes in the dryer before I took her home. Rayner's wife heard the shower running and woke up. When she saw Leigh come out of the bathroom wearing Rayner's clothes, she jumped to the wrong conclusion, so we had to leave in a bit of a hurry."

"I think I'd be a little scared of the woman who could get Rayner to kick his friends out of the house," I said.

"Yeah, no kidding," Paul said. "Anyway, I knew I was late to pick you up, so I came up with the skinny-dipping story. I told Leigh it'd be better for her if she just let the old bastard lay it on me."

Leigh tumbling off her bicycle into an icy creek was more plausible, I supposed, than her collaborating with Paul to commit a heinous double murder. Wasn't it?

"I guess that explains why you were acting so weird," I said.

"What do you mean?"

"You know," I said. "When you picked us up. You were just acting weird, that's all."

Paul lit another cigarette and sighed angrily.

"Well, Rocky," he said, "what can I tell you? Watching the love of your life fall to pieces right before your eyes might make you act a little *weird*. Knowing that you played a big part in her being so royally fucked up—yeah, you know, that might make you act a little *fucking odd*. It might drive you out of your own *fucking mind* every now and then, don't you think?"

By then we had reached the school. I pulled the truck to a stop at the curb in front of the loading dock.

"You never told me that before," I said.

"What?" he asked.

"That Leigh was the love of your life."

"Christ," Paul said, exasperated. "Do I have to say it?"

We sat alone in the darkness. Behind us, the police cruiser was at the far edge of the parking lot, presumably trying to look inconspicuous.

"If Leigh is the love of your life, Paul," I asked quietly, "why'd you let her go off on her own? Why didn't you come after her?"

"I've been asking myself that question for a long time," he said. "But you know what, Rocky? You can't change the past. You just have to find a way to live with it."

I couldn't help myself.

"Paul?" I said.

"What?" Paul asked.

"What shoes was Leigh wearing when you found her that night?" I asked.

Paul opened the door and stepped out. He flipped his cigarette into the grass behind him.

"Shit, Rocky," he said. "If you really believe I had something to do with what happened to those people, surely you don't think I'd have any trouble lying to *you* about it."

25

THE NEXT DAY, AS we sat under our tree at lunch, Cinnamon surprised me with an unexpected proposition.

"Hey," she said. "I want to come over to your place today. After school."

"Why?" I asked.

"To see the murder house," she said.

I doubt I was very successful at concealing my excitement.

"Yeah," I said. "Sure. OK."

"Great," she said.

"Paul can give us a ride back for rehearsal," I said. "He lets me drive."

Cinnamon nodded.

"Cool," she said.

Idiot, I thought. Just shut up already. What did Paul say? Girls don't like it when you act like you care.

"I can't wait to meet your mom," she said. "Do you think she'll like me?"

"No," I said.

A fluttering of voices rose up from the crowd at the end of the yard.

Cinnamon stood and trudged through the tall grass, me trailing after. We arrived at the fence just in time to see Leigh Bowman setting her bicycle with the wide seat and the basket on the handlebars into the bike rack in front of the annex before calmly walking inside.

"Maybe she's going to read to them," Cinnamon said.

Leigh's surprising appearance at the annex somewhat dampened my excitement about taking Cinnamon home with me and showing her Twin Oaks. The rest of the afternoon, the halls were atwitter with the rumor that Leigh Bowman had turned herself in to the police. I overheard one voice say she'd had the murder weapon in her bicycle basket. Someone else claimed to know for a fact that her father was forcing Leigh to testify against Paul Askew. The word had already been circulating for days that Judge Bowman's influence was the only reason Paul and Leigh hadn't been arrested already. Everyone seemed to expect an announcement that the case had been solved on the five o'clock news.

By the time the bell at the end of eighth period rang and the herd flowed out from a dozen different doors and down to the buses and the cars in the student lot, Leigh's bicycle was gone. When Paul's truck pulled up to the curb in front of the loading dock, the rubberneckers shifted their attention, drawing away from the annex to form a line at the edge of the sidewalk, staring and pointing at Paul like he was one of the giant pandas at the National Zoo.

"What's with them?" he said as Cinnamon and I climbed into the truck next to him.

"You don't know?" I said.

We told him what we had seen that afternoon during lunch period.

"Shit," Paul said. "I told her not to do that."

"Do what?" I asked.

"Leigh's crazy, but she's not ignorant," Paul said. "She knows what people are saying. Somehow she got it in her head that she ought to just go down and introduce herself to the task force boys. Set the record straight, so to speak. I told her it was a bad idea. So did Rayner. And Miss Anita. And Judge Bowman. It might be the first time that old bastard and I ever agreed about anything."

He lit a cigarette and reached across me to offer the light to Cinnamon.

"It's probably fine," he said. "You only need to talk to Leigh for about a minute to see how harmless she is."

As we reached the midpoint of the driveway, Twin Oaks came

into view at the top of the hill, rising up from the pasture. Even Cinnamon had to stop and stare speechlessly when she got her first full glimpse of the white columns across the long field, greener every day with the onset of spring. The yellow crime scene tape still encircled the house, but there was no sign of any vehicles or police presence in the driveway.

Paul parked and went in to check on the Old Man, leaving us alone at the fence looking up at Twin Oaks.

"Shall we?" I said.

When we reached the house, we stopped in front of the yellow tape, which fluttered in the light breeze. Cinnamon bent and deftly ducked under the sagging plastic as if it were electrified.

"Where do I look?" she whispered.

"Here," I said.

I stepped up to the window first and peered through. The sight was the same—the sliver of space between the shades revealing the dark, almost black stains on the floor and the rusty characters on the wall. I stepped back so Cinnamon could take my place at the window.

"Wow," she said. "This is heavy."

"Yeah," I said.

I should have been thinking about important things—the gruesomeness of what had happened on the other side of that door, whether Paul and Leigh were responsible for it, how they were going to get out from under the weight of the gossip and suspicion, and so forth. Instead I thought of whether Cinnamon was impressed—whether she genuinely liked me and whether the next time she kissed me it would be on the mouth instead of the cheek. So distracted was I by these thoughts that I had been staring at the sheriff's department squad car coming up the road past our house and toward the driveway of Twin Oaks for at least five seconds or so without registering it. By the time I reacted, the patrol car was turning through the gate.

"Shit," I said.

"What is it?" Cinnamon asked.

"Come on," I said.

We dashed down to the end of the porch and dropped into the mulch of the flower beds. Ducking around the side of the house, we huddled against the wall and waited as the car pulled in and came to a stop. We heard the doors open and slam shut, followed by voices I recognized as they drew closer to our hiding place.

"I don't suppose we can take down this dreadful yellow tape," Patricia said.

"It won't be long, ma'am," Bobby Carwile said. "We'll be finished here in another day or two. Then we'll have a crew come out and take care of everything for you. I can recommend a good cleaning service also, when you're ready."

"That won't be necessary," Patricia replied. "I'll take care of it."

"Don't be ridiculous, Patricia," said Charles Culver.

"It's what Mummy would have wanted," Patricia said.

"What Mummy would have wanted?" said Charles, derisively aping Patricia's bogus accent.

"That's right," Patricia meekly replied.

"Please," Charles said scornfully. "You sound like a fool."

Cinnamon couldn't resist peering around the corner for a look. There was no point in trying to stop her; besides, I wanted to have a look myself.

The three of them faced the door together, preparing to enter: Carwile in his usual navy blazer, tie, and chinos; Charles in a tan trench coat that hid his soft frame, making him look somehow more imposing than I remembered. Patricia wore a calf-length tweed skirt, a tan camel-hair blazer, and a patterned blouse buttoned to the neck. She'd cut her hair into a pageboy style that had the effect of making her look curiously sexless.

Poor Patricia, I thought. She was so dazed. All the pompous bluster had gone out of her, replaced by a faint hint of anguish.

The three of them stepped inside and shut the door behind them.

"Let's go," I whispered.

We scampered over into the trees.

"Wow," Cinnamon said. "That was freaky."

The field between the two houses was bordered on one side by Boone's Ferry Road and on the other side by woods that lined the path down to the barn. To avoid being seen from the windows of Twin Oaks, we walked through the trees, listening to the wind.

"So that was Patricia, huh?" Cinnamon asked.

"Yeah."

"And the other man, besides the cop—that was her brother, Charles, right?"

I nodded.

"He seemed like kind of an asshole," she said.

"I've never heard him talk to anyone like that before," I said. "I haven't hung around him much, but still. I'm sure they're both pretty messed up about what happened. Paul says people grieve in different ways. Like, what's the right way to act after your parents get murdered?"

"Maybe they did it," she said.

I hadn't given much thought to that possibility; I'd been too worried about whether Paul and Leigh were responsible to consider anyone else besides devil worshippers and Manson acolytes.

"I don't know," I said. "I don't think so."

It couldn't have been Charles, or Patricia, I thought. Both of their whereabouts at the time of the killings were well known. Charles had been out of the country on business. Patricia had been in Maryland with Nelson Waltrip, spending a long weekend going to the races at Pimlico and visiting friends in Annapolis. The police had to send someone out to the track to find her when the bodies were discovered.

We came out of the woods behind the stable, out of sight of the house. Looking up at the shuttered door of the hayloft, I remembered what Paul had found in the straw by the blankets. Was that the right way to act after your parents have been murdered? Maybe there wasn't a better one. Maybe it wasn't her idea—Nelson Waltrip might have begged or persuaded or even *forced* her to do it. Maybe it hadn't been them at all—maybe it had been left by the killers, or even by Brad Culver himself, getting a little action on the side. Maybe that's why it happened; maybe the killer was just a vengeful cuckold who had covered his tracks with the devil-worship stuff and the bullet in the leg.

Cinnamon reached into her bag for a cigarette and lit up.

"What are you thinking about?" she asked.

"Nothing," I said.

But I was thinking about a lot of things: About how frumpy and plain Patricia had looked back on the porch of Twin Oaks, and how the sight of her looking that way had made me both sad and a little embarrassed, as if I'd wanted her to look sexier so that Cinnamon would be impressed, or jealous, or even a little threatened. About everything that had happened in and around the stable, from the night I'd found Culver staggering drunk and helped him back up to the house, and what happened afterward with Patricia, to the day Leigh interrupted us and drove me off to make her confession. And I thought about Cinnamon—how much I wanted to be taken seriously by her, how I had hoped things would turn out that afternoon, and how differently they were going.

"Sorry," I said. "This is a little weird."

Cinnamon puffed out a bit of smoke and smiled. There we were—me and my Cinnamon Girl, alone in the woods with the whispering wind and sun-dappled ground beneath the spare shade of early spring leaves.

She stepped toward me. I reached tentatively for her hips.

"It's all right," she said. "I want you to."

I kissed her—thanks to Patricia, I thought—less inexpertly than she might have expected.

It would be silly to say that we were in love. After all, I had only ever kissed one girl before—one woman, to be more precise. But the sensation that came over me in that moment was completely, overwhelmingly, sublimely *new*. And though Cinnamon was no innocent, nor was I, what passed between us there felt pure and good and true.

. . .

WHEN WE REACHED the house, we found Leigh's bicycle leaning against the front porch steps. Back in the Royal Chamber, we found the Old Man in his armchair, Leigh on the couch facing him, a book open on her lap. Paul sat next to her, one leg propped across his other knee, stroking his beard. They looked so natural together, as if they'd never been apart.

"This is Cinnamon," I said.

"Cinnamon?" the Old Man asked. "What the hell kind of name is that?"

"Oh, hush, Mr. Askew," Leigh said. "I think it's lovely."

To my surprise, Cinnamon blushed.

"We were just about to have tea," Paul said. "Would you care for some?"

"Sure, I'll have some *tea*," Cinnamon said, sniggering slightly, as if taking tea in the afternoon was a ritual unique to the Boone's Ferry bourgeoisie.

Paul went to the kitchen. Leigh closed her book and placed it on the coffee table. She looked different. She had on makeup—nothing garish, just a touch of blush and eyeliner and pink lip gloss. She'd spent a little more time on her hair, which was still short but had grown enough to look less severe. She wore a navy V-neck sweater and a pair of new jeans. I wondered whether someone had advised that she try to look more normal.

"What are we reading?" I asked.

"*Rebecca Recalls*," Leigh said.

"I've heard of that book," Cinnamon said. "People have been passing it around at school. It's supposed to be pretty twisted."

"It's a true story," Leigh said.

"Do you mind?" the Old Man said. "It was just getting good."

"Sure, Mr. Askew," Leigh said.

The Old Man crossed his arms and nodded. Leigh resumed her reading.

Rebecca Recalls was the true story of how the author, Dr. Susan Gregory, was treating a patient named Rebecca for depression after the stillbirth of her baby. Using hypnotherapy, Dr. Gregory helps

Rebecca recover lost memories of years of ritual abuse at the hands of a satanic cult, which she'd been brainwashed to forget. Through hypnotherapy, Rebecca recollects that her own mother—a closet devil worshipper—had offered her up years earlier as a pawn to the cult, which included numerous highly placed members of the local community. According to the text, these putative civic pillars regularly participated in child rape and sacrifice for the pleasure of the Evil One. To hide their activities, the cult members brainwashed their sex slaves and performed their human sacrifices with babies stolen from the maternity ward at the local hospital. There, numerous doctors and nurses who were also secret cult members manipulated indigent single mothers into believing that their babies had died of natural causes; in some cases they were able to seduce the mothers themselves into joining the cult. Dr. Gregory teaches young Rebecca about the love of Jesus and helps her to be "born again." With God's help, doctor and patient do battle against the nefarious cult, ultimately taking on the devil himself. It would all have seemed ridiculous were it not so effectively unnerving.

Paul had returned with the tea tray and sat down as Leigh read. The Old Man drifted off and began to snore. Leigh folded the book shut, and the four of us rose quietly and retreated up the stairs to Paul's room. Paul took his chair by the window and lit up; Leigh sat on the floor next to him, where she could reach up to steal the occasional drag from his cigarette. I sat on the bed next to Cinnamon, who fired up one of her own, tipping her ashes into a saucer on the bedside table.

"That's some book you brought this week, Leigh," I said. "How did you pick that one out?"

"Oh, everyone in the Bible study is reading it," she said. "With everything that's happened, the director of Christian education at Holy Comforter has decided we all ought to get up to speed on the latest knowledge of SRA."

"SRA?" Cinnamon asked.

"Satanic ritual abuse," Leigh said.

"I thought you were talking about those standardized tests we took in elementary school," Paul said.

"You hush, Paul Askew," Leigh said. "You know precisely what I'm talking about. SRA has been all over the news, with the McMartin Preschool trial and whatnot."

Even before the Twin Oaks killings, congregants of various churches had been circulating books and pamphlets containing information about cult activity and satanic ritual abuse. Still, no one—least of all Leigh—could pretend that the sudden interest in SRA around Spencerville had much to do with the McMartin Preschool trial. The whole town knew about the bullet in the leg by then, and Leigh's bizarre scaling of the roof of Twin Oaks, and the borrowed track shoes. Everyone also knew that Paul and Leigh's alibi was dubious and that they both had good reasons to hate the Culvers, who lived just a few hundred yards away from us. It certainly didn't look good that the murders had occurred within two months of Paul's showing up out of nowhere after seven years missing, as if he had come back to settle a score. Add to that Paul and Leigh's former association with a child-molesting hippie guru and the rumors of Leigh's horrific late-term abortion, which seemed to bear discomfiting resemblance to the grisly narrative of *Rebecca Recalls*.

"How does one become an expert on satanic ritual abuse?" Paul asked.

"Some of the leading authorities are survivors," she said. "It's a true story. These cults are spreading all over the country."

"I was in what most people would call a cult," Paul said. "So were you. Do you think we have repressed memories of satanic ritual abuse?"

"I've thought about that," Leigh said. "But no, Paul. As much as I've tried to forget, I remember it all."

None of us knew what to say. It was the first time I'd heard Paul make any overt reference to New Nazareth, the first time Leigh had mentioned it since she'd first told me the story.

"We saw you over at school today," Cinnamon said to Leigh. "What was that all about?"

Leigh laughed.

"You were right," she said to Paul. "She is very direct."

"Sorry," Cinnamon said. "Just curious."

"I don't mind," Leigh said. "It's pretty simple. Since people have been saying such awful things about me, I thought I should just go have a talk with Mr. Carwile. He's such a nice man. He was very interested in what I had to say."

"I'm sure he was," Paul said.

"So what did you tell him?" I asked.

"Everything I could think of," Leigh said. "Everything they wanted to know."

"I wish you would have listened to Rayner, Leigh," Paul said.

"Please, Paul," Leigh said. "The day I look to Rayner Newcomb for advice on anything is the day I have myself committed."

I glanced at Cinnamon, expecting to catch her stifling a giggle. Instead she looked on earnestly.

"Embarrassing as it was, I told them about falling into the creek and then ending up over at Rayner's with Paul. Then they started asking about me and the Culvers—about Charles and the wedding and so forth. We ended up talking a lot about the past. You have no idea how good it felt to just unload all those things. When I told them about climbing up on the Culvers' roof to see the angels, I realized that I hadn't even thought about it much myself since it happened. Boy, that was crazy of me, wasn't it?"

No one said a word.

"It was pretty simple," Leigh continued. "I'd stopped taking my Thorazine. I was tired of feeling . . . well, tired. Numb. Half-asleep. I'd been feeling so good lately, so good that I thought I was ready to be—I don't know—*normal* again. It's very hard to accept that this is who I am now—that this is what it will always be like."

Paul reached down and grasped Leigh's shoulder. She took his hand and kissed it.

"Well," Leigh continued, "I had been thinking for a while that I'd like to see Mrs. Culver and apologize to her for how I had embarrassed her family. And I wanted to give her back the ring and tell her that I wasn't angry with Charles about the way things ended between us. I had Paul back, after all. It seemed like it was meant to be."

She squeezed his hand.

"Right when I got to Twin Oaks," she said, "I had my vision."

"Your vision?" Cinnamon asked.

"Of the angels, swirling around above me. I know everyone thinks I'm mad," she said, "and I understand the chemical explanations. But these visions are more real to me than anyone here in this room."

She smiled.

"The world we see is just a partial impression of what's all around us," she said.

She studied the palms of her upturned hands.

"To see such beauty," she said, "is overwhelming."

"I get that," Cinnamon said. "Totally."

Paul lit another cigarette.

"You've really got to quit, Paul," Leigh said.

"I quit everything else that's bad for me," he said. "Let me have this one thing."

"For your health, darling," she said.

"You sneak one every now and then," he replied.

"Only because you're a terrible *enabler*," Leigh said.

Here they were, thrown together again, playfully chiding each other like an old married couple. Wasn't that what I'd always wanted?

"What did you think the police thought of your story?" I asked.

"Oh, I'm sure they just think I'm a loon," Leigh said.

"Do you think they believed you about being over at Rayner's on Thursday night?" Paul asked.

"You never know," she said. "There's no love for Rayner Newcomb on the Twin Oaks Task Force."

"He has that effect on people," Paul said.

"So how did you and Bobby Carwile leave things?" I asked.

"Unresolved," she said.

I walked to the window and looked out across the field to Twin Oaks. The patrol car had left with Charles and Patricia and whatever they had come for.

"They were there earlier," I said. "Charles and Patricia. With Bobby Carwile. But they're gone now."

"We went over to peep at the murder house," Cinnamon said.

"That's what the kids at school are calling it," I said.

"We almost got caught," Cinnamon said.

"They drove up while we were there," I said. "We had to hide behind the house. Did you know Charles was in town?"

"I saw him yesterday, over at Kiki Baumberger's," Leigh said. "I went over to see Patricia, and he happened to be there. We had a nice visit, all things considered."

"Sounds a little awkward to me," said Cinnamon.

"It was a bit chilly, to tell you the truth," Leigh said. "I don't think Charles is convinced I'm not somehow responsible for all of this. Then again, he's the first to point out that a lot of people over the years have wanted his father dead."

"How is Patricia?" I asked.

"Oh, she's distraught," Leigh said.

"She'll feel better once she collects her inheritance," Paul said.

"But there is no inheritance," Leigh said. "Mr. Culver lost almost everything in the same deal that ruined your poor father. They'd been living off Charles for months. Patricia had no idea her father had been paying her allowance with money given to him by Charles."

The Culvers' lives had seemed to go on completely untouched by the disaster that had left us penniless and on the verge of losing our home. It had never occurred to any of us that Brad Culver might have been just as broke as the Old Man. Again I remembered what Paul had told me—that the Culvers would get theirs. Boy, did they ever, I thought. Once more I thought of Patricia—how desperate she must have felt, losing her parents that way and also learning that she was going to have to find a way to survive just like the rest of us mortals.

"Poor Patricia," I said, almost unconsciously and with complete sincerity.

"She's understandably mortified," Leigh said. "She and Charles don't have the chummiest relationship. But for now, she's going to have to depend on him."

"Or get a job," Paul said, lighting another cigarette. "Bless her heart."

26

AT THE NEXT REHEARSAL, we ran Cinnamon's scenes as Alan's mother. Cinnamon struggled vainly to put on the guise of a sorely repressed religious fanatic. I tried to reassure myself that she would be more convincing in costume. Observing her awkward efforts, I began to suspect that Rex LaPage's casting of Cinnamon was not a gesture of charitable goodwill but rather one of perverse irony. To her credit, Cinnamon went at it gamely, with a sort of wink-and-nod self-awareness.

When Cinnamon was done, LaPage called for a ten-minute break to go over lighting cues with the stage crew. We drifted to the rear of the house. Cinnamon took a seat in the back row and lit up.

"What'd you think?" she asked.

"You were great," I said. "Really."

"Don't make fun of me," she said.

"I mean it," I said.

Cinnamon abruptly stood and pointed.

"Look," she said.

Someone was striding purposefully down the aisle toward the stage. When he reached the orchestra pit, his face came into the footlights. It was Paul.

"Excuse me, sir," Mr. LaPage said, his voice high and shrill. "Can I help you?"

I ran over to Paul.

"It's my brother, Mr. LaPage," I said.

Whispers fluttered among the students lingering in the wings and scattered around the house. Richard's brother, they must have been saying. The murderer. For weeks the cast and crew had politely ignored the elephant in the room—that is, the fact that one of the play's two leads slept under the same roof as the prime suspect in the Twin Oaks slayings. But I knew people were talking about it. Now here he was, right in their midst—the Boone's Ferry bogeyman himself.

"What is it, Paul?" I asked.

Rayner must have found something out, I thought. Paul was going to be arrested. He'd ditched his tail somehow and risked everything to say a hasty good-bye before running away again, this time forever.

"Come on," Paul said. "You've got to come with me."

"We're in the middle of a rehearsal, sir," said Mr. LaPage, a little more politely.

My mind flashed back to that unforgettable day when I stood in the hallway outside the principal's office at my elementary school, Paul beside me in his navy blazer and Macon Prep regimental tie, asking me to follow him out the door.

"I can't," I said.

"Rocky," Paul said. "It's the Old Man."

WHEN WE REACHED the hospital, Miss Anita and Leigh were already there, waiting in the hallway.

"Is he dead?" I asked.

"No, darling. It's not his time," Miss Anita said, as if to suggest she was not guessing. Leigh looked less certain. She had been with the Old Man when it hit, Paul had said.

"Go to your father, boys," Miss Anita said.

He lay in the bed with the covers pulled up to his chin. My mother sat beside him, caressing his forehead. I came closer and leaned down toward the Old Man's face. He slipped his hands from beneath the covers and clutched mine and pulled me down so that his sour breath filled my nostrils.

I looked down into his watery eyes. His chin quivered violently. My hands began to throb with pain as he clenched them tighter. It seemed impossible that anyone on the verge of death could have such a grip. He seemed desperate to say something to me—some last bit of wisdom to serve as a lantern on the shadowy path of the future—but he was unable to find the words. This frightened me more even than the shaking or the horror in his eyes—the Old Man rendered incapable of speech.

I peeled my hands from his stiff, powerful fingers and moved to my mother's side. Paul took my place on the bed. The Old Man pulled him down so that their faces were almost touching and mumbled something incoherent. Paul softly hushed him, as if he were trying to lull an infant to sleep. At last the shaking subsided. The Old Man's hands relaxed and fell to his side, and his eyes slowly narrowed and closed. His chest rose and fell, exhaling a long, raspy gasp.

Paul stood up from the bed and tiptoed to the door. My mother and I followed him out into the hallway.

"Is he dead?" I asked for the second time.

"No," my mother said. "No, honey, he's not dead."

Of course he wasn't dead. The machines attached to the wires on his chest and shoulders still beeped. Peering back into the room, I could see his medicine-ball belly still rising and falling.

My mother reached for Paul's shoulder as if she wanted to hug him. For a moment it seemed as if they were on the verge of making their peace with each other. She stopped short, however, when she looked past him down the hallway, where she saw Bobby Carwile making his way toward us, followed by a uniformed sheriff's deputy.

"Oh, my," my mother said.

Carwile grasped his hands in front of his waist.

"Hello, Mrs. Askew," he said. "Paul."

"What do you want?" my mother asked, her voice curt, almost angry.

"We just need you to come along and answer a few questions for us, Paul," Carwile said. "Help us rule some things out."

"What if I say no?" Paul said.

"I'd rather you didn't," Carwile said.

"Surely you know why we're here," my mother said. "Must you do this now?"

"It's all right, Alice," Paul said. "My truck's in the visitor lot, Bobby. I'll meet you over at the school."

"Why don't you just ride with us, Paul?" Carwile said.

"What for, Bobby?" Paul said. "My escort isn't going to let me skip town."

"It'll be easier if you come with us, Paul," Carwile replied. "Understand?"

Paul's eyes widened. Even with the beard disguising the rest of his features, I could see that he was startled—even afraid. The look on Carwile's face was almost pleading. I realized what was happening. Paul was being arrested; Bobby Carwile just didn't want to cuff him and read him his rights in the hospital with all those people around and the Old Man on the other side of the door, fighting for what was left of his life. Carwile was trying to be a gentleman about it all.

"All right," Paul said. "I guess you can give me a ride."

Miss Anita and Leigh returned just as they were taking Paul away.

"Where are you taking him?" Miss Anita said.

"Pardon me, ma'am," Bobby Carwile said.

"Shame on you, young man," Miss Anita said, as if he'd made some minor breach of social etiquette like refusing to open a door for a lady.

"It's all right, Miss Anita," Paul said.

"I'm coming with you," Leigh said.

"That would be fine, Miss Bowman," Carwile said.

"She's not going anywhere with you," Miss Anita said.

Carwile looked at Paul as if appealing for his assistance. Paul shrugged.

"Her father's not going to like this one bit, young man," Miss Anita said.

"Mrs. Holt—" Carwile started.

"It's all right, Miss Anita," Leigh said. "I want to go with Paul."

She smiled and took Paul's hand. Together they started down the long hallway, flanked by Carwile and his deputy. We stood still as the four of them disappeared around the corner. As soon as they were gone, my mother turned without a word and started down the hall toward the pay phone, where she placed a call to Rayner Newcomb.

27

IT WAS MORE THAN a little strange walking the halls of Randolph High with everyone knowing my brother was in the field house annex, under arrest for murder. There was one upside, at least as far as Mr. LaPage was concerned: after Paul and Leigh's detainment, the box office saw an unexpected spike in advance ticket sales. Normally the spring play would attract no more than a dozen audience members who were not blood relatives of someone involved in the production. By opening night, however, all three of our scheduled performances had sold well over a hundred tickets— this for a play without a single show tune. The final Saturday night performance was nearly sold out. People must have thought it would be a sort of fun-house thrill, seeing a creepy play about madness a few hundred feet away from the building where the town loon and her evil hippie boyfriend were being detained, perhaps about to confess to what everyone had already decided they were guilty of.

Paul, at least, would never give them the satisfaction. My mother remarked that the task force boys could have saved themselves a lot of trouble if they'd just asked her how often Paul or Rayner had ever been made to admit to anything.

Paul had been booked, but Leigh was being held under something called investigative detention. No one was allowed in to see them but Rayner and the lawyer Judge Bowman had hired to represent Leigh.

"Prentiss Bowman's behind all of this," Rayner explained.

He had come to meet with my mother in the waiting room at the hospital after sitting through the first round of Paul's interrogations. The Old Man had just recovered consciousness; my mother was taking great care to hide the reason for Paul's absence from him.

"He's brought in a hotshot trial lawyer from DC," Rayner said. "They want Leigh to pin it all on Paul."

"And what does Leigh say?" my mother asked.

"Not a chance," he said.

"She told you this?"

"They won't let me see her," he said. "But if she'd given them anything they could use, the DA would have charged him already."

"So he's arrested but not charged?"

"That's right," Rayner said. "They can hold him for up to seventy-two hours. After that, they've either got to charge him, apply for an extension from the attorney general, or let him go. They have to let Leigh go tomorrow."

According to Rayner, Judge Bowman had reminded Leigh that with a word he could have her recommitted. Her choices were either to detach herself from Paul or to get hauled back to the funny farm in a straitjacket.

My mother sighed and buried her face in her hands.

"Don't worry, Mrs. Askew," Rayner said. "They've got nothing on us."

"Us?" my mother said.

"Well, they were with me on the night in question," Rayner said. "I'm the alibi."

The way he said it—smirking, almost smarmy—did nothing to allay my fear that Paul did in fact have something to hide.

THE OLD MAN was stable enough for us to go home. The next morning, my mother went back to work, and I went back to school. It was Thursday—the night of final dress rehearsal for *Equus*. That week, as we drew closer to opening night, the whole production had been overtaken by a mood that could fairly be called funereal. Only Mr. LaPage remained undaunted. For my own part, Paul's arrest had conveniently given me something else to worry about.

That day in English class, we were studying Yeats. "The center cannot hold," said Mrs. Worsham, reciting the famous lines from "The Second Coming."

"The ceremony of innocence is drowned," she said. "Surely some revelation is at hand."

The words felt weighted with personal import. Thoughts spun through my mind like Yeats's infernal rotating gyre, the tail of which descended down toward Twin Oaks, its facade gray, the eponymous trees in its foreground withered and sick with disease. I couldn't help imagining Paul as Yeats's apocalyptic messiah, the "rough beast" sent to unleash the "blood-dimmed tide" onto the Culvers' plush pile carpet.

FRIDAY MORNING, WITH opening night looming, Mr. LaPage decided to pull me into the office for a heart-to-heart, right in the middle of class. I leaned against the door while he settled into his desk chair.

"How's your daddy, honey?" he asked.

"He'll live, I guess," I said with a shrug.

"Is he going to be able to go home soon?"

"I don't know. Probably. I hope so."

"And your mother?" he asked. "How's she holding up?"

"OK," I said.

"She's a tough one, you know," he said. "A steel magnolia."

"I know," I said.

He stroked his beard and smiled gently.

"We can use Dylan, you know," he said.

Dylan was the name of my understudy.

"You can walk away," he said. "We'd all understand."

"I know," I said.

"I'll even tell everyone you came down with the flu," he said.

"I want to do it," I said. "The show must go on, right?"

LaPage smiled. He stood and rounded the desk and drew close to me.

"You can use it, you know," he said. "All the things you can't control. You won't think about it once the curtain rises. But it will be inside you. Right here."

He reached out and gently touched his finger to my chest.

"Find your deepest fear," he said, "the scariest place in your heart, and draw on it. You can do that."

"I'll try," I said.

Rex sat back on the edge of his desk. He crossed his arms and smiled.

"All life is performance, you know," he said. "And the performance is life."

Later I would wonder whether LaPage's little pep talk was more about saving the play than about consoling the mess of a kid I happened to be at that moment. Regardless, I walked out of the room believing every word.

A chill rain fell that day, but I knew Cinnamon would still be out in the yard past the pavilion, under our tree. I found her there, smoking as usual, gazing down the slope toward the throng of rubberneckers at the edge of the fence nearest to the field house annex.

"The natives are restless," Cinnamon said.

"Did something happen?" I asked.

"Leigh showed up a while ago," she said. "She came out with two old men and got into the back of a BMW."

"Judge Bowman and his lawyer," I said.

"That's not all," Cinnamon replied. "You're never going to guess who just went in."

"Who?" I asked.

"Your old girlfriend," she said. "And her new boyfriend."

"What are they doing in there?" I asked.

"Shit if I know," Cinnamon replied.

After school we hung around on the loading dock while I waited for my mother to swing by so that I could sit with the Old Man at the hospital until it was time for me to report back to Randolph for the play. Cinnamon smoked as we looked down the hill toward the field house annex, hoping to see something—some new arrival or departure that might ease the looming dread. I imagined Paul in a small room lit by a single naked lightbulb, smoking impassively while Bobby Carwile and some other more ill-mannered and imposing detective put the screws to him.

"Everything's going to be fine," she said. I nodded, but I couldn't tell her what I was thinking: that soon everything would again be as it had been for all the years before Paul showed up like a bomb dropped out of the sky that snowy February night. Leigh Bowman would go back to being an object of pity, destined to be an old spinster, pedaling around town on her bicycle with its basket full of titles from the Christian bookstore. The Old Man would continue to wither, and my mother along with him. Cinnamon would leave for California. I would go back to being another aimless, anonymous kid collecting classic rock records. And Paul would be in prison, body and soul.

THE OLD MAN was asleep in his bed when we arrived. I sat with him while my mother went to the nurses' station to sign another stack of paperwork. A few moments later, to my surprise, Leigh Bowman appeared in the doorway. I stood and motioned to her to take the seat by the bed. The Old Man opened his eyes and tilted his head toward us. When he saw Leigh there, his dry lips formed a weak smile. He shifted his hand on the bed so that the palm faced up. Leigh reached up and held it.

"Are you all right, Leigh?" I said.

She smiled and nodded weakly. Her eyes were dark and heavy with worry and weariness.

"I came as soon as I could," she said.

"I know," I replied.

"My father," she said, "has decided to involve himself."

"I know," I repeated.

"I suppose I can't hate him for thinking the worst of me after everything I've put him through," she said.

Her voice was shaky. I hoped she wasn't on the verge of another one of her episodes.

"What happened in there, Leigh?" I asked.

"It wasn't so bad," she said. "Poor Bobby Carwile. He'd rather confess to the crime himself than say an unkind word to a lady. My father, on the other hand—well, I shouldn't have been surprised. Do you know what he's saying now? That I've *repressed* it all. He wants me to talk to yet another psychiatrist who will help me remember. I know how badly he wants to get rid of Paul, but I never dreamed he'd stoop so low."

I thought of Leigh alone at the same table where I'd envisioned Paul being questioned by angry policemen in shirtsleeves, smoking cigarettes beneath a harsh white light. This time, however, it wasn't the police but rather Judge Prentiss Bowman and a gray-haired man in a white doctor's coat.

Leigh looked up suddenly.

"Do you think we did it, Rocky?" she asked. "I know what everyone else in town thinks. I know what my *father* thinks. What do you think?"

She watched me expectantly—almost imploringly. I didn't know what to say. I couldn't summon a single word.

"Oh, Rocky," she said.

The Old Man tugged on her hand. When she looked up, she met his mournful gaze. He couldn't have known what we were talking about or what had upset Leigh so. Without his hearing aids in, he was almost completely deaf. Regardless, the tenderness in his expression appeared to calm her. I wondered whether the love in his eyes could make up for the contempt she must have seen in her father's. Despite his many flaws and failings, the Old Man was never afraid to love, even when it broke his heart.

"Who would have dreamed one day I'd be interrogated like a common criminal in the Randolph High Field House Annex," she said. "I never even went inside that building when I was a student."

Her eyes drifted to the window. I imagined her thinking of

herself at sixteen, not quite carefree but beautiful and full of ardor, waiting in the parking lot at Randolph High for Paul's purple Nova to come rumbling along.

"My father can't comprehend how I would want to take up with Paul again after what happened," she said. "I'm sure plenty of other people feel the same way. You understand though, don't you, Rocky?"

My voice returned to me.

"Sure," I said. "I mean, you are a little crazy, right?"

She laughed.

"More than a little," she said.

She smiled sadly. Tears welled in her eyes.

"It all seems so remote now," she said. "Like the people we were back then never even existed."

I knew exactly how she felt.

"You once told me you wanted to forget the past," I said. "That you wanted to file it away and pretend that it never happened."

"But we don't get to do that, do we?" she said. "Even if we forget it, it's still there, like a snake in the grass, ready to strike you if you stumble too close to it."

Her glance fell back to her lap.

"I thought I'd gotten over people pitying me," she said.

I moved behind her chair and placed my hands on her shoulders. She turned her head and looked up at me. I lifted a hand to brush a wisp of hair from her face. The Old Man looked on with drowsy eyes. He hadn't yet asked for Paul. I wondered how long we would be able to put off telling him what had happened.

"I had a surprise visitor today at Daddy's house," she said.

"Patricia," I said.

"Yes," she said. "How did you know?"

"Cinnamon saw her today at school, with her boyfriend," I said. "Going into the Field House Annex."

"I didn't think they'd met."

"She saw Patricia the day I took her to look at the house," I said.

"Oh, right," Leigh said.

"Why are they here?" I asked.

"Patricia has to sign some sort of paperwork for the task force and answer a few questions about her parents and the house. She drove over as soon as she was finished. You might say she was my angel of deliverance."

"How's that?" I asked.

"Well, once she arrived, my father had to leave me alone."

She laughed uneasily.

"Patricia and Nelson are going to spend the night with Kiki Baumberger. I made the mistake of telling her your play opened tonight. I'm afraid she might come."

It seemed oddly appropriate that Patricia should be there.

"We had a long talk," Leigh said. "Her parents' deaths have really opened her up emotionally, I think. I told her Paul and I had nothing to do with what happened, and she swore she believed me. She was very philosophical about it. She said that when people are afraid, they need a face for their fear."

"She's right about that," I said.

"She asked about you, Rocky," she said. "We didn't talk about your little secret. I know she knows that I know about it. I'd never say a word—especially not in front of Nelson. Still, the way she talked about you—it was almost tender. She wanted to know all about what you've been doing. About Cinnamon. About the play. She seemed happy that things are going so well for you, in spite of all of *this*."

Her hand leaped up from her lap and flapped out like a bird with a broken wing before resettling back inside the folds of her cotton dress.

"I have to admit," Leigh said, her voice falling to a murmur, "I've felt very angry with Patricia in the past. I thought the things she did to both of us were deliberately cruel. She kept asking me to forgive her. I told her there was nothing to forgive. But she insisted that she was at fault—that I hadn't been miscast by mere circumstance. Those were her exact words—'miscast by mere circumstance.'"

I had no trouble believing Patricia would say something like that.

"Do you know what she said to me then?" Leigh asked.

I didn't answer; I had grown somewhat distracted by the thought of Patricia in the audience at the debut performance of *Equus*. Did she know the play? She must have—it was just her sort of thing. Would it stir anything in her to see me act out the role of the lovesick stable boy?

Leigh kept talking. My thoughts were elsewhere, but I was paying just enough attention to hear something that stunned me—something so unbelievable I had to ask Leigh to repeat the words in case I'd misunderstood what she'd said.

"I'm sorry," I said. "What did she say?"

"She was very sweet," Leigh murmured. "Very contrite."

"Could you say it again, please?" I asked.

Leigh sighed as if exasperated.

"You should pay better attention, Rocky," she said. "She told me, 'You know, Leigh, it's as if I'm the devil and you're the sacrificial lamb.'"

28

MY MOTHER RETURNED FROM signing forms. Leigh had drifted over to the window, where she stood gazing out at the gray sky over the parking lot.

"Tell her, Leigh," I said.

"Tell her what?" said Leigh.

"What is it?" my mother asked.

I blurted out what Leigh had told me about her conversation with Patricia.

"Is this true, honey?" my mother asked. "Did she say those things to you?"

Leigh nodded.

"What do you think it means?" Leigh asked.

"I don't know," my mother said. "Did you tell the police about this?"

"No," Leigh said. "She only left my house an hour ago. I came straight here. I just felt terrible."

"About what?" my mother asked.

"About not being here to read to Mr. Askew," she said.

My mother looked like she wanted to scream.

"Well, I think you should tell the police that she said that to you, Leigh," my mother said. "I think we should go there and tell them right now."

"All right," Leigh said with a drowsy shrug. "If you think so."

I rode in the backseat while Leigh sat up front next to my mother. Her head was tilted gently toward the blur of the landscape and the buildings lining Memorial Avenue as the car sped toward Randolph High School. When we arrived, my mother parked in front of the annex and led Leigh up to the door, with me following behind. We were met there by the same brawny deputy who had accompanied Bobby Carwile when he came to the hospital to pick up Paul.

"I'm sorry, ma'am," the deputy said. "I can't let y'all in."

"Miss Bowman here has something important to tell Mr. Carwile," my mother said. "Is he around?"

The deputy asked us to wait outside. A moment later, Bobby Carwile appeared.

"Tell him, Leigh," my mother said. "Tell him what she told you."

"Who told you what, Miss Bowman?" Carwile said.

"It might be nothing," Leigh said. "Just something Patricia said."

"Now, Miss Bowman, I'm not sure your daddy will like it much if he finds out you've been talking to me without your lawyer," Carwile said.

"You're going to want to hear this, Mr. Carwile," my mother said.

"All right then," he said. "Come on in, Miss Bowman."

"I'm coming with you," said my mother.

"I can't let you do that, Mrs. Askew," Carwile said.

"It's all right," Leigh said. "I want her there."

Carwile appeared to consider the request.

"You can't see Paul," he said. "And he'll have to stay out here." Carwile nodded at me.

"Why?" I said.

"All right," my mother replied.

She started through the door and then stopped and turned to me.

"Don't be late," she said. "Rex is depending on you."

"Are you serious?" I said.

She kissed me on the cheek.

"Break a leg," she said.

INSIDE THE THEATER, I found Cinnamon backstage, smoking a cigarette with Marcus Vaughan and Todd Ackley, the stage manager.

"Hey," she said. "You're early."

I told Cinnamon what Leigh had said about Patricia, and what had happened afterward.

"Wow," Cinnamon said. "That's creepy."

"I'm sure it doesn't mean anything," I said.

"Maybe it does," she said.

I shrugged my shoulders, afraid to hope.

"We were just going to get something to eat," Marcus said. "You guys want to come?"

"Sure," Cinnamon said.

When we walked out to the parking lot, my mother's car was still there in front of the annex.

"That's a good sign, right?" Cinnamon said.

We rode in Todd's car over to McDonald's. I didn't have any money, so Cinnamon bought me a Quarter Pounder with Cheese. I wasn't hungry but ate anyway, knowing the long night I had ahead of me. When we were finished eating, the three of them smoked cigarettes, flicking their ashes into one of those flimsy aluminum ashtrays stamped with the golden arches. Afterward we killed time driving around in Todd's car, listening to music. When we arrived back at Randolph, my mother's car was gone.

Backstage, we found the rest of the cast in the green room, huddled together, pale with nerves. Even the usually boisterous Blake Burwell sat silently in a motley leather club chair, chewing his fingernails.

"What are you worried about?" Cinnamon said. "All you have to do is stand there clenching your butt."

I left to go to my dressing room. Marcus Vaughan was already there, applying the makeup that was supposed to make him look like a shrink nearing the end of middle age. On the dressing table in front of him sat a vase filled with red roses and baby's breath.

"My parents," he said. "You've got something also."

He pointed to my side of the table, where I saw an unmarked envelope underneath a hard pack of Camel Lights.

"I didn't think you smoked," Marcus said.

"I don't," I replied. "It's an inside joke."

"Oh," he said.

"Well, I'm heading out. See you in a few."

"OK," I said.

After Marcus had left, I picked up the envelope. I recognized my name written in Paul's sloppy script. I took out the letter and began to read.

Rocky,

Funny, right? Sorry for the lousy gift. It's the best I could do. Give them to Cinnamon—we need to get her smoking a classier brand.

Sorry I won't be there to see the show. With a little luck, I'll get out in time to catch the last performance. Rayner says they've got nothing on me. He's the lawyer, right?

I'm sure you're wondering what's been going on in here. It's not so bad. They ask the same questions, I give the same answers. Mostly I just sit around reading. Rayner brought me a stack of books and a carton of cigs. If I had a turntable and a window to stare out of, it'd be just like home.

Cinnamon gave Rayner a copy of your play to pass on to me. I'm not sure I understood it. But one part stuck with me. When Alan's mother comes to see the shrink at the beginning of act 2, she says, "Every soul is itself." I know the mother is supposed to be nuts, but that seemed like a pretty good way of looking at things. "Every soul is itself." I couldn't say it any better.

—Paul

I placed the letter on the table and looked up at the mirror. I stared at myself for what seemed like a long time. I tried to remember what Paul had looked like when he was my age, searched for the traces of his features in my face, looking for our common inheritance—the evidence, as it were, of our connection. I thought of myself at nine years old. I wondered what I must have looked like to him on that cold spring night standing in front of Twin Oaks beneath those two great trees, tall and forbidding in the darkness.

I was still there when Cinnamon came in, dressed in her frumpy schoolmarm's costume. Without a word, she wrapped her arms around me and held me there until I stopped shaking.

WHEN I HAD collected myself, we went out to the wings. We found my mother and Leigh in the center of the tenth row.

"You see?" Cinnamon said. "They made it."

"But no Paul," I said.

"Maybe tomorrow. Oh, God," Cinnamon said.

"What is it?" I asked.

"They came," she said.

"Who?"

"My parents."

I had never seen Cinnamon's parents before. I had begun to wonder whether they even existed, but there they were: a tall, slim man with high cheekbones, a shock of salt-and-pepper hair, and a full gray beard that spread out from his face and descended to his collar, accompanied by a shorter, heavyset woman in a billowing floral-print dress, her long, dark hair tied up in a loose, messy bun at the base of her neck. They didn't look like anyone from Boone's Ferry but seemed somehow less eccentric than advertised.

Having been so preoccupied with studying Cinnamon's parents, I didn't notice until I looked back toward Leigh and my mother that Patricia Culver had entered the auditorium and taken a seat a few rows behind them. Next to her sat Nelson Waltrip. Together they looked like a frosty shrew and her troublesome nephew, sent out with Auntie to get a little culture.

Behind us, we heard the voice of Mr. LaPage.

"Two minutes to curtain, lovebirds," he said. "Let's go."

I walked out onto the stage. The houselights fell, the curtain rose, and there I was standing under a single spotlight, my head tilted against Blake Burwell's shoulder.

As the play progressed, whenever I found myself in the shadows between my scenes, with Marcus off to the side reciting Dysart's gloomy monologues, I closed my eyes and thought of Paul, alone in the field house annex with Cinnamon's tattered copy of *Equus*, reading along. I felt as if I were performing for him—or at least for my memory of him. I realized then that, in a certain sense, it was Paul and not me who most resembled Alan Strang. At some point, every boy feels the urge to lash out at something, to be cruel and violent, to curse the world for its frail humanity. But only a few have the will—be it born of courage or recklessness, folly or sublime wisdom—to act and, by their action, transform themselves. They will pay for their courage, of course; the world does not treat its *others* lightly. But so will the rest of us—the ones who love them—haunted as we are by our envy of their bright, burning beauty, which we can bear neither to look at nor to turn away from.

By the end of the first act, the mood in the theater had become palpably tense. Something strange and unexpected was coming over us all. This weird, ill-chosen play, which so many of the virtuous denizens of our priggish little town would have considered "indecent" and "inappropriate for children," had transformed into a vehicle for a collective act of catharsis. Even Cinnamon, the queen of detachment, was swept up in the communal rite of expiation. As the second act began and we played out the final, bitter confrontation between mother and son, Cinnamon's usually stiff, almost comical line readings became abruptly natural and filled with urgent sincerity.

In the scene, the psychiatrist Dysart walks in to find Dora Strang upbraiding Alan. The mother has come not to visit her son but rather to be exonerated—to be reassured that she is not responsible for the boy's shocking, senseless violence or for his madness. Alan Strang gives her no such satisfaction—just a stony stare of silent, sneering contempt.

"Don't you dare give me that stare, young man!" Cinnamon wailed.

The script called for her to slap me at that point. We had practiced the slap so frequently and playfully that I no longer flinched. This time, however, her hand whipped out with stunning force.

The sound of the contact echoed through the theater. Someone gasped (probably my mother). I felt a stinging welt begin to rise on my face.

"Don't you dare," she said again, more softly.

Marcus Vaughan entered from stage right. The pillar of light moved away from me. I stood still in the darkness as Cinnamon argued with Marcus, the bitterness in her voice rising with its pitch.

"Whatever's happened has happened *because of Alan*," she said. "Alan is himself. Every soul is itself. If you added up everything we ever did to him, from his first day on earth to this, you wouldn't find why he did this terrible thing—because that's *him*."

I glanced out into the audience and found my mother. I recalled how often she had made similar speeches to my father about Paul—the "born manipulator," the "bad kid." I wondered whether she felt Paul's presence hovering over the whole proceeding, as I did.

Not long after Dora Strang's final words to Dysart, Alan meets Jill—like Patricia, a seductress, though one who has no other motive, literally, than a roll in the hay. As the flirtation and the overtures continued, my eyes kept drifting away from Becky and out into the house, where Patricia sat watching as I reenacted our private history in front of an unwitting audience.

"Take your sweater off," Becky said.

"What?" I replied. It was my line—no problem there—but I was asking the question sincerely, as if I had forgotten where I was and what I was supposed to do.

"I will if you will," Becky said.

I pulled the sweater over my head and dropped it. We kissed lightly and then awkwardly descended to the floor together.

Since all the scenes leading up to the maiming of the horses are recalled from the recesses of Alan's memory in a therapy session, Dysart is also onstage, conversing with Alan as the action takes place. The critical moment involves Alan's hearing the stamping of horses' hooves beneath him and sensing the disapproving glare of his imaginary horse-god, Equus.

"When I shut my eyes, I saw Him at once," I said to Marcus.

As I loomed over Becky Mayhew, describing the vision of a foamy horse's hide replacing the nape of the beautiful girl in repose, I saw neither Becky nor Equus but instead Patricia Culver, looking up at me from a blue plaid blanket.

"NO!" I cried, leaping up and backing away. "Get out," I said, less forcefully at first than I was supposed to. I repeated the words, louder. Becky fled the stage. I mimed the blinding of Blake Burwell and the rest of the horses and then fell to the floor as the horror-movie sound track of stamping hooves echoed through the theater. The shame and wrath were genuine. Rex LaPage had been right all along: Everything in life is performance. And the performance is life.

Marcus Vaughan spoke the final lines. The stage went black. When the lights came up, the lot of us stood spread out across the stage, Marcus Vaughan and I at the center, flanked by Blake and Becky and Cinnamon and the others as we took our bows. The audience looked a bit shell-shocked but managed to summon a round of generous if not rousing applause. A scattered few rose to their feet, clapping slowly and steadily, as if unsure what had so moved them.

When the curtain fell, LaPage met me at center stage.

"My God, Richard," LaPage said.

He didn't have to say anything else. Looking back, I know that it wasn't technically the best performance I ever gave, but sometimes it doesn't matter—something just happens, and while the performer can never be completely delivered forever from his own limitations, he is, however briefly, lifted above the world.

Cinnamon clutched my arm as we walked offstage.

"Sorry for hitting you so hard," she said.

"Did it leave a mark?" I asked.

"You might call it your first tattoo," she said.

She kissed me. I wrapped my arms around her, full of gratitude and relief and something that felt like love. It must have looked strange, seeing the two of us, still in costume as mother and son, brazenly canoodling.

The euphoria faded. I felt a bit faint.

"What's wrong?" Cinnamon asked.

"I need a minute," I said.

"Do you want me to come with you?" she asked.

"No," I said.

As the others went off to greet the backstage well-wishers, I headed back alone to my dressing room. When I opened the door and entered, I found Patricia, sitting in my chair.

"Rocky," she said, "that was magnificent!"

Her tone was dry, as if she meant to make me wonder whether she was mocking or genuine.

"You're not supposed to be back here," I stammered.

"Oh, rules, rules," she said. "You were always so guilt-ridden, Rocky."

She stood and examined herself in the full-length mirror. I noticed that she was holding Paul's letter with both hands.

"What a sweet note," she said. "It's very biblical, isn't it?"

"What do you mean?" I asked.

"Saint Paul, writing letters from prison," she said.

This time, the bitterness under her words was plain. The exhilaration I had felt before I walked through the door had faded into an uneasiness bordering on fear—though of what, I couldn't say.

Patricia bent to the table to smell Marcus Vaughan's roses.

"I have to go," I said. "People are waiting for me."

"I just wanted to see you, Rocky," she said. "Nelson and I are leaving tonight. Our visit this afternoon with the police has made him a tad uncomfortable. So we've decided to take a little trip. I'm afraid I might not see you again for a very long time, if ever."

"Where are you going?" I asked.

"It's better that I don't tell you," she said.

She sat down and crossed her legs and folded her hands over her knees. Her face was pale and puffy, as if she had not slept for some time and had no hope of rest in the near future. The tone of her voice turned dreamy and wistful.

"I'll hate to leave the horses. Reggie most of all," she said. "But they belong to Charles, not to me. I expect he's already planning to sell them."

She smiled. For a moment I saw a flicker of the Patricia I'd fallen for—the illusion of vulnerability, the sense that there was a sweet, wounded little girl beneath the icy surface.

"Isn't it funny, you being in this play?" she said. "I imagine it's been therapeutic for you."

"I don't know what you mean," I said.

"But you do, don't you?" she said. "Honestly, I had such plans for you. But our mutual friend Leigh Bowman had to spoil that for me also, didn't she?"

My throat was dry. I licked my lips and drew in a deep breath.

"Are you the devil, Patricia?" I asked.

She stood and walked toward me. My back was against the wall; I couldn't get to the door without pushing her away.

"Every soul is itself, Rocky," she said.

I could smell the scent of her nape and feel her breasts pressing against me.

"I suppose this is good-bye, then," she said.

I did not notice her hand slipping forward between my legs until she was clutching my scrotum as if she meant to tear it off. Before I could cry out or even gasp in pain, she had disappeared out the door.

A few days later, we learned that in the midst of our performance, down the hill at the field house annex, Bobby Carwile had been on the phone with the commonwealth's attorney, trying to determine whether he had enough probable cause to hold Patricia Culver and Nelson Waltrip for questioning.

In retrospect, Patricia had been extremely reckless, sticking around for a high school play. But her choices were always enigmatic. In any case, the police had missed them—they were in the wind.

PAUL WAS RELEASED in time to see the final performance of *Equus*. Afterward he and Leigh stayed for the cast party, which was held onstage in the theater. There was a champagne tower and a case of sparkling apple cider. Rex LaPage ceremoniously popped the cork on the first bottle and began pouring its contents into the top glass until it overflowed into all the others. A few couples danced, including Cinnamon's parents, who performed a respectable Carolina shag to Al Green's "Let's Stay Together." I stood and held Cinnamon's hand as we leaned against the door to the loading dock. At the center of the stage stood Paul and Leigh, their arms wrapped around each other, swaying back and forth, bathed in light.

29

NOT LONG AFTER PATRICIA DISAPPEARED, the Twin Oaks Task Force moved out of the field house annex and disbanded. Bobby Carwile went back to the mundane crimes and misdemeanors of rural Spottswood County. Instead of being shunned, Paul was received as a hero by the regulars at the Wahoo—he couldn't buy his own beers for over a month. Once again, people smiled and whispered "Bless her heart" at the sight of Leigh Bowman cruising along Bonny Lane on her bicycle with a basket full of books.

Before fleeing, Patricia had left behind a terse note for the task force investigators proclaiming her and Nelson Waltrip's innocence. Ironically, in their note, Patricia used the scapegoating of Paul and Leigh to explain her and Nelson's decision to run. How can the police be trusted, Patricia wrote, if they were willing to frame innocent people based on nothing more than rumor and superstition?

A reexamination of the evidence, however, supported a rather damning case against them. The day before the murders, Patricia and Nelson had in fact gone to Baltimore, as the task force investigation had confirmed months before, to spend a long weekend going to see the races at Pimlico. They were seen at the track by friends, and they had been found there when the police were notifying the victims' families. This seemed to have been part of their plan from the beginning. After a day at the races, they had purchased tickets to an art house double feature of the original James Whale–Boris Karloff *Frankenstein* and *Bride of Frankenstein*—again, details the detectives had already confirmed. The box office cashier didn't recall having seen either of them.

The police searched both Patricia's and Nelson's cars and found nothing. Later, however, they discovered that on the day the murders were believed to have occurred, Nelson Waltrip had rented a car in Baltimore. The mileage added to the car roughly matched the distance of a round-trip to Spencerville and back. Despite the car's having been cleaned several times between rentals, the crime scene investigators were able to find microscopic traces of Brad and Jane Culver's blood in the cracks between the seat cushions. The knife was never found; the detectives assumed Patricia and Nelson had dropped it into the James or perhaps the Chesapeake Bay, along with Brad Culver's .38 handgun, which had been used to inflict the postmortem leg wound meant to cast suspicion on Paul.

After a brief manhunt, the police learned that Patricia and Nelson had driven directly to Dulles, where they booked tickets on a red-eye to Heathrow. The Spencerville DA contacted the FBI, who contacted Scotland Yard. Patricia's and Nelson's names and photos were added to the wanted posters that appear in federal buildings and American Express offices, but that was the end of it. Apparently, Patricia knew how to disappear.

What was Patricia's motive? Why would Nelson Waltrip kill for her? Had he acted alone? Just as had been the case after Leigh's wedding, the town would have to content itself with rumors—of which there have been and will continue to be many. For some, it was money: after all, Patricia had been surprised to discover she would inherit nothing after her parents' estate was settled. For others, it was revenge—though such a grisly fate seemed a heavy price to exact for not being allowed to major in English at Oxford. Only two people know the truth. Thus far, they have yet to be seen again. At least one of them, however, was heard from.

Two weeks after Patricia and Nelson vanished, I received a typewritten letter with no return address, postmarked in London:

Dear Rocky,
I'm sorry for how things went when we saw each other last. I was
under a bit of stress. It was wrong of me to punish you for things I
brought on myself.

I doubt you'll believe it, but I never meant for Paul and Leigh to come so near to being blamed. Perhaps that's why I said what I did to Leigh. Isn't it reassuring to think there's a small shred of humanity left within me?

If there had been time, I would have told you everything. But you have inklings, don't you? Remember that first night at the stables? Did you never wonder what my father was doing there when you found him? Why I would be down there so late at night, alone? Did you think I was waiting for you?

You did save me for one night, I suppose. It made no difference to me by that point—he'd been coming to me like that for years. I suppose he thought he had me too well trained to turn against him. You've no idea what it feels like to be used that way by your own father. As for Mummy—I don't think she approved, exactly, but she seemed to prefer his coming to me over anyone else. There were others before me, I think. She must have liked having someone who would keep him close to home.

You know why I'm telling you all of this, don't you? I saw the look on your face when you found him there, Rocky. I knew what you wanted to do. It was then that I first thought you were going to be the one I'd been waiting for. I might even go so far as to say that you gave me the courage, and the inspiration. Leigh and her madness intervened, which was fortunate for you, I suppose. I had to find another friend. Still, you should know, what happened—it was for you too. If you don't believe me, ask William.

Don't hate me. I gave you quite a gift, after all.

She left the letter unsigned; furthermore, she had typed everything, including the name and address on the envelope. Why had she done those things? It's not as if there was any mystery about who had sent it. Had she dictated it to Nelson Waltrip? Had he written it for her, without her consent? No, I thought. Even if she'd told him everything, he couldn't have written it alone—that was Patricia's voice. Every time I looked at the letter, I could practically hear her reading it aloud.

Were any of Patricia's allegations against Brad and Jane Culver to be believed? There was no evidence to confirm them—just the letter—and one would have to regard the claims of someone like Patricia with extreme skepticism. But when I thought of that early morning when I found Brad Culver reeling and drunk, skulking around outside his barn while Patricia waited within, I had little doubt that what she'd written about her father was true.

And what about William? What did he have to do with anything? *If you don't believe me, ask William*, she wrote. Was that her last manipulation? One final red herring, like the bullet in Brad Culver's thigh?

Clutching the letter in my hands, I walked out into the yard and down to the fence where I could see Twin Oaks, once again empty and spectral.

Paul appeared beside me. I offered the letter for him to read. When he was finished, he slowly folded it and passed it back to me.

"Here," he said.

He handed me his Zippo. I lit the end of the paper and held it aloft until nothing was left but smoke and ash borne away on the wind.

A FEW YEARS LATER, on a short visit home from college, I ended up at the Wahoo, drinking draft beer at one of those graffiti-strewn tables with a few old high school friends. We had just ordered a third or fourth round when I looked up to see William at the bar, sipping a Coke and smoking one of his menthol cigarettes. I felt a twinge of uneasiness when my eyes met his, as if he'd been watching me like that for some time. I peeled away from my friends and made my way to the bar.

"William," I said.

"Whassup, Rock," he said. "How's your pops?"

I slid onto the stool next to him.

"Hanging on," I said. "He's over at Saint Bernard's now."

"How 'bout your momma?" he asked.

"She's doing all right, I guess," I said. "Getting along."

"Y'all sell that house yet?"

"Yeah," I said. "A few years ago. Not long after—well, you know."

William puffed on his cigarette and sipped his Coke. I told him about the family that had moved into our old home: a doctor from out of town, with a wife and two young kids—a practical man who wasn't bothered by the idea of waking up across the field from the "murder house." I told him about the little three-bedroom ranch house we'd moved into, near the nursing home where we'd moved the Old Man after his condition had again worsened.

"Miss Leigh still come by to read them books to your pops?" he asked.

"She sure does," I said.

"How 'bout that brother?" William asked. "He still around?"

"Yeah," I said. "He's got his own place now, but he's still around."

"What about the big house?" he asked. "What they gonna do with it?"

At that time, Twin Oaks still sat empty. Charles Culver had put it up for sale and left Spencerville forever. For years, the house continued in its former state as an abandoned curiosity for the local history buffs and the next generation of thrill-seeking teenage trespassers until it was quietly purchased by a wealthy preservationist from Richmond.

But I knew none of this then, as I sat at the bar next to William, nursing my beer while he sipped a Coke and smoked his Kools.

"I don't know," I said.

A peculiar sadness overtook me. It was as if I were realizing for the first time that William and I had never really been friends.

We sat there staring at each other wordlessly for an uncomfortable moment. It might have seemed to an observer that we had nothing to say to each other, but the opposite was true. I knew precisely what I wanted to say to William—what I wanted to ask him.

"Too bad about Miss Patricia, huh?" he said. "You ever wonder where she at?"

"No," I said. "I guess it scares me a little. Every now and then,

I get this weird feeling, and I turn around, expecting to find her standing there, staring at me with that cold look of hers."

"Don't you worry none, Rock," he said. "She ain't never coming back."

William turned his head to me and looked directly into my eyes.

"Guess they'll never know what really happened out there," William said.

The way he said it made me shiver. *Ask William*, Patricia had written. I thought of Nelson Waltrip. He had never seemed tough enough to take down Brad Culver alone, much less with Jane Culver right there in the room with them, no matter how drunk they were.

William stamped out his cigarette in the ashtray, all the while staring at me, as if I were supposed to sense some private communication from the look in his eyes. But I could never read William, even if he wanted me to.

"I guess they won't," I said.

William slid off his barstool. He picked up his flat-brimmed University of North Carolina ball cap from the bar beside him, set it squarely on his head, and offered me his dry, smooth palm.

"Tell your pops I said hey," he said.

I took his hand and held it.

"I will," I said.

His hand slipped from mine. He walked away from the bar and out the door to the street. When he was gone, I picked up my glass of beer and emptied it in one long swallow, my heart pounding in my chest.

Now, years later, I'd like to run into William again sometime. I might have the courage to ask him a few of those questions I didn't dare to ask back then. But I haven't seen him since.

SIX YEARS AFTER the killings, I was living in a one-bedroom dependency on an old farm just outside Charlottesville. Earlier that May, I had walked the Lawn at UVA and received my diploma, with the Old Man and my mother and Paul and Leigh looking on. At the end of the summer, I would be packing up and moving to New York to take my chances.

One hot afternoon a few weeks after commencement, I went out running down the rural roads leading out to the working horse farms—the kind of places Patricia Culver and Nelson Waltrip must have frequented during their brief time together in Charlottesville. The road was quiet, the only sound my footfalls and the wind in the trees. So absorbed had I become in the rhythm of my stride and my breathing and the hypnotic blue green of the fields off to the left that I did not notice the storm clouds blowing in from the south, sheltered from my view by the steep woods lining the road. The heavens opened up, drenching me so rapidly and thoroughly that my clothes clung to me like paste. The sunlit rain created a surreal air—the weeping of angels or the devil beating his wife, depending on your preference.

I turned and ran back home. When I entered my little cottage and saw the flashing red light on the answering machine, I already knew that the Old Man was dead.

I picked up the receiver and called Paul.

"Time to come home, brother," he said.

As I drove down US 29 to Spencerville, I rolled down all the windows and left the radio off so that I could be alone with the humid, blustering winds and the rise and fall of the highway over the long stretches of misty green-and-blue hillsides and the lavenders and oranges of the sun setting in the stillness after the rain. At times I could feel thick tears streaking my face in the cool, damp air. But mostly I found myself calm and smiling, thinking about the Old Man the way I wanted to remember him, before Twin Oaks and the Culvers, before Leigh even—back when it was just him and me and my mother, and Paul.

My Old Man has been dead now for almost twenty years. But he's still with me, every time I look in the mirror, in the lines growing around my eyes in such a way that there is no mistaking from whom they have been inherited. These lines—this resemblance—

seems evidence of some small victory: something of his that Paul and I would always share.

I MADE A game run at the life of a working actor. There were touring companies with the big-name musicals, and Shakespeare in the Park, and bit parts on all three versions of *Law & Order*. A few commercials and small roles in independent films, a lot of bartending, a pilot for a *Friends* knockoff that might have been "the big break" if the network had picked it up. Along the way, perhaps sensing the need for a fallback plan, I followed the path of my first mentor, Rex LaPage, and earned an MFA at NYU. I fell in and out of love the way young men do until I met a girl I couldn't live without—a publicist at a literary press with a wild head of Black Irish curls, a wicked sense of humor, and a genuine reverence for the collected works of Neil Young. I had to break the Old Man's rule: a fifth-generation Mainer, Susan is as true a Yankee as any girl could ever be. Still, she lives every day with both a tireless love for lofty dreams and a sound sense of how hard the world can be to dreamers.

As the years passed, I wearied of closing the bar at 3 a.m. before eight o'clock casting calls that were far more frequently fruitless than not. Susan's press was bought up by a German conglomerate, causing her office culture to shift from quirky and lively to corporate and paranoid. When we started talking about having children, we began considering the possibility of a different kind of life for ourselves—someplace greener and quieter and gentler. We weren't ready to admit defeat, I think, so much as wishing to exit gracefully.

Susan and I spent Christmas that year with my mother and my stepfather, Charley Giffen—Old Giff, headmaster emeritus of Macon Prep. A year or two after the Old Man died, a mutual friend invited my mother and Old Giff to a dinner party and made sure they were seated next to each other. The old wounds had scarred over by then, and before long they were laughing about that awkward meeting in Old Giff's office and agreeing that things had worked out for the best. A year's courtship followed, and then a wedding in the chapel at Macon, where my mother served a brief term as the school's First Lady. Now, retired to a quaint little beach house on the South Carolina coast, my mother is as happy as I have ever seen her. She and Giff while away the days antiquing, reading on their screened-in porch, and strolling hand in hand along the shore in front of their waterfront love nest.

I didn't have the nerve to ask him myself. Instead, Susan approached my mother, who passed the word on to Old Giff, who brought it up with me when we were enjoying a scotch on the porch after Christmas dinner.

"Your mother tells me you're considering teaching," Giff said.

"Yes, sir," I said.

"There are always openings," he said. "You would have a number of options."

"Thank you," I said.

"There's one in particular I happen to know about," Giff said. "I called to confirm that the position is still available this afternoon."

I didn't have to ask where.

Now I am a teacher, and a director of school plays, and a costume designer, and a set builder and dresser, and a dorm counselor, and a JV cross-country coach, and all the other things that come along with this life, which is far from perfect but still rich and busy and full. Unbeknownst to my students, I hold the distinction of being the only student ever expelled from Macon Preparatory Academy to return as a faculty member. Susan went to work in the marketing office at Saint Bernard's, the nursing home where the Old Man spent his final days, and where Leigh Bowman continues reading to the elderly and infirm—with guidance from Susan on appropriate titles. There is much life about us—namely our two girls.

In the classroom and on the stage, I often find myself imitating my dear friend Rex LaPage, stealing his mannerisms and his favorite sayings—"Once is luck; twice is skill," "Draw on your deepest

fear," and so forth. Occasionally I have to stop myself from referring to one of my young thespians as "honey." As for Rex LaPage,
he managed to survive the dubious judgment of staging a play like
Equus with a bunch of sheltered high schoolers in the land of the
religious right and has since gone on to become an éminence grise
in the world of Virginia high school theater. Susan and I are regular guests at the home of Rex and his partner, who host lavish
dinner parties where Rex takes great pleasure in getting his guests
soused on champagne and brandy alexanders.

On one of those well-lubricated evenings, I reminded Rex of the
time he'd pulled me into his office on the opening night of *Equus*.

"Do you remember what you told me?" I said. "I've never forgotten it. You said, 'All life is performance, you know. And the
performance is life.'"

Rex's lips curled into a wry, purse-lipped smile.

"Did I tell you that, honey?" he said. "Shame on me."

THE MONTH AFTER *Equus*, Cinnamon graduated and left for California, to join her sister in the tattoo parlor on Venice Beach. I
can't say it didn't hurt to see her go, but I think I understood even
then how young love is a little like a high school play. A thing that
seems insignificant to everyone else takes on the greatest importance. And then, quite suddenly, it's over. You feel a certain emp-
tiness, but you survive it and go on.

Though we exchanged many letters over the years, I did not see
Cinnamon again until after college, on a trip home from the city to
visit Paul at his new place out in Holcomb Falls. Her hair was long
and black and streaked with red, her arms wrapped in the sleeves
of ink she'd designed for herself. She was back for good, to open
up her own tattoo and piercing business. For my graduation gift,
she said, she wanted to give me something special.

"Anything you want," she said. "Any*where* you want."

"All right," I said. How could I refuse?

No dragons or tribal armbands for me; certainly no dancing

bears, dolphins, or mushrooms. Instead, on the inside of my right forearm, a line from our old friend Neil, in delicate cursive:
Only Love Can Break Your Heart.

LEIGH BOWMAN MOVED out of her father's house to be Miss Anita Holt's companion and live-in caregiver. Miss Anita actually outlived Prentiss Bowman; without warning, his cold, hard heart gave out on him while he was, of all things, playing tennis. Down four games in the second set of his weekly match, Bowman mishit a serve that went careening off the frame of his racket and over the fence. "God-DAMN IT!" he bellowed. His face red with fury, he marched off the court and disappeared down the hill to collect the errant ball. When after several minutes Bowman had not returned, his partner went after him and found him crumpled on the ground, already dead. Less sympathetic observers pointed out that, fit as he was for his age, Prentiss Bowman might have lived to ninety if he wasn't such a sore loser.

Leigh made Paul wait for five years before she finally agreed to marry him. "Miss Anita needs me," she said, but I suspect it took her that long to convince herself that she could endure another wedding, and to fully believe she deserved another chance at her own happiness.

In time, over Leigh's objections, Miss Anita moved into Saint Bernard's.

"Get on with your life, child!" she said.

Leigh and Paul were wed—again, you might say—at the center of a field in the shadow of Otter Peak. Leigh wore a sleeveless white satin dress and a garland of flowers and ribbons in her hair, which was once again long and lustrous in the afternoon sun.

They settled in Holcomb Falls, where Paul had bought an old farmhouse with a barn in which he'd started his own finish-carpentry business. Just down the road lived Cinnamon Kintz, who, after a long string of bass players and at least one aspiring actor, ended up with one of Paul's carpenters—an ex-drummer. The shrinks seemed to have worked out Leigh's brain chemistry

ONLY LOVE CAN BREAK YOUR HEART

by then. Her episodes had fallen off almost completely—unless you counted her visitations in Bible study and prayer group, a gift presumably inherited from Miss Anita, which everyone around her regards now as evidence of a beatific, beatified soul.

THIS SHOULD BE the part of the story where I describe the moment when, at long last, Paul confessed: When he cursed the foolish child he had been, and rued the day he'd left us all, and shed mighty, streaming tears over the sins of his wayward youth. When he opened up and explained what had happened in New Mexico and afterward. What it had felt like to find out what had happened to Leigh when she came home and ended up on that table out at the rehabilitation center. How hard it had been to screw up his courage and return to us, and how he had done it as much for himself as for me or my mother or Leigh or even the Old Man, whom he loved—whom he had always loved, even when Paul's heart was warped with anger and confusion. But Paul never said any of those things.

The day after we buried the Old Man, I drove out to see Paul. We spent the day alone together in the barn where he built custom cabinets and furniture. Paul taught me how to use a sander and a lathe; how he separated the quality lumber stock from the culls; how he hammered and clamped and bound the raw pieces into something beautiful and, hopefully, permanent. We hardly spoke—just a word or a nod when necessary. The room filled with the sounds of cassettes played on Paul's portable tape deck, the notes reverberating off the aging boards of the roof and walls.

Even in moments of deep concentration, Paul wore that calm, happy Buddha's smile beneath the cover of his lengthening beard. I found myself smiling as well, caught up in the pleasure of learning something new: of working, of feeling the ache of labor creep into my shoulders and the palms of my hands, the sweat dampening my shirt, my breath quickening, the sound of my own heartbeat louder in my ears. As we worked together, I came to an understanding about Paul: how he found himself in the moment of formation, how he learned that his truest sense of self came through the abandonment of consciousness in the act of creation and the act of repetition.

As we worked together that day, I knew I had never felt so close to Paul, nor he to me. When people build something together—be it abstract or physical, spiritual or material—the circle closes around them. They find that elusive peace that, as that other Paul once wrote, passes all understanding.

When we were finished, we walked up to the house. Paul took two beers from the refrigerator and led me out to the porch. He lit up a Camel Light with the old Zippo. We sat down on the front stoop together and sipped our beers, watching the sun set over Otter Peak until the air around us turned cool and blue and the crickets sang in the high grass that filled the long green space before us.

JUST THIS SPRING, Paul finally left us, for good. Leigh had managed to wean him off the cigarettes, but three decades of three packs a day had taken their toll. When they found it, the cancer had already spread from his lungs to his liver and pancreas. There was nothing to be done, the doctors told him, but wait and manage his pain. Leigh was already an experienced home nurse, and anyway, she had always wanted to be the one to take care of him.

Paul and I were just settling into the easy, later stage of siblinghood, where we could truly know each other as friends. Funny enough, even then, we only ever seemed to do the same thing we had always done together. Once a week I drove out to Holcomb Falls with a stack of records on the seat behind me—sometimes alone, sometimes with Susan and our girls. Together we would drop a needle on some old Stones or Beatles or Neil Young and sit by the fireplace or, on warm afternoons, out on the porch, laughing and talking, occasionally singing along, sometimes just listening.

For me, a vinyl record will always be a sacred object; the practice of sliding the disc from its musty sleeve and settling it onto the turntable and hearing the warm crack of the needle finding its groove, a sacrament—my Holy Communion.

On the last of our Sunday afternoons together, I sat alone with Paul on the porch at his place. The windows were open. Paul was stretched out on a recliner and covered with blankets, positioned so that he could see my girls in the yard tossing a slobbery tennis ball to his and Leigh's dogs. Beside them stood Susan and Leigh, laughing and talking. Inside, the stereo was playing Joni Mitchell, which always reminded us both of Leigh when we first fell in love with her. Watching Leigh stoop to help my laughing children pry the ball from the mouths of the prancing dogs made my heart swell.

"I wish I had been able to give her children," Paul said.

I looked over at Paul. His face was wet with tears.

"She would have been a wonderful mother," I said.

"I know it," he said, his voice cracking. "It's my one regret."

"Your one regret?" I asked.

"That's right," he said.

"Just one?" I said. "My, Paul. I have so many."

He rubbed his eyes slowly and smiled.

"You shouldn't, you know," he said.

Now that Paul is gone, I think I know what he meant. When I look into the eyes of my children, I know that no good can come from regrets. For if even a second of my life before them had been different, my perfect, beautiful girls might not exist—or else they would be some other people. And though I wouldn't know otherwise, I can't bear the thought of their being anything other than exactly who they are, no matter what the future holds for them—even if it means that they might face what Leigh has faced, or if, through some unforeseen weakness, I should fail them the way Paul once felt he had been failed. That's the risk we take when we love. This was my gift from Paul—his legacy, you might say. Only love can break your heart. And who wants to live without love?

ACKNOWLEDGMENTS

Thanks to all my teachers, especially Patricia Worsham, Jim Ackley, Nick Radel, Lynne Shackelford, Jim Edwards, and Elizabeth Stuckey-French, and to my colleagues and students at Montgomery Bell Academy, especially Sean Kinch, Michael Kelly, and Will Norton. Many thanks to Brad Gioia, for continuing support and the opportunity to be part of an extraordinary community. Thanks also to Margaret Renkl and all the good folks at Chapter16.org and Humanities Tennessee. Very special thanks to Haywood Moxley, colleague, mentor, and dear friend, and to Frank Simpson, the finest coach I've ever known.

Deepest gratitude to Gail Hochman and Andra Miller, whose gifts to me and to this book are beyond measure, and to Rachel Careau, copy editor *nonpareil*, and to everyone at Brandt & Hochman and Algonquin.

Thanks to Charlie White, Will and Julia Hoge, Glen Rose, Barbara "Catfish" Petersen, and Robert and Carissa Neff. To all my family, especially Susan (Mom!), Bess, and Eleanor; Tom, Laura, Kate, and Thomas; Tom P.; Brian, Carroll, and Phillip; Lee-Lee, Muchi, and Tico.

To Bob Shacochis, venerable master, in whose debt I will forever remain.

Lastly: thanks (and apologies) to Sir Peter Shaffer, one of the finest playwrights of his age, and to Neil Young, for a borrowed title and the sound track of a life.

ONLY LOVE CAN BREAK YOUR HEART

A Faithful Invention: A Note from the Author

*

Questions for Discussion

A Faithful Invention

A Note from the Author

THE ORIGIN OF *Only Love Can Break Your Heart* dates back to 1978, when my half sister—I'll call her Caroline—stole my six-year-old sister out of her sickbed and disappeared. I have no recollection of that day. The story was told to me years later by my mother, after Caroline attempted suicide by swallowing a bottle of Tylenol capsules, and I was finally introduced to the many particulars of a tragedy that had been unfolding around me for as long as I'd been alive.

In 1978, Caroline was in her early twenties. She wasn't living with us anymore by then, but she was at the house frequently, to do laundry or borrow money, or maybe just to harass my mother— her step-mother—whom she hated, for reasons that were both obvious and inexplicable.

When Caroline showed up that day, my mother was in a bit of a bind. Our father was out of town on business. My mother needed to stop by the pharmacy to pick up medicine for my sister, and to pick me up from preschool. She had called several friends but hadn't been able to find anyone. Caroline offered to babysit. My mother didn't trust her, but rather than wake her feverish child and drag her out into the cold, she accepted the offer. When my mother returned maybe twenty minutes later, Caroline's car was gone and so was my sister.

CAROLINE WAS WHAT people used to call *wild*. A college dropout, she couldn't hold down a job or make up her mind about what she wanted to do with herself. She had a lot of long-haired, guitar-playing boyfriends who smelled like dope and trouble. She treated our father like an ATM and never let an opportunity pass to put him at odds with my mother. Unbeknownst to her much younger half siblings, she had long exhibited behavior that suggested deeper issues than a "wild" streak: threats of violence, teary ultimatums, arrests, hallucinations, and, above all, unrelenting anger and sadness.

In spite of all of the trouble she caused, Caroline had always held a peculiar sway over me. When she still lived with us, she would often invite me into her room while she smoked and listened to her collection of classic rock records. She had long, straight hair then, parted down the middle, like a young Judy Collins. She told me, in confidence, that I was her favorite, and I believed her. She gave me my first rock records—*Best of the Doobies* and Crosby, Stills, Nash, and Young's *So Far*. My favorite song was "Helpless." I would sit and listen to that song over and over, hypnotized by Neil Young's strange, keening voice, the shimmering reverb guitar, and the sparse, resonant piano. I still have that record, and it still floors me, with the combined power of beauty and nostalgia—as Neil might say, "Dream, comfort, memory to spare."

ANY PARENT WHO has lost a child for even a few minutes understands the agony my mother suffered in the hours after Caroline ran off with my sister. Finally, with darkness falling, Caroline's car rolled up to the curb, stopping just long enough for my sister to climb out before speeding off down the street. My sister walked slowly up the sidewalk, still in her nightgown, clutching a Slurpee from 7-Eleven. My mother met her halfway and embraced her, sobbing with gratitude and relief. Where have you been? my mother asked. They'd just been driving around, my sister said. She'd been bored and vaguely miserable, but was otherwise unharmed.

NEAR THE BEGINNING of *Only Love Can Break Your Heart*, six-year-old Richard "Rocky" Askew is unwittingly abducted by his half brother, Paul—a charming but difficult nineteen-year-old with a troubled history and a taste for Neil Young and the Doobies. Shortly afterward, Paul disappears. Rocky's childhood becomes defined by the absence of his beloved brother and by his involvement with Leigh Bowman, Paul's emotionally traumatized ex-girlfriend. Years later, Rocky and Leigh become entangled with Rocky's new neighbors, Brad and Jane Culver, and their twenty-nine-year-old daughter, Patricia, who move into an imposing colonial mansion known as Twin Oaks, situated at the top of a rolling hill adjacent to the Askew home on the outskirts of Spencerville, a small town at the foot of the Blue Ridge Mountains in Virginia. A grisly double-murder in Spencerville with alarmingly personal implications forces Rocky into a reckoning with the past and the present that is both traumatic and regenerative.

Only Love Can Break Your Heart is a coming-of-age novel, but it is also a Southern Gothic and a murder mystery in which the damsel in distress is a prime suspect. It is a story of fathers and sons and brothers, of love and betrayal and reconciliation. As much as anything else, *Only Love Can Break Your Heart* is a faithful invention: a deeply personal fiction, steeped in emotional truth, which I consider to be more accurate than the facts.

I think we read and write stories because we want to make sense of what bewilders us—about the people we love; about our families and communities; about the acts and moments in which we are shaped, and scarred. For me, the art of fiction comes down to being honest without telling the truth. I couldn't write truthfully about my half sister; that story isn't mine to tell. Instead, I simply began with a sound and a place and an image that still haunts me: a small child in a car with someone she trusts, oblivious to the hazards of love, jealousy, and madness.

Questions for Discussion

1. Rocky's relationship with his brother, Paul, is largely framed in terms of their shared interest in classic rock music. Discuss the role of music in the novel—the sense of nostalgia it evokes and the way the characters (and perhaps readers) construct their identities around their rock music idols and the songs they love.

2. *Only Love Can Break Your Heart* is set in a particular sliver of the small-town upper South. In what ways do Spencerville and the Boone's Ferry neighborhood resemble other communities in different regions? In what ways are they unique to their particular time and place?

3. Several critics have classified the novel as Southern Gothic. What aspects of the story evoke the Gothic mood or genre? Is there something distinctly Southern about the story's Gothic elements?

4. The point of view in *Only Love Can Break Your Heart* presents the adult Richard Askew describing events beginning in his early childhood through his teenage years. How does the narration balance the perspectives of innocence (through the eyes of a child) and experience? Can you relate to the sensation of discovering as an adult the significance of things that were happening to or around you as a child but you were too young to comprehend at that time?

5. At the novel's outset, through Rocky's eyes, Paul Askew initially appears to be the quintessential rebel-without-a-cause of his era. Gradually, that rebellion turns malicious; once Paul reappears, he

must live down his past sins and prove himself to be trustworthy. What evidence does he provide of genuine reform? Does Paul really change, or does Rocky simply gain a clearer understanding of his character?

6. How much of Paul's teenage persona is attributable to his taking on the persona embodied by his rock music heroes, especially Neil Young? How much of it derives from his troubled past? Is Rocky's recollection of Paul as a teenager accurate?

7. The character of Anne, Paul's mother, plays an important role both in the shaping of Paul's rebellious character and in instigating some of his more reckless choices. Anne is especially representative of the destructive effect of alcoholism, both on its victims and their families. Discuss Anne's influence on Paul and the circumstances surrounding her own personal tragedy and its collateral consequences.

8. The central relationships in the novel are between the two brothers and their father, but by the conclusion of *Only Love Can Break Your Heart*, it becomes clear that the women in the story are its most powerful characters. Discuss the roles of these women and the ways the men both unwittingly and consciously rely on them.

9. Leigh Bowman is both the tragic victim and the heroine of the novel. How does she evolve over the course of the novel?

10. Rocky suggests early on that Paul and Leigh "were star-crossed from the beginning, and she was doomed to love him, come what may" (page 32). How does Paul and Leigh's relationship compare to other examples of good girl–bad boy relationships in literature, popular culture, and/or real life? What do you think of Paul's treatment of Leigh after his mother's death? Why was Leigh's attempt

to move on from Paul with Charles Culver destined to end in disaster?

11. Both Leigh and Patricia are examples of women who have been damaged by the men in their lives, particularly their fathers. Discuss the different ways Leigh and Patricia cope with the abuse they've suffered at the hands of men.

12. For most of the story, Patricia seems to be a coldly manipulative presence, using Rocky and others to amuse herself or achieve her own aims. But by the end of the story, details come to light which may explain (if not excuse) her actions. Is there any sense in which Patricia might be viewed as a sympathetic character?

13. William is the only African-American character in the novel, a fact that points toward the persistence of racial segregation and inequality in Southern communities, well into the 1980s and beyond. At times, William's presence also provokes the Old Man's latent racism. Rocky yearns for a genuine bond with William, only to discover that the barriers between them preclude true friendship. How do you feel about the way William is portrayed in Rocky's memory? What do you make of Rocky's last meeting with William at the Wahoo? Is William's role in the story troubling or unsettling? Why?

14. In the Boone's Ferry milieu of Spencerville, wealth isn't enough to gain acceptance into the social elite, a condition symbolized by the Spencerville Historical Trust's refusal to sell the Twin Oaks mansion to the Old Man before later ceding it to the Culvers because of Jane Culver's family ties to Old Virginia. Are such class distinctions still relevant in the twenty-first-century South? What are the implications of the survival or disappearance of the caste system that defined Old South society in the ever-changing world of the New South? Do such distinctions have any relevance outside

of provincial towns like Spencerville? Are they exclusive to the former Confederate states, or are similar hierarchies in place in other regions of the country?

15. At a particularly difficult point after the Old Man's stroke, Rocky describes his father's life as "not just the rise and fall of a small, forgettable man, but the story of the American Century" (page 185). What does he mean?

16. Discuss the character of Miss Anita Holt. How is she a crucial mentor both for Alice Askew and for Leigh Bowman? Is she truly clairvoyant? What effect does her perceived ability have on her status among the women of Boone's Ferry and her significance to the story?

17. The author has openly discussed that the murders in the novel are based on an actual case from 1985 in his hometown of Lynchburg, Virginia, the basis for the fictional Spencerville. The case was the subject of a feature article in *The New Yorker* magazine (www .newyorker.com/magazine/2015/11/09/blood-ties). Read about the real-life case and compare and contrast it to the characters and the case portrayed in the novel.

18. After his comically disastrous ouster from private school, Rocky restarts his life in public school and eventually finds a means of establishing his own identity through auditioning for a production of *Equus*. Discuss the role of the play in the novel, both in terms of its thematic parallels to earlier events and its significance to Rocky's coming-of-age narrative.

19. Discuss the character of Cinnamon Kintz. Is she an unlikely love interest for Rocky? In what ways do her differences help Rocky develop as a person? How does her free-spirited attitude contrast with the more repressed and conservative environment in which Rocky is being raised?

20. Many significant events in the novel take place offstage or in the past and are conveyed to Rocky through storytelling: Paul's ghost story versions of the history of Twin Oaks and the John's Gap myth; Leigh's account of her and Paul's western odyssey and what took place afterward; the Old Man's stories of his early life, both pre- and post-dementia; Patricia's tales and her letter to Rocky near the novel's conclusion. How does the adult Richard Askew use these stories to make sense of the troubled history of his family and his own extraordinary rites of passage? Does storytelling play a similar role in your life?

21. In a recent interview for the American Booksellers Association, Ed Tarkington made the following remarks: "If there's one thing I've learned from the people I've met who've connected with the book, it's this: We are all on the same journey. Everyone struggles as Rocky does to find a sense of purpose and identity. Every family deals with unexpected and inescapable challenges that sorely test them in every way imaginable. Every family has that loved one who is just broken for one reason or another and can't get it right. Everyone has to face down shame and regret, and everyone has to find a way to forgive themselves and others and keep on living." Do you agree with this assessment? In what sense do the experiences of the characters in *Only Love Can Break Your Heart* resonate with your own experience?

GLEN ROSE

Ed Tarkington received a BA from Furman University, an MA from the University of Virginia, and a PhD from the Graduate Creating Writing Program at Florida State. A frequent contributor to Chapter16.org, his articles, essays, and stories have appeared in *Nashville Scene*, the *Memphis Commercial Appeal, Post Road Magazine*, the *Pittsburgh Quarterly*, the *Southeast Review*, and elsewhere. A native of Central Virginia, he lives in Nashville, Tennessee.